"The author knows about the ᴸ

Death in the Blood Moon

"Full of beautifully detailed descriptions of Lake [Superior] as well as interesting facts about the native Ojibwe . . . Wonderfully written characters throughout the book made me feel deeply connected to the storyline. . . Even though this is a work of fiction, LeClair's characters and their ability to put all differences aside for the greater good gave me a hopeful feeling in what sometimes feels like a time of such division in the real world today. . . Characters, locations, storyline—every aspect of this book was completely enjoyable. I look forward to reading the other books in this series, as well as future books by this very talented author.

—*Reader Views*

Dead Astern

"A great, bounding thrill ride . . . *Dead Astern* is the book Agatha Christie might have written if she'd loved the sea and had known how to trim a sail. Jenifer LeClair offers readers an engaging tale that is a strong, seagoing version of the locked-room mystery. With several well-plotted twists, lots of riveting scenes on the bounding main, and plenty of fascinating sailing information along the way, *Dead Astern* is an exciting excursion sure to please anyone willing to sign on for the voyage."

—William Kent Krueger
New York Times Bestselling Author

Apparition Island

"With a mastery of details and a sailor's sense of land and sea, LeClair has given us another memorable story on an eerie island off the coast of Maine . . . a real gift for those who like their mysteries straight from the sea."

—Steve Thayer
New York Times Bestselling Author

"LeClair handles the island's rugged terrain and its rugged inhabitants equally well."

—*Publishers Weekly*

"Jenifer LeClair provides her fans with another thrilling investigation in a consistently excellent series."

—*Midwest Book Review*

"LeClair skillfully brings the setting into the mind's eye with wonderfully descriptive detail."

—*Foreword Magazine*

Cold Coast

"Brie is so likable and the plot so involving, it's not surprising this series has won several awards."

—Mary Ann Grossmann
St. Paul Pioneer Press

"This engaging police procedural vividly captures the Maine background. . . . The eccentric Mainers add depth to a fabulous step-by-step investigation."

—*Midwest Book Review*

"*Cold Coast* is superbly written. The characters are easy to follow and well developed. . . . Brie is a strong female protagonist but in an endearing way, not the stereotypical hard-nosed female law enforcement officer. The descriptions of the harbor and the coast are exceptionally vivid. . . . 5 Stars—excellent read!"

—*Reader Views*

"Tense . . . keeps the reader guessing until the final outcome . . . full of wonderful descriptions of life on a sailing vessel."

—*Armchair Reviews*

Danger Sector

"If you love sailing, grab this title and prepare to be immersed. . . . A strong sense of place and a fine little closed-room drama make this seafaring read a real pleasure."

—*Library Journal*

"Intelligent and well-written . . . The strong, smart protagonist is Minneapolis homicide detective Brie Beaumont."

—*St. Paul Pioneer Press*

"Recommend this agreeable mixture of adventure and crime."

—*Booklist*

"LeClair combines police procedure, finely-honed investigative skills, psychological insights, and suspense . . . in this haunting story of unrequited love, deceit, and murder [that] involves all five senses. A creative imagination, a love for sailing, and gifted communication skills combine to make Jenifer LeClair a top-notch storyteller."

—*Reader Views*

Rigged for Murder

"A winning combination of psychological thriller, police procedural, and action adventure. It's a five-star launch for [LeClair's] aptly named sea-going series. . . . Tightly written and intricately constructed, LeClair's *Rigged for Murder* is first-class storytelling in a setting so authentic you can hear the ocean's roar and taste the salt from the sea."

—*Mysterious Reviews*

"An engaging New England whodunit."

—*Midwest Book Review*

"A strong plot, non-stop action, and first-class character development combine to make this an exciting, page-turning adventure novel."

—*Reader Views*

"A debut mystery that is so well written you will hunger for more . . . well-developed characters and superbly good writing."

—Once Upon a Crime Mystery Bookstore

"*Rigged for Murder* is an exciting mystery with a little romance thrown in. The setting for this novel is unique and gives the reader insight into life aboard a sailing ship."

—*Armchair Reviews*

"The characters have depth and movement . . . LeClair gets the sea and the sailing just right."

—*Books 'n' Bytes*

"*Rigged for Murder* is a fast-paced story which rings true both aboard and ashore on island communities. The characters are real, the situations are downright scary, tension is palpable."

—John Foss, Master/owner,
Schooner *American Eagle*, Rockland, Maine

SEA SMOKE
AND MIRRORS

ALSO BY JENIFER LECLAIR

Death in the Blood Moon
Dead Astern
Apparition Island
Cold Coast
Danger Sector
Rigged for Murder (Book 1)

SEA SMOKE
AND MIRRORS

JENIFER LECLAIR

FOG HARBOR PRESS
St. Paul, Minnesota

Fog Harbor Press
4411 Wood Duck Drive
St. Paul, Minnesota 55127

Cover Design: Rebecca Treadway / ATRTINK

Library of Congress Control Number: 2021910056

LeClair, Jenifer.
  Sea Smoke and Mirrors: a novel / by Jenifer LeClair – 1st ed.

ISBN: 978-1-7336084-5-9

10 9 8 7 6 5 4 3 2 1

Printed in the United States of America

To mariners, young and old, who take to the seas for a living, and to all those who wait for them.

"Everything is rising to the surface,
summoned by the light . . ."

—*The Sea Inside*
by Philip Hoare

Prologue

Tuesday, November 14
The Gulf of Maine
Off Starkhaven Island

Night slid seamlessly into the grayness of dawn. No fan-fare on the eastern horizon. No wind to punch a hole in the pea soup that blanketed the waters off Stark-haven Island. Like a phantom, the white lobsterboat material-ized from the fog so close to Abe Winter's boat that, steady-nerved as he was, it gave him a start. So thick o' fog was the morning that even the sound of the boat's engine could not be heard as the craft ghosted up to Abe's port gunwale.

"Hey man, how about a warning next time? Toot your horn or give us a shout, eh?"

The other man just nodded. "Wicked thick this morning."

"What brings ya over this side o' the island?"

"Got hot coffee and danish. Would you like some?"

Abe Winter hesitated for a moment, studying the other man—wondering—as the faint voice of caution made a futile bid for his attention.

"Sure. Raft up and come aboard."

Those would be the last words Abe Winter would ever utter. As he went forward to shut off the motor on his trap hauler, he felt something ice cold and razor sharp slice into his neck. The shock sent him to his knees, robbing him of his only chance at a defense. He fought wildly but futilely to pry the wire from his neck and in the seconds that remained, he flailed his arms and legs trying to fell his attacker. It only brought the end sooner, as every movement seemed to cinch the garrote tighter. He'd always been a scrapper, though, and he had no intention of leaving this earth without one helluva fight. A strong wind came suddenly out of the north, clearing the fog, and Winter caught a final glimpse of his beloved island. As consciousness slipped away like the sea beneath him, one thought burned like a hot brand on his mind. *I made a mistake.*

Chapter 1

January 5
Rutledge Boatyard
Lincolnville, Maine

Outside, the January wind howled in from the northeast, preparing to deliver another gut punch of winter. Ten more inches of snow were predicted for the coast over the next twenty-four hours. Protected from the full force of the wind, schooner *Maine Wind* rocked gently next to the wharf that was its winter home. Inside the belly of the ship, Brie Beaumont and John DuLac could hear the wind whistling around the rigging as they went about their work in one of the aft cabins. A small propane heater, safe for use below decks, provided portable heat that they could move from cabin to cabin as they worked.

They were in the process of installing sinks in the passenger cabins to replace the wood casks and stainless steel washbowls that the passengers had previously used for their morning ablutions. Throughout the fall, John, the captain of *Maine Wind*, and Scott Hogan, his first mate, had run water lines to each of the cabins from the water storage tanks down in the bilges. The last step of installing the small sinks in the corner of each passenger cabin was now under way.

George Dupopolis, the ship's cook, and Scott were working on the same task in the amidships compartment, staying warm with a heater identical to the one in the aft compartment. George had also fired up Old Faithful, the ship's woodstove, so if need be, any of them could take a break and go forward to the galley, where a pot of hot, dark coffee and a loaf of George's warm sourdough bread roosted on top of the stove.

Brie and John exchanged an occasional fiery glance as they passed the wrenches back and forth and scrambled up and down from the floor, fitting and tightening the connections. Since Brie had moved back to Maine from Minnesota in November, their shared life had fallen into a rhythm of work and pleasure. Far from the life of a homicide detective that she had lived in Minneapolis, the hands-on work of maintaining a sailing schooner provided a kind of balm for a spirit weary of violence and death, weary of the world she had been steeped in for fifteen years as a cop and then a detective.

"Well, that looks good." Brie stood with hands on hips, arms akimbo, studying their work. Strands of hair from her long, blonde braid had worked themselves loose, and she swept them behind her ears. "Should we check on the guys? See how they're coming along?"

"Sure," John said. "It's time for a break, anyway. We've just got one sink left to go back here."

They slipped on their parkas against the biting wind and headed up the companionway ladder and along the starboard deck to the amidships compartment.

John called down, "Hey, guys, wanna break for coffee?" They had worked right through the lunch hour and into mid-afternoon, making use of what puny heat the winter sun had to offer.

"Sounds great," Scott called up. "We'll meet you down there in a couple minutes."

Brie and John went down the ladder to the galley. The heat from the woodstove, carrying notes of sourdough and dark-roasted coffee beans, rose up to meet them like a warm embrace. Before long George and Scott joined them. George had brought a small cooler aboard from which he retrieved butter for the bread, sliced prosciutto, a jar of black olives, and a block of cheese. He laid everything out on the galley table that was designed in the shape of the ship's bow, with long benches that ran behind the table along *Maine Wind's* hull. The warm loaf of bread and coffee were brought to the table.

Winter's muted light came down the companionway. It fell across John's face, and Brie brushed a fleck of debris from his dark hair. George lit one of the hurricane lanterns above the table, and now the interior of the galley with its gold-hued oak glowed in the lamplight. Everyone sat down to eat. Brie loved this space, not just for the memories of George's wonderful meals cooked at sea on the woodstove, but because of its womblike feeling of warmth and safety. She loved coming down here after the watch, late at night when they were under sail. The feel of the sea beneath her as the bow rose and fell; the creak of the timber and how the pots and pans swayed gently on their hooks above the stove, in time with the motion of the ship through its watery realm.

The four shipmates sliced bread and laid on meat and cheese and, together, made short work of the pot of coffee.

"We should be done with the sinks in the forward cabins today," Scott said. "How are you two doing?"

"Just one cabin to go," John said.

"So what's next?" Scott asked.

"Really not too much until we do the haul out in the spring. We're waiting on delivery of the new foremast. Could be a few weeks before it arrives. It will need to be milled and fitted, which can begin as soon as it gets here. Otherwise, there's scraping and painting of the bottom. That will happen, as usual, in March or April when she's hauled out."

Just then Brie's phone rang. She fished it out of her pocket and saw it was Dent Fenton from the Maine State Police.

"Excuse me, guys. I should take this." She got up and walked over to the companionway, thinking it might be news about Garrett Parker. If so, she didn't want to pollute the mood in the galley until she knew what was up.

"Hello, Lieutenant," she said into the phone.

"Hello, Brie. You sound apprehensive."

She smiled. "Just fitting my tone to the anticipated information."

"Well, whether it's good or bad, I'm not calling about Parker."

Now Brie wasn't sure whether to be elated or deflated. "So what's up, Dent?"

"I'm wondering if you might be willing to meet with me at headquarters in Augusta. There's something I'd like to run by you, and if it's okay, I'd like John to be there too."

"What's this about, Dent?"

"It involves a case we're working on, but I'd rather talk in person if that's okay."

"That's fine. When do you want to meet?"

"Today's Tuesday. Would Thursday work? Say about eleven o'clock?"

"I think so, but I'll have to check with John. I'll call you back if there's a problem. Otherwise, we'll see you in Augusta on Thursday."

They ended the call, and Brie went back to the table. She noted the curious look on John's face, but he said nothing. It was rare for Brie to receive phone calls, and since the escape and disappearance of Garrett Parker in November, the possibility of his reappearance hung ominously over them—a kind of psychological sword of Damocles.

Brie didn't comment on the call but instead helped George pack up the remaining food.

"Well, I guess we should get back to it," John said. "May as well finish up today if we can."

The four of them headed topside. Scott and George disappeared down the amidships companionway, and John and Brie went aft and back down to their work in the stern compartment. John gathered up the tools and Brie carried the heater, and they moved over to the port side of the ship to the cabin just forward of John's.

"That was Dent Fenton on the phone."

John didn't look up, but she saw his jaw stiffen. "So what's up?" he asked. Instead of looking at her, he picked up a piece of pipe and knelt down next to the wall where a second pipe protruded.

"He didn't say exactly. Something about a case they're working on. He said it's not about Parker, though."

She thought she saw his shoulders relax when she said that.

"He wants to meet with us on Thursday at Maine State Police headquarters in Augusta."

"Why us? Why not just you?"

"I don't know, John. He asked if you could be there, too. That's all I know."

John shrugged. "Well, okay."

"So, Thursday's all right?"

"I guess so," he said noncommittally.

They got back to work fitting the pipes for the last sink, but the feeling of levity that had carried them through the rest of the day seemed to have evaporated, and they worked on in strained silence.

Brie had first become involved with the Maine State Police after solving a murder aboard *Maine Wind* last May. At the time, she was on leave from the Minneapolis Police Department. She had come to Maine in March of last year, a year after she had been shot in the line of duty, a year after her partner, Phil Thatcher, had been killed in the same incident, a year after she had first begun courageously but unsuccessfully battling PTSD.

In October, after six months aboard *Maine Wind*, and at the end of the sailing season, she had gone home to make decisions about her life and career with the Minneapolis Police Department. She hadn't intended to investigate her partner's murder, and for that matter was not allowed to formally investigate it. But she soon learned that all her decisions going forward, as well as her ability to reclaim herself from the ravages of PTSD, appeared to hang on solving the case of Detective Phil Thatcher's murder. But that decision had led her into dark territory with surprising and unforeseen consequences. And now, through the most bizarre and convoluted course of events, a man who had been a fellow detective and, she thought, a friend had become her arch nemesis. Had stalked and nearly killed John and placed the darkest of clouds over their relationship at a time when they had just begun their life together—at a time when happiness should have been a constant for them.

"Brie, could you lift that a little higher?"

Lost in her thoughts, she was letting down her end, literally. She lifted the small sink up a bit so John could check that the pipes were going to fit properly. Then they drilled and installed the mountings for the sink and hung it in place on the cabin wall. John knelt back down on the floor and caulked and threaded the pipes into place.

"It seems odd that Dent Fenton would want me at a meeting. You worked with him and Marty Dupuis last summer on several cases. But what do I have to do with any of it?" The question lingered in his brown eyes.

"Don't know, John. I haven't got a crystal ball, and Dent didn't seem to want to get into it, whatever *it* is, until we meet."

"Huh," was all he said. "Well, if it involves a case, I guess this wouldn't be the worst time to get involved. There's not much going on these next couple of months."

"But John, you're forgetting that I haven't signed back on with the Maine State Police since being back here. They deputized me last summer when we worked together on the case in Tucker Harbor, and I kept that status until I went back to Minnesota in October. But the fact is, I haven't decided whether I want to continue in police work, even as a consultant."

"Dent Fenton knows firsthand what a good detective you are. Of course he's going to try to draw you back into the fold. You can't blame him for that."

"I know that, John. I guess we'll just see what he has to say on Thursday and go from there."

"One step at a time, eh?"

"Funny thing. The deputy I worked with up in northern Minnesota in October—Claude Renard—that was his saying. 'One step at a time.'" Brie wondered if she should take it as a sign. Unconsciously, her hand came to her chest where the small medicine bundle hung that Claude and Joseph Renard had given her when she'd left Grand Portage for the last time.

John pulled her close, kissed the top of her head, played with her long braid. "You know, somehow the unknown isn't so scary now that you're a part of it."

"Thank you, John. That's the truth, isn't it?"

"Let's go home. Eat some of that wonderful soup you made last night."

"It's a deal."

They packed up the tools, bundled into their parkas and headed topside. George and Scott were just loading things off the deck onto the wharf. The winter sun was turning in early as it did every night at this time of year. They all said goodnight and headed for their trucks.

Chapter 2

On Thursday at eleven o'clock, Brie and John sat in Lieutenant Dent Fenton's office in the two-story red-brick building that was the headquarters for the Maine State Police in Augusta, Maine. Icy pellets of snow pinged off the windows behind his desk, and the smell of stale coffee from the pot on the burner behind the desk gave the room a caffeinated vibe—albeit not a good one.

The snowstorm that was predicted to be in and out by the end of Wednesday had stalled, dropping another four inches so far today. Ergo, the drive from Camden to Augusta had been a slog, and what was normally accomplished in an hour had turned into two hours of icy treachery. The kind that was helped not at all by John's four-wheel-drive truck. The kind where all the overconfident idiots in their four-wheel drives end up decorating the ditches along the way.

At 11:05 Dent Fenton entered the room. He was carrying a small tray with three mugs of coffee that didn't smell like it had been made in the last century either, but broadcast a rich, curl-up-in-your PJs aroma.

"Sorry I'm late, guys. Got caught up in another meeting." He handed around the coffee. "Thanks for braving the weather. How are the roads?"

"Moving from bad to worse," John said.

"In that case, we'll get right to it."

He sat behind his desk and studied them for a second. His heavy brow bone always gave him an air of gravitas. He had short red hair and glacial blue eyes, and there was something in his manner that branded him a cop through and through.

"You've probably heard or read about the four lobstermen who've disappeared from their boats without a trace over the past sixteen months."

"I heard about the first three cases," Brie said.

"The fourth man went missing in mid-November," Dent said. "You didn't come back to Maine until the end of November."

She nodded.

"All of them went missing in the waters off Starkhaven Island. Four lobsterboats found at sea with no one aboard."

Situated as it was, twenty plus miles from the mainland, Brie knew the seas off that island could be notoriously large and dangerous. She also knew the lobstermen on the outer islands were a different breed, fishing year round, often in treacherous conditions.

"People generally have no idea what a dangerous profession lobstering is," John said. "And I know, every year, lobstermen are lost at sea. But four in that span of time, all in the same waters . . ." His gaze shifted to the window behind Dent. It told the story of ever-decreasing visibility. In a few seconds he looked back at him. "Do you think their disappearances might be connected?"

Dent smiled. "You're thinking more and more like a cop."

"Yeah, well, you know who's to blame for that." He gave Brie a nod.

"I take it there's been an investigation into the deaths," Brie said.

"To the extent possible," Dent said. "Understand that none of the four bodies was ever found. In the first two cases, death certificates were issued in absentia, recognizing presumption of death but not the fact of death, with the stated cause in each case 'presumed drowning.' The problem with the investigation is the islanders themselves." He looked at Brie. "As you know from some of the cases you've worked with us, there is no police presence on the islands, and law enforcement from outside is not always welcomed. The islanders are self-regulating, and they tend to close ranks. Whatever their issues are, they want to deal with them themselves. So investigations often fall flat. And when you're talking about the outer islands—a place like Starkhaven—well, the effect is amplified."

"The islanders out there live a life apart, and they like it that way," John said.

Dent looked from one to the other of them. "Here's what I think," he said. "I think we have a killer out on Starkhaven, and he or she is targeting lobstermen. But we have no clue as to the 'why' or the 'who.' Which brings me to why I called you here today." He turned to Brie. "I would like to send you and John out to Starkhaven, undercover. You cracked that missing person's case—the case of Amanda Whitcomb—out on Sentinel Island this past summer, and you did it without any kind of official status."

"It was just coincidental that I was there and got drawn into the case," Brie said.

"Which made the outcome even more impressive," Dent said. "And you ended up solving not one but two mysteries."

They fell silent. It was a thick silence. John finally spoke. "You said you wanted to send both of us out there. What is your plan, Dent?"

Brie glanced over at him, stupefied that he would even entertain the idea of getting involved in such a plan.

"We've been looking at the possibility of sending someone out there undercover since the third death occurred. This fourth death in November has put a sharp point on the situation. Once again, we sent detectives and the Evidence Response Team out to Starkhaven to go over the boat and interview the families and acquaintances of this recently deceased lobsterman—Abe Winter is his name—to try and learn if he had any enemies or who might have had a motive to kill him. To try and discover how he might be linked to the other victims or if the supposed killings appeared to be random.

"But like the other three cases, we were met with a lot of resistance from the natives and outright stonewalling. In fact, I have to say that it's been nearly impossible to get any traction at all with this fourth case. Folks out there seem almost intent on denying what's happening."

"That's fear, plain and simple," Brie said. "Nothing like denial to give people a false sense of security."

"But that can't be allowed to stand," Dent said. "Starkhaven Island is under Maine State Police jurisdiction. The folks out there may want to be left alone to solve their own problems, and that's fine, up to a point. But if we feel others are in danger, we can't just sit on our hands. So, the consensus among the brass is that we should mount an undercover investigation.

"I recommended you to the chief in December, Brie. He's aware of the fine work you have done with the department. If you're willing to entertain the idea, I'll sketch things out for you. You certainly don't have to give us a decision today."

"Here's the thing, Lieutenant," John said. "If this plan involves me, I have a ship to float, as you must know. I could be available until mid-March, but not much later. So given those parameters, I'm willing to listen."

"And you, Brie. Are you open to this?" Dent asked.

"I'm open to listening, Dent, so go ahead and sketch away."

"Okay, then," he said. "Well, we started by looking into whether there was any tax forfeit property out there. Something that might have belonged to a family that had been in the lobster trade, since to lobster out there you need a territory, and those aren't easy to come by."

"So did you come up with anything?" Brie asked.

"Surprisingly, yes. There's a property out there that went into probate a few months ago. The owner, one Nathan Ross, died with no will and no apparent heirs. Ross owed back property taxes, so the State of Maine has taken possession of the property. We're working with the county and the state to use that property in our undercover investigation. Best part. The guy was a lobsterman. He had a territory out there."

Brie had learned over her time in Maine that not just anyone can get into lobstering. One needs a territory—a part of the ocean bottom that each lobsterman claims as his own. They are not easy to come by and, for that reason, they are usually inherited.

"Not to throw in a monkey wrench, but John isn't a lobsterman."

"But he is a mariner—a man of the sea. So being out on it wouldn't intimidate him. How about that though, John? Any lobsterboat experience?" Dent asked.

"Like lots of young guys on the coast, I worked as a sternman one summer when I was eighteen. So, yes, I know my way around a lobsterboat. I assume this guy, Nathan Ross, also had a boat out there. Do you know the status of that or his traps?"

"I'll check the state license bureau for his boat registration and lobstering license. And I'll see if Maine Marine Patrol can check on the status of his lobsterboat out there."

"So what would the setup be?" Brie asked.

"As the story would go, John would have a familial connection to the property and to the island—maybe as Ross's nephew or cousin, whom the State of Maine has managed to locate. And, as the story would also go, he has paid the back taxes and taken possession of the property. Because of his familial connection to Ross, we assume he'll be accepted on the island."

"But what if someone should recognize him or know him?" Brie asked. "Believe me, and I know what I'm talking about, this is always the greatest danger in any undercover op."

"What are the chances of that, John?" Dent asked.

"Slim to none, I would think. We windjammer captains give that island a wide berth. Yachtsmen and sailors generally aren't welcomed out there. What's more, the harbor is too small to accommodate a ship the size of ours."

Dent nodded.

"So are you thinking we'd be posing as a married couple?" John asked. He turned and studied Brie in a way that put a butterfly in her chest.

"That's the plan," Dent said. "If you two don't mind being a bickering old married couple."

"Maybe we'll be newlyweds," John said, turning to her again.

For whatever reason, the room was starting to feel uncomfortably warm to Brie. She shifted in her chair.

"Wouldn't it be better if you sent another detective out there undercover with me?" As soon as she said it, John turned away, but too late. She'd already seen the hurt look on his face. *Oh boy*, she thought to herself.

"Well, as a matter of fact, I am. I'm sending Jack Le Beau. He's going to pose as your elderly grandfather, living with you and John."

Just hearing Jack's name made Brie warm to the plan. Jack Le Beau was the retired detective whom she'd worked with throughout the case on Apparition Island. Jack was a sweetheart, and his giant Newfoundland dog, Angus, had galumphed his way straight into Brie's heart.

"Would Angus be coming, too?" she asked, a spark of interest in her voice.

It was the first spark that Dent had observed, and a smile spread slowly across his face.

"Jack has informed me that, much as he loves *you*, Brie, to not bring Angus would be a deal breaker."

"You know, if I didn't think of Jack as somewhat of a grandfatherly figure, I might be jealous," John said.

"And the fact that you can admit that shows just what a grownup guy you are," Brie quipped. She reached over and took his hand so there'd be no hard feelings.

"We were actually hoping that your cook, George Dupopolis, might get involved as well."

"Oh, yeah? And who's he supposed to be? Brie's long-lost brother from another mother?"

That brought a deserving laugh and lifted the thin veil of tension that had hung over the discussion.

"We thought he'd make a perfect sternman," Dent said. "He looks the part, and we know he won't be getting seasick. After all, if you can cook below decks for twelve hours a day at sea, you're about as acclimated as anyone will ever be. And as to his relationship to you two? Well, we were thinking he might be your cousin, John. You know, keep it in the family. They like that out on the islands."

"Great. So John will be out at sea pulling lobster pots. Jack will be working the geezer crowd. George will be working the other sternmen. And what is it exactly that I'll be doing?"

"Work your way into the fabric of the community," Dent said. "Do what you're so good at, Brie. Investigate." Dent sat back in his chair and took down some of his coffee. "We've been working the grapevine throughout the department for info about Starkhaven Island. We've learned there's an active group of quilters out there. Don't suppose you sew, Brie?"

She gave him a withering look, but finally relented. "I'm not really the crafty type. However, my Granny Beaumont did teach me how to quilt when I was a girl." She thought about her grandmother's beautiful handmade quilt that had hung on the wall in her Minnesota apartment for so many years and now hung in the house she shared with John. "Every summer when we came to Maine, I would quilt with my grandma. I'm pretty sure I could hold my own in that group."

"Great. That's one more angle we can work then," Dent said.

"I'd like to look through the case files for the four victims. Get a feel for what went on out there with the investigations. Find out if any suspects came to light during the interviews."

"I thought you might ask. I have them right here." He patted the stack of files on the left side of his desk. "But I have to warn you; what's in these is pretty thin."

He opened his drawer. "I have your shield. I kept you on active status when you went back to Minnesota. I hoped you'd return and work with us again at some point." He set the badge wallet on top of the desk.

Brie stared at it for a beat or two, uncertain what she felt about receiving it. "Why don't you hang on to it, Dent, until we make a decision about all of this."

"Fair enough. If you decide to go ahead with the plan, and if George is able and wishes to join you, I'd like to schedule a meeting for Monday. We have all the pieces in place, and if you are willing, we'd like to get the ball rolling on this as soon as possible. Will that give you enough time to make a decision?"

"I'll get back to you before end of day tomorrow," Brie said. That gave her and John today and tomorrow to reach a decision and to talk to George about the plan.

"Great. I'll talk to Jack Le Beau and ask him to save Monday morning in case we decide to go ahead."

"If that's it, I'd like to get back on the road," John said. He nodded toward the window. "Conditions are rapidly deteriorating out there."

"Absolutely," Dent said. He stood up, signaling they were done. "You two be careful driving back to Camden."

They shook hands, and Brie and John bundled into their parkas. Brie gathered up the files, and they left Dent's office and made for the truck.

Chapter 3

Outside the door of the Maine State Police Headquarters, Brie and John made a dash for his truck, heads down against the lash of the wind. Wind that whistled around the corners of the red brick structure, piling drifts of snow against the walls. They tumbled into the truck, and John started the engine and headed out onto Hospital Street and north toward Route 17.

Conditions were near whiteout as they drove east out of Augusta. The wipers created two small dome-shaped windows on an arctic world, and around those windows snow encrusted the windshield as if they were viewing the blizzard from inside an igloo. And blizzard it was. Coming from Minnesota, Brie was well acquainted with the look and feel of one.

"Can you imagine living out on Starkhaven in this kind of weather?" she asked.

"It wouldn't be that different from the coast," John said. "Same raw cold, straight off the Atlantic. The seas would be huge out there, though."

They were both silent for a few minutes, contemplating the thought of it.

Finally Brie spoke. "I've been a cop for a long time, John, and danger is part of the territory. But I wouldn't want to put you in jeopardy in any way. Or George, for that matter. That's the reason I asked Dent why they didn't send a cop with me out there."

"I understand that, Brie. But just anyone won't fit the bill. First off, they need someone who knows the sea and is comfortable with it. Even though this is Maine, you can't just snap your fingers and come up with someone. And I would think, to carry this off, we'll also have to be believable as a couple. I'm hoping we've got that part nailed at least."

Brie smiled. "You're right. I'm just surprised you're open to this plan. I mean, there's usually lots of work at the boatyard this time of year."

"Scott will be there, and I can always get Ed Browning to lend a hand."

Ed had served as mate aboard *Maine Wind* in the past. Brie had met him last summer when he took over for her while she was on the case up in Tucker Harbor. Still she had to wonder about John's willingness to leave the boatyard and join this op. *Is he an adrenaline junkie?* She'd never thought of him that way but had to admit that life at sea aboard the schooner was a high-adventure proposition—often unpredictable, sometimes dangerous.

"Look at it this way, Brie. It'll get us off the mainland and away from the possibility of Garrett Parker showing up and ruining our day some day."

"Yeah, well, I'm sure his plan would be to ruin more than our day." *But there it is,* she thought. *The reason for his willingness.*

They drove in silence for the rest of the trip, John squinting at the road, and Brie with her body clenched every time they hit a patch of ice. She was thinking about retired detective Jack Le Beau and the case that had brought them together.

Dent had plans for him to pose as her grandfather, if they decided to go through with the undercover operation on Starkhaven Island. Within American culture Jack would certainly be considered elderly, even though, in his mid-eighties, he was sharp as tacks and more physically fit than some thirty-five-year-olds she'd known. Brie had come to dislike the word *elderly* after working the case with Claude Renard near Grand Marais, Minnesota, and coming to know the ways of the Ojibwe. To Native Americans, such individuals are known as elders, which carries a very different connotation—one of respect, wisdom, experience, influence, governance. Jack Le Beau was an elder, and the plan for him to participate in the operation on Starkhaven, to her way of thinking, greatly increased the possibility of its success.

After battling treacherous road conditions for nearly two hours, they turned onto Route 1 and headed north. Eight miles up the road they descended a long, curving hill and entered the coastal town of Lincolnville. What would normally have been a one-hour drive had stretched to over two. Just beyond the town, they turned into the boatyard and parked the truck.

George was in the office, manning the phone, just in case anyone was thinking about going sailing on a day like this. It made Brie think about some of the outrageously blue days out at sea under full sail, and for just a moment the howl of the blizzard was transmuted into the roar of the wind in the canvas, and she could almost feel the warm July sun on her face.

John's dog, Barnacle—better known as Barney—lay on the floor next to George. He thumped his tail on the floor as soon as John and Brie came through the door.

"I think we'll close up shop for today," John said. "Conditions are deteriorating rapidly."

"No arguments from me." George stood up and reached for his coat on the back of the chair, and Barney arose looking expectant.

"I wonder if you'd mind stopping by the house. There's something Brie and I would like to run past you. In fact, why don't you plan to spend the night so you don't have to drive back down the coast."

"Sure." For a moment he looked like he wanted to ask a question but decided against it. That made sense; George being a take-it-as-it-comes kind of guy.

They headed out the door. "You can ride with us, if you like, and leave your car here," John said.

George nodded, and they piled into the truck with Barney and George taking the back seat. "Got any plans for dinner?" he asked as they pulled away.

"Not a plan in sight," John said.

"In that case, let's stop at the general store and grab some supplies. I'll make spaghetti and meatballs for dinner."

Brie rubbed her hands together. "That sounds great, George. I'll help."

"You're on."

They parked across from the Lincolnville General Store—undoubtedly the prettiest building in town, with its stately red and white frame exterior. It was of traditional Maine architecture—big house, little house, backhouse, all strung together. A white pillared porch wrapped around the front and side of the store, where, in the summer, tables and rocking chairs invited you to "set a spell." Large arch-top muntined windows on either side of the front door lent a feel of grandness to the structure and poured natural light into the interior. Inside, a lovely wide pine floor ran vertically toward the back of the store, drawing you into a treasure trove of good things. Fresh-baked breads and pastries, fresh produce, wines, and cheeses, and a deli with different soups and sandwiches appearing daily.

As they stepped through the front door, a crowd of wonderful aromas greeted them. The warm savory smells of bread baking; the sharp notes of roasted coffee; the sweet aroma of fruit, baked into pies. Even with the storm raging outside, the place was buzzing—everyone stocking up so they could hunker down.

The three of them walked up and down the aisles gathering what they needed. Fresh tomatoes, garlic and herbs for the sauce, greens for a salad, ground beef for the meatballs, boxes of pasta, fresh parmesan cheese from the deli area, a loaf of French bread from the bakery, and a bottle of Chianti.

John paid for everything up at the front register and they were on their way. His house lay on the outskirts of Camden. On a good day it was a ten-minute drive—today, twenty. During the season *Maine Wind* was docked in Camden harbor, so whether going to the ship or the boatyard, he was just minutes away. He had chosen his house carefully, knowing that traffic on the coastal highway was a snarl at least four months of the year.

The house was in the upper part of Camden, north of the commercial area of the village. The pickup crunched over a foot of fresh snow as they pulled into the driveway and made their way up to the house. It was a small two-story frame house, painted white with Prussian blue trim, with a lovely covered front porch and a wide yard, ringed by forest.

They bailed out of the truck and made a dash for the front door through the driving snow. Stomping their feet off, they unlocked the door and hurried inside. There was a small entry area to the right of the door with a coat rack, a rug for boots, and a Windsor parson's bench for sitting and pulling them on and off. Brie set the files down on the bench and took off her boots. A hallway ran past the foot of the stairs and straight back to the kitchen. The living room was through an archway to their left and beyond that, forming an "L," the dining room.

They hung their coats, and Brie headed into the living room. Barney made a beeline for his bed in the kitchen. Beautiful pumpkin pine floors ran throughout the downstairs. None of the furniture in the living room matched but, taken together, was a collection of coziness. Every piece invited you to curl up, stay awhile, and peruse a book from one of the bookcases under the living room windows. There was a freestanding woodstove in the corner of the room and a built-in niche that held logs.

"I'll get a fire started," John said.

"I'll make some hot coffee," George said.

"I'll help," Brie added.

John got busy with fire duties, and George and Brie went into the kitchen. A large window over the sink looked out on the depths of a Maine winter. George ground the coffee beans while Brie washed out the pot. By the time they had the coffee brewing, a fire was blazing in the woodstove. Brie put out a plate of cookies she and John had baked the previous weekend. When the coffee was done, they all gathered in the living room and moved their chairs into a circle around the stove. Normally, on a day with such a heavy atmosphere, getting a fire burning would be an iffy proposition. But John's woodstove drafted like a locomotive. So, once the fire was in full stride, they could damp down the stove and bask in the warmth, with no worries of the blaze petering out.

George looked expectantly from John to Brie once they had settled in.

"Here's the deal, George. John and I met with Dent Fenton from the Maine State Police today. You know I worked with them last summer on a number of cases."

"Sure," George said. "Heck, Detective Dupuis was aboard *Maine Wind* with us for part of that last . . . very unusual cruise in October."

"Well, here's the thing," Brie said. "There's a complicated case they've been working on for quite a few months, and long story short, they'd like me, and John as well, to go undercover out on Starkhaven Island."

George's eyebrows went up. "Both of you? Starkhaven? In the middle of winter?" His incredulity momentarily brought the discussion to a full stop. He looked from one to the other of them, and suddenly clarity widened his eyes. "This is about the lobstermen out on Starkhaven. The ones that have gone missing."

"That's right," Brie said. "There have been four deaths in the past sixteen months."

"But those were accidents, weren't they? Seas too high to be out on. Guys careless with their gear. There's lots of ways lobstermen can end up in the ocean. There's this macho thing you hear about that goes on out there. Who can go out in the worst seas and pull their pots. Badge of honor for stupidity, if you ask me." George sat back and crossed his brawny arms on his chest.

Brie could sense resistance on the rise.

John studied him for a moment. "You're right about all of that, George. But four deaths in that many months in the same waters . . ." He let the comment hang there.

"You have to admit, it's awfully coincidental," Brie said. "And here's the thing. Cops don't like coincidences. Not ones that are racking up bodies. Starkhaven is under the jurisdiction of the Maine State Police, as are all the islands when a major crime occurs."

"But from what I've read, none of the bodies were ever recovered."

"That doesn't preclude an investigation. And to that end, the MSP has sent a team to the island after each presumed death."

John leaned forward. "Look, George, you've lived here long enough. You know what it's like. If you're from Away, folks don't easily trust you. On a place like Starkhaven Island, with their desire for isolation, 'from Away' could easily include mainland Mainers, especially if they are the police. Even when there's a crisis, those folks prefer to handle it themselves."

"So what makes you think you'll get anywhere even if you go out there?"

"I've been a cop for a long time, George, and I've taken part in things like this before. These ops cost money and, because of that, they are carefully planned. There are no guarantees, but we have to try. The police have a sworn duty to uphold the law. No matter how daunting the case or the circumstances, we have to press on. Because if we don't, who will?"

As she heard herself speak those words, something registered with her, possibly in a way it never had—in a conscious way—as if it were being written with indelible ink in an indestructible book. It was duty that drove her, that had for as long as she could remember. And although PTSD had sidelined her psychologically for a time, that sense of duty was why she had become a cop. She had never understood, even as a child, how people could look the other way in the face of need. Just pretend they didn't see, didn't hear, didn't understand. There can be no justice, no security without the duty-driven. She thought about the shield Dent had put in front of her that afternoon. The shield she had carried. She realized there was no option about picking it up again. That, for her, there would never be an option. When the call went out, she would stand, she would always stand.

John leaned forward and put his hand on her knee, and she saw absolute solidarity in his eyes.

George also leaned in. "So, I suppose you want me to hold down the fort while you two are out there. And, of course, I will. I'd never let you down, John."

"Actually, we'd like you to be part of the operation, George. Dent asked specifically if you might be willing to take part."

George pointed to himself, but no words came out. He couldn't have looked more dumbfounded had he been granted a fiefdom. "But what can I possibly do?" he finally said.

"It's all about eyes and ears, George. Lots of eyes and ears." Brie proceeded to tell him about the plan for the undercover op and what his role would be if he agreed to take part in it—about acting as sternman aboard John's lobsterboat and immersing himself in the island's lobstering trade. About being their eyes and ears among the other sternmen on the island. She also told him that Jack Le Beau, retired Maine State Police detective, had been recruited by Dent Fenton and was onboard with the plan. "He'll be traveling with us and posing as my grandfather."

What she couldn't tell him because she didn't yet know was that Dent Fenton had a key player out on Starkhaven Island. A kind of bona fide welcome wagon in a place where wagons and welcomes never got together. A linchpin in what was sure to be a complicated and potentially dangerous operation.

George sat for a moment looking dumbfounded.

"You don't need to give us an answer right this minute," John said. "Take time to think about it. See if being part of this makes any sense to you."

"We'll understand if you decide against it," Brie said. "But just know that your role in the operation could be an important one."

George nodded. "I'll give you an answer by tomorrow."

"Perfect," Brie said. And with that they ended their meeting.

Chapter 4

After the meeting, George retreated to the kitchen to do some mulling, and we're not talking wine. Brie knew that he was most comfortable, did his best thinking, when surrounded by culinary paraphernalia. Of course, no better spot at such a time than his beloved galley aboard *Maine Wind*. But any port in a storm, as they say. So she soon heard him unloading groceries, opening cabinets, taking out pots, and sharpening knives. She smiled to herself, knowing George — knowing that this was simply his way of processing what they had just discussed. She also knew it was best to leave him to himself at such a time, so she went to the front entry and retrieved the case files from the bench where she had left them.

She walked into the dining room and sat at one end of the table, where she could look out the window and watch the snow deepening an already deep winter. Dinner wouldn't be happening for a couple of hours, which gave her time to go through the files. John had bundled up and gone outside to shovel a path to the woodshed. She spread the files out in front of her and chose the one with the earliest date—September 18, approximately sixteen months ago.

The name on the case file was Oslo Stumph. Brie marveled at the name for a minute, then opened the file and studied the picture of the first victim. He had been fifty-two years old at the time of his death. The photo, which had been enlarged and so was a bit grainy, showed him with a couple of guys at what looked like a backyard get-together. He was hoisting a beer in salute and looking slightly inebriated. He was ruddy and round-faced and mostly bald, and his smile showed a missing eye-tooth. He was also listed as divorced. There was a death certifi-cate—which stated "Death in Absentia." The cause of death was listed as "presumed drowned." Manner of death was recorded as "undetermined."

The file showed that a detective had been sent to the island and that the victim's parents, who also lived on Starkhaven, had been interviewed, along with a couple of Stumph's friends. After the divorce, Stumph's ex-wife had left the island and settled on the mainland, in Portland, with their children. The parents reported that he had always kept up on his child-support payments and that the children, one boy, one girl, had spent part of each summer with him on the island.

His friends, who had been interviewed, classified him as a jokester, but one source, who asked to remain anonymous, said that Oslo Stumph had a mean streak. When the detective pressed him for his name, the source refused to identify himself—said he wanted his name kept out of the record. There was little else in the file. This was the first death, after all, and understandably, it was presumed to be an accident, probably due to careless-ness. Brie noted the name of the detective in her notebook and moved on to the second case file.

The victim's name was Paul Le Fevre. She opened the file and studied his photo. He was handsome as could be. Dark curly hair, carved features. He actually bore a slight resem-blance to John. The record stated that he was thirty-eight years old at the time of death, in February of last year. Brie looked at the face in the photo for a few moments. There was something in his eyes, a hollowness that she could only describe as haunted —as if something had whittled away much of his vital essence. She wasn't sure why, but the thought came to her that he might have been suicidal. Of course she had nothing to base that on;

still she marked the thought, since Le Fevre had died at sea in an unexplained manner.

She read on in the file. There was no clue as to what had unfolded that day, but judging from the number of lobsters in the barrel aboard his boat, he hadn't pulled very many pots that morning, suggesting that he may have disappeared long before daylight. There was nothing particularly unusual about that, though. Lobstermen always put out to sea in the predawn hours.

Le Fevre's marital status was listed as widowed. One of the people interviewed after his death was his next-door neighbor. The detective had written that the neighbor was reluctant to speak ill of Le Fevre; said he'd been dealt a cruel hand, that his wife had died years before, and since then, he had turned to alcohol. The detective had asked the neighbor if she thought Le Fevre was alcoholic, and she reluctantly stated that she believed he was. The next question was about whether, in her opinion, Paul Le Fevre might have been working on his boat while "under the influence." She declined to comment, saying that no one could speak to that unless they were with him. Brie opened her notebook and made a note. "Ask about sternman —Le Fevre." She also made a note of the detective's name assigned to the case—a different detective than had worked the first case.

The name of the third victim was Cliff Gordon. He had been forty-eight years old when he disappeared. For some reason his picture reminded Brie of a wily fox. He had a narrow face, brush-cut dark blond hair and penetrating eyes. But even though he appeared clean-cut, his was not a face that inspired trust.

He had gone missing from his lobsterboat on July 22 of last year, roughly five months after Paul Le Fevre had disappeared. He was married and had a grown daughter who had left the island. The case file showed that two detectives had been sent to Starkhaven following the third death. The same two who had worked the first and second cases. It made sense, the thought being that they might have some purchase on the island—some shot at getting folks to cooperate, since they'd investigated the previous cases. The thought was wrong, though. As Dent had mentioned in their meeting, by the third death out on Starkhaven Island, virtually no one was talking. In fact, the islanders had turned from a guarded willingness to be interviewed about the victims to a kind of collective stonewalling. Also evident in the record was a disturbing degree of dismissal of the alarming events that were unfolding. As Brie had stated in the meeting with Dent Fenton: *That was fear taking the guise of denial.*

But in the case of Cliff Gordon, the third victim, both detectives had reported a strong sense of something buried below the surface of this man's life. Something no one would talk about, even though he was dead. Brie made a note of that in her notebook under his name. Closer to the surface was the obvious fact that his wife, Bess Gordon, was a victim of battering. The detectives had reported seeing bruising on her face and that she had her arm in a sling, as if her shoulder might have been injured or dislocated. They questioned her about the injuries and encouraged her to file a report about the abuse. The case file stated that she had merely shrugged and said, *Why? He's gone now, so what difference would that possibly make?* Their report stated that she was pretty shut down emotionally, showing no grief whatsoever.

Big surprise, Brie thought.

The detectives also noted that in their opinion, she would never have had the physical strength to kill her husband, even without one arm in a sling.

Brie moved on to the last of the case files. Victim number four. His name was Abe Winter. Once again she studied the photo clipped to the inside of the file. Winter had shoulder-length black hair that looked less than clean. He had a blank expression as if he might be slightly stoned. He looked a bit like a hippy from days of old. He had been thirty-three at the time of his death, approximately two months ago. He was the last victim and had been reported missing on November 14th. Near dusk, his boat was found going in circles a mile off the island. Once again, there was no clue as to what had transpired, but he had lots of catch aboard. That suggested he'd disappeared after daybreak — possibly late morning.

Abe Winter was listed as single in the report. His father had passed several years before, and Winter lived with his mother and worked what had been his father's territory. His mother had stated that Abe wouldn't hurt a fly and that he was a good boy. *Well, of course he was*, Brie thought. *Don't all mothers say that?*

It was clear to Brie from the reports in the file that the detectives had tirelessly worked the island, trying to gather information on this fourth victim. But while any number of residents readily classified Winter as a good guy, the detectives also noted a kind of low-frequency nervousness among the islanders they had interviewed that led them to believe there was a secret being kept, possibly wide-ranging in nature.

Something that might go to motive, Brie thought. She closed the last case file and sat thinking for a few minutes about what she had hoped to find in the files and what was actually there. After the meeting with Dent Fenton, she hadn't had very high expectations of what she would find in them. But the reports and the pictures *had* helped to give her a rudimentary sense of each of the victims. Enough so that the detective in her was already at work positing a number of questions.

The theory had evolved in the Major Crimes Unit that these deaths were all connected — that someone was killing lobstermen out on Starkhaven Island. The question was, what was the dynamic? Were they looking at a psychopath who chose his victims based on his own deranged parameters? Or was just one of these victims the real target, with the other murders used as clutter, so to speak, to confuse the investigation and hide the true motive?

Brie sat there mulling it over. There were too many deaths in too short of a timeframe for them to be coincidental. But could any of them have been an accident or even possibly suicide? Because if that were the case, it could easily skew the investigation. She knew any answer to that could only be revealed as the investigation unfolded, but she left it as a question in her own mind.

As she sat there cogitating, a third possibility reared its head, and it derived from the fact that there was no police presence on the island. Starkhaven was known as a lawless place and one where the fishermen handled matters themselves. Might these deaths have been motivated by some kind of vigilante justice? If that were the case, it would have to be considered a kind of subset of the first possibility—namely, that a psychopath was at work out there. In this scenario, each of the victims would have to have done something bad enough to warrant killing, at least in the mind of the perpetrator.

Brie wrote a short list in her small notebook and placed a question mark after each entry.

1. Psychopath?
2. Targeting one victim?
3. Vigilante justice?

She sat tapping her pen on the table and studied the list.

Finally she closed her notebook, sat back, and stared out the window at the gathering darkness of a Maine winter. She glanced back at the case files and sat fixated on them for a few moments. Beyond the questions that had arisen from them, she had noted a disquieting theme that ran through the interviews. A fatalistic outlook voiced by friends and relatives of the victims. *If the sea decided to take someone, they would be taken.* As if will or circumstance or good or bad decisions played no part whatsoever in these tragedies. The sea was their god, kind or malevolent—providing sustenance but taking payment when it so desired.

A chill ran through her at the thought of joining their ranks, not for her own welfare—she had danced with the devil her entire career—but for John. She feared for John. It was a fear new to her, because she had shied away from close relationships during her years as a cop. She'd never wanted to be with another cop, and yet cops were the only ones who truly understood the daily traumas they all faced and the toll that police work exacted.

She was still deep in thought when she heard George and John moving about the kitchen. She looked at her watch and was surprised to see that it was almost six o'clock. Two hours had passed since she'd sat down with the case files. She stretched her arms over her head and leaned back in the chair, feeling some of the kinks in her neck and back release. She stood up and set the files over on the sideboard that sat against the back wall of the dining room and headed out to the kitchen.

George was putting together a mixture of ingredients for the meatballs, and John was filling a pan of water for cooking the pasta. Over on the small table in the corner, a chess game was underway.

"Were you guys playing chess?"

"We were, but George thought he should get the dinner started."

"Only because I was losing badly," George said.

"Yeah, I kinda got lost in the case files. So what can I do to help?"

"You want to get the salad started?" George asked.

"Sure."

Brie got out the wood salad bowl and went to the fridge for the lettuce and other veggies. George had picked up a head of Bibb lettuce and a package of mixed greens at the general store. Brie tore the lettuce into big pieces, added the greens, and tossed it all with her hands. She covered the bowl with plastic wrap and put it in the fridge. She'd put the rest of the veggies on top when they were ready to eat.

George began to roll out the meatballs and put them on a baking sheet. Brie and John jumped in to help and in a few minutes they had the sheet full. George put them in a 350-degree oven to brown and started on the tomato sauce.

"So, anything interesting in the case files?" John asked.

"Well, none of them was what you'd call man-of-the-year material. From what I could glean from the reports, the victims seemed to have been a mélange of bullying, wife beating, alcoholism, and covert activities. Don't think we'll have to dig too deep to uncover motives."

"Maybe that will make things easier," John said, looking hopeful.

Brie smiled. "Knowing what the motive might be and figuring out who might have had it are two very different things. Especially in a place like Starkhaven, where the islanders are born tight-lipped." She leaned against the counter. "But it's always good to have a sense of ground zero."

"What's your gut telling you?" John asked.

Brie smiled at his saying that. In the nine months they'd known each other, he'd certainly learned a thing or two about how cops roll.

"Way too soon to tell. But even from the sketchy case files, I get a sense of secrets kept, almost as if that tendency were woven into Starkhaven's DNA."

"Well, when you figure how many generations some of those families have been out there, secrets would have to be almost as plentiful as lobsters."

"The trick will be to separate the ones that matter from those that don't."

They all got busy then with the last of the dinner prep. The meatballs came out of the oven and went into the sauce. George put the spaghetti into the boiling water and the bread into the oven to warm. John set the table, and Brie chopped and added the rest of the veggies to the salad. Finally, George whisked together a simple vinaigrette and got out a board for the bread. John opened the bottle of Chianti and poured it into the glasses on the table. The pasta was drained and added to the sauce, and George got down three pasta bowls and dished up one for each of them, topping them off with a drizzle of olive oil and some fresh parsley. The parmesan was grated and the bread brought forth from the oven and placed on the table alongside the plate of butter. Brie lit a candle and they all sat down at the dining room table to share the meal.

Brie made a toast. "To the warmth of home and to carefully thought-out decisions."

George smiled but said nothing, and for a few minutes the only sound was the wind picking up again outside as they tucked in. George's spaghetti and meatballs were wicked good comfort food for that cold winter evening. The aromas of baked bread and pan-roasted tomatoes, and the tart cherry essence of the Chianti, soon dissolved any anxieties of the afternoon.

After two glasses of wine and a second serving of spaghetti, George had loosened up enough to voice his concerns about the proposed operation out on Starkhaven.

"One summer as a sternman at eighteen isn't much experience for taking on those waters out there," he said, looking at John.

John turned to Brie, a question in his eyes. "I hope I would get something like a crash course out on the water to learn my way around the boat and the routine of hauling traps."

"That's a question for Dent if we agree to go ahead. It's essential that you feel completely competent to take on this role, or I'd say it's a deal breaker." She took the notebook out of the pocket of her flannel shirt, flipped to a blank page and made a note.

"And will we have any kind of a contact out there?" George asked.

Brie shrugged. "Probably not. There are no police on the island, as you probably know. But good question." She jotted another note.

"What I know, or have heard anyway, is that it's the wild, wild east out there," George said.

John laughed out loud at that.

George crossed his arms on his chest and sat back—body language that was not lost on Brie.

"I'm surprised at you, George," John said. "During that last cruise in October, we were well out to sea with a killer aboard and several other unhinged types lurking about, and you came through with flying colors."

George pursed his lips. "Yeah, that's true. But we were aboard *Maine Wind*, and you were in charge."

"Correction, George. I was in charge of the ship, but Brie was in charge of the situation, just like she was out on Granite Island last May. And look, here we are, safe and sound."

Brie for her part was not at all offended. She understood George better than he probably knew. She knew *Maine Wind* was his sanctuary to such an extent that he would always feel safe there even in the worst of times.

"You're right, Captain. I apologize, Brie."

"No need, George. I totally understand your concerns, and in fact, I have a whole list of my own, ready for the meeting with Dent. If we get that far, that is."

John asked if anyone might be up for a game of Scrabble —a clear ploy to change course.

"Yes, yes," Brie said.

"Great. We'll set the card table up in front of the wood-stove. And I have another bottle of wine."

They got the table cleared and cleaned up the kitchen, and within twenty minutes they were gathered around the card table with their wine and their game. George's words all seemed to revolve around food, as if he'd taken up refuge in the one thing he could completely control. And fortuitously, after an hour and a half, the game went to him. By that time Brie was yawning in earnest and, soon, by the power of suggestion, so was George.

"All right, you two. Time for bed before I have to carry both of you upstairs."

George took the front bedroom that was set up as a guest room. John loaned him some pajamas and told him where the extra blankets were. Then he and Brie retired to their room at the back of the house. A large bedroom that looked out over the woods. John, with the help of the guys, had installed a bank of windows along the back wall that faced east. The bed stood opposite them so they could wake to the sunrise and, sometimes, in the night to moonrise.

Brie washed up in the bathroom, got out of her jeans and shirt, and crawled under the down comforter. John soon joined her and they snuggled in together. The wind carved around the eaves, whistling and moaning updates on the storm outside, as the two of them created their own quiet symphony of passion—the perfect panacea for staving off the darkest depths of winter.

*　　*　　*

They woke to a pink and gold sunrise painted behind the evergreens that studded the woods. The storm had broken overnight, but arctic temperatures were predicted for the next few days, despite that deceptively welcoming sunlight. It didn't fool Brie much, being from a land where the sunniest, bluest days could quickly claim both nose and toes.

"Do you smell that?" she asked John.

"I smell you and you smell wonderful." He let out a low bear growl, reached over, and pulled her in. Brie let out a little squeal of delight and wiggled free and headed for the bathroom.

"A bear can outrun you, you know."

"Oh, yeah, just try. George's cooking is my elixir. Once I smell it, there's no stopping me."

Bearlike, John sniffed the air. "I detect hints of bacon and fruity notes of blueberries." He threw back the covers and pulled on his jeans. "Bet I can beat you down there!"

"Ah, go ahead," she said, her mouth full of toothpaste. "I don't mind letting you win this once."

But John was already out the door heading for the coffee.

Brie headed down the stairs within five minutes and found the boys in the kitchen, John drinking coffee and George whistling a sea shanty and looking all happiness and light. She took it as a sign that he might be coming around—or at least warming to the idea of the plan. On the other hand, it might just be the deep content he found in producing blueberry buckwheat pancakes in a state like Maine that had the best maple syrup. But don't tell the Vermonters that.

She jumped into action and started turning the bacon that was sizzling away in the big cast-iron skillet. John sauntered over to the dish cabinet and got the plates and set the small table in the corner of the kitchen that sat in a pool of sunlight beneath the window there.

Over those fabulous pancakes, George informed Brie that he'd thought it through and wanted to take part in the operation out on Starkhaven Island. And he assured her that, despite his trepidations the night before, he was all in and committed to helping the plan succeed.

"That's great, George. I'm glad you're in. But we still have some important questions to get answered before I'm giving this the green light."

"So what's the next step?" George asked.

"I told Dent Fenton I'd call him today by end of day. At the meeting yesterday, he said that if we decide to go ahead, he'd like to meet with everyone next Monday."

"Would you mention to him that George and I need to put in some time aboard a lobsterboat, so we know the drill?"

"I'll make sure to do that, John. George, how about you? Any questions you want answered when I call the lieutenant today?"

"Not that I can think of. But if any occur to me over the weekend, I'll write them down and bring them to the meeting Monday."

"Great. I'll give Dent a call after breakfast."

They lingered over their pancakes and hot coffee and enjoyed the winter sun that filled the kitchen. After breakfast Brie went to call Dent Fenton while the guys cleaned up. He set the meeting for 10:30 a.m. Monday at headquarters, where they had met yesterday. Brie conveyed John's concerns that he and George spend some time aboard a lobsterboat going over boat handling and lobstering procedures. Dent said he'd get on that and have a plan by Monday, and with that they ended the call.

Once breakfast was cleaned up, they showered and dressed and headed for the boatyard.

Chapter 5

John, Brie, and George arrived at Maine State Police Headquarters by ten fifteen on Monday. Brie spotted Jack Le Beau's SUV as they pulled in to park.

"Look, there's Angus," she said. "Let's go see him."

Jack Le Beau's big black Newfie had his giant head out the window of the Jeep, happily sniffing the January air. They piled out of the truck and Brie bounded toward him.

"Hey, Angus. Remember me?"

He let out an excited woof at the scent of her. For indeed, he would have identified and remembered her as soon as she had exited the truck, Newfoundlands being air-scenters. It had been three and a half months since they'd last met, and he was so excited to see her again that he did a little dance inside the Jeep. She held out her hand to be sure he remembered her and then gave him a hug.

"Angus, this is George, and you know John," she said.

George held out his hand so Angus could get his scent, and John patted his head and rubbed behind his ears. Brie fished a couple of dog treats out of her pocket that she had brought for him, and they all fraternized for a few more seconds before going inside.

They headed for Dent's office on the second floor. The door was ajar, so Brie knocked lightly and stuck her head in.

"Well, Brie, for heaven's sake." Jack Le Beau headed over and gave her a big hug.

"Jack, it's so good to see you again." She held him at arm's length. "You're looking good. You remember John, and this is George Dupopolis. He's our wonderful cook aboard *Maine Wind.*"

"George, it's good to meet you. Your reputation precedes you." He shook George's hand and gave his shoulder a welcoming squeeze. "And John, good to see you again. I believe we're all in for a very interesting time together."

Brie was standing to the side, smiling and taking Jack in. He was the healthiest, liveliest eighty-plus individual she'd ever met. Tall and lean with a shock of gray hair, and a musical voice that could have belonged to a fifty-year-old. They had worked together on the Apparition Island case—a case that connected to a very old cold case that Jack had worked as a young detective. They had forged a lasting bond while working on that case, and she was heartened to have him be part of this operation. Though retired, he brought to the op a lifetime of investigative experience. To her way of thinking, their chance of success doubled with him onboard.

Dent had brought in some extra chairs for a total of five. Brie wondered who the fifth chair was for. Not for long, though, because just then an officer from the Maine Marine Patrol entered Dent's office. He was a stocky guy, about five-foot-ten, with a broad, kind face and close-cropped brown hair.

"Ah, Rus," Dent said. "Thanks for coming. Everyone, this is Sergeant Rus Bellami from the Maine Marine Patrol. He'll be helping out with the op." He introduced Brie and Jack Le Beau first, giving a short summary of who they were, and then moved on to John and George. They all shook hands and passed a few icebreakers back and forth, and then Dent spoke up.

"Let's get started. We have a lot of territory to cover."

Everyone sat down, and Brie pulled out the case files and set them on Dent's desk.

"I've already filled Rus in on the plan for the operation. He was actually involved in the search and rescue efforts with the Coast Guard on each of our vics." He looked at Sgt. Bellami. "Is there anything you'd like to say about the cases, Rus?"

"Well, just that within a matter of three or four days, each case moved to a search and recover effort. But even with the Coast Guard's ability to study tidal drift and calculate where the victims might have gone into the ocean, none of the four bodies has yet to be recovered."

"What do we know about the weather on the days they disappeared?" Brie asked.

"That's one of the troubling parts to all of this," Sgt. Bellami said. "Assuming each of them disappeared on the day they were reported missing, then on three of those days, the records show that the seas were calm. But on all three of those mornings there was either heavy fog or sea smoke."

"Interesting," Brie said. "The killer could have used those conditions as cover. What about the other victim? How were the seas that day?"

"There was a swell running the day the second victim died," Bellami said. "We also know his death occurred before daylight."

"That would have been Paul Le Fevre," Brie said. "Why do you think he disappeared before daylight?"

"Because shortly after dawn, another lobsterman spotted his boat with no one aboard."

She remembered from reading the Le Fevre file that he'd had little catch aboard. An indication that he could have gone into the sea soon after heading out that day. It had been established that he'd had an alcohol problem. *Could he have been unsteady on his feet that morning—hung over maybe? Could he have fallen overboard in the darkness?* she wondered.

"I'd like to see any reports from the Coast Guard and the Maine Marine Patrol relating to the search and the sea conditions on those days," she said.

"I'll send you links to those," Dent said. "I assume you've gone through the case files. Any thoughts about any of the cases?"

43

"There wasn't a wealth of information there, but at least I got a rudimentary sense of the victims, and maybe some hints as to possible motives. What I didn't find were suspects. It seems the islanders weren't about to give up any, even if they had their own suspicions.

"My feeling—we're dealing either with a psychopath, or with someone bent on vigilante justice. Or, the other possibility, there's one of these four victims who was the target, and the rest were killed to create confusion—muddy the waters so to speak—to divert us from the true motive."

She turned to Jack Le Beau. "Have you seen the case files?"

"I went through them a couple of weeks ago when Dent met with me about the undercover operation. You're right, Brie. They're pretty thin, except, as you say, to give a general sense of the victims. But it's a starting place, and once we're out there, something to build on. I also agree with your thoughts on the three possible motivators in the killer's pathology."

"There's something else too," Brie said. "We'll need to learn a lot more, but in my opinion, there's one victim whose death could possibly have been an accident or even a suicide."

"Are you talking about Paul Le Fevre?" Jack asked.

"That's right." She wasn't surprised that his lifelong experience as a detective might have led him to the same conclusion.

"There's a certain sense of loneliness and desperation there," Le Beau said. "The loss of his wife and his descent into alcoholism. I checked the death records on his wife, Julianne Le Fevre. She died in childbirth, ten years prior to his death."

Brie nodded, reflecting on the fact. "It would skew the case, but I think we need to at least allow for the possibility. On the other hand, he may have been targeted like the other three. It's certainly too soon to draw any conclusions. And unwise to do so."

John spoke next. "There was a question about the status of Nathan Ross's lobsterboat and lobstering license when we met last week. Also, does anyone know what condition his territory is in out there? Are his traps still in the water?"

"When Ross died, the property went into limbo due to the back taxes owed," Dent said. "As far as we know, everything related to the property is still in place out there. But I think Rus has more on that."

"I went out to Starkhaven with my crew to check out the status of Ross's lobsterboat," Sgt. Bellami said. "We went in at a time of day when the lobstermen were out and cruised around the harbor enough so that even if we were observed, there was no focus on any particular boat. And with the deaths out there, the presence of the Maine Marine Patrol wouldn't be thought unusual." He turned to face John. "Nathan Ross's lobsterboat was there in the harbor. The registration is up to date, as is his lobster license. After we left the harbor, we cruised the waters out there until we found his lobster buoys and hauled up a couple of traps. They were empty but freshly baited."

"What does that mean?" Brie asked.

"Means the other lobstermen out there have been maintaining his traps and harvesting the keep."

"Is that legal?" she asked.

"No, but I don't think they care," Rus said. "They tend to make their own rules out there. Not worth making waves over either."

"In a way it works in our favor," Dent said. "The traps and the territory are being maintained and will be ready and waiting when you and John get out there."

"On another front, I'd appreciate it if someone got me up to speed on the boat. Engine specs, et cetera. And a crash course on lobstering wouldn't hurt. It's been a lot of years since I worked stern on a lobsterboat."

"No worries, John," Dent said. "That's one of the reasons I brought Rus in today. He's going to show you the ropes, take you through everything on the boat and also bring you out to a friend's territory in Casco Bay, so you can practice pulling and baiting traps."

"We'll take a look at the offshore forecast for the seas, but temps are going to be mild this week. I can schedule time with you any day," Rus Bellami said.

"Great," John said. "We'll set that up today before we break."

"Also, a bit of advice for when you get out there. Your best bet is to find a sternman who knows Ross's territory. He'll be your greatest asset. Pay him well. Find out the going rate, or percentage of the catch that's standard, and give him more, so he's loyal to you."

John nodded. "Thanks, Rus. Good advice."

Brie took out her small notebook where she'd written some questions and flipped through it.

"I know there's nothing like the law out there, but I'm wondering if we'll have any kind of a contact on Starkhaven? Anyone who will know about the op?"

"With an operation like this, it's always risky," Dent said. "But as fate would have it, there is someone I know and trust out there. His name is Mo Thorn, Mo being short for Mortimer, which was his mother's maiden name. Mo has deep roots out there. He's a lobsterman, the town manager, and also heads up the lobstermen's co-op on Starkhaven Island."

"Go on," Jack Le Beau said, leaning forward with interest.

"Well, our connection goes way back. When Mo was in his teens, he got a little too interested in Starkhaven's drug culture. Of course, drugs have been an issue on a number of the islands for decades, partly due to the lack of an organized constabulary in those places. Anyway, in Mo's case, his parents weren't going to tolerate such a thing, the Thorns being one of the dynasty families out there going back several hundred years. So they sent him off island the summer he was sixteen to work on a potato farm on the mainland, up near Calais. Potatoes are big business in that part of the state," Dent said, turning to

Brie. "As it happened, my uncle owned that farm, and I had worked there from the time I was fourteen. I was seventeen the summer Mo came, and we became fast friends. We've stayed in touch ever since."

"So have you talked to him about the operation?" George asked, speaking for the first time since the meeting had begun.

"I spoke to him on Saturday, after Brie had confirmed that the three of you were onboard with the plan."

"Has he given any sense . . . confided anything about who out there might, in his estimation, be capable of these crimes?" Jack asked.

Dent shook his head. "Even though he's a friend, he will only reveal so much. In that way he remains true to the island's 'ask us no questions and we'll give you no answers' M.O."

"What does he know?" Brie asked.

"At this point, just that I'm sending someone out there undercover, and that we will be using John's supposed connection to Nathan Ross and his property as a cover."

"Well, I like that he's a long-standing and respected part of island life," Brie said. "That could help lend credibility to our story, if he gets behind it. That said, though, I think we might want to hold some things back. Not give him one hundred percent of the picture."

"I agree with that," Jack said.

Dent nodded. "Okay, I get that."

"If I may," George said.

"By all means, George." Dent looked at him. "Feel free to jump in here."

"Well," George said, "I guess the plan is for me to go out with John and Brie as a brother or cousin, or something. Someone who will work Ross's former territory with John. But frankly, I think it would be more productive if I went out there on my own, independent of any of you, and settled down in the village near the docks and signed on to someone else's boat as a sternman." He looked around the group for a moment. "And here's why I think it would work. I read a little news item in the Portland paper about a month ago about sternmen leaving Starkhaven. They're kind of a nomadic group anyway, but apparently, with the disappearances out there, they've become skittish—decided there are safer places to ply their trade—seamen being a superstitious lot to begin with."

"Interesting idea, George," Dent said. "I like your thinking."

"I'd be way off everyone's radar," George said. "And hopefully in a position to keep my ear to the ground and gather information. What's more, what Sergeant Bellami said about John finding a sternman who knows Ross's territory is right." He turned to John. "It will also give us two different angles to work. And once I know who you hire, I can warm up to the guy down at the pub. Keep tabs on him that way."

"I like it," Jack Le Beau said.

Dent nodded. "Good thinking, George. We may have to deputize you."

"Nah, none of that." George shook his head. "I'm a true behind-the-scenes kind of guy. Playing this role will be a good fit for me. I'll hit the pub with the other sternmen and wait for loose lips to sink ships. And I don't need to wait for any of you. I can head out there on the next ferry and start to settle in. Also, as Brie is suggesting, I can be a part of the picture that Mo Thorn knows nothing about."

After his initial reluctance, George certainly seems to be warming to the plan, Brie thought.

"I know from visiting the island that there are some small trailers down by the docks that are rented by sternmen," Rus Bellami said. "Nothing fancy, but probably livable. And the pub out there, The Stern Man, has a reputation as a rough and ready place where that crowd hangs out."

George nodded. "I'll let my beard grow out and forage up some old clothes I use around the boat yard. Should blend right in."

"Speaking of clothes, what kind of gear will you need to acquire for lobstering?" Dent asked.

"Well, we've got our foul weather gear and sea boots we use aboard ship, so other than heavy gloves, I can't think of much we'll need."

"I'll go through your list of gear," Rus Bellami said. "Make sure you've got everything. I'd recommend wearing an inflatable PFD when you're out there. The lobstermen tend not to wear them, but they also tend to fall off their boats and drown every year. Just make sure you have one on. And that goes double if you're working alone out there on the boat."

"Don't worry," John said.

"Circling back to Mo Thorn, he'll put the word out on the island that Nathan Ross's nephew is taking over the homestead, the lobstering territory, and his mooring in the harbor," Dent said. "Don't worry, the word will get around fast, so your arrival won't come as too much of a surprise. And if you're related to one of the natives, they'll accept you. It might take a bit, but they will.

"The main thing in an operation like this is to blend in. Become part of the fabric of everyday life. Be neighborly but don't ask too many questions. Do more listening, less talking. And keep your eyes and ears open. Have I forgotten anything, Brie?"

"Nope. You're right about all of that, Dent."

He passed around manila folders that contained the identity and back story each of them would use in the operation.

"I've tried to go with stories that, whenever possible, parallel your lives. For instance, John, you were working in a boatyard in Lincolnville. If anyone calls there to check, whoever you have manning the phones can back up your story.

Plus you know the trade. And as fate would have it, Nathan Ross's sister, Helen, had a son named John. She's been dead for some time, but should anyone go record shopping, your name and family connection to Ross will jibe with the public records."

"So, what happened to the real John Ross?" Brie asked.

"Helen's son, John, dropped off the map when he was twenty-two—the year after his mother died of cancer," Dent said. "We tracked him down through the death records. He died in a motorcycle accident in California when he was thirty. Never made the news here. No obituaries. My guess is that, after his mother died, he cut his ties to Maine permanently. No evidence he ever knew his father."

"Well, that all works in our favor," Brie said. "No chance of the real John Ross showing up, throwing a monkey wrench into the works." She looked at Dent. "So what's my story?"

"In your case, you're a Minnesotan by birth who met John when he went to visit a friend out there. When you married him and moved to Maine, your elderly grandfather, i.e. Jack here, came with you. So Jack, we've given you the last name of 'Beaumont' for the op. Brie, your last name is Ross, just like John's. I'll count on you to give Jack some background about Minnesota."

"No problem," Brie said. "I've found since being here that Mainers seem to think we're a lot like them. I've often had them say, 'Maine—Minnesota—same thing.' So you can play into that, Jack. What's more, you don't have a Maine accent. That's a good thing."

"Nope. Grew up in Ohio. So no Yankee accent," Jack said.

"As for you, George, you're kind of a soldier without a cause," Dent continued. "You worked stern off Cape Cod and decided to move up to Maine. You come from Greek lineage and your family of origin are restaurateurs."

George nodded. "Most of that's the truth."

"So, you all get the drift, I think. There are enough touch-stones to the truth for each of you that you'll feel at home in these roles. Study them well. Don't play these characters; become these characters. You're going to have to work subtly and be clever to get those folks talking. It's not their way on any of the islands, but that goes double on a place like Starkhaven." He looked from one to the other of them. "Are there any questions?"

Nobody had anything to add.

Dent nodded. "Okay then. Rus, did you bring that ferry schedule for Starkhaven Island?"

"Right here." Sgt. Bellami fished it out of his pocket and studied it for a moment. "This time o' year, the ferry only runs once a month out there. This Friday's the day. Otherwise you'll have to wait another month."

"That gives us four days to have all our ducks in a row," Dent said. He opened his desk drawer and brought out a lock-box full of cash in small bills that had been allocated for their maintenance on the island during the op. He also gave John a cashier's check for $250—the fee for bringing a vehicle onto the island for more than thirty days—along with paperwork to be filed with the town office on Starkhaven.

"George, your idea of going out there before the others is a good one. But it's not going to be possible. But there's no reason anyone should connect you with the Rosses here," he nodded toward Brie and John, "if you steer clear of them on the ferry and afterward."

"That doesn't mean we won't be in contact out there," John said. "But we'll have to do it on the down low."

"There's no cell service on Starkhaven," Dent said. "But there is internet via DSL, which means you can email each other and stay in touch that way. That's also how we'll be communicating during the operation."

"Good to know," Brie said. "I have a laptop we can bring with. What about you, George?"

"I've got one at home. I'll pack it."

"Remember, it's DSL, so bring the appropriate cables," Dent said. "If you don't have them, our IT guy will fix you up."

"I assume since everything was left in place, that the house is furnished," Jack Le Beau said.

"Yes, I've confirmed that with Mo Thorn," Dent said. "But you might want to take a couple new mattresses and bedding. You, too, George. We'll pay for those, of course." He opened his desk drawer again and handed a prepaid VISA card to each of them. "Use these for anything you need to purchase for the op. The cash is for on-island expenses.

"John, you're taking your truck, so pack up the bed with anything you think you may need. There's a general store on the island. I advise you to buy your food there. Don't bring any with you. That will make the storekeeper warm to you."

"If I'm going to infiltrate the island quilting group, I'll need to pick up a sewing machine and some supplies, so I look the part. I'll bring my Granny Beaumont's quilt. She'll understand if I pretend it's my work, considering the circumstances."

"That'll be fertile listening ground there with the Starkhaven Stitchers," Dent said.

"They have a name? That's not at all intimidating."

Dent waved his hand in the air. "Don't worry about it. You'll be fine."

Brie chuckled. "Easy for you to say."

John leaned over to Rus. "Can we set a day to go over the boat and lobstering procedures?"

Dent stood up so they could use his computer, and the two of them moved around the desk to check the forecast for weather and seas. Wednesday looked to be the warmest and calmest of the few days they had to choose from, and Rus suggested they meet his friend at the ferry dock on Cousins Island near Yarmouth.

"George, you need to come along, too," John said. "Get comfortable with lobstering regulations and procedures, and hauling and baiting of traps."

George nodded. "Wednesday works for me."

"I'll drive you two to the meeting spot that day," Brie said. "That way I can continue on to Portland and get mattresses and a sewing machine."

"Good idea," John said.

"If you want to go on a different day, I can help manhandle those mattresses," George said.

"I'll be fine. Since time is short and we'll be near Portland, I should do it that day. But if you want to help me brainstorm a list of what we'll need on the island, that'd be great."

Dent turned to Jack Le Beau. "I know this doesn't give you a lot of time to prepare."

"Don't worry. I travel light. Angus and I will be ready to roll on the day."

"Great, then I think we're done here. We've got exactly four days to get this boat ready to float—metaphorically speaking. Call if I can help in any way. Otherwise, let's plan to touch base by phone the day before you leave for Starkhaven."

They started to get up.

"Wait, I almost forgot." Dent went back into his drawer and produced Brie's shield and service weapon. "You need to take these with you, just in case."

Brie picked up the gun and holster and clipped it onto her belt and pocketed the badge.

"Jack, I take it you'll be bringing your firearm as well," Brie said.

"Darn tootin'," Jack Le Beau said. "There's a killer loose out there. Can't be too careful. Anyway, if I didn't bring my gun, I'd probably be the only soul out there without one."

"One final thing," Dent said. He opened a small box that sat on the top of his desk. It contained a matching set of wedding

53

bands. He looked at John and Brie. "I now pronounce you man and wife."

"So, I guess we know what your moonlighting job is," Brie joked.

"There's a card in there for the jeweler. It's just a few blocks from here. Stop in there today so he can size those for you."

"Will do," John said.

They pulled on their coats and shook hands around the group.

"Can I take the case files with me so I can refer to them if need be?" Brie asked.

"By all means. The documents in those are copies," Dent said.

"So if the ferry goes down, I'm not in trouble."

"Hey," John said. "No joking about stuff like that. Like George said, we mariners are a superstitious lot."

"Aye, aye, Captain." She gave him a little mock salute.

They headed out of Dent's office and down to their cars. Brie walked over to Jack's SUV and gave Angus some more petting and one last dog treat. She turned to Jack. "See you Friday at the ferry dock." She gave him a quick hug and then headed for the truck with John and George.

Chapter 6

The next four days were a blizzard of activity. Scott Hogan, who served as mate aboard *Maine Wind* during the sailing season, and Ed Browning, former mate, agreed to split up the hours at the boatyard to man the phone and keep projects moving forward for the spring haul out. At John's request, Scott agreed to take care of Barney while they were gone, and in fact seemed eager for his companionship.

On Tuesday, the day after the meeting with Dent Fenton, Brie rose early to make the nearly two-hour drive to Cherryfield, Maine, where her grandmother, Isabelle Beaumont, lived. The goal was to spend the day reviewing quilting techniques. Granny Beaumont, as Brie called her, had a hot breakfast waiting when she arrived. She bustled around the large country kitchen, her slender frame and long gray braid in motion, as she pulled muffins from the oven and made fresh coffee. Before long, they sat down at the big table that filled the center of the kitchen. Brie was hungry from the drive up, and the scrambled eggs, sausages, and cranberry muffins took her right back to mornings at this same table when she had been a girl.

"Are you back in Maine for good then?" Isabelle asked.

"Well, I guess time will tell," Brie said. "I've resigned from the Minneapolis Police Department, given up my apartment there, and moved all my prized possessions here. So . . ."

"Sounds pretty definite to me," Isabelle said. "I, for one, couldn't be more delighted to have you back here. And I'll bet your sea captain feels the same way."

Brie smiled. "Thanks, Granny. Since I was a child, Maine has always felt like home. So maybe this was meant to be."

"Well, you're welcome here any time, my dear, for as long as you want to stay."

"Thanks, Gran. I love that you're here in Maine."

As soon as they were done eating, they got down to business. Brie marveled at how easily she slipped back into the routine of cutting, stitching, and fitting together the different geometric shapes. It was as if she had passed through a time warp and was twelve years old again, spending rainy afternoons in the quilting room of her grandmother's stately old house. And by the time she was ready to leave that evening, she was confident she could hold her own with the Starkhaven Stitchers.

Isabelle gave her granddaughter some books of designs to study, some quilting patterns and fabrics, and two quilts she had made that Brie could pass off as her work. She advised her granddaughter not to claim the quilt she had made for her as a college graduation gift as her work.

"Any expert quilter will recognize that as work that's above your level," she said. "But share the true stories of our time together when you were young. That should endear you to them and make them want to help you, which should go a long way to opening the door about other matters."

Wise advice, Brie thought. In fact, using stories from one's own life was an excellent strategy for drawing people out when working undercover.

On Wednesday, John and George met Sergeant Rus Bellami from the Maine Marine Patrol and headed out into Casco Bay with Sid Walters, a lobsterman Rus knew. The goal was to take them through a crash course in lobstering. Even though he hadn't hauled a trap in over twenty years, it didn't take John long to fall back into the familiar routine and, with Sid's help, acquaint George with the ins and outs of working stern. They also went over engine maintenance, and Rus gave John some manuals he had found online for the model of lobsterboat John would be operating—Nathan Ross's former boat.

At Sid's suggestion they motored south to the waters off Cape Elizabeth where the seas were running higher, so John could practice maneuvering the boat in rougher seas. Even though John was a master mariner, there's a world of difference between how a hundred-foot heavily ballasted schooner and a thirty-foot lobsterboat handle the seas.

That same day, while John and George were out on the water, Brie went on a procurement detail. Besides mattresses, she acquired bedding, towels, and some pots and pans. She also stopped at a bookstore and picked up an assortment of books to pass the long winter evenings. And finally, chocolate! She was willing to take her chances on getting everything else from the island store. But chocolate was not negotiable.

So it was that on Friday, with John's truck bed filled with mattresses, household goods, and their personal belongings, and the cab filled with John, Brie, Jack Le Beau and a very enthusiastic Angus, they drove onto the ferry in Rockland for the two-and-a-half-hour voyage to Starkhaven Island.

Starkhaven Island

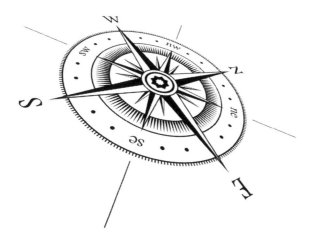

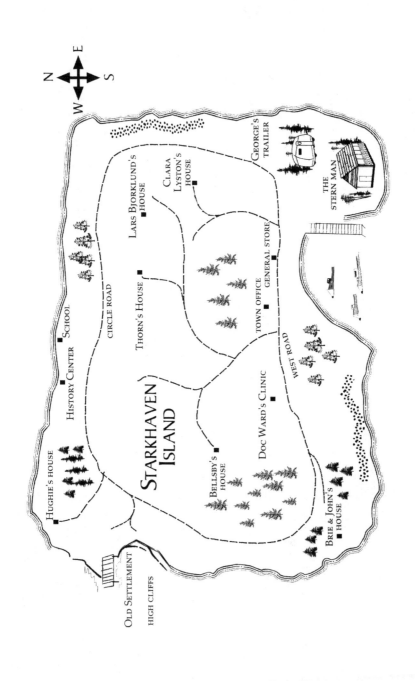

The Gulf of Maine
23 miles out to sea

Starkhaven Island lies so far from the mainland as to be but a distant relation. So distant that it seems it might up stakes one fine day and drift off into the North Atlantic unnoticed. Its kissing cousin, Starkhaven Rock, has been scoured by gales and great boarding seas since time out of mind, so that any trace of vegetation has long since disappeared from the annals of island memory.

The Starkhaveners, like the place itself, wear isolation as a second skin—a kind of anorak, or *imperméable*, as the French would say, against the possibility of any kind of close association with the greater sum of humanity.

The lobstermen of Starkhaven Island are hardened to near stone by the elements they battle year round. To fish the North Atlantic in the winter builds a certain kind of character. And the women who wait for them each day have grown generationally fatalistic. If the sea is intent on claiming a life, it will be claimed. Too much emotion is not helpful in such a place.

Chapter 7

The seas were calm as they chugged for Starkhaven Island. And the sky? Cobalt blue, as is so often the case on the most arctic of days. Sea smoke or arctic fog—that unique phenomenon that occurs when the cold North Atlantic is warmer than the frosty winter air above it—rose from the ocean like ghostly vapor and engulfed the ferry, making it seem as if they were sailing to some mythical land.

George had been the last person to board the ferry, and John had started to worry that he might miss it. But Brie had suspected this was just his way of separating himself from any connection with the three of them. Still, he cut it close. The deck hands were getting ready to let go the docking lines when he came trundling down the wharf carrying a large sea bag, and looking as scruffy as Brie had ever seen him look.

He jumped aboard, made his way up to the passenger deck, and sat on a bench, amidships, forward of where the three of them and Angus had stationed themselves. Of course, nobody aboard paid George any heed, as Angus was always the main attraction wherever he went. Big and black and furry as a bear, he made quite a statement. And since the sea is a Newfie's natural element, he lay down on the floor and went to sleep as if the voyage was just a normal, everyday occurrence.

For nearly an hour and a half, the ferry churned through the smoky sea with nary a sign of a swell. The drone of the engine lulled Brie toward sleep and for a while she dozed off. The few days leading up to their departure had been frenetic, to say the least. Between leaving the boatyard in order and figuring out what they needed to bring and then making sure it would all fit into John's pickup truck, they had put in some late nights.

Thirty minutes after she'd fallen asleep, her head resting against the portside window, Brie was awakened by Angus' large head in her lap. When she opened her eyes, he was staring up at her, and as soon as he saw her awaken, his long tail started thumping on the cabin sole. She scratched behind his ears, which accelerated the tail thumping. Finally, she fished a small dog treat out of her pocket and gave it to him. He started up from the floor, but Jack Le Beau gave him a stern command to "stay." Angus lowered his head to the floor and let out a heavy sigh of protest, which made Brie smile.

She turned and looked out the window so as not to encourage Angus. She was thinking about the case files and the four victims—all lobstermen. Of course, on an island like Starkhaven, one would be hard pressed to find a male age eighteen to eighty who did not lobster for a living. And the fact that they were lobstermen had somehow played into the killer's plans. He had used their isolation and vulnerability while at sea to prey on them. But there was no doubt in her mind that all the victims had known the killer or he never could have gotten aboard their boats. She ran through their names in her mind, picturing each one of them.

Oslo Stumph, ruddy and round-faced. Labeled as a mean guy by one of the interviewees, who had asked to remain anonymous. Was he mean, or rather a man who had loved his children, as his parents had described? Or was he both?

Paul Le Fevre, a widower. Handsome, possibly kind, but lost to alcohol. Was he suicidal? Had he ended it all in the predawn hours of that February day on the freezing North Atlantic? And if not, why did her detective's gut keep suggesting that?

Cliff Gordon, whose photo had reminded Brie of a wily fox. He had been abusive to his wife, but was there something else too? Both the detectives on the case had reported a strong sense of something buried below the surface of Gordon's life— something no one would talk about. Why? For a moment that single word overwrote everything else in Brie's mind. What occurrence could be so dark as to require such silence, even postmortem?

And finally, victim number four, Abe Winter, who looked like an unkempt hippy with his long black hair and checked-out expression. Once again the detectives had reported what they termed a kind of "low frequency nervousness" among those interviewed. As if there was something the islanders did not want brought to light. But did that something relate to his death? As usual, at this point in an investigation, there were only questions. A myriad of questions. A situation made even more complex by the fact of four victims. Her job, though undercover, was the same as always. Find the truth.

In the last forty minutes of the trip, the seas began to make themselves felt, and even though they were sailing up into it, Brie could feel the vessel begin to pitch and roll—ever so slightly at first, but before long, with serious intent. Not having been at sea for three months, her acclimation to the motion was long gone. She popped a piece of ginger gum in her mouth to arrest the slight feeling of nausea that was on the rise and stared out the window at the horizon, trying to breathe deeply through her nose. She glanced over at John, but he was sound asleep, chin on his chest. Next to him, Jack Le Beau was looking mildly distressed. She passed him the pack of gum, telling him it would help with *mal de mer*.

Within twenty minutes she got her first glimpse of Starkhaven Island. The place was beautiful. Covered with January snow, it sat like a brilliant white jewel in the midst of the deep blue sea. Arriving on such a day might make one wonder how the island had ever come to be called Starkhaven. But when one considered the actual fact of living here—the isolation, the physical, psychological, and emotional inbreeding that was bound to occur in such a place—maybe "stark" was apropos.

There was a swell running astern as they neared the breakwater that framed the eastern side of the harbor. As they made their approach to the ferry dock, the captain reversed the engines, bringing the vessel to a near stop, so he could maneuver the last hundred yards up to the dock. Once the lines were secured, Brie, John, Jack, and Angus made their way down to the car deck and climbed into the pickup, and as soon as the ramp was lowered they were motioned off the ferry by one of the crew.

Like with so many of the islands and coastal communities Brie had visited during her time on *Maine Wind*, the houses here were scattered about on the hill above the harbor, every one with a vantage of the sea. Colorful houses painted in various shades of reds, whites, and blues—New England colors—Yankee colors. But the waterfront itself was strictly reserved for the fishermen, with its array of docks, buildings for bait and gear, and holding areas for the catch.

They drove along the main road, passing the post office and then the general store. Through the front window a group of elderly men and one woman were playing cards.

"I think I might have to crash that game," Jack Le Beau said. "If they'll have me, of course."

"Remember what Dent said. If you're family . . . connected to someone on the island, they'll accept you. It may just take some time to build trust," John said.

"Have you thought about what will happen after the operation is over? They may never trust another outsider again, family or not," Brie said.

"On the other hand, if we catch a killer, it may bring the Starkhaveners some peace, whether they seem to want it or not," Jack said, sounding pragmatic.

John had stopped the truck in front of the town office—a simple white frame building with black shutters. They had been told that Mo Thorn—Dent Fenton's contact on the island—would meet them there when the ferry came in. They needed to drop off the papers required when someone was bringing a vehicle onto the island for more than thirty days. It was the perfect excuse to meet with Thorn and see what initial advice he had for them. John reached across and retrieved the manila envelope that held the papers from the glove box. Jack reached in back and patted Angus, and they piled out of the truck and stood for a moment looking up and down the deserted road.

The wind was up, and miniature tornadoes of powdery snow swirled up from the roadside. It felt strangely dissonant to smell the salt from the ocean on the wind while seeing snow on the ground. This was something Brie had never experienced, and she marked the moment with wonder. Everywhere, the low winter sun cast long shadows of buildings, spruce trees, even the flag pole planted before the town office. Coming from 45th parallel territory in Minnesota, Brie loved the low light of winter—the calm clarity of it—and sometimes wondered if there was an artist or photographer lurking somewhere deep inside her.

"I'm looking forward to running on the island on sunny days like this," she said.

They started up the walk toward the door, but Jack stopped them momentarily. "Time to affix our new personas," he said. "I'm Jack Beaumont and you two are John and Brie Ross. Don't forget."

"Got it, Jack," Brie said. "But remember, Mo Thorn knows who we really are, so the dynamic with him will be different, at least when we're meeting with him alone, as I suspect we are today."

"You're right. What was I thinking," he said.

"No worries, Jack. You're totally correct. We have to have our aliases firmly in mind at all times if this op is going to work."

A handwritten sign affixed to the town office door with duct tape, so the wind couldn't strip it away, read, "Lobstermen's Association Meeting, Tuesday, January 19, 7:00 p.m." John tapped it with a gloved hand, and Brie nodded. They stomped the snow off their feet and stepped into the town office.

Inside they found a large room approximately thirty feet wide by forty feet long. Four windows, spaced equidistantly along the side of the room, let in the midday sun. Straight-backed wooden chairs were lined up in rows, awaiting the next meeting. A wood lectern stood in front of the chairs and, from behind that, a man emerged from one of the two doors along the back wall.

"You must be Brie, John, and Jack. I'm Mo Thorn. I've been waiting for you." He motioned with his arm. "Come into my office."

They walked up the side of the meeting room and followed him into the office. He stood behind a desk that was littered with paperwork. Thorn had a full beard and curly black hair, and in his suspendered jeans and red flannel shirt, he reminded Brie of a lumberjack. He was easily six-foot-two with a powerfully built upper body which, not surprisingly, is the hallmark of the Maine lobsterman, who might have up to eight hundred traps in the water in a season and might haul up to four hundred of them a day.

Thorn's eyes seemed to look right into you and out the other side. And while not mean or malicious, Brie could tell that those eyes didn't miss much, and that Mo Thorn, at any point in time, might be aware of far more than the average bear.

He didn't offer to shake hands, but motioned to the three chairs across the desk from him. "Sit down." He waited a moment for them to get seated. "How was the ferry ride?"

"Smooth as silk most of the way," John said. "Started kicking up a bit the last half hour."

"Dent Fenton said you're a mariner. Ever do any lobstering?"

"Worked stern when I was eighteen," John said.

Thorn nodded. "Then you should be okay out there. Get yourself a good sternman. There are always a couple of them looking for work down at the harbor. They like to hang out at the pub down there—The Stern Man."

John nodded. "I noticed Nathan Ross's lobsterboat in the harbor when we left the ferry."

Thorn opened a desk drawer and took out a set of keys. "These will let you into the house, and there's one here for the boat as well. Just follow the road out of the village for about a mile. You'll see it just beyond the bend. House is furnished. Nothing great but livable. Will probably need a good cleaning. The general store should have what you need."

He paused and studied a sheet of paper on his desk. "You're going by the names John and Brie Ross." He looked up at them and they nodded. Then he turned to Jack. "And you are Brie's grandfather, as the story goes. Jack Beaumont. Is that right?"

"You got it," Jack said. "Those are our real first names, though."

"And you and Brie are both detectives with the Maine State Police?"

"That's right," Jack said. "In my case, retired detective, but I still help with the occasional case."

"I've put the story out on the island that the three of you are coming and what your relationship to Nathan Ross is. Since I'm the town manager, it shouldn't seem odd to anyone that I would know that."

"Do you know if Ross was still hauling his traps right up to the end?" John asked.

69

"As far as I know," Thorn said.

"You know how many he had in the water?"

"Not hard to check." Thorn opened a file drawer and pulled out a manila file folder. Inside, he turned a few pages and consulted a list.

"Looks like he put four hundred traps in last season. Only half his usual amount. Huh."

"Maybe he was finding it hard to keep up. We know now he had heart trouble."

"Maybe," Thorn said. "He didn't have a sternman."

"That common?" John asked.

"More than you'd think," Thorn said.

"Seems odd, with the amount lobstermen make, that my uncle would be delinquent on his property taxes," John said.

Brie watched Thorn carefully for his reaction. His face didn't change except to become more stone-like. But the vibe changed. He lowered his head and moved some papers around on the desk. Had there been a ticking clock in the room, the noise would have been deafening.

After a beat or two, he looked up at John. "I wouldn't know about that," Thorn said. "We don't mind other people's business, here."

Brie knew that was false. Both John and Dent had told her that everybody knows everybody's business on the islands. They're like small towns on steroids.

"Huh. Well, okay," John said. "Just curious. No worries, though. So, Dent said that you're also a lobsterman."

He shifted gears so seamlessly Brie almost smiled. *He's good at this*, she thought. She glanced at Jack and had the feeling he was thinking the same thing.

"Everyone here lobsters for a living," Thorn said. "I'm just ashore because you were arriving today. I came back in at noon so I wouldn't miss you."

"I'd guess it's more dangerous in the winter," John said.

"The seas are often large out here. But winter's a whole different game because of the cold. It slows you down physically and mentally. You watch yourself out there. And like I said, get a good sternman."

The words were meant to show concern, but somehow the tone or tenor of them felt more like a warning to Brie.

"So, is it hard being town manager and still keeping up with your traps?"

They were the first words Jack had spoken, and Brie could tell that the natural twinkle in his eye had disarmed Thorn, at least momentarily. She also knew that no detective, retired or not, makes idle conversation when a case is involved. Somehow, it all is working toward an end. It all goes to discovery. That tendency is hardwired in detectives. They don't just uncover motives. They also *have* motives or ulterior motives for what, on the face of it, may seem like casual or inconsequential questions.

Jack's question may have hit pay dirt.

Thorn seemed to sit a bit taller in his chair now that someone had acknowledged his importance. "I manage it," he said. "My ancestors have been on this island over two hundred years. We've always led the way. Watched over things."

Brie wondered if Thorn was really the shepherd he made himself out to be, or if he had just learned to believe his own narrative. Time would tell, she thought.

"With that in mind," Thorn continued. "There's something I need to say. Dent is a good friend or I'd never get involved in such a thing as this. It goes against all my island genes, because, out here, we like to take care of things ourselves. What's more, no one here can ever know that I was involved in this operation. I would be shunned. Maybe even driven off."

"Even if we are successful?" Brie asked. "Even if we catch the person responsible for these murders?"

"You don't understand, but maybe you will after being here a couple months. There's a code here. A code of trust. It's absolute. You don't ever break it."

"But didn't the killer break it?" she asked.

Thorn said nothing, but looked away, and she could tell from the expression on his face that what she had said did not compute, or maybe he just preferred not to think about it.

Finally he looked back at them. "You live in a place all your life. You think you know that place—those people. Then something like this happens—I mean the deaths—and you realize you don't know anything, really."

"That must be hard, considering your family's history here," Brie said.

He didn't respond to that but instead said, "Look, even my wife doesn't know about this operation of yours. All I've told her is that you three are coming to the island and she should make you feel welcome."

"That's fine by us," Brie said. "Our success depends on our objective remaining secret. Best she doesn't know."

"When it's all over, there may be hell to pay, though," Jack said.

"Believe me, that'll be the least of my worries."

There was another ticking clock silence after that, and Brie decided they had reached the end of the meeting. There was a pad of sticky notes on the desk; she wrote her email on one of them and handed it to Thorn. "From now on we'll communicate primarily via email," she said. She handed him the pad. "Would you please write down your email."

Thorn complied and handed the note to her.

"I know this is an uncomfortable situation, but we do appreciate your help and need you to be steadfast about it." She held his eyes for a moment to convey the gravity of the situation.

"I gave my word. I won't go back on it."

Brie nodded. The three of them stood and put on their coats.

"By the way, do you know who could hook up our internet service?" she asked.

"That'd be Josh Stevens. I'll give him a call and tell him to stop by your place later."

"Thanks."

"I'll walk out with you," Thorn said.

They filed through the office door and along the side of the meeting room.

"I plan to be at the Lobstermen's Association meeting on Tuesday," John said.

"Good idea. I'll introduce you to the other fishermen. You want to blend in as much as you can, as soon as you can. Become part of the fabric here. Let that settle in. Don't ask questions except about the trade."

John nodded and they went out the front door and down to the truck. They climbed in and John started the engine. Brie noticed Thorn standing at the front window of the town office, watching them. The look on his face could have frozen granite, and she couldn't help but wonder how well Dent Fenton really knew this guy.

Chapter 8

They drove along the road and before one could blink, they were out of the village. The last building they passed was a narrow white clapboard edifice. A barber pole next to the door offered all the explanation anyone might need. Through the large front window, two barber chairs optimistically hinted that a population boom might be in the offing.

"Yup. Think it's about time to get my ears lowered," Jack said. He studied the place as they passed. "Looks like they're closed, though."

Brie smiled. Jack was already into it. Devising ways to get the islanders talking. *If anyone can do it, he can,* she thought.

She turned to John. "You rattled Thorn pretty good with your questions about Ross and his property taxes."

"I noticed that," he said. "Interesting, huh?"

"He was defensive, that's for sure. And that bologna about not minding each other's business. Doesn't jibe with what you've told me about islanders," Brie said.

"No, it doesn't. Pure fiction." John tapped the steering wheel with his thumbs. "You gotta wonder where all Ross's money was going, though. Out here, off Starkhaven, these are considered the richest lobstering grounds in the world. You could get rich even with one hand tied behind your back."

"Well, it's a place to dig," Brie said. "It might connect to something."

"With few motives and even fewer suspects in these killings, we're gonna have to work all angles," Jack said.

For Brie, the clock was already ticking inside her head. It had only been eight days since their first meeting with Lt. Dent Fenton at Maine State Police headquarters. On the one hand that seemed like no time at all, considering the scope of this operation. On the other hand, it felt like a lot of time investigatively. Four lobstermen were dead, and the idea that they now had to take time to meld with this community troubled the detective in her. These cases were already cold and getting colder by the day. But that is the nature of undercover work; it takes time to produce results.

Thorn hadn't been very specific about where Nathan Ross's house was, but Dent Fenton had given them a picture of the property that the county had provided, so Brie knew what to look for. Beyond the village the houses spread out, as if each of them needed a lot of elbow room. The architecture varied from one to another, but there was one common denominator. Without exception, next to or behind each abode, a small to medium-sized mountain of yellow and green lobster traps rose out of the deep snow. Sometimes the mountain threatened to eclipse the house, while at other times, the hulk of a lobsterboat from days of yore accomplished the task. Lobster buoys hung helter-skelter from the sides of houses and outbuildings and sometimes, like ungainly Christmas ornaments, from the spruce trees that fringed the yards.

Up the road on the left, they passed a white house with navy blue shutters. A painted sign hanging from a post near the road read "Starkhaven Clinic." The second line read "Tobias Ward, M.D." Brie nodded at it. "Good to know there's a doctor on the island in case of an emergency."

Thorn had told them the house they sought was beyond a bend in the road about a mile out of the village. Within a few minutes of bumping along the snow-encrusted road, they spotted the place off to the left, on the crest of the hill. A small, weathered Cape Cod that had once been deep red, judging by the color under the eaves, but whose luster had long since faded under the glare of sun and lash of salt air.

An access road met the main road—known simply as West Road—at an angle.

"It's been plowed recently," John said. "Thorn must have gotten someone out here to take care of it."

They made a slight left onto the road and proceeded up the hill. Brie saw that there was a large outbuilding off to one side of the house. It would be big enough to accommodate John's truck, if not completely full of gear. Alongside it, the ubiquitous stack of lobster traps was well on the way to dwarfing the outbuilding.

John parked the truck at the end of the driveway in front of the outbuilding, which had an overhead garage door next to a normal entry door. They climbed out and let Angus escape from the back seat. He bounded about in the snow, euphoric to be let free in his natural Newfoundland element. John tried the door to the outbuilding. It opened and they walked into the building. As Brie had suspected, it was full of lobster buoys and piles of pot warp—the line that attaches the buoy to the lobster trap. An old Ford pickup roosted at the far end of the building.

"Huh, wonder if that works," John said. "Might be handy to have a second vehicle since we'll be off in different directions most days."

They backed out and headed for the house. Angus had flopped down in a snowdrift and was consuming huge mouthfuls of snow. They decided to leave him be for the moment while they explored the house. John fished out the key and opened the front door, and they stepped into a small entryway that had wood pegs on the wall for coats. A worn Mackinaw hunting coat in buffalo plaid hung there, as if Nathan Ross might just have returned home. Beneath the coat a pair of Bean boots sat on a rag rug.

They removed their boots and walked into the house. Brie hadn't known what to expect from a lobsterman living alone, but the place was neat as a pin. Pine floors ran throughout the downstairs, and in typical Cape Cod style, the stairs ascended directly in front of them, dividing the two sides of the house. To their right, the living room ran the length of the house and featured a red brick fireplace flanked by bookcases that held an assortment of books and magazines and a colorful collection of duck decoys. She had noticed a workbench in the outbuilding and wondered if Ross had carved these. She walked to the bookshelf and ran her hand over one of the decoys. It was fine, realistic work, both the woodcarving and the painting.

They explored the downstairs. While the furniture, rugs, and kitchen cabinets were worn from years of use, all in all things were perfectly livable. Brie investigated the upstairs. There were only two bedrooms, one large, one smaller, in which the beds themselves left a lot to be desired. The mattresses sagged and the bedding was worn. Before long, John and Jack came upstairs, and they got busy stripping the beds. They hauled the mattresses down the stairs and out the door to the outbuilding, where they stood them against the back wall.

They brought Angus in through the kitchen door, toweled him off, and laid his giant doggy pad in the corner of the kitchen. After exploring the house upstairs and down, he deposited himself on his bed and let out a heavy sigh, like he might be done for the day—like this was about as much change as a fellow could handle in one day.

They unloaded the truck bed, bringing the new mattresses up the stairs. Jack found a vacuum in the closet and gave the area under the bed frames a good going over before they laid the new mattresses. They made the beds using the new sheets, blankets, and pillows that the department had sprung for. And while the guys unloaded the rest of the truck, Brie went to check on the status of the kitchen and make a list of what they would need from the store. She was pleasantly surprised to find a decent supply of canned and dry goods. But everywhere the ghost of Nathan Ross seemed to linger. There were dishes stacked in the drainer as if he'd just washed them. Ground coffee had been placed in the coffee maker and water measured out in the carafe for the morning ritual. In the dining room, mail sat on the small desk in the corner, partially opened.

The refrigerator still held food, and Brie got busy cleaning it out. John showed up in the kitchen, said he was going out to check the level in the fuel tank, and disappeared out the back door.

The place had lots of windows, and the ones in the kitchen and dining room looked south toward the ocean. And while the house didn't sit directly on the shore, it stood on high ground and offered a fine panorama of the sea. Brie liked that a lot. It calmed her to look out over the vast expanse of water. The day had been sunny, if arctic feeling, but now from the window over the sink, she saw a front approaching from the southwest. Flat and iron-gray, it pressed down over the sea. She knew it would be rounding the compass—turning to the northeast. Getting ready to deliver another punch of winter. *Good thing we took the ferry today,* she thought. *Tomorrow will be a whole other story out there.*

John came back in the door. "Oil tank's more than half full, so no worries about heat." He started opening cabinets and looking inside. "I'm starving. Anything to eat around here? Breakfast was a long time ago."

They foraged around the kitchen and found an unopened jar of peanut butter and one of strawberry jam, and an unopened box of crackers. Brie opened two cans of chicken noodle soup, poured them into a pot and put them on the stove to heat. She discarded the water in the coffee carafe and scrubbed it out, and

John found a can of partially used ground coffee and scooped some grounds into a filter. They got the coffee brewing, and before long, Jack appeared in the kitchen. He'd been upstairs unpacking when the aroma of fresh coffee beckoned him.

"Now that smells like home," he said. "Didn't realize how hungry I was till I smelled the coffee."

Dent had told them to buy their food on the island, but Brie had packed some fruit anyway—one bag each of apples, oranges, and grapefruits. She pulled the apples out of a brown paper bag that John had set on the counter and washed and sliced two of them to go with their makeshift lunch.

They gathered around the small metal table, circa 1950s, that stood in the middle of the kitchen. The old Formica top that looked like black and white pebbles was holding up amazingly well considering its age. The four chairs were metal as well, with seats of red gingham fabric encased in thick vinyl that had yellowed with time. Brie marveled at them, wondering what the half-life of that plastic might be. They ate lunch and speculated about how George might be doing and whether he had found a place to stay. The day before they'd left the mainland, Brie had told him that if he came up empty, he should come up to the house. She'd showed him the picture of the house and told him where it was on the island.

After lunch, John offered to wash the dishes, and Jack said he'd dry, so Brie went into the dining room where the guys had left her sewing machine and quilting fabric on the table. The dining room lay to the left of the stairs across from the living room. She took the cover off the sewing machine and plugged it into the wall outlet. She laid the fabric in piles around the table and draped one of the quilts her grandmother had given her over the back of a chair in the living room. Should anyone stop in to visit, they would notice her staged sewing area. She wasn't sure how, but she planned to wangle an invitation to join the Starkhaven Stitchers.

She expected they would be guarded at first, but once she became part of the fabric of the group—pun intended—they were bound to loosen up. It was only one avenue they planned to work, but if anyone was likely to talk, Brie suspected it would be the women.

She went back to the kitchen and finished the short list of supplies they would need from the general store. She asked John and Jack if they wanted to "go with"—a Minnesota-ism that always made John smile. At first they said "no," but she pointed out that this was a chance for them to be seen together and show how downright friendly and eager to join the community they were.

"Well, when you put it that way, you don't give us much choice," John said, sounding mildly put upon.

"She's right, though," Jack said. "The Starkhaveners need to put a face to each of us. The more we're all seen these first few days, the more they'll begin to accept us as part and parcel of island life."

So with that in mind, they donned their coats and headed out the door and down to the truck. It was only two-thirty, but already the sun beat a path toward the western horizon. The wind gusted up the hill, filling the air with a prismatic flurry of powdery snow.

"It's beautiful here," Brie said. But even in the midst of that beauty, she felt the deep isolation of this place.

Chapter 9

As soon as George disembarked the ferry, he headed along the road in search of The Stern Man—the pub that Sergeant Rus Bellami of the Maine Marine Patrol had mentioned. It was known as the hangout on the island for both the lobstermen and the sternmen who worked for them.

George came upon the pub just down from the wharf a ways, a rectangular structure with weathered, gray cedar siding. An old-fashioned sign, hung from a black iron rod perpendicular to the building, depicted a brawny-armed mariner in foul-weather bibs, manhandling a lobster trap onto the gunwale of his boat as the seas sloshed around him. George entered through a heavy door near the corner of the building and stood there momentarily. The transition from the winter world outside to the dark, womblike interior of the pub rendered him momentarily blind.

As his eyes slowly acclimated, he surveyed his surroundings. The wide pine floor that ran the length of the pub had aged to the color of winter ale, and a massive carved bar that looked like it might have been raised from the *Titanic* sprawled along the back wall. Ladder-back chairs around oak barrels, made into tables with heavy wood tops, ranged throughout the pub, and a burnished tin ceiling and antique globe lights added even more character, if such a thing were possible. In his wildest dreams, George would not have expected to find such a place as this on Starkhaven Island.

He must have looked like a fish out of water because the barkeep beckoned him over. "Come. Sit. Have a pint. You must be new here."

George walked over to the bar and extended his hand. "George Dupopolis," he said. "Just arrived today."

"Ah," the barkeep said. He looked George up and down. "Sternman, looking for work?"

"That's right," George said.

"I'm Kieran McTavish. What'll ya have?"

"I see you've got Guinness on tap. I'll have that." An outsider might have thought it a bit early to imbibe, but not on a lobstering island where, as George well knew, the fishermen will wrap up a ten-hour day by 2 p.m.

McTavish drew off a schooner of Guinness and set it in front of George. Kieran McTavish was a tall, wiry man with close-cropped gray hair and long, slender hands. Definitely not the hands of a lobsterman. He wore a plaid broadcloth shirt, rolled at the forearm, with a fitted vest over the top—a look that somehow fit the pub to a T. George placed him in his mid to late 50s.

"This is quite a place. Not what I'd expected to find out here."

"And what were you expecting to find *out here*? Mud huts?"

"Didn't mean no offense," George said, leaning into his longshoreman persona. "It's just . . . the place has a feel. Kinda elegant."

McTavish softened a bit. "Old man Thorn built this place decades ago. It was his pride and joy."

George knew the name Thorn from their meeting with Dent Fenton and decided "old man Thorn" must be Mo Thorn's father or grandfather.

"There've been Thorns on this island for over two hundred years," McTavish said, continuing the story. "So, it's no surprise this place was built by the Thorn clan. Old man Thorn and his wife liked to travel to England and Scotland. Apparently, he took a liking to the pubs over there and decided to build one in the same vein right here on the island. That was in the 1960s. Like I say, it was his pride and joy. Also his gift to Starkhaven and its people. For over fifty years, the pub's seen weddings and wakes, births and birthdays and all other manner of holiday celebrations. But mostly it's a refuge for the island's hardworking lobstermen."

George fully understood the appeal of the place to the fishermen—the rich yeasty smell of brew, the welcoming darkness and visual warmth of the pub after a day spent in blazing sun or wailing salt winds. As one who lived at sea five months of each year, he knew the comfort he and the crew took in retreating to *Maine Wind's* galley in the warm belly of the ship after a long day at sea.

For a moment George was lost in a familiar longing for his beloved galley and woodstove.

"Strange time o' year to be looking for work. You from the mainland?"

The barkeep's question startled George from his brief reverie.

"Cape Cod," he said. "Lobster fishery's collapsing down there."

"I've heard a bit of it. What's causing that?"

"Waters are warming. It's just gotten too warm for lobsters. The ones that aren't dying off are moving farther out. Some fishermen have to go out fifty miles to catch 'em. At the same time, word is there's a lobster boom going on up in Maine. So I thought I'd try my hand up here."

"Why Starkhaven?"

George noted his tone had changed a bit from congenial to slightly suspicious. *An islander dyed-in-the-wool*, he thought.

"I ran into a guy in a bar in Portland had worked stern out here. Said I might find work, as some of the sternmen had moved off. Something about people dying. What's all that about?"

McTavish polished the glass in his hands but didn't look up. "Wouldn't know," he said. And just like that the subject was closed.

George decided not to push his luck and took another tack. "So, I don't suppose you know where I might find lodging? Took a chance coming out here spur of the moment. Did you know the ferry only runs once a month? Crazy, huh?"

McTavish looked up and smiled enigmatically. He set the glass down. "There's a place for rent out behind the pub here. A small trailer. Nothing fancy, but livable. I stayed there when I first came out here many years ago. Since then, it's mostly sternmen like to rent it. Belongs to the owner of the pub here, Mr. Mortimer Thorn, but I handle the arrangements."

George drained his glass and set it on the bar. "Be glad to take a look," he said. "Don't need nothin' fancy, as you say. Place to eat and sleep's all. Don't suppose you know anyone's lookin' for a sternman?"

McTavish nodded toward the door. "Post your name up there."

George turned and noticed a small cork board on the wall by the door.

"If anyone comes askin', I'll tell him where he can find you."

George nodded and stood up. "Mind if we take a look at that trailer now?"

"Sure. Boys will be coming in off the water soon, so now's a good time." McTavish retrieved his coat from behind the bar; George shouldered his sea bag, and they headed out the door.

After being inside The Stern Man, George had to shield his eyes against the brightness of the afternoon. They walked around back. Off to one side, about twenty yards behind the pub, a small Airstream trailer, no more than twelve or thirteen feet in length, squatted in a semi-circle of spruce trees. Or maybe landed might be a better description, considering its vintage aluminum, funky '50s spaceship vibe—all rounded and silvery and ready for take-off.

George laughed out loud. "Wow. That's a blast from the past."

"Don't get too excited. As you'll see, the inside can use some TLC."

McTavish ferreted out the key, unlocked the door, and he and George climbed inside.

He's not wrong about the TLC, George thought. *But then I'm not planning to make a career of the place.* "What's the price?" he asked.

"Three hundred a month," McTavish said.

George looked around. "Well, it ain't beautiful, but for that price, I'll take it. Providing there's heat and water."

"There's both," McTavish said. He went outside and turned on the propane. Back inside, he pulled out a lighter and lit the pilot on the small wall furnace and then the refrigerator. "Toilet works and there's a water line runs out from the pub," he said. "I'll turn it on soon as I get back inside."

George nodded, took out his wallet and paid McTavish three hundred dollars in cash. The barkeep stuffed it in his pocket, told George where the island store was for supplies, and left him to his sorry digs.

After he left, George gave the place a quick inspection, which didn't take much more than sixty seconds, considering the size of the trailer. The linoleum floor, while probably not the original, looked like it'd been rode hard and put away wet. The walls and overhead were covered with the original wood paneling, typical in vintage Airstreams, but years of damp salt air had left them in a sorry state. The grain was raised and bubbled in places, and where the finish had worn away, the wood had turned a weathered gray.

A kitchenette with a small range and sink lay to the right of the door, along the front of the trailer. Across from the door was a tiny bath with a toilet and claustrophobic little shower stall. Left of the door sat the small fridge and beyond that a dinette table with two stubby benches covered in bulletproof orange vinyl. As for the mattress on the bed at the rear of the trailer, George could only wonder what might inhabit it. Across from the dinette was a shallow storage closet with a broom, mop, some trash bags, a tall, narrow waste receptacle and an area to hang clothes, if you didn't mind them smelling like the trash.

George found a plastic bucket and some cleaning supplies under the kitchen sink. He tried the water. It was on. He let it get hot, then wedged the bucket under the faucet and filled it halfway. He poured in some cleanser and started to mop the floor while contemplating what to do with the ratty mattress. When he was done mopping, he relocated the trash can to the kitchenette, just to the right of the entry door. He had found a roll of duct tape under the kitchen sink and devised a way to wrap up the dilapidated mattress using cut-open trash bags and the tape. When he was done, he manhandled it out the door and around behind the trailer. Looking at it there gave him a sense of satisfaction. He dusted off his hands and went back inside.

He unpacked his sea bag and hung up a few of his shirts. There were a couple of shelves in the closet where he placed his jeans, two sweaters, socks, and underwear. Next he pulled a folded-up air mattress, small hand pump, and a set of flannel sheets from his sea-bag and laid them on the board where the mattress had sat. Last out of his bag came a medium-sized saucepan, a ten-inch sauté skillet, a small wood board, a good chef's knife, and a few of his favorite utensils. If you were George, there were certain things you did not leave to chance. Seeing his own pots on the stovetop made him feel okay about the rest of the place. He took a small notebook out of his pocket and wrote a short list of items. He also wrote out a post to place on the board inside the pub. It said: "Sternman for Hire: Inquire at trailer behind pub." He pulled on his parka and headed out the door to find the general store.

He was thinking about his luck landing a place this close to the pub. It meant he could manage to see McTavish on a daily basis and develop some rapport with him. Because if anyone knew things about the islanders, it was bound to be the local bartender. And though he'd hit a stone wall when he mentioned the deaths and the sternmen leaving the island, he planned to find ways to put a chink in that wall.

Since he was here and part of this whole setup, he intended to be a contributing factor. The way he saw it, the more each of them did, the quicker they'd be able to solve the case and get back to the mainland. With four of them working different angles, it couldn't take that long to uncover the truth. He would later look back and smile at his naïveté as an intricate web of deceit and buried secrets began to tighten around them.

Chapter 10

As John parked the pickup across from the general store, George emerged carrying a sack of groceries and headed along the road in the opposite direction from where they'd come. If he noticed them, he didn't show it and didn't look their way.

"Do you think he already found a place?" Jack asked.

"I'd say so, since he's carrying groceries. Didn't waste any time, did he?" Brie asked.

"No time to waste when it's this cold outside. It's find a perch or perish," John said. "Anyway, it never takes George long to land on his feet."

"The way he runs the galley aboard *Maine Wind*, I'd say he's hardwired for efficiency," Brie said.

She gave Jack a gentle nudge, and he opened the passenger-side door and climbed out. She and John followed, and they headed across the road and up onto the covered porch outside the store, where they stomped off their boots before entering. Inside the door, an assortment of aromas greeted them. First, fresh-baked bread, next the subtler notes of coffee and what smelled like homemade soup or stew.

There was no one at the one register near the door, so they picked up a basket and wandered down the aisle toward the back of the store, where all the good smells were coming from. The floor was pine like so many floors in Maine, and Brie worried about the moisture from their boots getting all over it.

Funny what one thinks about when entering an unfamiliar place.

"I'm back here if you need help," a woman called out.

They came around the corner of the aisle and saw a woman behind a small deli counter. There was a rack of fresh-baked bread behind her and on the end of the counter a giant, black soup kettle that, from the smell of it, held something wonderful.

"You must be the new folks moving into the old Ross place. Mo Thorn put out notice to expect you. I'm Mary Geary. Spelled with an 'ea' but pronounced 'Gary,'" she said. She was a tall, thin woman with pale eyes and red hair that was going gray, pulled back in a bun.

She seemed friendly and open. Not what Brie had expected, and she wondered if Mary might not be native to the island; might have moved here from Away. "We're pleased to meet you," she said. "I'm Brie Ross, and this is my husband, John Ross, and my grandfather, Jack Beaumont."

Mary had plastic gloves on and was making sandwiches, so she didn't shake hands but nodded warmly.

"It's sad how suddenly Nathan died. For a couple of months we all wondered what would happen to the place. Everyone worries when we lose any part of our year-round population. So you must be Nathan's nephew. Helen Ross's son."

"That's right," John said.

"I knew Helen growing up. She was a few years older, but on an island like this everyone hangs together. It's a one-room schoolhouse, grades one through eight—so more or less one big happy family. More like siblings than classmates, really."

So much for Mary being from Away, Brie thought. "So there's a school on the island."

"That's right. You two will, of course, be wanting to know that." She gave Brie a wink.

"No, I just meant . . ." Brie could feel herself color, which felt ridiculous, but on another level played right into her blushing bride role. She glanced at John. He was smiling at her obvious consternation.

"Well, it's the natural order of things," Mary said matter-of-factly.

Brie nodded. "Of course," she said and smiled. She was already planning to make Mary Geary a daily contact. She seemed friendly enough and obviously knew everyone on the island. If Brie played her cards right, maybe Mary would be a rich resource for understanding island dynamics. No part of their investigation appeared to involve Nathan Ross or his death, which had been determined to have been from natural causes. Still, by working that angle and learning more about Helen, Brie hoped to segue to other island families and slowly but surely get at the secrets that she suspected bound life together here.

"We'll leave you to your work and wander around and get the lay of things," Brie said

Mary nodded. "Just sing out when you're ready to check out. Gotta finish these sandwiches. The boys'll be coming in off the water soon, and the ones that don't have wives always hit the store here for hot soup and sandwiches."

"That soup smells great," Jack said. "What is it?"

"Vegetable beef barley," Mary said. "Would you like some?"

"Sure would! One of my favorites." He beamed at Mary, and now it was her turn to color.

Brie wasn't surprised. She smiled to herself. *Jack's a charmer. Maybe I'll send* him *to the store to gather intel, and I'll work other angles.*

Jack waited for his soup, and Brie and John walked over to the meat and seafood cooler that lay to the left of the deli counter. The setup allowed Mary to oversee both areas at once. As one would expect, there was some wonderful-looking seafood. They wandered up and down the aisles, and Brie added things to the basket. A bottle of milk, a carton of eggs, a couple of onions, a head of lettuce and a head of red cabbage, a loaf of sandwich bread, and a bag of ground coffee. Back at the meat counter, they bought some sliced turkey and ham for sandwiches and a piece of halibut to cook for dinner. Mary wrapped up the meat and fish and came forward to check them out.

"Nice meeting you," Brie said. "I'm sure I'll be back tomorrow for some more things once we get settled."

"I'll be here," Mary said. She gave Jack a smile.

It was a golden opportunity. "When we drove by earlier, I saw some folks playing cards," he said. "Can anyone join the game?"

"They get up a game most mornings," Mary said. "You stop down around ten-thirty. I'll introduce you."

"That sounds swell. I'll be down."

They headed out the door and across to the truck. Brie stared down the road looking for any sign of George, wondering where he had landed. Until they got their internet connection up and running, George was cut adrift, so to speak. He'd seen a picture of the house and knew generally where it was, but this being the middle of January, and without a vehicle at his disposal, he was unlikely to be dropping by. John started the truck, made a U-turn in front of the general store, and headed out of the village.

*   *   *

As George approached his new digs with his groceries, he saw a man peering in the side window of the trailer. He stopped in his tracks and watched for a moment, troubled by the intruder's boldness. Then he recalled the post he'd put on the board in the pub and relaxed a bit. When he got closer he called out, "Can I help you?"

The window peeper gave a start and turned around. "Lookin' for George. You him?"

"That's right," George said.

The man was slightly taller than him and built like a block house. He wore rubber bibs, Bean boots, a ratty parka and plaid bomber hat trimmed with what looked like real fur. One of his eyes opened farther than the other. *Probably from too much peeping,* George thought. "What can I do for you?" he asked.

"Saw your note in the pub. Said you're lookin' for work."

"That's right," George said again.

"You ever work stern on a lobsterboat?"

"Sure. Been workin' off Cape Cod. Lobster fishery's collapsing down there, so I thought I'd try my hand up in Maine. Heard some sternmen had bailed out here. So I came on out."

"Funny time o' year to head out to Starkhaven." The word 'year' came out 'ye-ah.'

"Lucky for you I did," George said.

"You're pretty cocky," the peeper said.

"I'm a hard worker and good at what I do," George said.

"Ayah? We'll see about that. Meet me on the dock tomorrow at oh-four hundred. We'll see if you can walk the walk."

"I'll be there," George said. "Didn't catch your name."

"Didn't throw it," Peeper said. "It's Hyden."

"Good to meet you, Hyden." George shifted the groceries to his left arm and stuck out his hand.

"Hyden's my last name. You can call me Trulie," the peep said.

"Great. I'll see you in the morning then, Trulie."

Hyden headed off. He had a rolling gait that marked him a mariner. George watched as he disappeared around the side of the pub, then he turned, unlocked the door to the trailer, and climbed inside. He was smiling as he deposited the bag on the miniscule kitchen counter. "Brie is not going to believe this," he said out loud. "Trulie Hyden! Really? Darn good name for a suspect, if you ask me." Truth was, though, George would always think of his new boss as the Peeper. That's just the way it was with him. First impressions always stuck.

George put the groceries away and headed back out the door and around to the front of the pub. Just inside the door, he removed his note from the board.

McTavish must have seen him because he called from behind the bar, "Trulie found you, eh?"

"Yeah. We're all set up. I start tomorrow."

At that, a couple of heads swiveled around and took him in. Obviously lobstermen, in from the sea. George nodded toward them by way of greeting, and they went back to their brews.

"Don't suppose you know who could hook up my internet?" George asked McTavish.

"That'd be Josh Stevens. He's our island handyman and IT guy. I'll give him a call if you like."

"That'd be great," George said. He headed out the door and back to his trailer, where he put on a pot of coffee and fired up the oven. To his way of thinking, a batch of chocolate chip cookies was the very best air freshener. The general store had everything he'd needed, so he got out a bowl and started in on the dough.

He was just pulling the last batch of cookies out of the oven when there was a knock on his door. He reached over and opened the door, spatula in hand. The tool belt and box stuck under the guy's arm that said "Modem" were a dead giveaway.

"You must be Josh."

"Right on, man. Kieran called. Said you just moved in. Needed an internet hookup."

"Yeah, thanks for coming out so quick."

"Well, not much of a work backlog out here." It came out "he-ah." "Although I do have another call out t'other end of the island. New folks just moved into the old Ross place. Two calls in one day. That's gotta be some kinda record."

The outlet was on the wall by the dinette table. George got out his laptop and set it there and left Josh to his business. Twenty minutes later, George had internet service. He paid Josh in cash and tipped him with cookies, and Josh went on his way.

George went and checked his connection and sent Brie a quick email telling her where he'd landed and that he'd already been hired. He didn't tell her the boss's name. Wanted to see the look on her face when he revealed that. When he was done he went back to the kitchenette and started his dinner.

*   *   *

Brie heard the doorbell and started out of the kitchen, but John had already gotten there and let Josh Stevens in. He took him into the living room and over to the front wall, where there was a phone jack just to the right of the small drop front desk that sat in the corner. Brie had set her laptop on top of the desk. Josh got busy setting up the modem and activating the landline and DSL connection. He warned John not to expect a lot of speed from the connection, and John told him they weren't worried about that.

Brie wandered back to the kitchen, washed some russet potatoes and put them in the oven to bake. Forty-five minutes later she put the halibut into the skillet where she had melted butter. She added some sliced garlic and, as the fish cooked, squeezed in some lemon juice. Not much was needed with fish this fresh. George had taught her that the less you do to it, the better.

Jack put a salad together while Brie cooked the fish and without too much fanfare, they gathered in the dining room to eat. Brie had pushed her sewing machine and fabric to the far end of the table. The sun had long since headed for its berth in the west, and Brie was longing for her berth as well. She and John had been up since six o'clock that morning, making sure the house in Camden was secured and checking their supplies before heading for the ferry.

After dinner, Jack fed Angus and then took him out the kitchen door to do his business. She and John were cleaning up from the meal when they heard the doorbell. Brie looked at her watch. It was six-fifteen. "I wonder who that can be?"

She and John headed for the front door. John flipped on the outside light and opened the door. A tall woman in a blue hooded parka stood there. She was holding two plastic storage containers.

"Hi, I'm Tam Thorn," she said. "Just wanted to stop by and welcome you to the island."

"Come in, come in. It's freezing outside," John said. They stepped back to make room for Tam in the tiny entryway. "This is my wife, Brie."

"Hi, Brie. Nice to meet you."

"Please, come in," Brie said.

"Well, okay. But just for a minute." She handed Brie the containers. "I brought some scones and a pound cake that I baked today."

"That's awfully kind of you," Brie said. She thought about the lukewarm reception they had received from Mo Thorn that afternoon and wondered if Thorn had sent his wife on a damage control mission.

Tam Thorn pulled off her boots and stepped into the small hall between the living and dining rooms. She pushed the fur-fringed hood off her head. Long black hair, tangled from the wind outside, fanned across the front of her parka. She was tall— every bit of five-foot-ten. She had broad shoulders and looked like she might have hauled her fair share of lobster traps over time.

Brie placed her age at mid-forties. She could tell that Tam had been pretty at one time, but the sun had taken its toll on her skin, and for whatever reason, she sensed the weight of the world rested on those broad shoulders. She had no doubt that being the wife of the island's alpha male would come with a unique set of challenges.

Once Tam had handed off the baked goods, she seemed at a loss as to what to do with her hands. She put them behind her back, then clasped them in front of her and finally stuck them in the pockets of her parka.

Brie saw she was anxious and decided that Tam was out of her depth in the role of welcoming committee. "That's an unusual name and a pretty one," she said, attempting to put her at ease.

"It's short for Tamara." She looked around the living room. "I've never been in this house," she said. "Nathan Ross kept to himself. Never married. It's nice, though."

"We're pleased with it. It's a wonderful opportunity for John."

"Mo told me you're Helen Ross's son. So you inherited the property?"

"That's right," John said. "There was the matter of some back taxes, but we were able to take care of those and clear the title."

Tam nodded.

"Would you like to come in and sit down?" Brie asked.

"Oh, no. I really have to get back." She looked like a filly ready to bolt.

Just then, Brie heard the kitchen door open as Jack and Angus came back in. A few seconds later, Angus came careening into the room. John caught his collar just in time.

"Angus, sit." John kept him firmly in hand till he sat.

Apparently, this was just what Tam needed. She went to her knees so she was eye to eye with Angus. "Well, hello, big boy," she said. "Aren't you beautiful." She rubbed his giant head and Angus wiggled frantically, but John kept a grip on him.

Jack came in from the kitchen and Brie introduced him. "This is my grandfather, Jack Beaumont. Jack, this is Tam Thorn. Mo Thorn's wife. She's brought us some wonderful goodies."

"Pleased to meet you. I see you've met Angus."

"He's wonderful," Tam said. "There couldn't be a better place for a Newfie than out here."

"You know your breeds, then," Jack said.

"Well, some of them. These dogs are known in Maine. The Canadian Coast Guard uses them for rescue operations."

It was just the ice-breaker they had needed. Tam stood back up. She seemed more relaxed.

Brie wondered what it must be like for the Thorns, who were used to being in control of pretty much everything on the island. Now the murders of these four fishermen—and murders they were in Brie's mind until something indicated otherwise—threatened that control. The people who ran the show were now forced to take a back seat to an unfolding drama, spiraling out of control. She wondered how much strain that fact might have imposed on their relationship. She also had to wonder, if Tam Thorn knew who they really were and why they were here, what her reaction might be?

"I should warn you that they may cut your gear." Tam studied John's face, waiting for a reaction.

"Who?" John asked.

"If it happens, you'll probably never know."

"So, that's how they welcome you out here?"

Tam shifted from foot to foot, ill-at-ease. "They might accept you, but while they're making up their minds, they'll be cutting your gear."

"I see." John looked at Brie. "Well, there's no point worrying about it till it happens."

Realizing she had slipped out of character, Brie tried to summon up a properly horrified wifely expression.

"You seem like nice people, so I just want to warn you about what can happen."

She said it in the most matter-of-fact way, like she was commenting on the weather. The subtext seemed to be, *You're on your own. Make or break, no one's coming to your rescue.* Brie couldn't help feeling a chill, thinking about the men who had died. No one had been coming to their rescue either. At that moment an uncomfortable thought winged across her mind like an unwelcome bird of omen. *Since the Thorns are seemingly in control of everything out here, what if they were somehow involved in the deaths?* The thought seemed outlandish, but the detective in her did not ignore it. She had learned long ago that her success in the investigative realm was equal parts hard work and gut instinct.

Tam said she really had to get back. Brie thanked her again, but as she turned to go, she noticed the sewing machine and quilting fabric on the dining room table. "Are you a quilter?"

"I am," Brie said. "Or I should say, I'm learning. I've only been at it for a year or so."

"We have a quilting group here on the island. It meets at my house once a week. Why don't you come? Meet some of the other wives."

"I'd love to. What should I bring?"

"Whatever you're working on. And your machine. I have a big room in my downstairs dedicated to the group and the work. Sometimes we do group projects and give the quilts to women's shelters or to the veterans' home there on the mainland."

"I like the sound of that."

"We're meeting tomorrow. Ten-thirty. Some are off island for the winter, so it's a small group right now."

She told Brie where her house was, then she put on her boots, pulled up her hood, and headed out the door.

Brie felt a little thrum of excitement. The plan they had constructed was working. Of course, their ultimate success would depend on how well each of them played their roles. Any good undercover op is nothing more than a vehicle for data collection, and the data to be mined here was all in human form. It was in the form of secrets kept.

Chapter 11

Brie stood in Tam Thorn's downstairs quilting room staring out the large windows at the raging nor'easter. They were sheltered from the worst of it here in the village, where the harbor faced southwest, but the Thorns' house stood high on the hill above the harbor, where the wind blowing across the top of the island could not only be heard but felt when the storm unleashed a violent gust or downburst.

Brie had dropped Jack off at the general store where, despite the snowstorm, the scheduled poker game was in full swing. The understanding was that she'd pick him back up in two to two and a half hours, depending on how the quilting session was unfolding. Since they were working with one vehicle, the plan was to get back home by around one o'clock so John could take the truck and head down to the pub, where he hoped to get a line on a sternman for his boat.

Brie turned away from the windows and observed the group of women who were clustered around the bar-cum-kitchenette, eating scones and drinking coffee. She guessed that this room had been designed as a large family or game room, complete with bar, running water, small oven and refrigerator. At some point Tam had obviously decided to use it for her quilting operation.

The house itself—three stories plus an attic—was impressive with its gold-hued, cedar shake siding and burnished metal roof that had to have cost a fortune. Sitting as it did near the top of the hill, it dominated the scene below it, and whether intentional or not, was certainly emblematic of the way in which the Thorns held sway over island life. Tam had told her that they'd had the house designed and built twelve years ago on the spot Mo Thorn had always fancied should be his. *After all, if one is the island kingpin, what better place than this to perch?* Brie thought.

She looked across the room. After the initial introductions, the women had gotten busy ignoring her and gossiping among themselves. She felt quite comfortable with the situation, her *raison d'être* being to spy on them generally, but she contemplated how it might feel if she were just what she appeared to be—a newcomer on the island, looking to be accepted. When viewed through that lens, the dynamic felt unpleasant, bordering on lonely. She paused a moment to soak in the feeling of how Brie Ross, not Brie Beaumont, might have felt.

Then she decided to give them the benefit of the doubt. Maybe they feared for her and for her husband alone on the sea, vulnerable to whatever evil lurked in this place. Maybe they had no way to convey that fear, island rules being what they were —namely, that one didn't readily share what one might know with a stranger. Or maybe the fear she sensed was born of tribalism, which always fears the new, the different. They were the new element. Tribalism always opposes change, and it would be strong in a place like Starkhaven with hundreds of years of history and a certain kind of inbreeding.

She consoled herself with the fact that things were bound to get better. As the French say about new liaisons, "The first time you're a stranger; the second time you're a guest; the third time you're a friend." Brie hoped it would play out like that, but for today, she was content to be a stranger. Today she would be a listener. After all, that had been Dent Fenton's directive for the op.

She stopped in front of a large table where the women had been assembling one of their group projects that Tam had mentioned the night before. As she studied the work, Tam approached and asked if she'd like to cut fabric for some of the pieces or if she'd prefer to sew.

"I'll be happy to work on cutting shapes," she said.

"When we're working together on a project, we try to rotate jobs each time. Keeps things from getting boring."

Brie nodded and Tam showed her what geometric shapes they needed from each of the three fabrics on the cutting table. She gave her a brief tutorial and then watched her cut several pieces before nodding.

"You've got this, girl." With that, she walked away, leaving Brie to the work.

Besides herself and Tam, there were four other women present: Jana Bjorklund, Bess Gordon, Sara Bellsby, and Clara Lyston. Brie recognized two of the names from the case files. Bess Gordon was the wife of Cliff Gordon, one of the lobstermen who had gone missing, and Clara Lyston was the neighbor who'd been interviewed about Paul Le Fevre. The files had revealed that Bess Gordon had been a victim of domestic abuse and that, at the time of Gordon's disappearance, the detectives had reported recent evidence of battering. She had refused to file a report at that time, saying, "What would be the point? He's gone now."

Brie studied Bess Gordon from across the room. She stood to one side of the large table where Tam was fitting pieces together that would be sewn on to the evolving quilt. Bess seemed content in the role of observer, at least at the moment. She was a thin woman, fortyish, with sandy brown hair. She stood with her hands in her pockets, and the vibe Brie got was that, whatever demonstrative might look like, Bess Gordon would be the polar opposite of that.

The division of labor played out as follows: Tam appeared to be the assembler-in-chief; Brie was assigned to cutting; Sara Bellsby was a sewer, stitching individual pieces together into blocks at her machine; Clara Lyston was the presser, working at the ironing board, and Jana Bjorklund manned the larger of the two sewing machines. Brie guessed she had the job of sewing the blocks onto the greater quilt.

Tam had told her that they were missing one of their regulars today—Lyla Stumph. *Good*, Brie thought. *That's one more name from the case files.* Oslo Stumph had been victim number one. She recalled that his wife had divorced him and had moved from the island years before his death, but that his parents still lived here. So she reasoned that maybe Lyla might be his mother. Of course she could just as easily be an aunt, or a cousin, since family roots run deep on these islands, resulting in many branches.

At first it seemed odd that two of the women in the group had names that matched up with the victims in some way, but Brie reminded herself that this was a small community. Tam had also mentioned that several members of the group had left for the winter. The fact is that many lobstermen make enough money to winter in warm places. John had told her that they'll cite the going price of lobster and claim they're just making ends meet, but the fact is many of them are wealthy, as is attested to by their fancy boats, trucks, and vacations.

One thing she knew; the killer was not part of that group. Since two of the deaths, Paul Le Fevre and Abe Winter, had occurred in the late fall or winter months, it meant that the killer was most likely here on the island, among them. Unless, of course, the final *coup de gras* had been dealt, and he or she had left the island—possibly under the guise of going south for the winter—never to return. But somehow her gut told her otherwise. It told her the killer was still here, emboldened by the fact that he or she had gotten away with murder, not once but multiple times.

Brie went on with her cutting, now and then delivering the pieces to Sara Bellsby, who sewed them together. Of the four other women present, Sara Bellsby took the prize for least friendly. She had a distant manner, as if the mere fact of Brie's presence was somehow a burden. She sported a boyish haircut, and a mild case of acne had hounded her into what Brie guessed to be her mid-thirties. Despite being rather stocky, Sara seemed to favor clingy clothes with lots of color and pattern, which told Brie she had spirit. But every time Brie delivered her cuttings, Sara would gesture with her hand in an aloof sort of way and say, "Just put them there." Brie wondered if she'd inadvertently done something to offend her but dismissed the thought, since all she'd said to Sara when they'd been introduced was, "Hello" and "Nice to meet you."

Jana Bjorklund, on the other hand, seemed open to her presence in the group. And while she never actually spoke to Brie, she would occasionally look her way and smile in a welcoming manner.

The fourth woman, Clara Lyston, seemed intently focused on her work of ironing the stitched-together pieces that Sara Bellsby continually passed to her. Lost in her own little reverie, Clara hummed quietly to herself as she worked the iron back and forth over the cloth. For whatever reason, Brie got the sense that this was Clara's way of convincing herself that she was happier than was actually the case.

All in all, it was one of the longest two hours Brie had, in recent memory, endured. By the end of the quilting session, she felt like she'd washed up on an uncharted island where nobody spoke her language, and so, after saying a quick thank you to Tam Thorn, she wasted no time getting out the door and into the solitary refuge of John's pickup truck, the wild lash of snow in between stripping away some of the anxiousness she felt.

*   *   *

Jack Le Beau sat in the front window of the general store playing Texas Hold'em with the three other intrepid individuals who had come out in the gale. Outside, trapped under the porch roof, the windblown snow swirled in large vertical eddies, occasionally pinging the window with icy fingers.

Inside, the aroma of homemade soup simmering back in the deli reminded Jack of what he loved about winter—the stark contrast between inside and outside. In the same way that you don't know happiness unless you've been sad, you can't know the real feeling of coziness unless you've been through a northern winter.

When he'd arrived that morning, Mary Geary, the storekeeper, had introduced him to the others, explaining that John and Brie Ross were the newcomers to the island—John being Nathan Ross's nephew—and that Jack was Brie's grandfather. One of the players named Dale Woodrow had asked where they had lived before, and Jack had filled them in about John's house in Camden and work at the boatyard. He'd also mentioned his and Brie's Minnesota roots.

While the three individuals surrounding him—two men, one woman—all seemed plenty lively, in American parlance they would all have been termed old folks. Jack didn't mind, though, and couldn't help smiling at youth's horrified perception of age. Little did they know that it could be the freest, happiest time of life, if one had just bothered to take care of oneself.

Biddy Firth, who sat to Jack's right, was a plain-spoken woman who didn't mince words. She had close-cropped gray hair, and though her skin had weathered to a nut brown, her blue eyes still sparked with life. Jack guessed she was north of seventy-five but by how many degrees of latitude was uncertain.

"Minnesota, eh? Never been there. What's it like?" Biddy asked.

"A lot like Maine, actually. Cold. Really cold in winter. People are hard workers. Independent minded. Like the outdoors. Like I said, a lot like Maine—just no lobsters." He made sure to pronounce the "r" like a proper Minnesotan would.

It was a description Brie had coached him on that went to the heart of what, in her mind, made Minnesota and Maine simpatico.

"Lots of lakes, though," Biddy said. "Saw a license plate from there once. Said 'ten thousand lakes.' Seems like they might be stretching the truth a bit."

"Nope, it's true. In fact, there may be more than that. When the last glaciers retreated ten thousand years ago, it left a whole lot of holes filled with water."

"Heck, we got almost that many lakes here in Maine," Marty Hawkins said. "And lots of lobsters to boot." It came out "lobstahs."

"Well, like I said, you got us there. But we got our walleye. Think you've got those in the lakes here, too, though," Jack said.

The other three shrugged like they'd never heard of such a thing as a walleye. Being from Starkhaven, probably born and bred, it wasn't surprising. These ancient mariners had lived and breathed all things North Atlantic. That meant lobster, cod, haddock, and halibut. No walleye to be had out here.

Jack was surprised at their openness. He'd expected tight-lipped silence from them—being an outsider and all. He guessed he might be the senior member of the group, so maybe that fact made him more acceptable. After all, he posed no threat to anyone's lobstering territory. So after a couple more hands were played, he ventured a question.

"So were all you folks lobster fishermen?" He included Biddy in that, knowing that any woman who had fished commercially would be insulted by being called a fisherwoman. They weren't alone in that, either. He also found the term absurd.

"We still are on nice days in the summer." As she said it, Biddy made a motion with her hand that included the other two. "My husband and I fished out here for fifty years. He passed a few years back, but I still put the boat in. Pull a few traps for old time's sake. If you're from here, you're born to it. No getting it out of the blood. One day you die, but you hope it's while you're pulling up a pot full o' bugs."

Jack Le Beau knew "bugs" meant lobsters, but he cocked his head to the side like he didn't get it.

"Bugs is lobstahs," Marty said.

Jack smiled, nodded, and took the hand currently in play.

Marty Hawkins was tall and lanky with a neatly trimmed gray beard and hair to match, new flannel shirt, tucked in, and well-fitted jeans. His buddy, Dale Woodrow—at least Jack had them figured for buddies—who sat to his right, was the night to Marty's day. Dale had the arms of a wrestler and the face of a stooge. Suspenders held up his baggy dungarees that were old enough to have been sewn by Levi Strauss himself. A triangle of worn tee-shirt bulged through a gap in his red flannel shirt where a button had gone missing. There was something about their back-and-forth banter that marked the two as boyhood mates, and Jack knew friendships that old pay little heed to externals.

He certainly could have asked them, but he'd chosen to keep a low profile on this first day. So, while the detective in him was busy making silent observations about his fellow players, outwardly he kept the questions to a minimum and erred on the side of listening. Occasionally, though, he caught them glancing at him as he studied his cards. There was something urgent in those glances. Were they wondering if he knew about the deaths of the lobstermen? Were they debating whether to tell him—to warn him, not for himself but for his grandson-in-law? Jack had spent his entire career as a detective picking up on vibes, and that sixth sense was as strong in him today as ever. The vibe behind those looks was one he knew well—fear.

Just before one o'clock he saw Brie pull up across the street in the truck.

"Time to cash in my chips, folks. My granddaughter's here to pick me up. Hope I can join you again."

"You come on down any time," Dale said, friendly as could be. "We're here most every day. Same time."

"Okay, then. Thanks." Jack stood up and put on his parka. "Gotta grab some of Mary's soup before I head out."

As he walked toward the back of the store, he could hear Biddy, Dale, and Marty continuing their game. The soups today were chicken dumpling and fish chowder. He bought a quart of each and a loaf of roasted garlic bread that had just come out of the oven.

"Thanks for introducing me to the group, Mary. Nice to meet some folks so soon after getting here."

"You're welcome, Jack." She glanced up at him. "You get bored at home, come on down. I'll put you to work."

He nodded. "Okay. Well, best be getting along. Brie's waitin' on me."

He gathered up his purchases, moved through the store and out the front door where, head bowed against a stinging wind, he crossed the road to the truck.

"Whatcha got there, Jack?" Brie asked as he climbed into the truck.

"Soup for lunch and a loaf of warm bread."

"Wonderful. Just what we need today." She switched on her wipers against the storm, made a U-turn and headed for home. "How'd the game go?"

"Just three others there today—two guys, one gal. All older and all former lobstermen. No names that match up with the case files, though. How about the quilters?"

"It was like being the new girl in high school. Nobody talking to you. Couple of familiar names, though. Bess Gordon and Clara Lyston. Their names showed up in the case files.

And Lyla Stumph was missing today. I figure she's somehow related to the first victim, Oslo Stumph."

"Well, our job in these early days is just to assemble a who's who on the island," Jack said.

"You're right. That's why it's so important to work our way into the fabric here, wherever possible. Learn the unwritten stories. Who hates whom. Who's sleeping with whom. Who's angry and why. Who thinks they have a score to settle."

"I get the sense it won't be easy," Jack said. "But I'll tell you something. There's fear here, just below the surface, just beneath the routine of island life."

Brie nodded. "I sense it too. We just have to lean hard on the fact that we belong here. That John has a birthright here. That's what we all have to project."

They drove in silence for the next few minutes with the defroster puffing away and Brie squinting through the windshield. As they neared the turnoff, she switched the truck into four-wheel drive and turned onto the long driveway that led up to the house. The deepening snow seemed a metaphor for an island steeped in secrets—secrets thick as the arctic fog, where death might again come for an unsuspecting lobsterman.

Chapter 12

John sat at the bar in The Stern Man, nursing his schooner of beer. He liked his brew, but at just east of two o'clock, it was a bit early for him. However, the email George had sent the night before informed him that this was where he'd most likely find a sternman. So here he sat, waiting expectantly.

He'd no more than come through the door when the bartender, Kieran McTavish, had guessed his identity and greeted him with, "You must be Nathan Ross's nephew."

John introduced himself and was pleasantly surprised when McTavish said, "You look just like your mother, Helen."

"Did you know my mom?" John asked.

"No, but Nathan used to show me pictures of his sister. Seems like they were close. You were in some of those pictures as a little tyke. But seeing you as an adult; well, you're definitely Helen's son."

"Thanks, mate. That's nice to know," John said, contemplating the irony of it all.

"So I suppose you'll be looking for a sternman," McTavish said.

"Ayah."

"Too bad. There was a guy just arrived yesterday lookin' to work stern, but Trulie Hyden snapped him up."

"What happened to his guy?" John asked.

"Left the island recently. There've been a few others too. They're a nomadic lot."

John nodded. He knew the real reason they were leaving but didn't mention it, waiting to see if McTavish might bring up the deaths. He didn't.

John withdrew into his beer, not wanting to ask too many questions. He'd just ordered a second round when a big Scandinavian-looking fellow came in the door. He was tall, six-four, maybe, somewhere south of mid-life, brush cut blond hair, full beard, the face of a Viking.

"Yorkie. Come on in. Shut the door fast. Storm's a beast."

The man squinted in the direction of McTavish's voice, blind from the arctic brilliance he'd just closed the door on. "Supposed to keep right on through tomorrow. Helluva wicked blow." He took a few moments to let his eyes adjust to the low light of the pub and then walked toward the bar, eyes on John the whole way.

As he approached, McTavish introduced him. "This is John Ross. Nathans Ross's nephew, just come out from the mainland to take over his uncle's place." Turning to John, he said, "This is Lars Bjorklund. Known as 'Yorkie' here abouts."

Bjorklund took his seat around the corner of the bar from where John sat, so they half faced each other in a catty-corner fashion. He had eyes the color of the North Sea, but John sensed kindness in this giant of a man.

"Pleased to meet you, Lars." John extended his hand. He stayed away from "Yorkie" as it seemed presumptuous.

"Welcome," Lars said. His eyes appeared to agree with his greeting.

John thought that was a good sign. "Thanks. Buy you a beer?" he asked.

Lars waved that away. "I should be the one buying. You're the new guy." He gestured to John's brew. "Put that on my tab, Kieran, and draw me one of the same."

"Thanks," John said again. He noticed Lars looking at his hands.

"You ever lobster before?"

"Just one season when I was eighteen. Worked stern."

"You got workman's hands. What's your trade?"

"Worked in a boatyard in Lincolnville," John said.

"Boat builder, eh? And you gave that up to come out here in the middle of winter?"

"Opportunity knocked," John said. The look exchanged by Lars and McTavish was fleeting, but John caught it. It translated to, *Opportunity or risk?* But neither mentioned the deaths of the lobstermen.

"Didn't know my uncle very well," John said. "Only remember him coming to the mainland a few times when I was growing up. Mom passed twenty years ago. After that Uncle Nate and I kinda lost track of each other. Not sure how she'd feel about me coming here."

"Didn't know your mom," Bjorklund said. "She moved off long before my time, but you've got a birthright here. Don't let'em push you off."

John studied his beer. "Thanks, man." Now he knew the vibe he'd picked up was true. "Suppose they'll try, though," he said.

"They may," Lars said. "Stand your ground."

Just then the door opened and in came a snow-encrusted human. The three of them stared in his direction until he pushed the hood off his head.

"Fin," McTavish said, surprised. "When did you come back to the island?"

"Took the ferry out yesterday." He nodded in Bjorklund's direction. "Yorkie."

"That ferry wouldn't be running today," Lars stated unequivocally.

"Nope. 'Bout as bad as it gets out heah." He hung up his coat, walked over, and sat next to Lars at the bar.

Fin was young, maybe twenty. Six feet tall. All wiry strength, shaggy dark hair, good features. John had noticed him on the ferry yesterday.

McTavish drew him off a beer, appearing to know just what he liked. "Thought maybe you were gone for good," he said, sliding the glass across the bar.

"When I left the island, so did I. But I like the life out here. Thought maybe if I saved up long enough, I could get a boat of my own." The young man stared into his brew. "Wicked expensive, though, to get into the trade."

"This is Jim Finrude," Lars said to John. "We call him Fin. He's been working stern out here for a couple years." He told Fin about John's connection to the Ross property.

Fin extended his hand. "Pleased to meet you," he said, showing his mother had taught him well. "Saw you and your wife on the ferry yesterday. That's quite a dog you got there."

"Angus is his name."

"Yeah? What is he?"

"Newfoundland."

Fin nodded, impressed. "He'll be likin' this blizzard, then."

"Yup," John said. "It's his favorite season. Never more happy than when he can lie in a snow bank."

They talked on a bit, dogs always making a good ice-breaker. Fin mentioned he was rooming with his aunt, who'd lived on Starkhaven since birth. "We get along well, and she's got extra room. Never wants to charge me, though, so I make it up by working around the place, doing repairs, upkeep."

"Nothing wrong with that," Lars said. "Too many young people don't carry their weight."

"They wouldn't make it long out here, then," Fin stated matter-of-factly.

"Gotta girl here, too, don't you?" McTavish asked.

"Isa Firth. It was her encouraged me to leave. Look for work on the mainland." He and Lars shared a look that said they both knew why but weren't about to say.

John knew perfectly well why Fin had left Starkhaven.

The conversation wore on a bit and finally John said, "I'm looking for a sternman, Fin, if you're interested. I need someone to help me get acclimated to the waters out here and my uncle's old territory. I'll pay you top dollar."

Fin went silent for the first time. He looked into his beer for a long moment and finally took a draught. He set his glass down and studied John's face, as if what kind of a man he was would be written there. "I'll think about it," he finally said. He stood up. "I should be going. Leave your contact info with McTavish here. I'll be in touch." He shook hands with Lars and headed for the door.

Things went silent for a time after Fin left. John ordered another beer for himself and Lars. He was just beginning to think the party was over when Lars spoke.

"You have to forgive Fin his curt behavior. He's gun-shy, that's all. He worked stern for Abe Winter for two years. Thing is, Abe went missing from his boat two months ago. Fin was under the weather that day. Hadn't gone out hauling with him. Don't know if he feels guilty or it just spooked him, but he left the island shortly after that."

"Look, I've read about the deaths of the lobstermen out here. Knew about all of it before my uncle died."

Silence stretched out again. McTavish busied himself polishing glasses.

John finally said, "The chance to inherit this property. Work in the lobster trade . . . it's a dream a lot of men have who've grown up in Maine. I'm no different. How could I pass that up?" He took a long, slow drink. "My wife is worried, though. I know that."

Lars put a hand on his shoulder. "You'll be fine. Good reason to get a sternman, though, and treat him well. You never know, Fin may come around."

"So all these guys who went missing off their boats were hauling alone?"

"That's right," Lars said.

"Is that common?"

Lars took a swallow. "Fifty percent of lobstermen don't use a sternman. Saves money, I guess. Personally, I wouldn't be without one."

They retreated into their beers after that. When he'd finished his, John stood and shook hands with Lars. "See you around, mate," he said. He wrote his phone number down on a napkin and gave it to McTavish in case Jim Finrude checked in. The Stern Man was a true port in the storm, and John reluctantly left the coziness of the place and headed back out into the gale.

*   *   *

Later that evening, Brie, John, and Jack were at home starting dinner prep in the kitchen. The plan was for sloppy joes. Jack had just finished putting food out for Angus. Brie had gotten out ground beef, an onion, and the chef's knife, and John was stirring up some boxed brownies for dessert, when a sharp cry rang out. As the knife hit the floor, the guys both whipped around to see her holding her hand. John darted over and steered her to the sink. He saw the blood running down from where she had pressed one hand over the other.

"Let me take a look," he said gently.

Brie looked away, not wanting to see the damage.

A second later, John said, "Sorry, babe. This will need stitches."

Brie let out a groan. "Really?"

"Yeah. Sorry. We packed the first aid kit from the ship. Do you want me to take care of it, or do you want to head down to the island clinic? We saw it yesterday—remember?"

"How deep is it?" Brie asked.

"Pretty deep," John said. He pulled a clean towel out of the drawer next to the sink and wrapped it tightly around her hand.

115

"Maybe we should visit the doc, then."

"I'll get your coat," he said.

Angus, sensing trouble and undoubtedly smelling the wound, had sat directly next to Brie and was leaning into her leg. Jack encouraged him to come away so Brie could get the coat around her. In the entry she stepped into her boots, and John steered her through the door and out to the truck.

They drove down the long driveway and turned right onto the road.

"You know there are better ways to get out of cooking dinner." He reached over and gave her leg a squeeze.

"And here I thought I was being clever. How'd you know?"

"Deductive reasoning. It's rubbing off on me, living with a detective."

"Actually, I never thought I'd say this, but I like working in the kitchen. Slicing and chopping and sautéing. My work as a detective has always been pretty cerebral, and there's something calming about the hands-on work in the kitchen. Helps the mind shift into neutral. Sometimes that's when the best things come to you."

She let out a yawn. "George would not be happy, though. He taught me knife skills aboard *Maine Wind* and told me to always work with a sharp knife. Said a dull blade can slip off the food and cut you." She held up her towel-wrapped hand. "Exhibit A. What's more, I think my mind was somewhere else."

"On the case?"

"Well, that *is* why we're here, after all."

On the outskirts of the village, they pulled into the driveway for the island clinic, and Brie again noted the name on the sign. Tobias Ward, M.D. The lights were on in the house, and she heaved a sigh of relief.

"I guess it's not bad to make the acquaintance of the doc," she said. "Being who he is, he probably knows all the islanders."

"You didn't have to go to these lengths to meet him, though."

"Very funny. Let's go."

They climbed out of the truck and walked toward the front of the house. The doctor must have heard the truck, because as they approached, he opened the door. Brie figured if you're the only doctor in a place like this, you might have a sixth sense for when someone's in trouble.

"Doctor Ward?" she asked as they came up onto the porch.

"That's me, all right," the doc said in a reassuring way. He nodded toward the towel-wrapped hand. "Come on through, and we'll take care of you."

The doctor was John's height, around six feet tall, but stockier than he. Mid-sixties, Brie guessed. He had a broad, strong face with thick, salt and pepper hair that was more salt than pepper. He hunched a little—probably from too many years of leaning over patients—but intellect danced in his eyes, giving him an air of youthful vigor.

A hallway led from the front entry straight back to the kitchen. They passed through a door at the back of the kitchen and into a small waiting room that had a desk and a file cabinet tucked in one corner. Brie noticed there was a door to the outside. Folks that lived here would know to come around the side of the house to the clinic entrance.

"You must be the new folks," the doctor said over his shoulder.

"We're the Rosses. I'm John and this is my wife, Brie."

A short hall off the waiting room led to two small examining rooms—one on either side of the hall. The doc flipped on the light in the room on the left and asked Brie to sit up on the table.

"Sorry we have to meet this way, but as you might guess, it's not the first time it's happened," he said.

"I bet it comes with the territory."

Doc Ward smiled. "Making a lobstering joke, while wounded?" He winked at John. "You got a live one here."

"I'll say. Likes to juggle with knives."

The doc darted John a quick look and then smiled, seeing the twinkle in his eye.

"Let's see what we've got here."

Doc Ward was a big man, but his touch was gentle as could be. Brie was grateful for that, because by now her hand was throbbing.

He unwrapped the towel from her left hand and inspected the wound. "Why don't you lie back," he said. "I'm going to put your hand in a solution to clean the wound while I prep everything."

Doc Ward brought the table up to a reclining position, and Brie sat back. He took her blood pressure and nodded like he approved, and then prepared a solution of warm water and a disinfecting soap. He carefully lowered her hand into the solution and got busy preparing his small operating area.

John came and stood by Brie. "How're you doing?" he asked.

"Feeling stupid," Brie said.

"No need for that," the doc piped up. "We all make mistakes."

"Did you grow up on the island?" John asked.

"Nope. Grew up in Rockland. The Army put me through medical school. I did my residency at the VA Medical Center in Vermont and then was stationed in the Middle East, in a field hospital, for most of my active duty."

"So your specialty must have been surgery," Brie said.

"Actually, I had two. Internal medicine and general surgery. Makes me a perfect fit for an island community, I guess."

"What brought you out here, Doc?" John asked.

"After my wife died . . ." He paused and looked over at them. "Cancer," was all he said, but Brie could read the pain that still lived in him and thought about how helpless a doctor must feel to lose his wife to cancer.

"I think I went through some kind of crisis. It wasn't that I didn't serve a purpose on the mainland in the clinic where I worked. I just needed to do something more. Feel more essential, I guess. Once you've been a battlefield surgeon, there's a part of you that's forever changed. Every day, it's life or death. After my wife died, I decided I wanted to go where I'd be *that* indispensable. People die in these remote island communities —things like heart disease, diabetes, pre-natal problems, early-stage cancer; they can all go undiagnosed. I feel like I've made a real difference out here. And that's enough. I don't need a lot of money. The folks here are so grateful for what I do. No better payment than that. Been out here for almost nine years now." Tobias Ward shook his head. "Don't know where the time's gone."

"So much for retirement, eh?" Brie said.

"Well, I'm not quite there yet but don't plan on it," the doc said. "It's overrated anyway. Good for the brain and the spirit to have meaningful work. Look at the men out here. They don't retire. Even the old-timers still go out and pull some traps."

"Some places they'd call that workaholism," Brie said.

The doc smiled. "No prescription for that yet, but give 'em time. I'm sure they'll come up with some kind of a pill," he said with slight disdain.

"It's all about remaining relevant, don't you think?" John asked.

"That's what I think, young man." He moved over to Brie. "I have to put some Novocain in to numb things up. This will sting."

Brie nodded.

The doc went around the wound with the needle doing several injections. At a point he looked up. "Brave girl," he said. "Didn't even flinch."

She smiled and shrugged. What she couldn't tell him was that once you've been shot and your life has hung in the balance, you have a different perspective on pain.

The doc worked confidently and efficiently suturing up the wound, which put Brie at ease. When done, he put a non-stick pad over the stitches and wrapped the hand with gauze.

"You'll have to keep this dry," he said. "And change the dressing every day." He put some supplies in a bag, along with a sheet of instructions for wound care, and handed them to John. "Call me if you see any redness or oozing. If you need to, take some Tylenol for the pain. Stay away from NSAIDs; they can increase bleeding. I'll see you back here in ten days to remove the sutures."

Brie nodded. "Thanks a lot, Doc."

"Can we pay you now?" John asked.

Doc Ward waved that off. "Don't worry about that tonight. Stop in any time, and we'll settle up." He walked with them to the front door. "From now on, stick to juggling with balls." He gave Brie a wink.

Then they were back out into the driving snow. John put an arm around Brie and steered her toward the truck. He helped her into the passenger side and came around and climbed in.

"How're you feeling?" he asked.

"Really tired. Don't know why."

John chuckled. "Your body's gone through a shock, that's why. It can sap your energy."

"I guess."

"Plus we didn't have dinner. You must be hungry."

"Now that you mention it," Brie said.

"I thought you might ask the doc about the deaths of the lobstermen when he was talking about people dying out here."

"Yeah, well, it didn't seem like quite the right time. But I'm guessing the doc is a deep well of information, so I need to get him talking about what he knows. Maybe when I go back to get the stitches removed."

"Sure," was all John said. They were approaching the house, and he turned onto the access road and made his way up the long hill and parked the truck.

They climbed out and made for the house, and as they came through the door, the smell of cooking greeted them. They left their boots and coats in the entryway and headed for the kitchen. Jack was stirring a pot of soup and had four sandwiches grilling on top of the stove.

"Thought I'd take over the dinner detail," he said.

"Thank you, Jack. We were just saying how hungry we were."

Brie went over to the stove. "Umm, grilled cheese. My favorite. And tomato soup. Perfect."

"Sloppy joes didn't seem like quite the right ticket for an injured hand."

"This is comfort food," she said.

"I put the brownies in the oven, too, and made hot coffee." Jack nodded toward the coffee maker.

"I could go for some of that about now," Brie said.

"So, how did it go?" Jack asked. "Stitches?"

"Yeah," Brie said. "The doc knows his business, though. He got me fixed up just fine. Have to keep it dry, that's all, and change the dressing."

"John and I can help you with that. I'm sorry it happened, though."

"It's my fault. I should have sharpened that knife."

"Still, it's a bummer," Jack said.

Over dinner they compared notes about who they'd met that day and whether any of the names might link to the case. John mentioned his hope that Jim Finrude would take him up on his offer to work stern on his boat.

"He might be a valuable resource since he was Abe Winter's sternman. If he decides to bite, I may be able to slowly finesse some information out of him about the other lobstermen." He also told Brie about his encounter with Lars Bjorklund at The Stern Man. "He seemed pretty open and supportive. Told me to stand my ground if they cut away my traps."

Brie nodded. "That's good. We'll all keep working our angles. Gathering intel. But right now, I'm beat. Think I'll turn in early."

Jack nodded. "Me, too. I just have to get Angus out to do his business."

"I'll take care of that, Jack," John said. "You go on up. I'll be up in a few minutes, Brie."

Upstairs, Brie changed into her pajamas, brushed her teeth, and took a Tylenol. Her hand was throbbing again and to abate that, she tried focusing on some of the details of the case. But she was glad when John climbed in next to her and drew her close. And fortunately, he knew just how to make the pain go away.

Chapter 13

The storm that was supposed to end on Sunday changed its mind and raged on for another two days. By midday Tuesday the island was digging out. The sound of plows scraping roads and snow blowers clearing walkways filled the clear, cold air. Twenty-four inches of new snow had been dumped in one fell swoop, and Starkhaven Island dazzled like a flawless white diamond set between layers of blue sea and sky.

Jack had taken over the cooking detail, at least until Brie's hand began to heal. So while John was out clearing the way to the outbuilding, Jack made French toast and coffee, fried sausages, and squeezed some oranges for fresh orange juice.

"I'm heading down to the harbor after breakfast," John said as they ate. "Dig out the boat and check to see what I need to bring aboard to start hauling traps. Will you two be okay without the truck, or do you want to drive me down?"

"We'll be fine," Brie said. "Plenty to do around here, and it's only a mile walk into town."

"Well, it's supposed to be in the thirties later today," John said. "So not too cold if you want to take a walk. Keep your hand warm, though. When I get home, I'll check out that old truck in the outbuilding. See if I can get it up and running."

"Sounds good," Brie said.

"Thanks for a great breakfast, Jack. Let me clean up."

Jack waved that off. "You go on down to the harbor. I've got this."

John gave Brie a kiss. "Wish me luck, guys."

"Luck!" Brie and Jack chimed together.

"Be careful out there on the water," Jack said.

"When it comes to the sea, careful is my middle name." Then John was out the door.

*   *   *

The harbor was a bustle of activity. It seemed like all the lobstermen on the island had converged at the same moment. A few moorings sat empty, so some had already taken to sea. The rest were in the process of readying their boats. As John walked down onto the wharf, he spotted Jim Finrude talking with Lars Bjorklund. John studied the flotilla of small dories at the foot of the ladder, wondering which one had belonged to Nathan Ross.

"It's the red peapod there."

John turned to see Finrude pointing down at a classic one-man double-ender, known as a peapod.

"Thanks, Fin. I was wondering which one was mine."

"That offer to work stern still stand?"

"Sure does."

Fin nodded. "Okay then, let's get to it."

Fin climbed down the ladder and perched in the bow of the peapod. John handed him a small snow shovel and broom and then stepped aboard. He freed the docking line and took the oars. As he rowed out, he noticed Lars watching them and gave him a nod, wondering if he'd had anything to do with Fin's change of heart. If so, he was grateful.

They climbed aboard and secured the peapod to the float. It was an older model lobsterboat, but Fin said Nathan Ross had kept her up.

"Not sure if she'll start. She's been sitting for a few months."

John went forward and flipped the switch for the bilge blower. He was encouraged when it started right up. He waited four minutes to evacuate any dangerous fumes from the engine compartment, then put the key in and turned the engine over. She started right up, and he and Fin gave each other a high-five. John let the engine run, and they got busy clearing the deck of snow.

Within fifteen minutes they were carefully maneuvering out of the harbor with John at the helm and Fin standing by in the house to give directions.

"Nathan's traps are up the west side of the island," Fin said. "We all noticed that he didn't put nearly his quota in this season. Some of the guys had asked him about it, but he never really said much. Then when he died suddenly, we knew why."

"It was a sudden heart attack," John said. "Maybe he was struggling. Knew he couldn't keep up with that many traps."

"He worked alone," Fin said. "Never used a sternman."

"So I've heard. You'd think he would have hired one and put in all his traps, though. Would have offset the cost."

"There's lots of guys just like to work alone," Fin said. "About fifty percent of lobstermen, in fact."

John nodded. "Yeah, I get that."

Today the waters south of the island were protected from the wind and seas. But even though the wind had dropped after the storm had passed, the seas grew larger as they left the lee of the island and headed north. John felt a thrum of excitement—the same sensation he always felt going to sea. And even though this was not a sailing vessel like *Maine Wind*, nor the start of a new season or voyage, he still loved the act of taking to the sea. In the winter he worked on maintaining the ship, but always with an aura of anticipation that knows return to the sea is not far off.

"Ever lobstered before?" Fin asked over the roar of the engine.

"When I was eighteen, I worked stern one summer. Strange, but being out here, it seems like just yesterday."

"How long's it been?"

"Twenty-two years."

From the look on Fin's face, John knew that didn't compute. And how could it? Probably more years than Jim Finrude had been on planet Earth. To a young man of twenty or twenty-two the thought of forty is unimaginably old, and John could feel Fin surreptitiously studying him, trying to work it all out.

After a few more minutes skirting the waters off the island, Fin said, "We'll be coming up on Nathan's territory."

John throttled back a bit as Fin watched out the window of the house. Within a few seconds he left the house and made his way up to the bow. John slowed the boat and they kept going, but by now Fin was looking around and down into the water. John took that as a bad sign. Finally Fin came back into the wheelhouse.

"There's nothing here," he said.

"What do you mean?" John felt the alarm grow on his own face.

"The bastards cut 'em. Cut 'em all."

John idled the engine so the boat rose and fell in the swell. He left the wheelhouse and walked to the bow. The January cold stung his face but was no match for the cold reality of several hundred traps now on the bottom with no way to retrieve them. All the buoys painted with Ross's colors—the ones assigned to him on his lobster fishing license—were nowhere to be seen. Gone. Even though this wasn't his real profession, he still felt inner rage at the act and wondered how exponential that feeling would be if it were his family's livelihood down there.

Fin joined him at the bow.

"Who do you think did this?"

"No way to know," Fin said. "And if you ask, everyone will deny it. Best to act as if nothing happened. That'll bug whoever did it. What they want is a reaction. Best not to give 'em one."

"You think it was one guy or a group?"

"No way to know. But it's a lot of traps for one guy to cut. Not unheard of, though. There was this one lobsterman—Oslo Stumph. He cut traps the way some guys cut grass. If anyone looked at him wrong, he'd cut their gear. This one guy, Alan Bellsby, married his way onto the island. Stumph didn't like it and made it his mission to singlehandedly drive the guy off."

"Oh, yeah? Did it work?"

"No. But only because Stumph went missing from his boat and was never seen again." Fin clammed up as soon as he said that—like he'd stepped over some invisible line. "We should get back inside."

The boat rose and fell in the swell as they made their way back to the wheelhouse.

"You think this Bellsby guy had anything to do with Stumph's disappearance?" John asked.

Fin's head whipped around. "No, man. That's crazy. The sea took him. It happens that way. Every year lobstermen go missing. Sternmen go overboard too, but they usually make it out alive. When you work alone, though, the way lots of guys do, it's a dangerous gig."

John throttled up the engine and steered the boat in a long arc to port and headed back toward the harbor. He regretted making the comment. Fin was already spooked enough about Abe Winter's death. He didn't want to lose his sternman before they'd even pulled one trap.

*   *   *

After John left for the harbor and breakfast was cleaned up, Brie and Jack sat down at their laptops to write their reports on the operation. They detailed who they had met on the island so far and how any of those contacts might link to the case. The reports, though somewhat preliminary, were designed to give Lieutenant Dent Fenton a sense of how the early days of the operation were unfolding. Brie described their first meeting with Mo Thorn, as well as her initial contact with the Starkhaven Stitchers, including who was in the group. She also mentioned that John had attempted to hire Jim Finrude, who had worked as a sternman for Abe Winter—the fourth victim.

After they were done with their reports, they spread the case files out on the table in the dining room and spent an hour together looking back through them. But nothing new emerged, and the only potential motives gleaned from the files seemed to connect to Oslo Stumph's bullying ways and Cliff Gordon's abusive nature. They agreed that if they could find someone on the island that linked to those motives, they'd be getting somewhere.

"The more names we put with faces, and the more human dynamics we become privy to, the farther along we'll be," Brie said.

"It's just going to take time." Jack sat back and stared out the window.

"There's a web of human connectivity here, and as we learn where all the strands are anchored, things *will* come to light."

"I agree," Jack said.

"With that in mind, I think I'll take a walk around the top part of the island. See what's what. You wanna come with, Jack?"

"I think I'll take Angus and wander down to the village. Need anything from the general store?"

"How 'bout some of Mary's soup *du jour*?" She gave Jack a wink.

"You're on."

*   *   *

A few minutes later Brie was out the door in her boots, parka, and stocking hat, walking down the driveway to where it connected to the main road. Her map of the island had showed that the road carried on beyond their property, bent north for a ways and then east, where it followed the spine of the island and eventually bent south and back down to the harbor. The island was approximately a mile and a half long, so to make the whole loop was around three miles.

Jack had learned from his poker group that the island school and church sat up along this road. Brie wondered what else she might find. The temperature today was just below freezing but, with the bright winter sun and calm winds, it was a perfect day for a winter walk. The deep, fresh blanket of snow dazzled under the midday sun, and she fished her sunglasses out of her pocket and put them on. When she came to the crest of the hill where the road bent east, the salt air engulfed her senses. She stood for a minute and breathed deeply, looking out to sea. In the distance a few lobsterboats plied the waters, pulling their traps. She wondered if one of them was John. He'd told her that Nathan Ross's territory was off this end of the island.

After a few minutes of pinch-yourself happiness that a Midwesterner like Brie feels having come to live by the sea, she carried on along the road, breaking into a jog. Her boots weren't conducive to full-on running, but it was good enough for now. She hadn't been out for a run since they'd landed on the island, and it felt good to push herself a bit as the road began to rise. Within a few minutes, though, she was forced to slow to a walk when her injured hand began throbbing.

The road flattened out and ran like a narrow ribbon through dense spruce forest. Occasionally a pickup truck would drive by, and sometimes the driver would stop, roll down his window, and greet her with, "Ross, right?" as if he were checking to be sure she actually belonged here. As if she had only one name that mattered, and it mattered only because it marked her as some kind of appendage to another islander, either past or present.

A group of three buildings came into view a ways down the road. In the middle, the island church was unmistakable with its traditional white steeple. There was a house on the nearside of the church and beyond it, the island schoolhouse. As she got closer, she saw that the white clapboard house displayed a decorative sign next to the front door that read, "Starkhaven History Center." It seemed fitting somehow that the spiritual, educational, and historical components of the island should be grouped together.

"Well, what do you know?" Brie said to herself. She felt a little spark of excitement at the existence of a history center on the island, because with it came the prospect of discovery. And discovery is the life blood of any investigation. It was unknown what those discoveries might be, but for Brie the sign on the building may as well have said, "Fertile Ground." She headed up the walk. The hours on the sign indicated the center was open. She knocked lightly on the door and then stepped inside.

There was a large front room that would have been the living room in days gone by. The walls were lined with framed photographs, and the room itself was filled with display cases that held documents and artifacts connected to Starkhaven's long history as a fishing and lobstering community. Stacked in the far corner of the room next to the fireplace, several old wooden lobster traps attested to the fact that earlier lobstermen had not only hauled traps but also had had to build them.

Within seconds a tall, thin woman with straight, shoulder-length black hair and blue-framed glasses appeared through an archway from the next room. Her shoulders were stooped, as if the weight of the island's history sat heavily on them.

She studied Brie for a moment and then said, "You must be our newcomer."

"Well, one of them, anyway. There's also my husband and my grandfather." She held out her hand. "Brie Ross."

"Pleased to meet you, Brie, and welcome to the island. I'm Faith Babcock. I run the history center here on Starkhaven."

"It's somehow fitting that it should be up here with the church and the school," Brie said.

"Many years ago this was the parsonage for the church, back when the island had a full-time minister. Later on it was rented by a number of families who tried but failed at island living. The property is owned by the town, so it was an easy enough decision to turn it into a history center and archives for Starkhaven's records."

"Now that we've moved here, I'm really eager to learn more about the island."

"Well, you're welcome here any time." Faith said.

"My mom was a history teacher, so I guess it's in my blood to want to connect more deeply with the places I live." She paused for a moment and looked at Faith. "I'd be happy to help out, if you ever need a hand."

Faith Babcock gave her a curious look, and Brie hoped she hadn't overstepped.

"I guess I'm just looking for ways to fit in," she said, looking down at the floor, feigning shyness. "My husband has the boat and the lobstering, but I . . . ." She let her voice trail off.

"I think I know how you feel," Faith said. "It's hard coming to live on an island when you haven't grown up that way. You probably don't know this, but most of the kids who grew up here in the past went to boarding school for high school."

"Really?" Brie said. "That's interesting. Is that what you did?"

Faith nodded. "My husband and I both did. We were just a year apart. In those days, the island was just too far from the mainland to commute. Now, of course, with the really fast lobster boats, you can get out here in an hour, but it was different back then."

131

"So the school here is just for the elementary grades."

"That's right."

"But you came back to the island."

"Yes, but not right away. My husband wasn't sure he wanted to live here—lobster for a living. We married after high school and lived on the mainland for a number of years. But eventually we were drawn back here."

"So, it's in the blood, you might say."

"I believe it is," Faith said. "It's not uncommon for kids to leave here and struggle in the bigger world. I'm glad I lived away for those years, though. If you're from here, you can always come back. But I was gone long enough that I think I lost some of my islandness."

Brie didn't ask what that meant, but she thought she knew. She thought maybe Faith was referring to the close-minded tendencies—ones that sometimes bordered on superstition—that were so pervasive here. Tendencies that made it difficult for outsiders, even the law, to get at the truth.

"I think I know what you mean," she said. "I'm not sure people here see *me*, but rather just an appendage to my husband's name and history here."

That must have gotten to Faith, because she said, "You know, if you're willing, I could use some help here."

"Really?"

"A couple years back, the town purchased a microfilm machine for the history center. I know it probably seems like old technology, but what people don't know is that microfilm, when properly stored, has a shelf life of five hundred years."

"Fascinating," Brie said. But though she pretended to look surprised, she knew from her police work that while records had gone digital, the department still maintained its microfilm archive for just that reason.

"When we got the machine, I started with the birth and death records and then moved on to the island newspapers."

"There's a newspaper?"

"There was until ten years ago, when the woman who was the last of the line that had been responsible for producing the paper passed away. It's left a hole here, but so far no one wants to take on the work of resurrecting it."

Brie nodded. "So you're committing that archive of newspapers to microfilm."

"I started with the oldest issues first. The *Starkhaven Signal* goes back to the nineteen fifties, so I'm slowly working my way forward in time."

"Well, I'd be happy to help," Brie said.

"It *would* free me up to work on some displays I've promised to make for the school library," Faith said thoughtfully.

"Should we set up a schedule for when I'll come in?" Brie asked.

"That's not really necessary," Faith said. "I'm here every weekday from about ten to three. Just come on up when you feel like it."

"Great," Brie said. "It will give me some kind of a routine to follow." She paused. "Tam Thorn invited me to take part in the quilting group, and I am, but this is really more my cup of tea."

Faith smiled at her in a discerning way. "Seems like it would be."

Brie could tell that Faith was not one to be easily fooled. "Well, I'll let you get back to your work." They said goodbye and she headed out the door.

She looked along the road to the east, wondering what else might be down that way, but decided to save it for another day. She turned and headed back in the direction she'd come from. She'd gone about a quarter of a mile when a pickup truck came up from behind. The driver stopped next to her and ran down his window.

"Ross, right?" he asked.

Again with the Ross question, Brie thought. "Right," she said, trying to keep sarcasm at bay.

He didn't ask her first name and she didn't give it, nor did he give his. But the guy had movie star good looks, and there were lobster traps in the bed of the truck, so not too hard to guess what he did.

"Can I give you a lift?"

"No, I'm fine. It's not very far."

"Okay . . ." He studied her for a few moments like he wanted to say more. "I'll see you around."

Brie nodded and Mr. Hollywood ran up the window and drove on, but she could see him studying her in his rearview mirror.

Maybe I should have taken the ride, she thought. *Figure out who this guy is and where he might fit in.* "Oh, well, too late now." She laughed to herself.

In a few more minutes the road bent south and soon the house came into view up on its hill. John's truck was behind the house, and she could see him and another guy loading lobster traps into the bed from the pile next to the outbuilding. She wondered if he'd found a sternman. She carried on down the hill to the driveway and headed up toward the house. John saw her coming and motioned her over.

"Brie, this is Jim Finrude. He'll be working stern on my boat. Jim, this is my wife, Brie."

"Nice to meet you, Jim." She held out her hand. "Glad to hear you signed on."

Jim nodded. "Nice to meet you, too. You can call me Fin, if you like. Everyone here does."

"Sure." She turned to John. "So, I guess you're planning on adding more traps."

"Yeah, to replace the ones now lost to Davy Jones," John said.

"Oh, man. Really?"

"Yeah. Definitely not a good start to my lobstering career."

"Tam warned us. I guess she was right," Brie said.

"We'll put some more in tomorrow. See what happens."

"It's all you can do," Jim said.

"Well, I'll go inside and make some coffee. Come on in when you're done, Fin. We'll give you a sandwich."

"That'd be great."

Brie headed in the house. Jack was in the living room reading. Angus lumbered up from the floor and came over to greet her, nudging her with his giant head, in case she hadn't noticed him. She shed her boots, hung up her parka and headed out to the kitchen to start the coffee. Jack came out and they put together some ham and cheese sandwiches. Jack had brought soup from the general store. It was tomato bisque today. They put it on to warm.

"How's Mary?" Brie asked.

"Pretty as a rose bush in winter."

"I see." She gave him a knowing nod.

"Missed the poker game, though. Got there too late."

"Maybe tomorrow," Brie said.

"Sure."

Within ten minutes the guys came in, and they gathered around the table in the kitchen to share lunch.

After lunch John drove Fin home. He was back within fifteen minutes, and the three of them took their coffee into the living room to talk about the day. John went first, telling Brie about the sinking feeling—no pun intended—he'd had at finding his traps cut.

"I actually think Fin was angrier than me. He called them bastards and a few other things I won't repeat. His advice was to act as if nothing has happened, since they'll be looking for a reaction. Don't know how I feel about that, though."

"Yeah, me either," Brie said. "I think if I were you, I'd want them to know I was hopping mad."

"It's a cruel act when you figure that's someone's livelihood out there," Jack said. "That gear doesn't come cheap, either."

"Here's the silver lining, though," John said. "The fact of it happening to me got Fin talking about Oslo Stumph."

"Really?" Brie and Jack both perked up at the mention of the first victim in the killings. "What about him?" Brie asked.

"According to Fin, he was a gear cutter extraordinaire here on the island. If anyone looked sideways at him, he'd cut their gear. Apparently the worst case was a guy named Alan Bellsby, who married his way onto the island, as Fin told it."

"Huh, I think his wife is in the quilting group. But go on," Brie said.

"Fin said that Oslo Stumph cut Bellsby's gear relentlessly. Made it his mission to single-handedly drive the guy off the island. The vendetta only stopped because Stumph went missing from his boat."

"Wow, that's motive." Brie could hear the excitement in her own voice. "Good work, John."

"Yeah, almost makes losing that gear worth it. I asked Fin if he thought Bellsby had anything to do with Oslo Stumph's disappearance."

"And?"

"The question seemed to completely shock him. His response was, 'No, man, that's crazy. The sea took him.'"

"Ah," Brie said. "Well, if he were to allow for that possibility, then he'd have to wonder about Abe Winter's disappearance as well. Maybe that hits too close to home."

"Maybe," John said. "Like you said, fear and denial go hand in hand. He was certainly reluctant to sign on again as a sternman after what happened to Winter."

"Raises another question of where he was the day Abe Winter disappeared. Why he wasn't aboard."

"Lars Bjorklund told me he was sick that day," John said.

"You thinking Fin may have had a motive?" Jack asked.

"Well, you know how it is in the beginning. Pretty much everyone is a suspect. But one thing we've now learned: Alan Bellsby had a compelling reason to do away with Oslo Stumph. Like I said, nice work, John."

"Well, before my head gets so big it won't fit through the door of the outbuilding, I think I'll go out and try to get that old truck up and running."

"I'll give you a hand," Jack said.

"Don't forget about the Lobstermen's Association meeting tonight," Brie said.

"Right. Important for us to be there. You want to come, too, Jack?"

"I think I'll let you and Brie cover it, if that's okay."

"No problem," Brie said. "Let's plan to get there a little early."

John nodded, and he and Jack bundled up and headed outside with Angus in tow.

*   *   *

At 6:45 that evening, John and Brie headed into the village for the meeting. The Maine Lobstermen's Association, which dates back to the 1950s, is a statewide organization whose membership includes those who are or have been actively involved in the lobster fishery in Maine. The MLA works to sustain both the industry and the resource and is proactive at the local, state, and federal levels on issues that affect the fishery. Brie knew there was no option but for John to join the association, even though, tonight, he felt little goodwill toward the lobstermen of Starkhaven Island.

He parked the truck across the road from the town office, and they headed inside. "You find a seat, Brie. I'm gonna use the bathroom."

She chose two seats in one of the middle rows of chairs, laid her coat across them, and headed up to the front of the room where coffee was set out. She was filling her cup when she felt someone standing a little too close to her. She set the cup down and turned, nearly colliding with the rough-looking character. He looked a little wild about the eyes and before she could speak, he started in.

"What are ya doin' here? Keepin' track of your husband?"

"And who might you be?" Brie asked, trying to keep a neutral tone.

"He don't need baby sittin', ya know. Just like we don't need baby sittin'."

Brie squared her shoulders. "Oh, yeah? Well, maybe you do, considering some of the childish behavior here." She stepped even closer. "Did you cut John's traps? Were you the one?" She poked a finger into his chest.

He swatted it away. "Best you know your place. It ain't here."

She was about to ask if he meant the meeting or the island, when Mo Thorn stepped up to the lectern and called the meeting to order.

Brie headed for her chair. As she sat down, she glimpsed George out of the corner of her eye. He looked horrified. Just then John sat down next to her.

"Saw you talking to Trulie Hyden."

"Is *that* who that was."

He must have caught the contempt in her voice because he turned to her. "What'd he say?"

"Nothing. Just some sexist bullshit."

John started to say something, but Thorn banged his gavel to silence the group. Just then Fin arrived and sat to John's left.

Thorn proceeded to call the meeting to order. There was discussion of the recent catch and how the numbers compared to last year, along with the going price of lobster. The main item up for discussion involved the changes to bait usage and regulations. In the past couple of years, lobstermen had been forced to move away from the use of herring for baiting their traps. Apparently, the new regulations reduced use of herring by seventy percent. Several alternate sources had been explored, the most promising being the blackbelly rosefish, a species related to the Atlantic redfish, but most commonly found off Uruguay. Several members weighed in on the pros and cons of use and cost of that bait in comparison to others, and a fifteen-minute discussion ensued. As it continued, John pointed out a few of the villagers he had met to Brie, including Lars Bjorklund, Marty Hawkins, Dale Woodrow and Kieran McTavish.

Mo Thorn was just getting ready to move on to the next item on the agenda when Fin stood up from his seat and spoke in a forceful voice.

"I just wanna say that whoever cut away John Ross's traps should be strung up."

A moment of charged silence followed and then a murmur of muted voices.

"Sit down, Fin. You got no stake here, so you got nothin' to say."

The comment came from behind them, but John didn't turn around to see who had spoken. Fin stood his ground, feet apart, arms crossed on his chest.

Lars Bjorklund spoke up. "He's not wrong. Nathan Ross was one of us. Born and raised here. What would he say? This is his nephew."

"Not till he proves himself," someone mumbled.

"How's he gonna do that with all his gear at the bottom?" Fin said.

That was met with silence, but not a conciliatory one.

Lars stood up. "Haven't we lost enough without driving off good men?"

Brie knew he could only be talking about the lobstermen that had been lost over the past sixteen months.

Now the room buzzed with voices. Finally Mo Thorn banged his gavel several times. "The room will come to order," he said forcefully. "Anyone wishing to speak will ask to be recognized." He cast a steely look around the room that came to rest on Jim Finrude. "You've had your say, Fin. Now, I'd like you to sit down. We will go on to the next item on the agenda."

Fin sat down and John leaned over. "Thought you said I should act like nothing happened," he said, *sotto voce*.

"That's right," Fin said. "Doesn't mean I have to."

Mo Thorn moved on to the final item, which involved some new guidelines for ordering from the lobster smack. The lobster smack, which looks something like an oversized lobsterboat, but with the house at the rear, is the vessel that brings all manner of lobstering supplies, along with fuel and bait, to the islands and transports the day's catch back to the lobster pounds on the mainland. A vital link in the industry, it made the trip from Rockland to Starkhaven Island daily. John made a few notes in the small notebook he'd brought. He had told Brie he needed to order more traps and supplies to keep his territory up and running.

Within a few minutes, Thorn brought the meeting to a close. John stood up, grabbed his coat, and headed for the door. Whether lobstering was his real life or not, Brie sensed he felt humiliated. She saw Lars Bjorklund moving in the same direction.

Outside, Lars caught up with John as he crossed the road. "Don't let 'em win. You go home and get more gear together and get back out there tomorrow."

John stopped and turned. "Thanks, Lars." He paused a beat, looked at the other man. "Guess those buoys were no use to me anyway. I got different colors now."

Lars studied him for a moment, then let out a broad smile and clapped him on the shoulder. "That's the spirit."

They left it on a high note, and no one mentioned the cost of the traps attached to those buoys. Lars went his way, and John and Brie climbed into the truck.

"Well, that was interesting," she said.

"I'll bet. Especially for someone in law enforcement."

"The willingness to willfully destroy another's property speaks to the general lawlessness that can come from living too far off the beaten path. And it's just a stone's throw from that kind of attitude to vigilantism." She stared out the window into the darkness. "I'm afraid, even if we catch the killer, the tribalism here may run too deep for the lesson to be learned."

"What is the lesson?" John asked.

"That fear only begets more fear. And fear is diametrically opposed to change."

Chapter 14

Two nautical miles out to sea, George leaned over the gunwale and hooked the buoy with the gaff, led it forward, and fed the line into the hauler. There were two traps on each line and when the first one broke the surface, he brought it up on the gunwale and processed the lobsters inside, measuring each to determine the keepers, throwing the others overboard. Looking for females with eggs or a notched tail and returning them to the sea.

They had been on the water since four a.m. It was now 7:45 and the sky was just beginning to brighten in the east. Arctic fog or sea smoke covered the water on this calm, frigid morning. The boat rocked in the small swell as George pushed the trap overboard and waited for the next one on the line to appear. A grueling process that would be repeated up to four hundred times until half of Trulie Hyden's traps had been emptied and re-baited. That would take anywhere from eight to ten hours, depending on the catch and the sea conditions.

This was only George's second day out on the boat, on the job. But on Saturday, the day after he'd arrived on the island and been hired by Trulie Hyden, he'd been on the dock in the pitch dark at four a.m., as Trulie had instructed. Of course there was a blizzard in progress, and most guys would have stayed in bed. But George had given his word, and he followed through. He had figured he'd wait ten minutes and then head home, but to his surprise, Trulie pulled up in his truck right at four o'clock. Trulie hadn't had to get out of bed either, but apparently he wanted to see what kind of guy he'd hired. He told George to get in the truck and then drove and dropped him so close to his trailer door that two more feet and he'd have been inside. That morning marked the beginning of mutual respect between them.

Trulie called from the house. "Let's break for some food."

George turned off the hauler and headed into the house. Trulie had cranked up the heater inside and poured out hot coffee for them. Even though George had brought his own thermos, Trulie shared his. George noticed his hand shook a bit as he poured.

George pulled out a big-wide mouth thermos full of hot soup. He had brought an extra cup for Trulie. "Here you go, boss. Try this."

"No, I shouldn't take your soup. You're the one out there in the cold."

"That's okay, I got plenty," George said. He poured hot chicken soup into the second cup and handed it to Trulie. "It's homemade."

"Really! You got a missus somewhere around that trailer?"

"Nope. I like to cook." George fished a ham sandwich out of his pail.

Trulie took a sip and his eyebrows went up. "That's wicked good. Thank ye kindly." He eyed George with interest as he sipped his soup. Finally he said, "You aren't afraid of a hard day's work, are you?"

"Nope."

"Where'd that come from? Most guys have to toughen into this job."

"It's not my first rodeo. I worked stern off Cape Cod. But my work ethic, that's thanks to my parents. They owned a restaurant in New York City when I was growing up. It was a humble establishment at first, but it grew. My family is Greek. Everyone worked in the restaurant, aunts, uncles, cousins. From the time I was five, they were finding little jobs for me."

"So, that's why you can cook so good," Trulie said.

"That'd be it," George said.

"Well, we should get back to it. I'll come out and help with the next batch. See if we can get out of this cold a little quicker."

"Whatever you say, boss." George was sorry he'd thought of him as the "peeper." Trulie was turning out to be an okay guy. But then he thought about the scene at the lobstermen's meeting the night before. As he exited the house, out of the corner of his eye, he saw Trulie open a pill bottle and shake a couple into his hand and swallow them.

*   *   *

Jack Le Beau drove the old truck into the village and parked in front of the general store. It wasn't anything fancy, but he and John had managed to get it running, and it was handy to have a second vehicle. Brie had told him to take the truck, since she had no plans for the morning.

His three friends were already there, hanging out at the back of the store, eating hot scones and drinking coffee.

"Morning, Mary," Jack said and tipped his imaginary hat, which was comical since Jack was not a hat guy and never had been. Used to drive his wife crazy in the middle of winter, he recalled.

"Morning, Jack. Hot coffee?"

"Wouldn't miss it. I'll bid on a couple of those scones, too."

"They're goin' fast. Better jump in before the price goes up."

"Now, Mary. You wouldn't do that to me."

She blushed a little, and Biddy poked Marty Hawkins in the ribs. "See what I told you?"

"Oh, stop it," Mary said.

The poker players took their goodies to one of the tables up front and settled in.

*　　　*　　　*

After writing up her report on the lobster wars between Oslo Stumph and Alan Bellsby, Brie pulled on her coat and boots to take Angus out for a romp in the yard.

"C'mon, boy. Let's hit the snow." Angus came bounding out of the living room and careened into the kitchen where he pressed himself, all a-wiggle, against the kitchen door. Brie had to use the door to budge him out of the way, and as soon as it was open a foot, out he shot. She had brought his long rope toy outside, and they played tug-of-war, chase, and flatten the snow until finally Angus flopped down in a snow drift.

Brie walked to the edge of the property, where the hill sloped down toward the ocean and a house a good distance below, and looked out to sea. Thick sea smoke rose off the water in the distance, and for a moment she felt the press of absolute isolation that was this place. She turned away from the sea and took a tour around the house, inspecting the volume of snow on the roof—an inbred Minnesota obsession.

When she got to the far side of the house, she stopped in her tracks. There were footprints up close to the house that ran from one window to the other. She turned to see if they continued around the house, but Angus had romped through that area and would have obliterated them. She felt the hairs rise on her neck, and she actually turned and looked behind her, suddenly consumed by the thought of Garrett Parker. She walked up close to the tracks and recognized the tread of an L.L. Bean boot. That narrowed it down to pretty much everyone on the island. She just hoped it *was* someone from here, as the specter of Garrett Parker continued to give her the willies. She shook off the feeling. With the ferry running just once a month, she was pretty sure she didn't have to worry about him showing up. No, someone from the island had left these.

Still, she decided she wouldn't share this with John. No point worrying him. She went back in the house, brought out a tape measure, and measured the tracks. Then she brushed them away and called Angus back in the house.

*   *   *

The poker game had been underway for an hour. As usual, they were bidding with quarters, just to keep it interesting. Today, it was Biddy Firth who was taking no prisoners. During the deal she turned to Jack.

"So, I hear Jim Finrude is working stern for your grandson-in-law now."

"That's right," Jack said. "John is happy to have him, too, since Jim knows the waters."

"I'm sorry about his gear being cut away," Marty Hawkins said. "Bit of a scene at the MLA meeting last night. No call for that. We need to all get along."

"That'd be nice," Jack said.

"Personally, I'm glad Fin is no longer working for Abe Winter, though," Biddy said.

"Why's that?" Jack asked.

Biddy shrugged. "I think Fin might eventually have been led astray. Abe was known to be connected to drugs on the island."

"You shouldn't speak ill of the dead," Marty said.

"Maybe not, but still, I'm glad. He and my granddaughter Isa are dating, and we all know where that leads on this island.

And it doesn't take long either. I'm just relieved he's working for a better guy." She fixed Jack with a suspicious eye. "Your grandson's not into that stuff, is he?"

"John, no way. He's a straight arrow."

"Because word on the island was that his uncle, Nathan Ross, was into the drugs," Biddy said. "Nearly cost him his stake on the island, too."

Jack nodded, thinking that would explain why he didn't have money to pay his property taxes. "Well, I don't see John ever going down that road."

"You could have said the same for most guys that lobster out here," Dale Woodrow said. "Truth is, the job takes a physical toll on the body. A big one. And if the pain gets bad enough, the straightest arrow will take those drugs if they can lay hands on them. It's the ones making a profit off all that pain that should be stomped out. They should suffer in due measure to the suffering they've brought." Dale's face was beet red.

Jack didn't say anything but noted the emotion behind Dale's words. It was becoming clear to him what the motive had most likely been for the murder of Abe Winter if, in fact, Winter had been pushing drugs. Dale's words didn't necessarily make him a suspect, but they did shine a light on why someone might have decided to eliminate Abe Winter.

Marty reached over and placed a hand on his friend's shoulder. "It's best not to dwell on the past," he said to Dale.

Jack half expected Dale Woodrow to lash out at him, but Dale met Marty's eyes for a moment and then nodded. "You're right," he said in a subdued voice. But in that meeting of the eyes, Jack sensed a bond of absolute solidarity between the two men and wondered what might lie behind it.

Within a half-hour the game came to a close. Dale, Marty, and Biddy headed out the door to their vehicles, but Jack stayed behind, hoping to talk to Mary. He walked to the back of the store to see what the soup *du jour* was.

"I heard some raised voices during the game," Mary said. "Feelings running high about something?"

"Biddy brought up the subject of Jim Finrude working stern for my grandson, John. John has told me Fin used to work on Abe Winter's boat."

"That's right," Mary said. "A couple months ago, Abe Winter disappeared from his boat while out hauling."

"John mentioned he'd heard that. Very tragic." Jack paused for a moment out of respect for the fact. "Anyway, Biddy said she was happy Jim no longer worked for Abe Winter."

"It's no secret that Jim is dating Biddy's granddaughter."

Jack nodded. "Now, I have no idea about any of this, but Biddy said Abe Winter had been connected to drugs on the island. That's when things started to heat up. Dale got very emotional about the subject of drugs, painkillers in particular, and those involved in supplying those drugs. That was what you heard."

Mary nodded but turned back to her work. "Dale has cause for that," she said quietly. "His son left the island a few years ago. He later died on the mainland."

"I'm very sorry to hear that," Jack said.

"It was known on the island that he'd become addicted to opioids. That addiction eventually tore him from the island in search of stronger drugs. He died six months later from a fentanyl overdose in Portland. Of course, it hit Dale really hard, not having his son to pass his territory on to." She looked back at Jack. "You need to warn your grandson to be careful. Not get involved with those drugs, even if someone offers them."

"I will, Mary. But is it true what Biddy said? Did Abe Winter deal drugs?" He knew he was treading close to a line that at any moment could shut down the conversation.

Mary's shoulders stiffened a bit. "Like most things, I think there's probably more to the story than that. Sadly for Abe Winter, he was the face of the problem on Starkhaven, and he paid for that, I fear. But I also fear that the heart of the beast may lie elsewhere."

While a bit cryptic, it was pretty easy for Jack to extrapolate a number of things from Mary's comments. First that, while part of the problem, Winter may also have been a kind of sacrificial lamb. On the face of things, he was the island drug dealer. But Jack knew well that most street corner dealers are just go-betweens taking one hundred percent of the risk for a small piece of the action, while the big guns keep most of the money and stay well out of sight.

"When you say he paid, are you saying his death was not an accident?"

Mary stopped and turned and eyed him for a moment. "I like you, Jack, but I'm not sure you've been here long enough to be asking such questions. Whatever our problems may be, we like to keep them to ourselves. They will all be dealt with in time."

"That's fair, Mary. Just write it off to me being a nosy old coot."

A slow smile spread across her face. "Somehow that's not the vibe I get from you." She opened the oven and put two large trays of cookies inside. "Sometime, when we have time, I'd like to know more about this place you come from—Minnesota. Right now, though, I have to get these cookies finished. The boys'll be in off the water soon and clean me out of whatever I can get baked."

Jack nodded. "If I could just bother you for some soup and a loaf of French bread, I'll get out of your hair."

"No problem."

A few minutes later Jack was out the door, heading for his truck, with a baguette tucked under one arm and two quarts of fish chowder cradled in the other. Brie would be happy to know that he was the bearer of one other thing as well. A motive for Abe Winter's murder.

*   *   *

George and Trulie made it in off the water by two o'clock. Trulie rowed them ashore, and George asked if he'd like to stop into The Stern Man for a pint.

"There's a couple things I need to do on the boat yet. You go on ahead. I'll catch up with you later."

"You need help out there?" George asked.

"Nah. You get outta the cold. You done enough for one day."

George nodded and headed off the wharf and steered himself toward the pub. Trulie was an okay guy who seemed to have a heart for the one shouldering the arduous work of hauling his traps. That told George he'd come up through the ranks, probably working stern from the time he was a boy. Trulie had mentioned that it had been his father's territory and that his parents were both gone now. George thought about how Trulie's hand shook as he'd handed him the coffee, and the pills he'd surreptitiously taken. Both worrisome signs that Trulie Hyden might be hidin' something.

George pushed open the heavy door to The Stern Man and stepped inside. A wave of warmth engulfed him, accompanied by the rich, yeasty smell of beer. Blind from the outside world, he stood for a moment, wrapped in that dark sensory womb, in no hurry for his vision to clear. But slowly the pub's interior swam out of the darkness, and George made his way to the bar. But now, unexpectedly, he was smelling cinnamon, nutmeg, and cloves.

"Whatcha brewin' there, McTavish?" he asked.

"Toddy," the barkeep said. "Hot buttered rum. It's popular with the boys this time of year. I always have some heating this time of day."

The frigid dampness of hours at sea had seeped into George's bones, and the thought of the hot toddy was as delightful as it was unexpected. "I'll take one," he said.

A few moments later, Kieran McTavish set a steaming mug in front of him, the dollop of butter still melting on the top. The happy mariner's version of chai tea if ever there had been one.

George took a sip and suddenly felt unreasonably happy.

"Ah, see," McTavish said, watching him. "Just what the doctor ordered."

George smiled and wrapped his hands around the mug. "You're a good man, McTavish."

Just then the pub door opened, and the guy he'd heard called "Fin" at last night's meeting stood there letting his eyes adjust. George hadn't met him yet but knew John had hired him as his sternman. He also knew from his emails with Brie that Fin had worked for Abe Winter, the fourth victim.

Fin made his way over to the bar. He gave George a nod and sat one stool away from him.

"You must be the new guy here," he said. "Heard you're working for Trulie."

"George Dupopolis," George said, extending his hand. "Yeah, Trulie hired me right away when I got here. Seems like a good guy."

"Jim Finrude." He shook George's hand. "Everyone calls me 'Fin,' though. Yeah, Trulie's okay. Lost his sternman a few months ago. Guy moved off suddenly." He turned to McTavish. "I'll have a toddy, Kieran."

Fin took off his hat and ran a hand through his shaggy black hair. George couldn't help but notice that, with the long hair, Fin bore a slight resemblance to the picture of Abe Winter that Brie had showed him from the case file. But unlike Winter's dazed, somewhat slovenly appearance, Fin was sharp-eyed and, shaggy hair aside, presented a pulled-together aspect.

George ran through the bit about the lobster fishery collapsing on Cape Cod and that being why he'd come up to Maine.

151

Fin nodded. "Yep, we got all their lobsters now. But who knows, if things keep heating up, they'll all be up in Canada eventually."

George nodded and sipped his buttered rum.

"So, what brought you out here?" Fin asked.

"Ran into a guy in Portland who'd worked stern out here. Said I might find work on the island."

"You chose well. These are the richest lobstering grounds on earth, or so they say. No brackish water from the rivers. The water's cold and there's a mix of shoals and deep water trenches around the island."

"Perfect habitat for lobster," George said. "So, who do you work for, Fin?"

"Just started with John Ross, who came out here to take over his uncle's territory."

"How's that going?"

"Good. I like the guy. Doesn't let the gear-cutting get to him. Just plows on. You gotta admire that. Just hope he knows what he's getting into."

It was said in a cryptic way, and George studied him for a second, wondering if he might say anything about the dead lobstermen, but he didn't.

"Yeah, I was at the meeting last night. Heard the whole thing. Sucks. Don't know why some of these guys have to be such cavemen. Not like there aren't enough lobsters to go around."

"That's for sure," Fin said.

The pub door opened, and Trulie Hyden came in and hung up his coat by the door. He made his way to the bar and sat next to Fin and ordered up a pint.

"How's it goin' with the new guy?" he asked, not looking at Fin.

"Going okay," Fin said.

"It's good you came back. We've lost enough good men."

"Thanks, Trulie." Fin took a sip of his toddy.

George thought about what he knew of the four lobstermen who'd died and wondered if "good men" was an apt description for all of them. Of course, some sternmen had moved off too, so maybe Trulie was including them in the good men club. Or maybe, to him, "good men" just meant "hard-working men." Trulie didn't elaborate, and they all drank in silence for a while.

At a point George looked over and noticed that Trulie was sweating profusely. Droplets ran down the side of his face and neck, despite the fact that the temperature in the pub was far from hot. George was about to ask him if he was okay, when Trulie suddenly turned to Fin and said, "I need to talk to you outside." He stood up from his stool abruptly, eyeing Fin.

"Sure, man. No problem." Fin finished the last dram of his toddy and made his way to the door. They donned their coats and headed outside.

George slapped some money on the bar and headed for the back door of the pub. McTavish was nowhere to be seen at the moment, so George had an easy escape out the back of the pub. As soon as he was outside he could hear voices coming from around the side of the pub. He crept to the corner and listened. Trulie sounded desperate.

"Look, man, you gotta help me out."

"I can't help you, Trulie. I'm not involved with any of that."

"You gotta know where Abe got the stuff. You worked for him for two years."

"I'm telling you, I don't know, Trulie. Look, man, I think you need help."

"Don't need any help. Just need the painkillers. I've been trying to stretch out what I got left, but I'm in trouble, man."

"Why don't you talk to Doc Ward?" Fin said.

"The doc's hard core. Won't give out nothin'. Others have tried. Believe me, I've asked around. No one'll admit to knowin' nothin'. Meantime, I'm losin' it. Gonna have to go to the mainland if nobody here will help me."

"Don't do that, man. Look what happened to Tom Woodrow. You can beat this."

"I know you know something. You gotta."

George peeked around the corner and saw that Trulie had grabbed Fin by his coat. The air around them was electric—charged for a storm.

Fin pushed him off. "I told you, I want nothin' to do with any o' that. It destroys lives. You need to go to the doc. Tell him what's going on. He'll have drugs that'll help you beat this. You're better than this, Trulie."

Trulie reached for him, but Fin stepped away.

"Don't ask me again, Trulie. I'm warning you." The words had an ice-hard edge to them.

"You have anything to do with Abe's disappearance? Word was you weren't on the boat that day." Trulie's voice suddenly rang with suspicion.

"You nuts, man? You think I'd kill Abe? I was home sick that day. You can ask my aunt. And by the way, how would I even pull that off? I got no boat. How would I get out there? Walk on the water?" Fin didn't wait for a response but headed for the road, walking fast.

Trulie yelled after him. "Somebody's doing it. It's too many deaths. They can't all be accidents like everyone says. I'd watch my back if I was you."

Fin didn't respond. Just kept on walking, and after a moment or two, Trulie skulked off in the opposite direction.

George headed for his trailer. He knew it was time to meet with Brie and Jack. He took out his backpack and loaded it up with a few supplies he needed to make dinner. He'd buy some lasagna noodles at the store on the way up the road. The winter sun, as void of warmth as Fin's words had been, was already low in the January sky when George left his trailer and headed west along the road.

Chapter 15

George had seen a picture of the Ross property when they were setting up the operation with Dent Fenton, and an email from Brie several days ago had told him how far along the west road the house sat.

It was just after four o'clock when he rang the doorbell. He heard a deep "woof" and then an excited scuffling around on the other side of the door.

"Angus, back," came through the door, and then it opened. "George! What a wonderful surprise. Come in."

Brie stepped aside and ushered him in, and Angus squeezed into the tiny entryway to properly welcome George with lots of wiggling and slobbering. Brie hauled Angus out of the entry, and George hung up his coat, slipped off his boots, and stepped inside. He looked to right and left at the living room and dining room.

"Nice place. Sure beats my digs. Not that I'm complaining, of course. I'm so tired after hauling traps all day, I could sleep on a bed of nails."

"John's in the outbuilding painting buoys, and Jack is taking a nap," Brie told him.

"The house is pretty isolated, so I didn't worry too much about anyone seeing me. Anyway, this time of day most of the lobstermen are in front of their tellies."

"I've got hot coffee in the kitchen, George. Or would you like a beer?"

"Coffee would be fine, thanks. I brought some supplies to cook dinner if you'd like."

"Sounds great. What are we having?"

"How about lasagna?"

"Ooh, that sounds delicious. It's a lot of work, though."

"Not that much if I can get some help from my messmate."

"No problem," Brie said.

"I wanted to meet with you and Jack. I've got some information that connects to the case."

"I'm glad to hear that, George. Feels like things are moving at a snail's pace, but then that's just the nature of undercover work."

"See, it doesn't feel like that to me. But I don't have a cop's perspective."

"In a normal investigation, things move very fast, the first forty-eight hours being critical to whether or not the crime will be solved. But like I say, this is different. Three of the four deaths are already cold cases, and number four, Abe Winter, is cooling down fast.

"We'll wait to get into the information until Jack and John are here. Why don't we assemble the lasagna, and while it's baking we can have our meeting. I know you must be up at the crack of dawn, so we won't keep you long after dinner."

"I thought I kept early hours on the *Maine Wind*, being up by five a.m., but out here I have to be up by three thirty in the morning to grab a bite and get down to the dock by four a.m."

"Brutal," Brie said. "Especially in the dead of winter. I'll think of you from my cozy bed."

"Thanks a lot."

She smiled. "You're welcome."

They got busy with the lasagna prep. Brie filled a large pot of water to cook the noodles while George chopped some onion and garlic and got them sautéing. Then he added in a pound of

Italian sausage and browned it with the veggies. He had brought a large bag of spinach, and Brie washed and dried it and, in another pan, cooked it down with some olive oil.

They made sauce and the cheese mixture, and Brie drained the noodles. They were just starting to assemble the layers when Jack came down from upstairs.

"Well, George. How nice to see you. The wonderful smells wafted upstairs, making for a very nice end to my nap."

"Hey, Jack. Good to see you. It gets kind o' lonely down there in my frumpy little trailer, so I thought I'd make dinner for everyone."

"Brie pointed out your vintage Airstream the other day."

"'Vintage' is maybe a bit too kind. But I'm looking on all of this as a rare adventure and a chance to finally help Brie with a case."

"How's that going?" Jack asked.

"It's interesting. When you plant yourself in the community, before long you start to notice things. Hear things."

"That's the beauty of undercover work," Brie said.

Just then they heard the front door open. "Something smells great," John called.

"George is here," Brie said.

"Well, no wonder." A few moments later John came into the kitchen and gave George a man hug and then went over and sniffed at the lasagna.

"We'll get this into the oven and then let's sit and have a meeting," Brie said. "George and Jack both have some information to share about the case."

George finished assembling the lasagna and put it into a hot oven, and John opened a bottle of red wine and got out some glasses. Brie collected her notebook, and they headed into the living room and sat down.

"George, why don't you go first? How's it going with Trulie Hyden?"

"He seems like a good guy. Appreciates the hardship of working stern, that's for sure. He's obviously been at this for a lifetime, and that may be part of the problem. I think he may have a drug problem. I saw him popping pills when we were out on the water today, even though he tried to keep it on the down-low."

"Opioids, maybe?" Brie asked.

"Could be. He came into The Stern Man after we got back in today, and even though we'd just come in from a freezing day on the water, he was sweating profusely. It wasn't hot in there, either."

"He could be coming down with something," Brie said. "But that's also a symptom of opioid abuse."

George nodded. "Well, that would explain what happened later." He turned to John. "I also met your sternman, Jim Finrude, in the pub today. That's where things got interesting."

"How so?" Brie asked.

"After we'd been talking for a while, Trulie came in. And like I say, he just seemed off, what with the sweating and all. At a point he said he needed to talk to Fin outside, and they left the pub. Something felt odd about it, so I snuck out the back door of the pub and was able to listen in without their knowing."

"Go on," Brie said.

"Trulie was pressuring Fin pretty good. Saying Fin had to know where Abe Winter got 'the stuff'—obviously meaning drugs. Fin tried to tell him that he needed help. That he should go to the doc. Trulie cut him off—said the doc was hardcore. 'Won't give out nothing,' were his words. Trulie kept pressuring Fin. Grabbed hold of him at one point. Then things really heated up. Fin pushed him off. Said he wouldn't have anything to do with drugs. Warned Trulie not to ask him again.

"That's when Trulie brought up Abe Winter's death. Accused Fin of maybe having something to do with it. Fin told him he was nuts. That he'd been sick that day. That's when Fin broke it off and walked away. But Trulie yelled after him, 'It's too many deaths. They can't all be accidents. I'd watch my back if I was you.'" George looked from Brie to Jack. "Hard to say if that was a concerned warning, but to me it sounded more like a threat."

Brie sat back in her chair. "The fact of the killings has caused a kind of unraveling—a distrust that is slowly eroding the fabric of the island. The people here may cling to the idea that the sea has taken these men, but deep down, they know different. And while they may hew to a kind of party line, in the meantime, truth is there, staring them in the face."

Jack leaned forward. "I think you're right, Brie. And that's good work, George. Establishes motive in the death of Abe Winter. And it connects to something I learned today, as well."

"Let's hear what you've got, Jack," she said.

"Well, it also pertains to drug use on Starkhaven. The whole thing started with Biddy Firth at the card game today, talking about how she was glad Fin wasn't working for Abe Winter anymore. When I asked why, she said that Abe was known to be connected to drugs on the island."

"I'm surprised she would divulge that to an outsider," Brie said. "And why all the interest in Fin?"

"Because he's dating her granddaughter."

"Ah, I see."

"That would be Isa Firth," John said. "Fin's completely gaga over that girl. Talks about her all the time."

"Biddy said she feared Fin would have been led astray if he'd kept working for Abe Winter. Even asked if John here was into any of that—meaning drug use."

"So, she's not unhappy that Winter met his end," Brie said.

"Well, she didn't say that, but it certainly solved her worries about Fin," Jack said. "Even so, she's leery of Fin working for John. Said that word on the island was his uncle, Nathan

Ross, was into drugs and that it almost cost him his stake on the island."

"I guess that answers the question about why his property taxes fell into arrears," John said.

Jack continued. "I told Biddy she didn't have to worry about John ever going down that road. Well, that really got Dale Woodrow going. He's one of the guys comes to the card game," he told George by way of explanation. "Dale talked about the physical toll lobstering takes on the body. Said that if the pain gets bad enough, the straightest arrow will take those drugs."

"It's basically the perfect set-up for whoever is pushing them," John said. "An island full of lobstermen with work-related pain."

"Just talking about it, Dale Woodrow looked mad enough to kill. Said the ones making a profit off all that pain should be stomped out."

"Were those his actual words?" Brie asked.

"They were," Jack said. "Turns out Dale lost his son to drugs. After the game broke up, Mary told me the tragic story. When the opioids weren't working anymore, Dale's son started going to the mainland. He left the island for good a few years ago and later died from a fentanyl overdose in Portland, Maine." Jack looked at Brie. "Portland is known to have a significant opioid problem."

"You know what?" George said. "When Fin was arguing with Trulie about the drugs, the name Tom Woodrow came up. Trulie mentioned something about going to the mainland if he couldn't get what he needed here, and Fin said, 'Don't do that, man. Look what happened to Tom Woodrow.'"

"Certainly gives Dale Woodrow a motive for killing Abe Winter," Brie said. "Assuming Winter was his son's drug source here on the island. But what about means and opportunity? Any thoughts, Jack?"

"Dale claims he still pulls a few traps now and then. Marty and Biddy, too. Even though they're up in years, they've all said they keep their boats up and go out in the nicer weather."

"My guess is they're letting their territories to one of the other guys on the island and taking a cut," John said. "I can ask Fin, though."

"Why don't you do that," Brie said. "So assuming we have means—a boat—and therefore opportunity, could Dale Woodrow have pulled it off, at his age?"

"He's a big guy. And while not super agile, you have to remember he's spent his life on the sea," Jack said. "If he got aboard Abe Winter's boat and took him by surprise, he might have pulled it off. Maybe knocked him out and sent him overboard. Maybe even strangled him. The problem is that Dale, Marty Hawkins, and Biddy all said they pull their boats out of the water for the winter. I think Dale's boat would have been out by the time Abe Winter was killed in November. And one of the other deaths occurred in February. Assuming we're looking for one killer, that would take him out of the running."

"Can you try to find out when he takes his boat out?" Brie asked.

"Sure. I'll work on that," Jack said.

Brie looked at George. "I'm very interested in what you overheard between Fin and Trulie. Sounds like Fin is pretty down on drugs."

"He said they destroy lives. And he didn't just say it, either. The words were emotionally charged."

"Whether he claims he was sick or not, Fin has to be considered a suspect," Brie said.

"But he has no boat. How would he have gotten out there?" George asked.

"Not sure, but in a harbor full of boats, he might have found a way."

John had been mostly silent during the meeting, but now he leaned forward. "So, we know that drugs are a problem on the island. Abe Winter was involved in distributing them, and maybe it cost him his life. We know they've mucked up lives all over the place, from Nathan Ross to Tom Woodrow to Trulie Hyden and who knows how many others. We also know from what George overheard that apparently Doc Ward will have nothing to do with prescribing opioids. So with Abe gone, it's created a drug vacuum."

"Maybe yes, maybe no," Jack said.

"What do you mean?" Brie asked.

"Well, when Mary, down at the store, told me about Dale's son dying, I asked her if it was true about Abe Winter sourcing the drugs. Her response was interesting. She admitted that Winter was the face of the problem on Starkhaven, but she also said, 'I fear the heart of the beast may lie elsewhere.'" Jack looked at Brie. "Winter may have been a small fish in a big pond. If so, he could have been working for as little as free drugs."

"Drugs and territories go together," Brie said. "And just like lobster territories, drug territories are carefully guarded. My take on all this is that Starkhaven is someone's drug territory. Abe Winter was probably just a stooge for someone who rules the drug roost here. Does that bring anyone to mind?"

"Sure does," Jack said. "Thorn."

"That would be my thinking," Brie said.

"Really?" John said. "Even after what Dent told us about Mo Thorn being sent off island when he was young as a punishment for his involvement with drugs?"

"All that tells us is that this may have been a pattern since he was young," Jack said. "Over time, he could have turned his predilection into a money maker."

"Maybe I can rattle his cage," Brie said.

"You need to be careful," John said. "Thorn's got a lot to protect here."

"So, could he be the killer?" George asked.

"That would surprise me a great deal," Brie said. "If he *is* behind the drugs on the island, why would he, of all people, rock the boat? Kill his own dealer? Bring the law out here to scrutinize everyone? No, I don't think he's the killer, but probably just as dangerous if hedged in. I do think, considering the profiles of these victims, that he might want to watch his back."

"You mean the killer might have him in his sights?" George asked.

"If these are vigilante killings, then I'd say yes. Of course, we don't know enough to make that judgment yet. There are a lot of pieces that would have to fit together."

"I should check the lasagna." George got up and headed to the kitchen. He was back in a couple of minutes and announced that the dinner was out and cooling.

"We're making progress," Jack said. "More than I would have expected at this point in the game. We have strong motives in two of the killings and have identified three suspects—Alan Bellsby in the death of Oslo Stumph, and Dale Woodrow and Fin as possible perpetrators in Abe Winter's death." He looked at Brie. "I'm also interested in what you said earlier about a slow unraveling of trust on here on Starkhaven."

Brie closed her notebook. "My thought is that as this erosion of trust unfolds, the islanders will become more suspicious of each other—i.e. Trulie accusing Fin—but also more willing to talk. As outsiders who arrived after the deaths, we are in a perfect position to be the ones the islanders may talk to.

"There's a tipping point in every human dynamic. Maybe this fourth death was just that, compounded by the fact that folks here depended on Abe Winter to get their fix." She looked at Jack. "Remember in Abe Winter's case file, it stated that detectives had noted nervousness in those interviewed, as if some wide-ranging secret were being kept. Well, now we may know what the secret was."

"The tipping point you mention. I think it's already happening," Jack said. "At the card game today, they made direct reference to the deaths of the lobstermen as well as the drugs. That surprised me, as well as Mary's willingness to tell me Dale Woodrow's story."

Brie nodded. "But before we can begin to assemble any patterns—draw any conclusions—we need to learn more about the other two victims, Paul Le Fevre and Cliff Gordon. We know some things from the case files, but we need to drill down, learn more about those two. We need to find out who had motive in their deaths, and then where all these motives may ultimately converge."

"Due to the number of deaths involved, it's an extremely complicated and challenging case," Jack said.

"But our plan is working, isn't it?" John asked.

"Better than I expected," Brie said.

"Lasagna, anyone?" George asked.

Jack stood up. "We've all earned it. Let's eat."

They headed out to the kitchen and while Brie and George assembled a salad, John and Jack set the table in the dining room and poured out some more wine. George's lasagna was a winner. Warm and comforting, with rich tomato sauce, thick noodles, and gooey cheese. They lingered over it, soaking in the comfort of food and wine and togetherness.

At 7:30, John drove George back down to the village, and Brie and Jack cleaned up. Because John's wakeup time was no kinder than George's, they were all tucked in bed by shortly after eight o'clock. But sleep proved elusive for Brie as she thought about who had been lurking around the house last night and why. It was a brazen act. Did the intruder hope they would find the tracks? Were those tracks meant to intimidate? Was it merely someone curious about them, or was it a killer with a sixth sense? A sense that a trap was being set and that his days of freedom were numbered.

Chapter 16

Saturday, January 23rd

On Saturday morning Brie drove to the Thorns' house above the village for the weekly get-together of the Starkhaven Stitchers. She was arriving late on purpose so as to miss the pre-quilting socializing, during which she had been keenly reminded of her outsider status. *They can't shun me if I'm not there*, she thought and smiled to herself as she bumped along the road.

She was also thinking about her early days at the history center with Faith Babcock, who had been giving her small tasks and also beginning to teach her the process of microfilming. A large archive of island newspapers, letters, and photographs was waiting to be filmed, and Brie sensed that her offer to help had given Faith hope they might finally conquer the backlog.

Within a few minutes the road climbed to where the Thorn house overlooked the village, offering a postcard view of the small harbor. It was a cold, clear blue day with calm seas. Most of the lobsterboats were out fishing, but a few rode at anchor, bows to windward, facing the sea, as if yearning to be out there with the rest.

Brie parked the truck in the driveway behind the others. "Last in, first out," she said. "I like it." She climbed out, headed up to the door, and rang the bell. She knew everyone would be downstairs.

After maybe a minute, Tam Thorn opened the door. She stepped aside and let Brie in. "We thought you weren't coming," she said. Brie wondered if that had been cause for celebration.

"Thought I'd skip the social hour," she said.

Tam nodded. "It just takes time. Believe me, they'll warm up to you. When you didn't show up this morning, I gave them a little talking to."

"Totally not necessary," Brie said. "I'm a big girl."

"That's all well and good, but sometimes we can forget our manners, being so to ourselves out here."

Brie nodded. "Fair enough," she said, and they headed downstairs.

After a brief chorus of "Hello, Brie," the ladies followed their instincts and got right back to ignoring her. But uncomfortable as the dynamic felt, if created a perfect crucible for observation of who might melt down when the heat was applied.

All of the women were there from the previous week—Jana Bjorklund, Bess Gordon, Sara Bellsby, and Clara Lyston. Plus one woman she hadn't met. Brie assumed this was Lyla Stumph, who had been missing last week. From her age Brie guessed she might be Oslo Stumph's mother. At that moment Tam called her over to where the woman stood.

"Lyla, this is our new member, Brie Ross, who's just moved to the island. Her husband, John, is Nathan Ross's nephew. They've taken over Nathan's house, and John is learning the lobster trade."

"Hello, Brie," Lyla said. A slow smile spread across her face, and for whatever reason she cast a furtive glance across the room to where Sara Bellsby was already busy cutting material for today's work. "Have you ever done any quilting?" she asked.

"My granny taught me when I was young, and I used to quilt with her whenever we visited."

"Was your granny from Maine?"

"Yup. She's getting older now but still lives in Cherry-field," Brie said.

Tam called Jana Bjorklund over.

"Jana, I thought you could work with Brie today, doing assembly."

Brie knew from last week that "assembly" entailed pinning the new blocks onto the larger quilt for sewing.

"I'd be happy to," Jana said and led Brie over to a large table where the quilt in progress was laid out.

Brie hadn't paid much attention to Jana at the first meeting, except to note that she seemed amiable and had at least sent a few smiles her way. But, since then, John had met her husband, Lars, and had sung his praises. Lars was the one guy on the island who had encouraged John—told him to stand up to the bullying and gear cutting—and who had, to John's thinking, probably helped convince Fin to sign on as his sternman. Brie hoped Jana might be as welcoming to her as Lars had been to John.

"Your husband has been very kind to mine," she told Jana.

"Lars doesn't hold with a lot of the bullying and aggression some of the fishermen ascribe to out here. He's always said that without new blood we're doomed to go down."

"What exactly does that mean, if you don't mind my asking?"

"Just that too much inbreeding will eventually be the death of this place. Lars believes there's strength in diversity, but it's not a popular stance out here."

"That's wise, though," Brie said.

"Most here wouldn't think so."

Whether "here" meant this room or the island in general, Jana's message was clear.

The work got underway in earnest then, with each of them doing her part. The tasks were the same as last week—cutting, sewing together pieces into blocks, ironing, assembly, and the final sewing, but everyone had rotated to a different job this week. Today, Sara Bellsby and Bess Gordon were working together, and Bess was actually showing some sparks of life. Brie thought about the abuse she had suffered before her husband Cliff went missing from his boat. So, even though she'd gotten the cold shoulder from Sara, she gave her points for drawing Bess out.

Because the hands-on nature of the work was quite focused, Brie had a chance to surreptitiously observe the women. See what tensions, if any, existed among them. See who was friendly to whom and conversely, who was not. Now that she knew the story of Oslo Stumph cutting away Alan Bellsby's gear in an attempt to drive him off the island—a vendetta that had only stopped when Stumph went missing from his boat— she was aware of an almost magnetic repulsion that radiated from Lyla Stumph anytime Sara Bellsby got too close.

Oslo Stumph had been the first to die, sixteen months ago. Of course, his death would initially have been written off as an accident at sea. Just like so many others that had occurred down through time in these Maine waters. After all, lobstering is a dangerous profession, and the sea is a fickle mistress. But Brie could imagine that, with each passing death, the islanders would have become increasingly suspicious of each other. Because of Oslo's actions against Bellsby, Lyla Stumph would, of course, have fixated on Alan Bellsby. And that growing suspicion and hatred could have found a focus on Sara Bellsby as well. Or at least that was how Brie had it figured.

Interestingly enough, there also seemed to be an unsettled energy between Bess Gordon and Jana Bjorklund. Brie thought she had noticed it last week, but the sense of it persisted. Jana was clearly a warm and friendly person, yet she seemed to struggle around Bess, as if some invisible wall had been constructed between them. A wall they appeared powerless to remove. But it was just an impression, and Brie reminded herself not to read too much into the dynamics she witnessed, but rather to neutrally observe them.

Surprisingly, she soon warmed to the rhythm of the work, a feeling seeded in her girlhood by Granny Beaumont. But the job of collectively working on a task, working toward a goal, was also integral to her being a detective, since all homicide investigations are a team effort—the teams being composed of forensic scientists, evidence collection teams, medical examiners, and police detectives. Like raising sails at sea, the clearing of cases requires all hands on deck.

After an hour they took a break, and the women headed either toward the kitchenette for coffee or the bathroom. Brie headed for the bathroom, but Sara Bellsby got there first, so she waited her turn, and soon Lyla Stumph joined the line. A couple minutes later, Sara existed the bathroom, but the arctic draft emanating from her nearly froze Brie solid. Brie had experienced the same disdain from her last week but was even more curious now as to the why.

"I wonder why she's decided not to like me," she said under her breath to Lyla Stumph.

Lyla smiled the same enigmatic smile as before, looked Brie up and down, and said, "You'll find out soon enough."

Brie could have asked what that meant but decided this wasn't the time or place to get into it. So instead, she took refuge in the bathroom, using the few minutes of alone time to gird herself for the next hour.

An hour later the session wrapped up. Brie donned her coat and headed out the door. Fortuitously, Lyla Stumph was right behind her, while the others were still inside, busily gabbing. Brie started down the driveway, knowing this was an opportunity. She was framing up a question when Lyla surprised her by speaking.

"I saw you coming out of the history center last week. I live up that way."

Brie turned to face her, seizing the opportunity to engage her.

"That's right. I stopped in there last week, just out of curiosity. I met Faith Babcock." Brie waited a beat to see if Lyla would comment, but she didn't. "I've been looking for things to do on the island, and I thought the history center would be a good way to learn more about this place. I also asked Faith if she could use any help. Told her I wouldn't mind volunteering. She took me up on it. Turns out she's got a backlog of responsibilities. Just from looking around the center, I can tell that the island has a rich history."

"Oh, there's lots of history here," Lyla said. "Maybe too much history." It was another cryptic comment to which she clearly intended to add no addendums.

As a detective, Brie was no stranger to cryptic communication. Depending on who's playing the game and what motivates them—sometimes fear, but more often, holding power over another, as in "I know something you don't"—the job of extracting information can be as disagreeable as pulling a molar. Knowing that she and Lyla didn't have time here to unpack the island's history, Brie circled back to her comment outside the bathroom.

"I'm curious, Lyla. What did you mean by 'You'll find out soon enough,' when I brought up Sara Bellsby's seeming dislike of me?"

Lyla looked behind her to be sure no one was listening. She shifted from one foot to the other as if buying time. Finally she appeared to make a decision. "I'm just gonna say it right out. Alan Bellsby is a womanizer."

"Sara's husband?"

Lyla nodded. Again she looked Brie up and down. "He'll come after *you*. Mark my words."

"I'm married, Lyla."

"Won't matter. Mark my words." She glanced over her shoulder again. "My son, Oslo, rest his soul, hated that behavior.

Now Oslo had his struggles, but he was a faithful husband even after his wife took the kids and left the island. He hated what he saw Alan Bellsby doing. Playing up to the women here, married or not. Causing pain when he wasn't even from here. Someone from Away has no business coming out here, making trouble."

The comment hit a little too close to home, and Brie had to remind herself that their undercover operation here had a moral imperative.

"Oslo tried to put a stop to it. Warned him to leave the island women alone. Even cut his gear. Said someone had to do it." Lyla's gaze fell. "But he paid." She didn't explain the last three words, but turned abruptly and headed for her car. Brie heard her mumble, "Like I said, too much history."

Brie got into her car, backed down the driveway, and drove toward home. Alan Bellsby was already a suspect. Fin had told John about Oslo Stumph relentlessly cutting his gear in an attempt to drive him off the island. But apparently there was more to the story. She needed to ask John if he'd met Bellsby. But she had a sneaking feeling she already knew who he was—the guy who had twice now passed her on the road from the history center and stopped to make small talk. She had dubbed him "Mr. Hollywood" because, well, he was that good-looking. Had he used Sara as his way onto the island and into the richest lobster fishing grounds in the world? That's basically what Fin had told John—that he'd married his way onto the island. Now, Brie could see Bellsby going after Oslo Stumph, who was cramping his style, but, to her mind, it was a stretch that he'd fit the bill in the other killings. And if this case did boil down to vigilantism, it seemed more likely that Bellsby would have been the one with a target on his back.

No, her sense was that they were only beginning to scratch the surface of what lay beneath these crimes. But they had placed themselves well. Cast their net wide enough that they were positioned to gather a myriad of information. Would two months be enough to close the case? She believed it would. Could they all stay safe until then? She thought about the footprints outside the house, under their window, and a chill ran through her. It was her job to make sure they did.

Chapter 17

Tuesday, January 26

John steered the boat for the next bunch of buoys. Every day he and Fin set out a few more traps—testing the waters, so to speak. After the first few days of his traps being cut away, things seemed to have settled down. He wondered if what Lars had said at the Lobstermen's Association meeting a week ago had put an end to the mean-spiritedness.

Fin stood just outside the house, gaff in hand, ready for action. For several days he had been in a non-communicative funk. John had let him be, figuring he'd talk when he felt like it. Today the elements matched Fin's mood—gray and unsettled. Just after dawn, the seas had started making up, and now a stiff eighteen-knot wind pressed in from the north. John steered the boat into it as Fin labored at the gunwale, pulling, emptying, and baiting the traps. The lobstering territory that had belonged to Nathan Ross, and now John, lay west of Starkhaven, so today, the island offered little shelter from the callous lash of the wind.

They had pressed on, deciding not to stop for lunch, since the seas were building. But by one o'clock, conditions had deteriorated enough that John decided to call it for the day. He brought Fin into the house and steered the boat for home.

As they headed south, John noticed another lobsterboat approaching fast from astern. It is the job of the overtaking or give-way vessel to stay well clear of the stand-on vessel, but as John watched his mirror, the intent of the other boat became clear. As it passed to port, close enough to shake hands, John veered to starboard. He saw Trulie Hyden turn and grin as he passed. George stood behind the house, hanging on for dear life, looking equal parts appalled and bemused.

"What a maniac," Fin said. "I suppose that was directed at me."

"Why would it be?" John asked, even though he knew about the fight between Fin and Trulie over the drugs.

"Let's just say he's got issues, and he thinks I can help him."

"Something to do with Abe Winter?"

"Why would you ask that?" Fin sounded suspicious.

"Well, you worked for Abe Winter. Winter's gone now, so it doesn't take a rocket scientist to figure it might be related to Winter in some way."

"Yeah? Well, maybe it is. Maybe it's not."

"Look, Fin, I may be new here, but there's a few things I know. One, drugs are a problem on all the islands. Mainland, too. My wife's grandfather, Jack, plays cards with Biddy Firth, your girlfriend's grandma. Biddy has made no bones about the fact she's glad you're not working for Winter anymore. Told Jack she worried you'd be led astray. Even asked Jack if I was into the drugs."

"I'm sorry about that," Fin said. "She's pretty protective of Isa."

"Of course she is," John said. "Hey, it's no big deal. She told Jack that my uncle, Nathan Ross, nearly lost his stake here because of the drugs. Got way in arrears with his property taxes." John throttled back the engine, partly to smooth out the ride but also in hopes of keeping Fin talking. "It's a known fact that Abe Winter was dealing drugs. Opioids, from what I understand."

"Abe wasn't a bad guy," Fin said almost protectively. "He just got into something and couldn't get back out. I can tell you, the last couple weeks aboard his boat, he was off, man."

"How do you mean?"

"Scared. He seemed scared. When he went missing from his boat, I didn't know what to think. That's why I left the island. And Trulie—he's nuts. He accused me of having something to do with Abe's death."

"Maybe that's the drugs talking," John said.

"Maybe. But something's wrong out here. Trulie said four deaths can't all be accidents. I didn't want to think about it, but he's right. They can't all be accidents."

"Do you think Abe Winter knew he was in danger?" John asked.

Fin gazed out the window as thick, icy sleet started to fall. "I don't know. I just know he acted scared." He spread his feet wide against the pitch and roll of the boat. "And now, Trulie thinks I had something to do with his death."

"Did you?"

Fin stepped threateningly toward John. "Are you accusing me, too?"

"No, I'm asking you. I believe you're a man of your word, so I'm giving you a chance to answer truthfully."

"Then I'll say it once and never again. I had nothing to do with Abe Winter's death. I was home sick that day. What's more, you can check with Doc Ward if you don't believe me. When I got off Abe's boat, the day before he died, I was feeling awful. So, I went to see the doc. He said I had the flu and needed to rest in bed for a day or two. He would have a record of that appointment." Fin stepped away from John. "I was at home, at my aunt's house." He leaned against the side wall of the house. "I knew Abe was involved in dealing drugs, and I didn't like it, but I didn't kill him."

John turned his head and looked him directly in the eye. "I believe you, Fin."

Fin stared out the window at the converging elements as they cut a long arc southeast, heading for the harbor. John sensed

there was something more troubling him. Something he wasn't
yet ready to talk about.

*   *   *

When John got home that afternoon, just before two o'clock,
Brie was preparing to leave for her doctor appointment to get the
stitches in her hand removed. He told her it had been an event-
ful day on the water, and she promised to hear all about it as
soon as she got home. Then she was out the door. She checked
her watch as she headed for the truck. Plenty of time to get
there, since the doc's place was just down the road. She drove
down West Road, wipers on against the sleet that had begun to
fall, and on the outskirts of the village, she turned left into the
driveway for the clinic.

She parked in the driveway but, this time, knew to go
around the side of the house to where the clinic entrance was.
Inside, a warm, cozy waiting room greeted her. Having been
under duress, she hadn't taken much note of it the night she
and John had been here, but now she took it in. The walls were
painted a calm but hopeful green, and the chairs were uphol-
stered with a green and white leaf pattern. A coffee station held
two pump pots—one full of hot brewed coffee, the other with
hot water for tea. A tray of real coffee mugs hinted the doc
might be environmentally aware.

She was the only patient waiting, so she got a hot cup o'
joe, nabbed a couple magazines from one of the tables, and settled in. There was a desk in the corner for a receptionist, but
Brie hadn't seen one either time she'd been here, which led her
to believe maybe the doc flew solo. And why not, with such a
small island population?

In about five minutes she heard a little scuffling in the
hall and a woman appeared with a boy behind her who
looked to be about ten or eleven years old. He had his head

against her back, and she held his hand. Doc Ward was right behind them.

"Hello, Brie," he said as they came into the waiting room.

"Good afternoon, Doc."

"Annette, let me introduce you. This is Brie Ross. She and her husband just moved to the island to take over Nathan Ross's property. Brie, this is Annette Bryce and her son, Hughie."

"Pleased to meet you," Brie said. She peeked behind Annette's back and waved her hand. "Hi, Hughie." He was a handsome boy with dark hair and intensely blue eyes.

Hughie had started to rock from side to side and hid his face. Brie suspected he might have autism spectrum disorder.

"I'll be right back," the doc said. "I'm just going to prepare the room and get your file." He disappeared down the small hallway.

"Hughie's not normally like this," Annette said. "Something's got him spooked. He's been troubled since he got up today."

"Is he scared of the doc?"

"Oh, heavens, no, Tobias is the only doctor Hughie's ever been to. He's always liked him. No, some days are just like this. Usually, I don't get to know why." She looked back at Brie. "Your name is Ross, so your husband must have been related to Nathan."

"Yes, he's his nephew," Brie said. "Helen's son." Brie wasn't sure if that would mean anything or not, but Annette nodded like she understood.

"All ready for you, Brie," the doc said from behind them.

"I'll see you around the island, Annette. You, too, Hughie." She waved at him again. "I hope we meet again soon."

Annette and Hughie headed over to the coat rack for their winter gear, and Brie followed Doc Ward back to the examining room.

"So, any problems with the wound healing? The doctor asked. He gestured for Brie to sit up on the examining table.

"Nope. Other than some mild pain the first couple days, all has been well."

"Good to hear. Let's take a look." The doc examined the sutures in her left hand, then said, "We're fine to remove these." He picked up a miniature scissors that came to a sharp point on the end and gently began lifting and snipping the sutures. When he was done he studied the hand again to be sure the wound had closed properly. "It's healed well," he said.

"That's thanks to you, Doc."

"Not entirely," he said. "Some folks are just quick healers. Usually a sign of a healthy life."

"Well, I try," Brie said.

"So, any other problems or questions, since you're here?"

She wanted to verify what Trulie had said about the doc refusing to give out painkillers on an island where most of the men suffered from occupational pain. She could only think of one way to do it.

"My husband, John—you met him—struggles with a lot of pain, especially in his back. Is there anything you could give him?"

"That strapping young fellow?"

"He's forty, and before coming here he worked in a boat-yard. In fact, he started working at the Bath Ironworks in his teens to help support his mother, who was sick. He looks good, but I think parts of him are just worn out."

"Look, Brie, I'll tell you right out, I don't prescribe pain-killers. They're not the answer. But there are other things that can help. Tell John to stop by. I'll give him some topical patches and also show him some exercises that will help strengthen his core and help his back." The doc studied her seriously for a moment or two. "He can't make the mistake others on this island have made of turning to illicit drugs. That never ends well." He paused for a moment as if making a decision. "You and John have probably heard about the deaths of the lobstermen out here."

"We have, and . . . well, it scares me, Doc."

"Listen, Brie. There's a drug problem on this island. Specifically, opioids. Many of the lobstermen here are working impaired. Couple that with the fact that lobstering is one of the most dangerous professions, period."

"So you're saying their safety was compromised by the drugs?"

"That's what I believe. It only takes one bad judgment and you're overboard. The traps are heavy. They're working with lines and hydraulic haulers. It's very easy to lose your balance or get tangled in your gear. Just a little physical or mental impairment can turn fatal. Your husband will be safe as long as he makes the right choices. And I'm happy to help him do that."

Brie nodded. "Thank you, Doctor. I'll tell him." She stepped down off the examining table.

The doc fixed her with a kind smile. "Life has a cycle, Brie. Some die, some are born. Some leave, others arrive—just like you and your husband have recently. And who knows, maybe there will be little Rosses running around soon. This island and its population have been here for hundreds of years. It will go on, but we all have to do our part to keep it healthy."

"We'll try to do that, Doc," Brie said. "If you have time, I'd like to pay our bill."

"Sure thing. Let's step out to the desk."

The doc brought up her account on the computer and printed off an invoice for her. Brie had brought cash along, and they squared up. She thanked him and a couple minutes later, she was out the door.

She sat in her car for a few minutes, listening to the sleet assaulting the roof and thinking about what the doc had said. To his mind, the drugs were Public Enemy No. 1, responsible for all the deaths here in the past year and a half. The drugs had made those men vulnerable, and the sea had reached out and taken them. It's what the Starkhaveners had decided to believe. But she didn't buy it. She'd been a detective for too long not to know the feel of something amiss. She sensed it, lurking, just out of sight. And she was sure others felt it, too, because there was fear here, frozen in the long shadows of a clean, winter white world. But to disprove the doc's theory, she needed to find one of the victims who didn't fit the mold. Abe Winter was a drug dealer and very likely a user. Paul Le Fevre was an alcoholic and possibly also a drug user, because, often as not, the two go together. But what of the other two victims—Oslo Stumph and Cliff Gordon?

This wasn't a sprint to the finish like many investigations that were solved in forty-eight hours. There was still much to learn. Motives to bring to light, suspects to suss out, hidden history to unearth. No, how well they could play the long game would determine the outcome here.

Brie started the truck and headed out to the road. She turned left and drove into the village and parked across from the general store. She had decided to cook a chicken and needed to get some vegetables to add to the pot. She climbed out and headed across the street and called out to Mary as she entered.

"Hi, Mary. It's Brie Ross."

"Hello, Brie. Can I get something for you?"

"Just here for some vegetables and a chicken. I'll be back there in a minute."

"Sounds good."

Brie, never having cooked much before her season aboard *Maine Wind*, was constantly surprised at how much she enjoyed the process. It almost had the feeling of a beloved hobby. Of course, much of that was due to her affection for George, and his careful and kind tutelage when she was on the ship. George preferred to work without a messmate, but, that said, he was usually happy to have help in the galley. Although her work on the ship was topside, on cold or rainy days the galley was always delightfully cozy, and during her months aboard, it had become a place of safety, where her troubled soul could take refuge. She knew full well that her newly acquired love of cooking had everything to do with those experiences.

She moved along the produce aisle and picked up carrots, celery, and onions. She paused at the basket of garlic and picked out a couple of bulbs. Mary had Swiss chard today, and she added a bunch to her basket and then moved on to the back of the store to the meat counter. Mary was working next door in the deli/bakery and came over when she saw Brie waiting.

There were two chickens left in the meat case, and she told Mary she'd take both of them. She knew that, after a day on the water, John could easily eat one of those single-handedly. And cold chicken made great leftovers.

"Would you like me to cut it up for you?" Mary asked.

"If it's not too much trouble."

"No trouble at all." Mary picked up her cleaver and started whacking away. "This is my kick-back time. The boys are all in off the water, and the baking and deli work is done for the day. I get precious few customers this time of day, which is nice."

"I'll bet," Brie said. "Your days must start so early."

"I'm always down here by three a.m., starting the baking and putting out a few sandwiches for the boys heading out on the water."

Mary cut up those chickens like a pro, wrapped them up in white butcher paper, and taped them closed. As she finished, she looked up at Brie rather shyly.

"Do you think Jack, I mean your grandfather, might like to come to dinner some night?"

Brie was surprised that Mary, in a roundabout way, seemed to be asking her permission.

"Well, I can't speak for him, but I think he'd really enjoy that."

"I just thought . . . well, he's such a nice man."

"You know what, Mary? Nothing ventured, nothing gained."

"Good, then I'll invite him." She handed the package of chicken across to Brie. "These are raised by one of the families on the island."

"Really? How wonderful."

"There used to be lots of animals on the island years ago, when I was a girl. Sheep, pigs, chickens, even some horses. Animal husbandry was a much bigger thing back then, because we were so isolated. It wasn't that easy to get things from the mainland."

"It must have been nice," Brie said, imagining that earlier time. Truth be told, there was a part of her that cottoned to the thought of a simpler way of life. It was why she loved life aboard *Maine Wind*. But she was also enlightened enough to know that, while those times were simpler in one way, they had carried their own set of problems and challenges. Every coin has two sides. Take technology that brings with it certain freedoms, while stripping others away.

Brie paid for the groceries up at the checkout and said goodbye to Mary. She crossed the road to the truck and put the groceries on the passenger seat. She climbed in, started the truck, did a U-turn in the road, and headed for home.

Chapter 18

In the fading light, the temperature had started its descent, and the sleet was busily transposing itself to snow. As Brie neared the end of the village, she saw Lyla Stumph walking along with a bag of groceries. She stopped and powered down the window.

"Would you like a ride, Lyla?"

"Oh, my. That would be wonderful."

Brie put the truck in park, leaned over, and opened the passenger door. She shifted her bag of groceries to the back seat to make room for Lyla, who climbed in.

"Here, let me put your bag in the back." Brie relieved Lyla of her groceries and deposited them in the back seat next to her own. "It's a nasty afternoon, isn't it?" she said, banking on weather talk as a good icebreaker.

Lyla peered out the window. "It's been a wicked long winter, and looks like we're not done yet."

"You should be driving your car today, Lyla."

"Stopped running yesterday, but my husband's off island for a couple of days getting the boat repaired. Lars is stopping by tomorrow to take a look."

"Well, that's good. You'll have to direct me, Lyla. You said you live up near the history center."

"It's just north around the bend from your place," Lyla said.

"All right, then I know just where I'm going."

Brie put the wipers on and drove west, out of the village. The sleet had left a sheet of ice, and she could feel the truck fishtail a bit trying to find its footing. The going was slow with the ice and snow, but still, within five minutes they rounded the bend in the road beyond the Ross home. A quarter of a mile along the road, Lyla directed Brie to turn into a driveway on the right. A small, gray-shingled, Cape Cod-style house sat in a clearing surrounded by spruce. The shutters and front door were painted a deep red, which helped the house stand its ground in the midst of the thick spruce forest.

"Would you like to come in for a pot of tea?" Lyla asked.

"I'd love to," Brie said, thinking this might be a chance to learn more about Oslo and possibly some of the other victims. But she knew she would have to tread carefully so as not to raise any alarm bells. She collected Lyla's bag from the backseat and followed her to the front door.

Inside, the layout was just like their house. Long living room to the right and dining room and kitchen to the left. Brie set the bag down in the entryway, slipped off her boots and coat, and followed Lyla into the kitchen.

"You can set the bag there." Lyla gestured to the table in the middle of the room. It wasn't a large table but very sturdy and built of pine. Brie could imagine it doubling as a work-space.

Lyla got the kettle on and started laying out teacups. Brie walked over to a shelf that held cookbooks and studied the titles.

"So, how are you and your husband settling in?"

"Pretty well," Brie said. "Of course, it's a strange time of year to start such a life, but with the house vacant and the boat in the water, we thought we should come now."

Lyla nodded like that made sense. The kettle boiled, and she poured water into the pot and added several teabags. "Hope you like black tea," she said.

"Yes, that's fine."

When the tea was steeped, Lyla asked, "Do you like macaroons?"

"I love macaroons," Brie said, and she wasn't lying. It was something about their moist, coconutty essence.

Lyla brought the pot and the tin of macaroons, and they sat down at the kitchen table. For a few minutes, they sipped their tea. Brie could hear the wind outside the house ramping up.

"I'm sorry the girls at quilting haven't been more welcoming. I guess that includes me."

Brie was surprised at Lyla's contrition. "Well, I did talk to Jana a bit last time and also to you. So that's a start. By the way, thanks for the heads up about Alan Bellsby. I'll keep a lookout. I actually think he may have greeted me on the road one day, coming from the history center, but he didn't give his name."

"Well, believe me, he's not done," Lyla said.

"That must be terrible for his wife."

"If you ask me, she should have known he was after something. I mean, if you think about the two of them, they're not much of a match. I mean, he's very good-looking, and well, Sara, not so much."

"But people can be attracted for other reasons," Brie said.

"You're right," Lyla said. "And maybe they each saw some kind of opportunity."

Brie could see that the hardships of life on Starkhaven had long ago beaten any sense of the romantic out of Lyla. But then again, maybe she was right. Fin had told John the story of Bellsby marrying onto the island to gain a lobstering territory —an idea that Oslo, and maybe others here, had planted and nourished. Didn't mean there wasn't truth to it, but since Brie didn't know either Alan or Sara Bellsby, she wasn't about to judge.

"Lyla," Brie said gently, "Fin—Jim Finrude—told my husband about what happened to Oslo. How he went missing from his boat over a year ago." She set her cup down and looked Lyla in the eye. "I was so very sorry to hear about his death."

Lyla's eyes clouded, and she looked toward the window, where snow and darkness were quickly eradicating any visibility. "The island lost a good man the day my son didn't return. He used to watch over things here. All the time, every day. He was always watching over things and people. If something was off, something bad going on, Oslo made it his business to know about it and sound the alarm. Everyone knew that about him, and we all depended on him in that way."

Brie sat quietly listening, intrigued by what Lyla was saying. It sounded as if Oslo had been a self-appointed, one-man surveillance operation here on the island, or put less kindly, a snoop. And the implications of that were not lost on her. Whoever the killer was, she believed he might be working some kind of grand plan, and Oslo's covert activities would undoubtedly have posed a real threat to that. The fact that he had been the first victim suddenly took on a deeper meaning. Maybe he wasn't targeted because of his bullying of Bellsby or anyone else. Maybe he was targeted because the killer knew his reputation and feared it. Maybe he was targeted because the killer needed to clear the way for his *own* operation.

Brie knew it was a risk, but there would never be a better moment to ask the burning question. So, she proceeded cautiously. "Lyla, I'm just wondering. Have you ever thought that Oslo's death might not have been an accident?"

Lyla went silent. She set her teacup down and looked toward the window and, after a moment, turned and studied Brie, as if making some kind of decision. Finally she spoke.

"For a long time after Oslo died, I believed it had been an accident. But it always bothered me, because he was a careful person. Never involved in drugs or booze like some of the others. Oh, he liked a beer with his friends, but that was it."

Brie had to wonder, if the guy was such a saint, why his wife had left him. But she quickly tabled that thought as off-topic.

"Even after Paul Le Fevre died, I keep believing it was accidental," Lyla said. "After all, Paul was a drunk. Everyone knew about it. Used to go out on his boat hung over or, worse yet, still drinking. I always figured something bad would come of it, even though he seemed to be a nice man and had certainly had his share of tragedy."

Brie recalled that Le Fevre's wife had died years before.

Lyla leaned forward. "But when the other two died, that was too much for me. Others here think the sea has taken all these men, but I don't believe it anymore. And here's why. My friend, Marlis Winter, her son died last November. Same thing, just like the others. Went missing from his boat one day. Happened on a day his sternman—that was Fin—was ashore. Now Abe, though not a bad guy, was involved in drugs here on the island. He was the guy everyone went to. Oslo had known about it for a long time."

"Did Oslo know where Abe Winter was getting the drugs?" Brie asked.

"No, and that bothered him a lot. Bothered him that he could never seem to find out how Abe was getting them. But he knew Marlis was my friend and didn't want to make trouble for Abe."

Brie nodded, waiting for the meat at the center of all this.

"After Abe died, Marlis was so distraught. I tried hard to comfort her, having lost my son as well. One day she told me that, before he died, Abe had been excited about something. Said he'd figured something out. Something big. And it was going to put money in his pocket, so he could get his own place. Marlis asked what it was, but Abe wouldn't tell her."

"When was that?" Brie asked.

"Just a few days before he died," Lyla said. "Sadly, whatever he knew, he took to the grave with him. I've never believed for a moment that his death was an accident."

Brie thought about what Lyla had just said. The words she had used—"He'd figured something out. Something big that was going to put money in his pocket." To Brie that sounded like blackmail. Had Abe somehow stumbled on information that had revealed the killer? Had he stupidly decided to try and blackmail him? Or did it have something to do with the drug chain here on the islands?

Lyla spoke again. "I don't know who to trust anymore." She studied Brie. "Now, you folks just arrived, so I guess I can trust that you're not involved. That's why I've told you these things. But the others here? Well, who knows what's going on? Who knows who can be trusted?"

"I'm sorry, Lyla. I probably shouldn't have asked that question."

"Why *did* you ask it?" Lyla suddenly seemed troubled.

Brie looked into her teacup, framing her words carefully.

"Since we got here, I keep hearing little things. And John, my husband, has learned things from Fin. Fin was terribly troubled by Abe's death. He even left the island for a time. Maybe he feels responsible in some way since he was ashore the day Abe disappeared. But more than anything, I want to know because I'm worried about my husband. No, it's more than that. I'm scared for him. I fear he might be next."

Unbidden, Brie's eyes filled with tears, and at that moment she had to face the fact that she was actually afraid for John. They were playing a dangerous game out here, and she realized she had very real fear for his safely—fear she had suppressed.

Lyle poured out more tea and when she spoke, it was with great gentleness. "You shouldn't worry. You and your husband have no history here. What could anyone have against you?"

Brie felt the irony in her words. The killer would have plenty against them if he knew the truth of their sojourn here.

Then, as if to distract her, Lyla said, "I've seen your husband down in the village. The first time I saw him, I asked someone who he was. That's a fine man you've got there."

Brie smiled. "Thanks, Lyla."

"Not too many cold nights with a fella like that." Lyla winked at her, and Brie felt a weight lift from her chest.

"Well, I'd better get home and fix the fine man some dinner. That chicken in the truck will be frozen solid if I don't get moving." She stood and set her teacup next to the sink. "It was good talking, Lyla, and thanks for the tea."

Lyla showed her to the door, where Brie climbed into her winter gear. A few moments later she was in the truck, heading for home.

*   *   *

As soon as Brie stepped through the door, she knew she wouldn't be cooking dinner. A savory aroma filled the downstairs, telling her that Jack or John or both of them were hard at it. Angus wiggled around her in the pocket-sized entryway, making it tricky to get her boots off.

"Okay, boy. Gimme a second and I'll pet you."

That made him wiggle even more. Brie extricated herself from the entry and gave him a proper rubbing behind the ears and on his sides and then padded out to the kitchen.

"Thought, since you were delayed, I'd cook dinner," Jack said. "It's chili."

"Thanks, Jack. That sounds great." She stowed the chicken and produce she'd bought in the fridge. "Where's John?"

"Upstairs, napping. Seemed pretty tuckered out. Said the seas were active out there today."

Brie nodded. "What can I do?"

"Salad?"

"Sure." Brie got out the lettuce and some random veggies lurking around the fridge and started in.

Jack had cut a leftover baguette in half. He melted some butter, brushed it on, and minced up some garlic.

"Why don't you go check on John."

"How long's he been out?"

"Maybe an hour."

Brie nodded and headed upstairs. She peeked into the bedroom. John was lying there, eyes open, staring at the ceiling.

"Hey, you." She went and lay down on her side next to him. "Did you sleep?"

"Yup."

"Jack cooked dinner."

"Great."

"Somethin' up?"

"We can talk over dinner."

She propped herself up on one elbow and looked at him. "You sure?"

"Yeah. How's your hand?"

"Good. Doc took the stitches out. Said I was a quick healer. Don't know about that." She thought about the bullet wound in her side. Though it was long since healed, it sometimes still troubled her. Scar tissue, maybe.

She leaned over and kissed him. "Shall we go down?"

He turned on his side, played with a long strand of her hair. "If we must."

Their eyes met in silence—kindling flame.

"I'm thinking I need to turn in early tonight," Brie said. "Long day, you know." A lazy smile played at the corners of her mouth.

He brushed the hair behind her back and trailed a strong hand slowly to the end of her spine, where it paused, achingly still, at the end of its long, sensuous journey.

Brie leaned in, resistance being futile.

"Should I put the bread in the oven?" Jack called up the stairs.

"On our way," Brie called. She rolled over and stood up. But a glance backward as she left the room said, *This isn't over.*

A few minutes later they gathered around the dining room table to eat. Over dinner, Brie told the guys about her fishing expedition with Doc Ward about drugs. "Trulie Hyden was right. The doc *is* hardcore. Said he won't give out painkillers, period. Said there's a drug problem on the island. He also mentioned the deaths of the lobstermen—wrote them off to those men working impaired, due to drugs. Now, as a doctor, trying to put a lid on opioid abuse, I can see why he would believe that."

Jack had gathered some info at the card game about the hauling out of the lobsterboats. "Turns out Lars Bjorklund is Marty's son-in-law," he said. "Apparently, in October, he hauls out all three of their boats—Marty's, Dale's and Biddy's."

"Huh," Brie said. "So, that could put all three of them out of the running for any involvement with the death that occurred last February—Paul Le Fevre's—and the one in November—Abe Winter's."

"Well, at least we know for sure that none of them used their own boats," Jack said. "Which might be cause to eliminate them from the suspect pool."

"On another front, I gave Lyla a ride home from the general store today. She invited me in for tea, and of course I accepted. Over tea, I told her I had learned of her son's death and that I was very sorry. Well, that got her talking about Oslo. She described how he, quote, 'watched over things.' Made him out to be a kind of patron saint of the island, but in reality, I think he was the island snoop—gathering information on anyone and everyone."

Brie paused a moment, trying to picture him hiding behind bushes and listening at cracked doors and windows. "To my mind, that behavior could have created a strong motive in someone here. Someone who had a plan to systematically eliminate certain individuals from the island for whatever his reasons may be."

"In other words, Oslo Stumph's idiosyncratic behavior—acting as the island's unofficial P.I.—could have jeopardized the killer's plans," John said.

"Exactly my thinking. Which is why he may have been the first to go." She looked from John to Jack. "Now, I know Bellsby had a motive to do away with him, but I'm hard-pressed to see why he would go after the others. Seems it would have worked against his goal to settle on the island for the profitable fishing.

"And there's more. Apparently Lyla Stumph is a friend of Abe Winter's mother, Marlis." Brie told them what Abe had revealed to his mother about knowing something that was going to translate into a lucrative revenue stream. "That was just a week before he disappeared from his boat."

"Sounds like blackmail," Jack said.

"Yup."

"That may fit with something Fin told me today," John said. "He told me Abe seemed off that last week or so before he disappeared. 'Scared' was the word he used."

"Maybe Winter realized that he was playing with fire," Jack said.

"But if he had stupidly confronted the killer, tried to blackmail him, it would have been too late." Brie sat back. "So, maybe Abe Winter's death is not related to dealing drugs, and maybe the reason Oslo Stumph died had nothing to do with cutting Bellsby's traps or cramping his Casanova style."

"It's possible that's true," Jack said. "But I don't think we can come to any conclusions until we learn more about the other two men—Paul Le Fevre and Cliff Gordon."

"You're right," Brie said. "But I am encouraged that the activities we've plugged ourselves into here—the card game, the Starkhaven Stitchers, and John's lobsterboat—are producing intel. And there's another connection I hope to work. Paul Le Fevre's neighbor, whom the Maine State Police interviewed shortly after Le Fevre died, is in the quilting group. You might remember her name from the case files—Clara Lyston. I'm hoping to somehow get her talking about Le Fevre."

"Your connection with the history center is a good one, too," Jack said. "Keep working that angle."

"I will. I'm getting more established there day by day. By the way, Jack, just a heads up. I think Mary may be planning to ask you to dinner. I only mention it so you won't be caught too off guard."

"Ah, love is in the air." John smiled.

"Knock it off," Jack said.

"Oh, all right." He sat forward, more serious now. "On another front, not to alarm anyone, but someone has been aboard my boat."

"What do you mean?" Brie asked, feeling her heart speed up and remembering the emotions that had appeared, unbidden, when she was with Lyla.

"When I got down to the harbor this morning, I could tell someone had been aboard the boat. Things were shifted around. I put stuff in the same place day to day—a habit I formed years ago at the boatyard, so I'm not always looking for my tools."

"Could it have been Fin?" Brie asked.

"No, I asked him this morning. He said he'd never go aboard my boat without permission."

"So, what do you think it's about?" Jack asked. "Some kind of warning, maybe? Or someone just trying to rattle you?"

"I have no idea," John said. "They've stopped cutting my traps, but maybe this is the next tactic to make me feel unwelcome. We'll see if it happens again."

"I guess I'd be concerned about someone tampering with the engine," Jack said.

"There was no evidence of that. Anyway, the engine compartment is locked when I'm not aboard."

John was silent for a moment, thinking. "Unless it was Trulie Hyden. He seems to be coming unstrung." He told Brie about Trulie's crazy maneuver on the water—passing dangerously close to his boat while overtaking.

She immediately thought about the set-to she'd had with him at the lobstermen's meeting. "Guy's a loose cannon. Was George aboard?" she asked.

"Oh, yeah. Hanging on for dear life and looking aghast at what was unfolding."

"Trulie's need for drugs could be causing all kinds of erratic behavior," Jack said.

"Fin thought the shenanigans on the water today were directed at him. And we know, from the argument George overheard, that Trulie's got some vendetta against Fin. Thinks he knows something about where to get drugs on the island. Even accused Fin of having something to do with Abe Winter's death. But Fin told me today that Doc Ward can vouch for the fact that he was sick the day Winter died. Said he'd gone to see the doc the previous day, when he came in off the water, running a fever and feeling terrible. The doc diagnosed a case of flu and told him to rest for a day or two. Fin said Doc Ward would have to have a record of that visit."

"If that's true, it could eliminate Fin from the suspect list," Brie said.

"So, all the suspects we had on the list—Fin, Alan Bellsby, and Dale Woodrow—have been scratched?" John looked downtrodden.

"That may be true," Brie said. "But eliminating suspects can be a good thing. Helps us narrow our focus."

"I agree," Jack said. "It's part of any promising investigation. Lets you know you're getting somewhere."

John didn't look convinced, but Brie added, "It's kind of like an archeological dig. You always find the small stuff before you unearth the big stuff. However, it's too early to eliminate anyone from the suspect list. I'm just saying that Oslo Stumph's snooping creates another motive for someone to have done away with him."

The three of them finished their dinner in silence. John's describing his boat being boarded had gotten Brie thinking about the footprints she'd found outside the house.

"I didn't mention this before, but maybe now is a good time," she said. "I was out with Angus in the yard one morning last week, and I found footprints in the snow under two of the windows on the east side of the house."

Now it was John's turn to look alarmed. "Why didn't you tell us about that?"

She recognized his captain's tone of voice. The one he used aboard ship when one of the crew had misstepped. "I suppose I didn't want to worry you."

"I'm afraid I have to side with John on this one," Jack said. "You should have told us about that immediately. We're playing a dangerous game here. We're undercover with a killer on the loose. We need to be one hundred percent transparent about anything we discover—about anything that happens to us. That's why we do these informal debriefings. To keep everyone up to speed on everything."

"I apologize," Brie said. "It won't happen again."

John's expression softened a bit. "Look, I know you may have had another reason for not telling me." He studied her for a moment. "Garrett Parker. Right?"

Brie shrugged. "I suppose."

"And just who the hell is Garrett Parker?"

"It's a long story, Jack. I'll fill you in later," Brie said.

John pushed his chair back. "So, if that's all, I think I'll hit the hay. Today was a tough one out there."

"You go on up. I'll help with the clean up."

"Thanks for dinner, Jack. It was great." John headed for the stairs.

Brie and Jack carried the dishes to the kitchen.

"We didn't tell him that this is where it starts to get dangerous," Jack said. "Right now, we're in the middle. The eye."

"John's weathered plenty of storms. I think he knows."

A little while later, she crawled into bed next to him, hoping to pick up where they'd left off earlier, but, alas, the gentle snoring from his side of the bed told her it was not to be. She lay there thinking about Trulie Hyden's erratic behavior on the water that could have endangered John's boat and George as well. It was time to pay a visit to Thorn. The drug scene on the island was spiraling out of control. Something had to be done, and since Mo Thorn had his hands in everything here, she decided it was time to get to the bottom of the situation.

She closed her eyes as a parade of facts and faces marched through her mind. She observed them all from a neutral vantage, knowing the big stuff was yet to come.

Chapter 19

Brie knew that every Wednesday Mo Thorn stayed in off the water and worked at the town office, taking care of island business. So, today was the day to visit him. She intended to rattle his cage, see if she could pry some information out of him. And though it wasn't their primary mission here, still, being a cop, she couldn't continue to overlook the drug problems on the island that were compromising lives and killing people. They had learned what had happened to Tom Woodrow, and Nathan Ross had nearly lost his stake on the island due to drugs. Biddy Firth had revealed that Abe Winter had been a user, and it was widely known that he had been the go-to guy for drugs on Starkhaven. And now, Trulie Hyden was right on the edge, displaying erratic behavior, making accusations toward Fin and acting crazy generally. She worried for George's safety, working stern every day aboard his boat.

So, after she'd finished writing her report to Dent Fenton, updating him on what they'd learned the past few days, she told Jack she was heading into town to talk to Thorn.

"Should we both go?" he asked.

"Might be better if it's just one of us. If he feels outnumbered, it could work against us."

"You're right," Jack said. "You go."

"You want me to drop you down at the card game?"

"Sure. May as well." He had finished his own report and closed his laptop. "You know, I've been thinking about how the poker game is a great metaphor for our operation here."

"Oh, yeah, how so?"

"Well, we have to be clever and strategic. Play our cards close to the vest—not give ourselves away with any tells. The truth is, though, in any undercover op, there's a huge element of luck and chance. But, if you play the game well enough and long enough, you're bound to come up a winner."

"I think we're playing it well enough," Brie said. "But I'm worried about the long enough. John hopes to be back on the mainland by mid-March. That gives us around seven more weeks to find the truth."

"All we can do is work the case," Jack said. "And have faith."

"It's no small part of the equation, is it?"

"Nope, and every detective knows that. You gotta believe."

Jack took Angus out to do his business, and then they bundled up and headed out to the truck.

Yesterday had brought a dusting of snow, but a heavy sky sulked over the island, threatening another bout of precipitation. Brie parked the truck across from the town office. Jack got out and headed for the general store, and she crossed the street and made her way up the walk to the town office. She pushed open the door and stepped inside. A still, gray light fell cheerless on the empty chairs. She removed her boots, not wanting to drag snow across the meeting room's polished wood floor, and made her way to the door of Thorn's office and knocked.

"Come in."

She stepped inside and noted that Mo Thorn hurriedly shoved something into his desk drawer when he saw it was her.

"Good morning, Mr. Thorn," she said, deciding to keep things formal. "Do you have a few minutes?"

He waved her over to his desk and gestured to the chair across from him.

"What can I do for you, Detective Beaumont? I suppose you're here to fill me in on this *investigation* you're running." The word rang with contempt. "Are you making progress?"

She sat down and squared her shoulders, preparing to do battle if necessary. "Some progress, but these things take time, and the fact of four victims complicates the investigation greatly."

"So, what *have* you learned?"

"Actually, any details about the operation need to stay confidential."

"I won't tell anyone."

"No, what I mean is that, during an investigation, no details can be revealed to anyone outside the police."

"So, it's a one-way street. I'm supposed to help you, but I don't get to know what's going on on *my* island."

"That's right. And by the way, is this *your* island?"

"You know what I mean."

"Here's what I know. Since you refer to this as *your* island, it's not hard to surmise that you are involved with the drug scene."

"Now, listen here . . ."

"No, you listen and listen well. We're here for a killer, but that doesn't mean I'm going to turn a blind eye to the fact that drugs are ruining lives out here."

"If you've done any digging, and I'm sure you have, then you know that Abe Winter was the drug guy here." His eyes went dark with warning.

"Sorry, I don't buy it. I think someone far more influential is behind the opioid scene here."

"And you think that's me. You do know that I could bring this operation of yours to a crashing halt any time I want, by revealing who you three really are."

"And I'm sure you know that running drugs is a felony."

"You have no proof of anything."

"No, but I could make it my business to get some." She matched his icy stare, degree for degree. "So, here's the deal. We'll agree to leave you here if you give up the name of the guy at the top—the guy who runs the drug operation in the Gulf of Maine. And you'd better hope it's not you. You'd better hope there's a bigger fish in this pond than you. You give up that person and agree to fund drug rehab for those in trouble here, and maybe you can avoid incarceration."

"You should be careful who you threaten."

"And you should remember you're talking to the law."

They seemed to have reached a stalemate, and for a few charged seconds, the two of them sat, eyes locked, possibly wondering which one would blink first. As it turned out, it was Thorn.

"Look," Brie said. "I'm going to ask you something. You've lived here your whole life. No one knows this island any better than you. Among the victims—the lobstermen who have died—is there any one of the deaths, looking back, that doesn't surprise you?"

Mo Thorn's answer came without hesitation.

"Cliff Gordon."

Brie started to say something, but Thorn cut her off. "I need to get back to my work, Detective. So, if you'll excuse me."

That translated to, *I'm done talking to you.*

Brie nodded. "Very well. I expect you will consider what we discussed."

Thorn didn't look up or acknowledge her remark in any way. She stood and showed herself out. At the front door she pulled on her boots and headed outside. She had agreed to leave the truck for Jack, so she started up the road toward home, happy for the walk. This was a complicated case, replete with intricacies and question marks, and outside, in the fresh air, the sky was literally the limit for her thoughts.

In response to her question about the victims, Thorn's choice of Cliff Gordon as the death that didn't surprise him had been immediate. Why? Was it because Gordon was an abusive husband who beat his wife? That could certainly give someone a compelling motive. Particularly someone related to Bess Gordon. Under her vigilante theory, Gordon could easily have been a target for a killer ridding the island of bad guys. She wasn't swayed one way or the other by Thorn's choice, but it did make her curious to learn more about Gordon. She decided she would do a little digging in the county records later tonight—look for a marriage license for the Gordons. See what Bess Gordon's maiden name was. See if it rang a bell—if maybe she had any family of origin here on Starkhaven.

It was time to learn more about both Gordon and Le Fevre. There were still plenty of missing pieces here, but the frame of the puzzle was assembled. The parameters of the case were in place, and Brie could feel herself working inward toward the heart. She knew that each investigation is a lot like a story unfolding, with the characters—the players—slowly revealing themselves. And truth is a funny thing. It likes the light. It wants to be seen.

*   *   *

Brie had plans to work at the history center in the afternoon. The temperature had warmed under the heavy atmosphere, so she decided she'd jog up the road to the center and back again when she was done. After taking Angus out for a quick romp around the house, she pulled on her running shoes and fleece jacket and headed out the door, down the long driveway, and then north along the road.

The snowpack on the road made for decent footing, if a bit slow. A few minutes later she reached the crest of the hill, where the road bent east. The ocean panorama spread out to the northwest, and she paused, as she always did at this spot, to take in the view. Under the overcast sky, the sea lay like a vast blanket of dark gray wool. As always, for Brie, the prospect of it brought a profound sense of peace. Where others might have felt isolation, standing here, looking out, she felt the thrill of the possible. The pull, the allure of the unknown had always beckoned to her. It was the reason she loved life aboard the *Maine Wind*. It was also the reason she had become a detective.

After a few moments, she turned from that long view and ran on, picking up her pace as the road flattened out. In a few minutes, she came to the history center and headed up the walk to the building. She stepped inside, removed her shoes and coat, and placed them to the left of the door where there was a coat rack. Faith Babcock heard the bell above the door and came down the stairs.

"Ah, Brie. I thought it might be you."

"Hi, Faith. How's it going?"

"Good. I'm working on a presentation I have to give next week at the school. I think I'll have you continue on the microfilming today. You seem to have the procedure down. Are you comfortable working by yourself?"

"Sure," Brie said. "We've had a couple of sessions together, so I think I know the ropes."

"Great. If any questions arise, I'm right next door."

Brie headed up the stairs to the room adjacent to Faith's office. It had been the smallest of the four bedrooms back when this had been the parsonage and was a perfect size for the microfilming process, which didn't require a lot of space. The other two rooms upstairs held the island archives, which consisted of copies of birth and death records as well as an extensive archive of photographs and letters—some dating back to the earliest days on the island—given to the center by island families.

Brie walked across the room to the back wall where a long table held the microfilm machine. An adjacent table was stacked with several piles of the *Starkhaven Signal*—the island newspaper from days gone by. The paper had been a bi-monthly publication—appearing every two weeks. But even so, over the six decades of its publication, that added up to a daunting number of newspapers that needed to be filmed. Working in her volunteer capacity, Faith had managed to document several decades of the newspapers over the past three years, and with Brie's help they were now working their way through the late 1980s.

Brie got started scanning the newspapers onto the microfilm. Here and there she would pause to read something that caught her interest. Short articles about people, usually young adults, leaving the island or returning home from school or military service. Articles about agriculture on the island or new technology being introduced to the lobster fishery.

Even though she'd only been at this work for a couple of weeks, she had already begun to understand the web-like nature of the island's population. The names, many of them already familiar to her, marched down through time in a steady but relentless stream of human history. A complicated pattern of interconnected relationships. Births, deaths, weddings, funerals. Everyone bound to everyone, like strands of fiber woven together, as island families intermarried over and over, so that virtually everyone here was related and had been for a very long time. She remembered Lyla's words. "Too much history."

She could see why Lars Bjorklund was eager to support new blood on the island—why he had welcomed the arrival of John and Brie and even Bellsby. The old ways of isolation—keeping newcomers at bay—had led to hundreds of years of inbreeding. The very name of this place, Starkhaven, attested to the island's history of isolation, so far from the mainland, brooded over by the power and pull of the sea in all of its moods. Lars was visionary enough to see that, without new blood, the island as a community could not survive. And now, malignancy in the form of a killer threatened to accelerate that eventuality. The close-knit fiber here had begun to unravel.

There was a knock on the door behind her.

"Brie, do you know it's after two-thirty?" Faith stood in the doorway, adjusting her blue-framed glasses.

"I must have gotten lost in the work." Brie checked her watch and, sure enough, over three hours had elapsed. "I've just got two pages left to scan of this paper. Should I finish it?"

"Sure, and then I need to close up."

Brie finished scanning the last couple pages of the newspaper she was working on, checking as she always did to be sure the pages appeared in miniaturized form on the microfilm. Then she turned off the equipment, tidied up the stack of newspapers she'd finished with, and flipped off the lights as she left the room. Faith was waiting for her downstairs. Brie pulled on her shoes and jacket and out they went with Faith locking up behind. They said goodbye and Brie headed down the walk.

She felt like stretching her legs after all that sitting, so instead of heading for home, she turned left and followed the road east along the spine of the island. She walked for a short ways to warm up her legs and then broke into a run. The sky was still gloomy as ever but as she ran, the smell of the spruce forest up here at the top of the island both calmed and invigorated her. Here and there a house peeked out of the forest, but largely, this was no-man's-land. She knew if she kept going the road would eventually bend south and meander down into the far end of the village.

She was deciding whether she'd run the whole loop when she saw a pickup approaching. The truck slowed as it got nearer, and she recognized the driver as Alan Bellsby. John had pointed him out one day when they were down in the village. Bellsby had stopped and greeted her twice before, once asking if she wanted a ride, which she had declined, but so far they had not exchanged names. He seemed to always pass by about the time she was heading home from the history center. Granted, it was the time of day when the lobstermen came in from the sea and, coincidentally, since John was one of them, the time she would be heading home from the history center. Still, she had begun to wonder if his timing was not just chance.

He stopped the truck next to her and ran down the window.

"Hello again."

"Greetings," Brie said.

"Nice day for a run, I guess?"

"Plenty warm enough," she said. "Can't let winter stop you."

"With that attitude, you'll do just fine here," Bellsby said.

"You think so?"

"Sure."

"Well, not everyone's been so welcoming."

"How about a ride back?" Bellsby asked.

Here was a golden opportunity to get a better sense of this guy that, so far, she'd only learned about indirectly. If she turned him down again, she might not get another chance, although, considering his reputation, she doubted he'd give up that easily.

"I was thinking of running the whole loop back to the house," she said. "But I guess I could do it another day."

Bellsby reached over and opened the door. "Climb in."

"Thanks." Brie climbed into the truck. It was quite warm inside and she pulled off her hat.

"You've got pretty hair," Bellsby said. "I don't think we've exchanged names. I'm Alan Bellsby."

"Brie Ross. But you already knew about the Ross part."

"Well, it's not too often we get someone new on the island. Word gets around, you know."

Bellsby had a laidback demeanor. Not exactly what Brie had expected. But maybe when you're that good looking you don't ever have to try too hard. He shifted the truck into gear, and they headed west along the road, retracing the route Brie had taken on her run.

Just past the history center, he said, "There's something I'd like to show you."

"What?" Brie asked.

"You'll see. It's something kind of cool."

Shortly after the road bent south, he slowed and turned right onto a narrow, gravel track. It was rutted, but passable. The road climbed, and they followed it for a ways as it carved through a tunnel of spruce that pressed in from both sides. After a few minutes of bumping slowly along in four-wheel-drive, they cleared the forest and came out on a high promontory overlooking the sea. It was a breathtaking panorama with the ocean all around them.

"Gorgeous," Brie said. But she was keenly aware of the isolation of the place and that she was here with a man she knew not at all. She felt his eyes on her but didn't turn to meet them.

"Look down there," he said after a moment or two.

She craned her neck in the direction he had nodded, and her gaze traveled down to the foot of the headland, to the shoreline that lay just north of them.

"What is that?"

"The remnants of what used to be a second settlement on the island a hundred and fifty years ago. Since you seem to like history, I thought you might like to see this place."

Brie got out of the truck and walked to the edge of the overlook and gazed downward.

Bones of old dories—the small, open boats that had originally been used to haul lobster pots, before the advent of the modern day lobsterboat—were abandoned along the shore. Skeletal stacks of wooden lobster traps rose in piles like hulking sentinels, and the gray ghosts of long-abandoned buildings, some missing roofs and windows but all listing precariously toward oblivion, still clung to the rocky shore. The remains of a bygone place and time on this remote and inhospitable corner of the island. The tide was coming in and the waves came ashore, caressing the old dories, beckoning them back to sea, promising a more appropriate watery grave.

She felt Bellsby step up behind her—a little too close for comfort. She moved back away from the edge of the precipice.

"They were so exposed to the sea here," she said. "Hardly any harbor. What would have made them think they could make it in such a place?"

"History has it that two of the dominant families on the island began feuding. It got so bad that one family decided to start their own town over here. Figured they could make it on the western side of the island since most of the wicked-bad weather comes in from the northeast."

"How long did this place survive?"

"Surprisingly, a number of generations. Eventually the feuding died down, and they all moved back to the other end of the island, life being easier over there."

Brie was surprised at Bellsby's knowledge of and interest in Starkhaven's history.

"How do you know about all of this?"

"Look, even though you haven't been here long, I'm sure you've heard the stories about me. That I just moved out here to profiteer because these are the richest lobstering grounds." He waited a beat for her to respond. When she didn't he continued. "Truth is I've wanted to live out here since I was a boy. Something about this place has always called to me."

"Didn't you know how unwelcoming they would be?"

"I did. I'd heard all the stories. But I wasn't going to let that stop me."

What she really wanted to ask was if he had married Sara, an islander, just to get a stake here. But she couldn't think of any non-incendiary way to phrase it. She was beginning to wonder if the stories about Bellsby's wandering eye were true or just some more island lore. Even if they were true, he certainly was different from what she had expected. Strange to say, but she sensed a loneliness about him.

They turned and walked back to the truck and climbed in. Once inside, though, the tone of things changed, and Brie wondered if his playing island history guide had just been a preamble to his real objective. He reached over and picked up a strand of long blond hair and let it slip slowly through his fingers.

"I'm married, you know," she said, turning to meet his look. She held up her left hand. "I happen to know you are too."

"That doesn't have to matter."

"It doesn't?"

"Not if only you and I know."

"Yeah, well, that's not how I roll." She studied his face. Being a cop, she felt confident in her ability to defend herself, but she didn't think it would come to that. She sensed no malice in him.

"Does it occur to you that this behavior of yours is what makes the islanders think you came out here just to take advantage?"

"Nobody knows about it."

"You can't really believe that. I think your wife knows. She's in my quilting group, and I have to say, she's been distinctly unfriendly. I've been told she's threatened by women who might catch your eye."

"You shouldn't believe everything you hear."

"If you knew me, you'd know I don't."

"Believe me, she wouldn't care."

"How can you say that? She's your wife."

"Let's just say we're pitching for different teams."

Brie took his meaning and nodded slowly. "But why would she marry you then?"

"Keeping up appearances."

"I can't believe anyone would care in this day and age."

"That's just the point. Out here, it's not *this day and age*."

"Did you know before you married her?"

"Of course not. Now, I know she isn't the most beautiful gal, but she's smart and funny. Really funny. I did love her."

"But now?"

"I don't know. Sara thinks it has worked out for both of us. She's got cover, and I've got my stake on the island."

"So, you're saying she doesn't care what you do."

"I haven't asked her, but I don't really think so."

"None of this makes sense."

"Actually it does. I'm her meal ticket. She inherited the house and lobster territory when her dad died. But with no one to work that territory, she has no income. There's not a lot of other industry on Starkhaven, in case you haven't noticed."

"But couldn't she have let out her territory to one of the other lobstermen?"

"It's possible, but except for a few sternmen who might want to break into the business, everyone else already has a territory and their hands full fishing it. And as for someone coming out from the mainland, the islanders would never accept that. What's more, it's not cheap getting into the trade— the boat, the gear, the license. It can take years to save up enough to get started. Not everyone's as lucky as you and your husband."

"I wouldn't call it luck. John is Nathan Ross's nephew. What's more, we had to pay off a lot of delinquent property taxes."

"Big deal. You ended up with a house, a boat, and a territory in the richest lobster fishing grounds in the world."

"Yeah, and you're not the only one who's unhappy about it. Someone's been cutting John's gear and going aboard his boat. That wouldn't be you, now, would it?"

"Of course not. After how I've been treated, I'd never do that. And I didn't say I was unhappy. It brought you to the island, didn't it?"

He slid a hand under her hair and along her neck. The hand was cold and she shivered.

"See, it's nice, isn't it?"

Brie removed his hand and placed it on the steering wheel. "We need to head back. I have to get home."

Bellsby didn't argue or press the issue, but started the truck and, after carefully maneuvering in a circle, headed back out the way they had come. At the main road he turned right, and they drove in silence. A few minutes later, he dropped her at the access road that led up to the Ross house.

As Brie climbed out of the truck, Bellsby said, "This isn't over, you know." The tone of his comment was neither teasing nor threatening but simply matter-of-fact.

Brie wished that she had that much confidence in the outcome of the case. She turned to face him. "I think you're wrong," was all she said.

She knew she was deceiving him. After all, she wasn't married, and she wasn't Brie Ross. But then again, she wasn't the one who had come looking for *him*. The cop in her was more interested in solving four murders and less interested in Bellsby's feelings. What was more, she wasn't about to burn any bridges that might help her navigate this case. So with that, she gave him a nod and closed the door. He didn't drive away immediately, and she could feel his eyes on her as she walked up the road toward the house.

*   *   *

Later that night, over dinner, Brie told John and Jack about her meeting with Thorn and how she'd laid down the law about the drug situation on the island.

"Toward the end of our meeting, I asked him a question. I asked him, of the four lobstermen who had died, if any of their deaths did not surprise him. His answer was immediate. Cliff Gordon."

"Did you ask him why?" John inquired.

"I started to, but he cut me off. Said he had to get back to his work."

"Which translates to, I've got the power—in this case, information—and I'm not about to share it with you." Jack sat back, disgusted.

"Well, I gave him an ultimatum about the drugs, so that was his counter play."

"Still, his immediate mention of Cliff Gordon tells us something."

"Yeah, it tells us he was the worst of the lot," John said. "But that's pretty obvious since he beat on his wife, don't you think?"

"Let's do a search of county records tomorrow, Jack. Locate a marriage license for Cliff and Bess Gordon. See what her maiden name was. Find out if she has any family of origin on the island. If she does, one of them would have had motive to do away with Cliff Gordon, considering the spousal abuse."

"We'll get on that first thing."

Brie also told them about her encounter with Bellsby and about the old settlement he had showed her up on the northwest side of the island. She noted that John looked dismayed and was willing to acquiesce to the fact that he may have had reason.

"So you got in his truck and allowed yourself to be driven to some godforsaken spot?" His voice had moved up a range.

"Look, John. This isn't an easy game out here. We're undercover, and as I see it, our only hope of gaining information is by interacting with the islanders."

"That's fine, but you still have this guy on your suspected killer list. Right?"

"That's true," was all Brie said.

"Did he come on to you? You told us what Lyla Stumph said about him hitting on the island women."

"I won't lie to you. He did come on to me. But I got no dangerous or malicious vibe from him."

"Was that before or after you went off into the middle of nowhere with him?"

Jack held up his arms in a timeout sign. "Let's just step back a bit here," he said. "First of all, John, you have to trust that Brie knows what she's doing and that, as a cop, she is always calculating risk. Also, I'm sure she has outstanding self-defense training. That right, Brie?"

"That's right."

"Secondly, there's no better way to get a gut sense of someone than to spend time with them. It's not something one can judge from afar."

John threw his hands up. "It's just . . . when does the danger ever stop?"

"It stops on the day she leaves law enforcement," Jack said. "Look, it's not easy being with someone who's a cop. If it were, their divorce rate wouldn't be through the roof. The person with that cop—spouse, partner, whatever—is daily relegated to territory that feels scary and helpless. It takes a special kind of person to bear up under that. I know. I was lucky enough to be married to that person for fifty years. The significant other has to trust in *their* cop's ability, and hand the rest over to God."

John lowered his head. "I get that. I've been trying to do that with every case she has worked on. I thought I'd get the hang of it, but it never seems to get easier."

"And, if you love that person, it never will," Jack said.

"You keep talking like that and you'll send John packing," Brie said. Now it was her turn to feel anxious.

Jack regarded him for a long moment. "Somehow, I don't think so."

Brie went on to tell them what Bellsby had said about his wife being gay.

"How did that come up?" Jack asked.

"I had leaned on him pretty hard for coming on to a married woman. That's when he told me his wife wouldn't care and why."

"Wow, that's kind of messed up," John said. "Why would she marry him?"

Brie related what Bellsby had told her. About wanting to come to this island since he was a boy. About what he had loved about Sara, and that he hadn't learned the truth about her sexual orientation until after they were married.

"So, he's caught between a rock and a hard place," Jack said. "He's finally on the island he loves, and he's got his lobstering territory, but at what cost?"

"I guess that might explain some of his behavior. Doesn't justify it, mind you, but may explain it," John said.

"Of course, that's his story. And until we get some confirmation, it's just a story."

She thought about Sara's hostile behavior at the quilting sessions, which didn't make a lot of sense if she was gay and didn't care who her husband took up with. On the other hand, maybe she saw Bellsby as part of her territory and was determined to guard that territory aggressively.

Jack drummed his fingers on the table. "You know, Bellsby's love for the island may be a reason to eliminate him as a suspect. My thinking—he wouldn't create that kind of chaos in a place he loves."

"Possibly not," Brie said. "On the other hand, though, his deepseated love for Starkhaven may have given him motive to clean the place up, vigilante-style. Since Oslo Stumph was Bellsby's chief persecutor, he would have been the obvious first choice for elimination. It'd be interesting to see how long Bellsby had been on the island before Stumph went missing from his boat."

"Fin should know when he came to the island," John said. "I'll see if I can find out."

"Or if I see Bellsby again, I'll ask him. Don't know why I didn't think about it today."

John leaned back and crossed his arms. "Too preoccupied with his good looks?"

Brie gave him the stink eye.

"Sorry. Kidding."

As they cleared the table, John told them that Fin had been in one of his black moods all day. "I'll tell you, for a guy in love, he sure seems to struggle with happiness."

"Maybe that's why," Brie said. "Maybe he can't see a path to his future with Isa Firth. Maybe you should talk to him, being older and wiser." She gave him a wink.

"Don't know about the wiser part," John said. "But maybe I'll give it a try. It's hard seeing him moping around. Working stern is hard enough without whatever else is weighing him down."

Brie could see how tired John was and sent him up to bed, telling him that she and Jack would clean up and close up the house. He just nodded and headed out of the kitchen. But later on when she crawled in next to him, he was still awake, and since he was, she got busy and showed him just how much he didn't have to worry about Bellsby.

Chapter 20

A lurid shade of red stained the eastern sky as the winter sun finally crept above the horizon. An oily sea rose and fell in ominous gray swells that portended mayhem down the line. The silver lining was the temperature that had languished in the forties the past few days and had the makings of a January thaw.

Out on the water, John and Fin had been hard at it for several hours before dawn broke. John was hoping to get done early, before the wind and seas started to build. They'd just finished a set of traps, and he idled the boat and called Fin into the house for coffee and sandwiches. When you start work at four a.m., you're ready for lunch about the time normal people are having breakfast.

Fin came into the house and perched on the stool in the corner. For three days he'd barely spoken a word, barely made eye contact with John. Clearly something was going on, and while John's main goal was to clear the traps and get off the water before the weather moved in, he needed to find out what was bugging Fin. While Fin had a girl, and lived with his aunt, what seemed to be lacking was a male influence in his life.

John handed him a mug of coffee and half a sandwich. "So what's going on, Fin? And don't tell me nothing, 'cause I'm not blind."

Fin shrugged and finished his sandwich in two bites. He swigged his coffee and stared down at the sole.

The boat rose and fell, and John spread his feet for balance, a stance he felt like he'd been born to after so many years at sea. "Look, anything you tell me stays right here, between the two of us. So, it's safe to talk."

"Won't help," Fin mumbled.

"That's pretty categorical for a guy who leads a kind of nomadic life."

"I hate my life. It's a dead-end."

"How can you say that? You've got a great girl. I know you love her."

Fin finally looked him in the eye. "That's just it. I want to make a good life for her. For us."

"And you don't think this is the way to do it?"

"Don't know." Fin's gaze returned to the sole.

"What's really bothering you, Fin? Because something has changed in the past week. If you tell me, maybe I can help."

"Someone's pressuring me to do something I don't want to do."

"If you don't want to do it, then what's the problem?"

"It's not that easy. It could mean money for me and Isa."

John leaned back against the side of the house. "Is it your family? Do they want you to leave your island existence? Do something else?"

"No, that's not it at all."

"How old are you, Fin?"

"I'll be twenty-two in a few months."

John nodded. "Here's what I know. If you don't hold true to your moral compass, if you decide to do something that goes against the grain, you'll never find happiness. Because you'll always be trying to get back to the man you were before."

Fin nodded, and John got the feeling he'd hit on something that made sense to him, so he decided to take a chance.

"Does this have anything to do with what your former boss, Abe Winter, was involved in? Does this have something to do with drugs?"

Fin sat silent, but it was a heavy silence, and John could see him struggling with the weight of it. Finally he spoke. "Let's just say that someone has offered to set me up with a territory if I take over where Abe left off."

John was dumbstruck at what he was hearing. "Are you at all aware that Abe Winter's activities may have gotten him killed?" He tried to keep his voice level, keep the mounting anger he felt under wraps. "Are you also aware that that would be the quickest way to lose your girl forever? You wouldn't have to wait for a killer to strike. Isa's grandmother would have your head on a plate."

Fin smiled—the first sign of hope John had seen in days.

"Look, Fin, who's pressuring you to do this? Give me a name, and I'll go to bat for you."

"I'm not gonna do that. It wouldn't be good for you or me. There are some people you don't mess with. After you're here for a while, you'll learn that."

"Look, Fin, don't do anything stupid. I have a feeling things will change for you."

"Really? How?" Fin's anger flared.

"Let's just say opportunities can arise." John was thinking about the fact that if Brie and Jack solved the case, they would be leaving the island, which could leave an opportunity for someone here.

Fin regarded him with a curious expression but didn't say anything.

John looked through the windshield. The wind was picking up. "We gotta finish up. Storm's coming in."

Fin nodded, and John put the boat in gear and headed for the next bunch of traps.

*　　　*　　　*

After breakfast, Brie and Jack sat down at their laptops to write their reports to Dent Fenton and also to begin a search of the county records. While they had learned a fair amount about victims one and four, Oslo Stumph and Abe Winter, it was time to focus on the other two men who had died, starting with Cliff Gordon. Brie had *him* in her sights because the abuse of his wife, Bess Gordon, created an obvious motive for someone to target him. By searching the public records, she and Jack hoped to learn if Bess had family here on the island, and if not here, then where?

Within forty-five minutes, they had completed their reports, detailing what they had learned in recent days, including the possibility that Abe Winter had stumbled onto the identity of the killer and decided to blackmail him. Once they had sent their reports off to Dent, each containing their own thoughts on the case and also including potential next steps they might take, they moved on to the county records.

They started their search with marriage licenses and certificates under the name of Clifford Gordon. If they could locate the marriage license, it would show Bess Gordon's maiden name. And locating the marriage certificate would show where the couple had been married, which could be an indication of where her relatives might be. They first searched the Knox County records, since Starkhaven Island was in Knox County. No luck. So they moved on to the neighboring counties of Lincoln and Waldo and found that the marriage license had been filed for in Waldo County. The license contained Bess Gordon's maiden name of Stafford. They also found the marriage certificate, which recorded that the couple had been married in the city of Belfast, in Waldo County, Maine.

"So we can assume that her family of origin may have been from Belfast, Maine," Jack said.

A check of birth records confirmed that Bess Stafford's parents had indeed lived in Belfast.

"It's not impossible that someone from the mainland could have killed Gordon," Jack said. "But it does seem unlikely, especially considering that there's a pattern to how these men died, and that pattern seems to point strongly to someone here committing the crimes."

"I agree," Brie said. "If Bess Gordon had been born here, had family here, the likelihood of one of her relatives being the perpetrator would be greatly increased. But as it is, I still think we're looking for someone who lives on the island. Particularly because two of the deaths were during cold months with more treacherous seas. No, I think the answers are here. We just need to keep digging.

"As to Paul Le Fevre, his neighbor, listed in the case file, is in my quilting group. Her name is Clara Lyston."

"Yes, I recall the name from the case file."

"I'm hoping to get better acquainted with her, see if I can get her talking, as I did with Lyla Stumph. It's just gonna take time."

"I think we're making good progress considering it's only been two weeks," Jack said.

They made a few notes in their respective notebooks and then Brie told Jack she was heading up to the history center.

"I think I'll get Angus out for a walk. Maybe saunter down to the village. Need anything from the general store?"

"Well, there's no plan for dinner yet."

"I'll surprise you," Jack said.

"Great."

Brie shut down her laptop and in a few minutes she was out the door heading up the hill. She'd gotten in the habit of walking to the center, which gave her a bit of exercise and time to think, out in the fresh air.

*   *   *

An hour after Brie arrived at the history center, Faith Babcock stuck her head into the microfilming room and told Brie she was heading over to the school to give her presentation.

"I should be back in about an hour and a half," she said. "Can you hold down the fort?"

"No problem," Brie said.

Ten minutes after Faith left, she got up and headed across the hall and into the room where the copies of the island birth and death records were filed. She went to the drawer that held surnames starting with the letter "S." She wanted to know if the name Stafford would show up at all in the island records. See if Bess Gordon's family of origin might have any connection to the island. But she came up empty. Not a Stafford to be found as far back as the records went.

She tried to think if there was anything else she should look up while she had the opportunity but couldn't come up with anything. She already knew from poring over the old newspapers that the names of all the victims—Stumph, Le Fevre, Gordon, and Winter—went back for generations here on Starkhaven. She went back to her work in the other room, and by the time Faith returned, it was nearly time to lock up. Brie finished the newspaper she was microfilming and shut down the equipment for the day.

Outside, she looked left and right, half expecting to see Bellsby's truck somewhere down the road. She turned and started for home.

The wind had really picked up since she'd left the house that morning. Even with the forest to the north, up here on the spine of the island she felt the bite of a nor'easter making up. *She's a-gonna blow.* The familiar refrain of the coastal Mainer played in her head like a dissonant little melody. She zipped her coat up all the way to keep the wind off her neck and picked up her pace.

As she came further along the road, she glimpsed movement off to her right in the woods. She stopped and looked carefully into the forest, eyes peeled for any sign of disturbance. She stood for a minute, letting her eyes adjust to the shadow of the woods. Suddenly she saw what had caught her eye. It was Hughie Bryce, the boy she had met at the clinic with his mom when she'd had her stitches removed. He was wearing snow gear that so mimicked the color of the forest, had it not been for his movement, he would have remained completely camouflaged.

At first she was concerned to see him there by himself, but as she observed him, she realized that he was intent on something up high in one of the spruce trees. He stood frozen for a moment and then ever so slowly lifted a small pair of binoculars that hung from his neck. His movements showed a studied concentration, a practiced stillness. Brie stood transfixed, observing the observer. At a point he must have sensed her presence because he turned, almost in slow motion, and saw her. She smiled and waved but didn't call out, so as not to startle whatever he was observing.

After a moment he motioned her to come, holding a finger to his lips to caution her to be quiet. Brie left the road and crept on silent feet into the forest and slowly, carefully up to where Hughie stood. His blue eyes glowed with the light of discovery, and he slowly raised an arm and pointed up into a nearby tree. Brie followed his arm and after a moment had to suppress a gasp of wonder. A large snowy owl was perched in the tall spruce, about a third of the way down from the top. Hughie, ever so carefully, took his binoculars from around his neck and handed them to her so she could see the raptor close up.

After a short period of observation, she carefully handed the glasses back to him, nodding and letting her eyes say thank you. He returned to studying the owl through the glasses, as if he might be memorizing every detail of its appearance. Eventually, as if it had lost patience with its perch being observed—because Brie had no doubt the white owl was duly aware of their presence—it took flight, and they watched it wing ghost-like up over the trees and soar in a graceful arc away to the southwest.

Brie motioned toward the road and Hughie nodded. She felt as if they had thoroughly bonded over the sighting of the snowy owl, but she also felt a level of concern about finding him all by himself in the forest. From observing him at the clinic, she suspected he might be autistic. When they came out on the road, she turned to him.

"Do you remember me, Hughie? I'm Brie. We met the other day." She didn't mention the where, as he had been agitated that day, and she didn't want to recall a negative memory.

He nodded. "Hooey," he said, giving his customized pronunciation of his name.

She looked back toward the forest where they'd been. "That was amazing, Hughie. I've never seen a snowy owl."

He beamed with pride.

"Can I walk home with you?"

Hughie nodded and pointed west along the road.

"You lead the way, and I'll follow."

He set off at a rapid pace as if on a mission to show her where he lived. A half mile down the road, beyond where it had bent south, Hughie headed down a road to the right or west that ran out toward the sea.

The road climbed and in a few minutes they came in sight of the house. It was a small, white Cape Cod, so common on the coast and islands here. But while the house was humble, the view over the sea was unparalleled. There was a wide lawn around the house and forest to the north and south, so while Brie had glimpsed other houses off in both directions, Hughie's house, tucked in between swaths of forest, was quite secluded.

Annette Bryce, Hughie's mom, must have seen them approaching because the front door opened and she stepped out. Hughie raced past her without a word, and Brie could see him beyond the door, peeling off his winter gear.

"Hi, Annette. We met the other day at the doctor's office. I'm Brie Ross."

"I remember you, Brie. Would you like to come in? Have some coffee or tea?"

"I'd love to, if I'm not intruding."

Annette waved that off and showed Brie in the door. She took off her shoes and hung her coat on the coat rack in the entry.

"I was coming from the history center and spotted Hughie off in the woods. I guess I was a bit concerned, so I stopped and waved to him."

"Oh, he's fine off on his own. He loves to go bird watching, and I try to give him as much freedom as I can. He has autism, as you may have guessed, but he's pretty high functioning. Everyone on the island knows him—watches out for him. It's pretty hard to get lost on an island. What's more, he knows Starkhaven like the back of his hand."

The inside layout of Annette's house was identical to Brie and John's place. The stairway ascended from the small central hall, while off to the right, the living room ran the length of the house, with windows at the back that looked toward the sea. The dining room lay to the left with the kitchen beyond. The walls were painted a soft cream color and the wide pine floor had aged to a cinnamon brown. Hughie sat at the far end of the dining room table, a large sketch pad in front of him, an array of pencils scattered about. Daylight poured through the window behind him as he worked with rapt attention, seemingly oblivious to their presence.

Brie and Annette passed through the room and into the kitchen. "I have coffee or I could make tea," Annette said.

"Coffee would be great."

Annette got down two mugs and poured out coffee. She set out a plate of oatmeal cookies, and they sat down at the table at the back of the kitchen, next to windows that overlooked the sea. Brie wondered about Annette and Hughie's situation here, whether there was a father and husband. But it seemed intrusive to ask.

"Hughie waved me into the woods where he was today and showed me a beautiful snowy owl. I've never seen one in the wild. It was amazing."

"Hughie is enthralled with the birds. We live in the right place for it, too. Being an island, we get the seabirds but also birds that nest on land, in the woods. There's a rich diversity here."

"Is that what he's drawing right now?"

Annette nodded. "He's quite the artist. It's a gift that some autistic children have around art or music. It brings me great happiness to know he has that gift. It fills his life."

Brie nodded. "I don't know if I've ever seen greater intensity of focus than the way Hughie studied the owl today through his binoculars."

They sipped their coffee and stared out at the sea.

"Looks like we're in for a blow," Brie said.

Annette nodded. "The winters out here are long and sometimes unforgiving." She studied Brie. "How are you and your husband settling in?"

"All right, so far," Brie said. "It's not the easiest time to break into a new life."

Annette nodded. "I heard about them cutting your husband's traps."

"It was tough at the beginning, but things are improving. John is the kind of guy who just presses on. And he's got a good sternman. That's been a big help."

"Who's his sternman?"

"Jim Finrude."

"Ah, Fin. He's a good kid. He was Abe Winter's sternman."

As if she'd ventured into forbidden territory, Annette Bryce became suddenly silent and stared out the window. Brie waited a bit to see if she might elaborate, but Annette seemed suddenly uncomfortable.

"Do you think Hughie might let me see his drawing?" she asked, trying to return to safe ground.

Annette looked back at her. "He might. Sometimes he lets me see his drawings and sometimes not. I never press him, though."

"Of course not," Brie said. "Do you think he's more satisfied with some than others? Is that why he may not let you see them?"

"I really don't know," Annette said. "To me they are all amazing. But that *could* be a reason. Anyway, you can ask him. He may let you see it. Especially since you shared the experience with him."

They talked for a while longer. Brie told her about the quilting group she'd joined and how it was helping her get to know some of the island women. Annette asked about her grandfather, aka Jack Le Beau. Brie told her he'd joined the card game at the general store and that he'd found a friend in Mary Geary. But she could tell it was time to get going, as talk was beginning to dwindle.

"I should be heading home. Thank you for the coffee, Annette."

"And thank you for paying attention to Hughie. So many people marginalize him."

"He seems like a wonderful boy." Brie stood and took her mug over to the counter. "I'll see if he'll let me take a peek."

She walked into the dining room with Annette behind her.

"Thank you for showing me the owl today, Hughie. I've never seen a snowy owl. Is that what you are drawing?"

He gave a slight nod.

"Do you mind if I look at your drawing?"

To Brie's surprise, Hughie slid the sketch book toward her. She stood for a minute, awed by his ability. He had almost photographically captured the snowy owl in the tree where they had observed it. On the page opposite he had started another drawing of the owl in flight as it had winged southwest away from them.

"These are amazing, Hughie. Thank you for letting me see them. You are a great artist." She slid the sketchbook back to him. "I have to go now, but I really enjoyed seeing you again and getting to see your house."

Hughie didn't respond, once again absorbed in his sketching. Annette walked her to the door and showed her out. Brie headed back down the road that gave access to the Bryce home and soon turned onto the main road. The northeast wind pushed hard against her propelling her along at a faster than usual pace. The temperature had dropped, and the first harbinger flakes of snow whipped around in the gusty wind. She reached the long access road and started up toward the house, eager for the shelter of home. Up ahead, John's truck was parked by the outbuilding. She felt the same relief she did every day, knowing he was in off the sea and safe.

*   *   *

John had brought home lobsters for dinner. They boiled them up in water with some seaweed, and Brie roasted some potatoes and broccoli to go along with, and the three of them sat down and shared a feast. Lobster for dinner was one of the perks of this job, and they ate it a couple of times a week.

Over dinner, Jack explained what they had found in the Waldo County records and that Cliff Gordon's wife appeared to be an off islander who had grown up in Belfast, Maine. Brie related that she had checked the island birth and death records for the name Stafford—Bess Gordon's maiden name—and had come up empty, leading them to believe that Bess was a transplant to the island.

She also told them about her encounter with Hughie and about observing the snowy owl. "I walked home with him afterwards, and though I'd met his mother briefly at Doc Ward's office, it gave me a chance to make a better connection with her and with Hughie too, for that matter."

"Not to use a poker metaphor, but we have to see every connection we make here as a chip in the pot that may pay off." Jack helped himself to a few more potatoes.

"Well, since you started it, there's no doubt this is a high-stakes game we're in," Brie said. "If we don't win it, I'm afraid this island may not see peace for a very long time. Fear and distrust are highly corrosive elements. The lack of resolution around these deaths has the power to tear apart the fabric of life here." She stared out at the complete darkness the storm had ushered in.

John reached over and took her hand. "We're doing everything we can."

She turned back to face him. "I hope we are."

He went on to relate the conversation he'd had with Fin about what had been troubling him lately.

"At first he'd say nothing, but finally he admitted that someone was pressuring him to do something he didn't want to do. After eliminating a number of possibilities, I asked him if it had anything to do with Abe Winter and what he'd been involved in. That's when Fin revealed that someone was trying to get him to take over for Abe Winter distributing drugs."

"Thorn?" Brie asked, anger simmering in her voice.

"He wouldn't give me a name. Said it wouldn't be good for him or me. But whoever it is is offering that boy things that are really hard for him to refuse. He desperately wants to make a good life for himself and Isa, so after some more prodding, he revealed that he had been promised a territory out here if he took over Abe's operation."

"Damn. I warned Mo Thorn just yesterday."

"Well, Fin's been in a funk for days, so I'd say all this unfolded before you confronted Thorn."

"Still, I get the sense that nothing I say is likely to stop that man. Did you talk some sense into Fin?" Brie asked.

"I tried. Told him that would be the quickest way to lose his girl."

"Did he listen?" Jack asked.

"I think he did. I mean, we know from the confrontation he had with Trulie Hyden outside the pub—the one George overheard—that he hates the idea of drugs. I was shocked he'd even consider such a thing, but like I said, he's desperate to provide a good life for Isa."

"I hope you impressed on him that that was the wrong way to do it."

"I did. And I'll keep at it. He's a good kid. I have to believe he'll make the right choice. And by the way, I asked Fin how long Bellsby has been living on the island. He said about two and a half years."

Brie nodded, thinking about the timeline of the deaths.

"We should try to round up George. See if he's got anything new for us," Jack said.

"If he did, I think he'd let us know," Brie said.

John stood up from the table and stretched his back. "We're in for a blow, so I probably won't be going out on the water tomorrow. If you've got anything for me to do around here, let me know; otherwise, I plan to sleep in and catch up on some reading."

"That sounds perfect. We're in," Brie said, happy to end the evening on a good note. "Jack brought some nice meat and vegetables from the store today, so tomorrow will be a perfect day for a big pot of savory beef stew and dumplings."

They cleaned up from dinner and headed upstairs shortly afterwards. When days start well before dawn, they need to end shortly after sunset. John was out almost before he hit the pillow. Brie had brought a book about birds upstairs that she had found on one of the bookshelves in the living room. She wanted to look through if to decide it Hughie might like it. Maybe she would visit him some day and bring him the book.

She had found a section about owls and in it a picture of a snowy owl. Its yellow eyes stared back at her from the page as if it could peer into her soul. The bird that she and Hughie had seen today was pure white, but the one pictured here had black bars on its plumage. Below she read that these were the markings of the female. The species is native to the arctic but sometimes winters in the northernmost reaches of the United States. She also learned that while owls are nocturnal hunters, the snowy owl is diurnal, meaning it hunts both day and night, this behavior being due to the fact that during the arctic summer daylight prevails 24 hours a day.

Brie closed the book, turned off her reading light and sat listening to the wind. Outside, the nor'easter held Starkhaven in its icy grip. Wind howled around the eaves of the house, and in the distance Brie could hear the roar of the sea. The wildness of it thrilled her. Some untamed part of her resonated with those raging elements. The sea was nothing to be trifled with, but to fall under its spell, to feel and witness its power as she had aboard *Maine Wind* was to be forever changed, as if some layer of banality, triviality, superficiality—call it what you may—had been forever scrubbed away and what remained was the core —simple, real, true.

Finally, lost in her thoughts of the sea and *Maine Wind*, she drifted off to sleep.

White hot lightning spears the sea, illuminating an unfathomable darkness that surrounds her. Brie struggles to keep her head above the surface as huge seas roll over her and thunder reverberates like a tremendous drum of doom. The great atmospheric flashbulb fires again, and she sees the knife wound on her hand has opened. Blood oozes from the wound drop by drop, and now she sees it also flows from her side, from the bullet she took nearly two years ago.

In the next strobe of light, she sees the island—Starkhaven Island. It seems impossibly far away. She sees a cliff. She knows the place. It is where she looked down on the old settlement. Hughie stands at the cliff's edge, and she is surprised she can see him from such a distance. He has a large white owl on his arm, as if he were a falconer of old. He sends the owl out over the troubled sea. It is nothing like the great golden eagle she'd dreamt of while in northern Minnesota last October. Yet there is a gravitas about the owl, with its majestic wingspan, as it soars like a white ghost above her. She has read about the significance of certain animals to the Native Americans and knows that owls symbolize death. And now the raptor circles above her, and she wonders if it portends her own death in this storm-swept watery grave. The white owl circles down, down in a great spiral. It lifts her from the water and wings away, not toward the island but out to sea. She struggles to be free and suddenly she is falling, falling through the darkness from a great height.

Brie woke with a start as if dropped from a high place. The dream hovered around her like a spectral presence. She felt for a small notepad she'd placed in the drawer next to the bed and in the darkness jotted a list of images from the dream before they could evaporate.

She got up and went into the bathroom for a drink of water. Back in bed, she lay thinking about the dream. Was it somehow a metaphor for the case? Was she floundering in a sea of victims, suspects, and motives? But what of Hughie and the white owl? And why were her wounds bleeding? Maybe the dream could be simply explained by the fact that she had been with Hughie today, had seen the owl, and that a storm was raging outside.

She thought about the symbolic dreams she'd had since being shot and nearly dying. Dreams that had sometimes led her to answers in cases she had worked. Dreams like she had never experienced before that time. She remembered the talk she had had with elder Joseph Renard while staying with him on the tribal lands of the Anishinaabe in Grand Portage, Minnesota, last fall. She thought about his words. *When you were shot, you hung between life and death. Between the two worlds. You would have drawn very near the spirit world. It is possible you brought back the gift of seeing when you returned. It is a great gift. One that can guide and also protect you.*

She decided not to make any judgments about the dream but to hold it close to her heart, as she did the small medicine bundle that Joseph and Claude Renard had given her when she had left Grand Portage for the last time. Her hand went to the small deerskin pouch she had worn since then, and in a few minutes she drifted into a peaceful, dreamless sleep.

Chapter 21

B y the next morning, the islanders were reminded that winter was not yet finished with them. A fresh, deep blanket of snow whitewashed the island, and one look out the window at the sea told any sane lobsterman that Mother Nature had granted him a day off.

As soon as daylight broke, the air hummed with the sound of snow blowers and industrious islanders pushing snow rather than pulling lobsters. Flurries continued to drift down sporadically throughout the day, but unlike most nor'easters that entrench themselves, delivering days of misery, this one had weakened by mid-afternoon. Or more to the point, a cold air mass, pushing down from the arctic, had sent it packing.

Brie and Jack put together a big pot of stew that simmered throughout the afternoon, filling the house with amazing aromas. After grappling with the snow, John affixed himself to an easy chair in the living room with his book and spent the day alternately reading and napping. Brie built a fire in the fireplace, and she and Jack got their books and hunkered down as well. No one mentioned the case, so as not to break that fragile spell of domestic bliss. Throughout the day, pieces of the dream from the night before drifted in and out of Brie's consciousness. She merely observed them, as one might observe a bird that alights and then is gone, but did not try to engage with them in any way.

Just after darkness set in, there was a knock on the back door. Brie opened it to find George there, cradling a bag of groceries. As soon as he stepped inside, he sniffed the air and knew they wouldn't be needed.

"I'd better be careful or you'll have my job aboard *Maine Wind*," he joked.

"That'll never happen, George. I need to be topside where I can smell the sea."

"So, where are the guys?"

"Sound asleep in the living room."

"Want to play cribbage?"

"Sure," Brie said.

"Before that, though, I brought some stuff to make bread pudding. I had some stale bread, perfect for the job."

He tucked the chicken he'd brought into the fridge for the next day and took two apples, raisins, cinnamon and vanilla, milk, eggs, and half a loaf of crusty bread out of his bag. Brie got out butter and sugar, and they went to work. Within fifteen minutes they slipped the baking dish into a 350-degree oven and sat down to a game of cribbage and mugs of hot coffee.

Brie asked him if anything notable had happened in the past week since she'd seen him.

"Really nothing much to report. Trulie Hyden continues to act truly crazy at times. I think he's in withdrawal from the drugs, but I'm not a doctor, so I couldn't say for sure. Too bad he won't visit the doc, as Fin suggested that day they argued. Maybe the doctor could give him something to help the symptoms."

"You could suggest it again," Brie said.

"Oh, no. No way. I have to work with the guy out in the middle of the ocean on a pitching boat. If I fall in some day, I wanna be sure he'll fish me out. I don't plan to get on his bad side."

It was the first time Brie had a window into George's true feelings about the danger of their operation. "Well, you should follow your instincts," was all she said.

George nodded and took a swallow of his coffee. "Most nights I hang out at the Stern Man. Observe who's there, who's hanging out with who. When Fin's there, he'll usually join me."

"So, have you learned anything from your observations?"

"Well, one thing I've noticed is that Lars Bjorklund and Alan Bellsby seem to be pretty tight."

"Really? That's interesting. I'll have to mention that to John, see if he has any thoughts on it. Bjorklund's wife, Jana, is in the quilting group. I've talked to her there and told her it was great that Lars stuck up for John at the Lobstermen's Association meeting. She told me Lars believes they need to bring new blood to the island. That could be why he's befriended Bellsby."

"But I think Bellsby's been here a couple of years, at least."

"Believe me, that's new for out here," Brie said. "Any other interesting tidbits?"

"Well, Kieran McTavish, the barkeep, is also pretty friendly with those guys."

"Isn't that the job of the barkeep?"

"I guess. But he seems to have a special connection with those two. He's got a boat, too. Don't know why that surprised me. I guess just about every man on the island has one."

"How do you know that? That he has a boat, I mean?"

"Saw him coming into the harbor one day as Trulie and I were mooring the boat. As we were finishing up, McTavish loaded a crate of lobsters into his dory and rowed ashore."

"Huh, interesting," Brie said. "Maybe he was out catching his dinner. Must have a few traps out there somewhere."

Within forty minutes the sweet aroma of apples and cinnamon issuing from the oven brought the guys out to the kitchen.

"Well, George! I should have known that wonderful smell had your stamp on it."

"Hey," Brie said. "Jack and I have been doing just fine."

"That's right," George said, coming to her defense. "I smelled some world-class stew as soon as I came through the door."

John held up his hands in surrender. They got the table set in the dining room. Brie put a loaf of French bread in the oven to warm, and George took the bread pudding out to cool.

They all gathered around the table, and Brie lit a candle against the darkness of the January night, and they did one of the most comforting things humans can do on a cold winter night. They shared a delicious hot meal, laughter, and conversation.

They made it an early night since John and George both had to be out hauling early the next morning. So, after the bread pudding—yes, as expected, it was mouthwateringly scrumptious—John drove George back to the edge of the village while Brie and Jack cleaned up.

Later, Brie lay awake in bed, wondering if she might be visited by another dream. Details of the case ran haphazardly through her mind. The thought of the calendar turning to February in three days was disquieting. She thought about Paul Le Fevre, the lobsterman who had disappeared from his boat last February. The thought of his death in that frigid water set her heart racing in a kind of vicarious horror. She turned over and studied John in the near darkness, willing him to stay safe out there. Then she tried some deep breathing to calm her troubled mind and finally fell into a restless sleep.

Chapter 22

John waited on the wharf for Fin. The thermometer outside the door this morning had read ten degrees. As he waited, gloved hands under his armpits, he hunched his shoulders up and down and stomped his feet against the cold. He waited there another fifteen minutes, but at 4:10 a.m. he climbed down into his peapod, freed the docking line, and pushed off. As he rowed for his boat, he passed Mo Thorn's lobsterboat. Mo had just started his engine and was preparing to head out.

"Where's your sternman?" Thorn called over.

"Don't know. Didn't show up today," John called back.

Thorn just nodded and steered his boat slowly among the others, threading his way toward the mouth of the harbor, where he headed west.

John climbed aboard his boat, went forward and tied off his peapod. Inside the house he stowed his lunch and coffee and turned over the engine, which was reluctant to come to life on this frosty morning. Outside the harbor, sea smoke rose off the ocean, mysteriously cloaking all that lay beyond. John turned on the heater in the house and after letting the engine warm up for a few minutes and watching the wharf in case Fin showed up, he released his mooring buoy and motored slowly toward the mouth of the harbor.

Outside the harbor John entered a mysterious realm. Sea smoke boiled off the surface of the ocean to such an extent that by the time he had motored a hundred yards beyond the mouth of the harbor, the island and its surrounding waters completely disappeared, as if a great cloak of invisibility had been cast over all of it. He throttled back his engine, ghosting over the still water at two knots and sounding his fog horn with one pro-longed blast once every one to two minutes—the signal for a power-driven vessel that is underway.

*   *   *

Brie woke to the same dread that had pursued her into sleep. It was still dark outside, and she felt for John, hoping he might still be there, but the bed was cold. In the early days of their being here, she had gotten up every morning to see him off, until finally he'd told her she needed to sleep and not to worry about him. He could easily make sandwiches and coffee, or if feeling lazy, pick up soup and sandwiches at the general store before heading out on the water.

She tried to go back to sleep but soon realized that it was hopeless, so she got up and went downstairs to the kitchen. John had left hot coffee in the carafe. She poured out a cup and headed into the living room to watch the sunrise through the east-facing windows. Angus lumbered in from the kitchen, lay down and rested his giant head on her leg. She stroked it gently, taking comfort in his presence.

After a half hour of slowly coming to life, Brie went out to the kitchen and made a pot of oatmeal for herself and Jack and then headed upstairs to get dressed. The Starkhaven Stitchers were meeting at 10:00 a.m., as they did every Saturday. She was hoping to somehow make a better connection with Clara Lyston, who had been Paul Le Fevre's next door neighbor up to the time he had died. She had talked to Clara briefly the past couple Saturdays but needed to figure a way to get her away from the group, in hopes of gaining some insight into Le Fevre's life. She knew from the case files that Clara had at least been willing to talk to the detective who had originally been assigned to the case. From his notes, she had determined that Clara was privy to some of the problems in Le Fevre's life.

So with all of this in mind, she started for the quilting group earlier than she usually did, hoping to somehow align herself with Clara when it came time to assign the tasks for the session. She pulled into Tam Thorn's driveway at 9:45 and wasted no time heading up to the door.

"Brie, you're here early," Tam said, seeming surprised.

"Just thought I'd catch a little of the social hour this time."

"That's great. Good to make that effort. It will help the others warm to you."

Brie studied her for a moment, wondering if maybe she knew something about the operation, but then realized Tam was just stating a fact. If you want others to warm to you, then you yourself have to make an effort to be part of things.

They walked downstairs where a couple of the women were busy in the small kitchenette. Brie was happy to see Clara there, along with Jana Bjorklund and Lyla Stumph. She greeted the others, making a special effort to send a warm smile toward Clara. She asked what she could help with and was given the job of cutting and plating coffee cake. The other members arrived, and after coffee and cake, Tam got busy assigning the jobs for the day.

When she got to Clara, she said, "I thought you could do the sewing of the full quilt today, Clara."

"I can do that," she responded.

"We need someone to help with that," Tam said.

Brie didn't hesitate. "I'll help," she said. And just like that, she felt like she'd accomplished at least part of her mission.

They got down to business. Progress on the charity quilt had been rapid with so many hands to do the work. The others had told her that they usually completed ten to twelve quilts a year, with some of them going to veterans' care facilities. Brie did like knowing she was part of something that would bring beauty and comfort to another's life. It was somehow a positive aside to an operation focused on murder. But she also reminded herself that at the bottom, at the foundation, of all murder cases is the drive for justice and the search for truth.

Her job in helping Clara was to hold and help guide the large quilt as Clara sewed on the squares being added. After an hour they took a short break, and Clara encouraged Brie to switch jobs and take over at the sewing machine.

She hesitated for a moment, but Clara told her that the beauty of working on charity quilts was that no one would judge if there was a tiny mistake here or there.

"It's very freeing," Clara's blue eyes twinkled. "Working on these group quilts has made me more adventurous about my own quilts."

"Are you making one right now?"

"I am. I'm working on a batik triangular block quilt."

"Batik fabrics are my favorite," Brie said. And it was the truth. She loved the interest and depth that batik patterning brought to the fabrics.

"Would you like to see it?" Clara asked.

"I'd love that."

"Why don't you come over to my house after we finish. I'll make us some lunch and show you what I'm working on."

"Okay. That sounds like great fun."

Brie couldn't have been happier. She considered this a stroke of luck—a chance to possibly learn more about Paul Le Fevre, the second lobsterman who had disappeared while at sea. They'd had good luck learning about victims number one and four, Oslo Stumph and Abe Winter, but now they needed to focus on the other two victims in order to locate more potential suspects and ultimately to narrow their field of suspects.

Brie had hoped to observe Sara Bellsby a bit more after her encounter with Alan Bellsby on Wednesday, but Sara was missing from the group today, eliminating that possibility. She reminded herself that there was always next week, and that gathering information on Le Fevre was far more critical.

The next hour seemed to fly by and soon the session was wrapping up. Clara told Brie she lived just down the road toward the east end of the village and suggested Brie follow her there. A few minutes later they pulled into Clara Lyston's driveway. While it couldn't claim the grand view that the Thorns' house did, the white saltbox-style house still offered a very nice prospect of the harbor, and Brie guessed the view from the second-story windows would be quite spectacular. But she was more curious about the house immediately to the east of Clara's, where she knew from the case file that Paul Le Fevre had lived. The well-kept gray-on-gray Cape Cod appeared to be closed up for the season. The driveway was deep with snow, and the window blinds and curtains were all closed.

Brie followed Clara up to the door and into the entryway. Unlike the straight, rather stark lines of saltbox architecture that the exterior displayed, the interior of the home glowed with color. Off to the left of the hallway, the living room walls were painted a deep red, and the furniture clustered companionably around the fieldstone fireplace on the far wall of the room.

"Your home is lovely," Brie said.

"It's the house I grew up in. My parents left the island twelve years ago. My mother had health issues, so they decided to move to the mainland. That was before Doctor Ward came to the island. Technically, they still own the house, but it will belong to me one day. I had hoped to fill it with a family, but as time goes by . . . well, I'm afraid that dream has faded."

Brie didn't know what to say. It seemed like such a personal comment to make to a stranger, especially in a place like

Starkhaven where the prevailing wisdom seemed to be that emotions are best kept under wraps.

"Still, we never can know what fate has in store," Brie said. "I met my husband in the most unlikely way."

Clara nodded like she heard what Brie was saying, but her expression was dubious. "Well, at forty-one, I fear that ship may have sailed." She gazed toward the window, but Brie felt a wave of loneliness roll toward her. She cast around in her mind for a response, but before she could come up with one, Clara said, "Would you like to see the quilt I'm working on?"

"Yes, I would."

Clara led her across the hall and into the dining room, where her quilting hobby had claimed the table. Laid out next to the sewing machine was a stunning batik fabric quilt, assembled in an ever-expanding pattern of triangles within blocks. Jewel-toned purples, blues, and reds blazed on a blizzard white background.

"It's amazing," Brie said. "I love the contrast of these vivid colors against the white fabric."

"I like working with vibrant colors in the winter. They lend warmth to a long, colorless season."

"The batik fabrics bring depth to the quilt."

"That's what I think," Clara said. "They're expensive, but the effect they create is worth it."

Brie noticed another quilt of tangerine orange and sun yellow. The opposite side was a verdant spring green. She walked over to it. "This one is wonderful, too. The colors are so full of what feels like hope."

Clara smiled wistfully. "You're very perceptive. As a matter of fact, it was made for someone who needed just that." She turned away. "The kitchen is this way."

Brie followed her through the doorway into a large, square country kitchen with a sturdy wood table and chairs in the center of the room. Clara moved over to the refrigerator. "Would ham and cheese be okay?" she asked.

"Sure," Brie said. "What can I do to help?"

"You could put the soup on." Clara removed a plastic container from the fridge and handed it to Brie. "The pans are under there." She indicated a lower cabinet, and Brie retrieved a saucepan and emptied the soup in.

Clara made a pot of coffee and then they assembled the sandwiches, each to her own liking. Clara laid out some place-mats on the kitchen table, and once the soup was hot and the coffee was ready, they sat down.

Brie told Clara about her home state of Minnesota, keeping to the story about meeting John when he came there to visit a friend.

"I met your grandfather, Jack, in the general store one day. He's joined the poker game, I see."

"That's been really good for him," Brie said. "He's a very sociable man, and meeting some other folks closer to his age has really helped him adjust to island life." She stared out the kitchen window. "The house next door looks closed up. Do those folks leave for the winter?"

"About half the families on the island bail in the winter. Some go to Florida and some to the southwest." She looked out the window. "Me, I've never minded the winter. It's a cozy time of year if you have the right hobbies. I have my quilting and I like to knit, and for exercise I like to split wood for the fire." Clara ran a slender hand through her sandy shoulder-length bob. "It's surprisingly good exercise."

They ate silently for a few minutes, dipping their sandwiches in the tomato soup and sipping their coffee.

"I've seen your husband down by the harbor," Clara said after a bit. "Name's John, right?"

"That's right."

"He's a handsome man, that's for sure."

"Thank you," Brie said. "He's kind, too."

"That's important, isn't it? More important than the looks, really. Don't you think?"

"I do," Brie said.

"Some of these guys here just have a mean streak, that's all." Clara's face went stormy. "Makes you wonder who they think they are."

Clara was silent for a few moments after that, and Brie wondered if her comments had anything to do with Paul Le Fevre. She knew from his profile that he was not a mean guy, but maybe he also had been bullied. Or maybe Clara was thinking about guys like Cliff Gordon who thought it was fine to brutalize their wives.

Finally, Brie broke the silence. "I do worry about John, though. He's new to lobstering, and . . . well, it's a dangerous profession." She waited a beat to see if Clara might take the bait, but no.

Brie looked into her soup, coaxing it back and forth with her spoon. Her gaze came unfocused. "I've heard about the lobstermen who've died the past year and a half, and well . . . I'm afraid for my husband."

After a second she glanced up. Clara was gazing out the window, her eyes moist with tears.

"I'm sorry," Brie said. "I shouldn't have mentioned it. They were your neighbors and friends."

"It's all right," Clara said. "It's just that one of the men lived next door." She nodded toward the house that was closed up for the winter. "He had his problems, but still, he was a good man in many ways. And like you mentioned about your husband, he was kind."

"What was his name, if I might ask?"

"Paul Le Fevre," Clara said.

Brie saw Clara's jaw quiver and knew she was fighting hard to hold back her emotions.

"You cared for him," she said in a gentle but unequivocal way.

That opened the floodgates. The tears poured down Clara's face, and she sobbed uncontrollably. Brie went around the table, pulled a chair close and put an arm around her shoulder.

"I'm so sorry my words brought back these painful memories."

Clara blotted her eyes and slowly got hold of herself. "It's all right," she sobbed. "I've just never been able to talk to anyone here about it."

"Why not, for heaven's sake?" Brie asked, hearing the surprise in her own voice.

"No one on the island ever mentions the deaths. It's like an unspoken rule." She took a sip of her coffee, and Brie saw that her hand was shaking. "I guess the thought is, if we don't talk about it, it somehow isn't real."

Brie again realized the power of being an outsider. It meant she didn't have to abide by these bizarre, unwritten island rules, and so, by association then, neither did the person she was talking to. She had seen the phenomenon unfold with Lyla Stumph and now with Clara Lyston.

"Tell me about Paul." She reached across the table and drew the placemat with her lunch over, so her physical closeness might buoy up Clara's courage.

Clara let out a long, ragged sigh. It was like a valve being opened, releasing the built-up emotional pressure of the past year since Paul Le Fevre had died.

"He was a wonderful man," Clara began. "But so broken." She stopped after that and stared out the window, and Brie could see her struggling with herself, possibly wondering if talking about Le Fevre's troubles was somehow akin to betraying him.

"It sounds as if he lived alone," Brie ventured, hoping to approach Le Fevre's troubles from a different angle.

"Yes, that's true," Clara said. "He'd been alone for many years."

"How old was he when he went missing?" Again, even though she knew the answer, it was a way to gently lead Clara to a deeper discussion.

Clara paused for a moment as if calculating something. "He was thirty-eight," she finally said, but it was said with conviction, attesting to the fact that she knew Le Fevre pretty well. And she was right. Brie knew from the case file that Paul Le Fevre had been thirty-eight when he died.

"You said he'd been alone for many years . . ." Brie let her voice trail off, hoping Clara would pick up the ball.

"Yes," she finally said. "Paul lost his wife ten years before he died." Clara reached for her coffee and as she picked it up, her hand trembled. She cradled it in both hands and took a swallow. The silence in the room felt suffocating, but Brie waited, trying to breathe into the situation for both of them, hoping Clara would reveal more of what she knew.

"She died in such a tragic way," she finally said. "We'd had a midwife on the island. But while Julianne was pregnant, the midwife—her name was Jenny Briggs—died rather suddenly of a heart attack. So, when Julianne's time came, Paul had no choice but to take her to the mainland in his boat. But I think they may have waited too long, because partway there, things took a turn for the worse. She was in terrible distress. Paul stopped the boat and tried to help, but she told him to keep going to the mainland. He radioed ahead for an ambulance, but by the time they got to Rockland, she was unconscious. She died en route to the hospital. They operated, but the baby had died in utero."

The tears came again. "Part of Paul died that day. And while he always remained the gentle, kind man that he was, he lost the rest of himself incrementally to alcohol. I tried so hard to show him I cared, but it just wasn't enough."

"Did you ever tell him how you felt?"

"Nooo." She drew out the word as if Brie were speaking a forbidden language.

"Do you think it might have helped?"

Clara shook her head. "I don't know. I hate to think it might have and that I didn't have the courage to share my feelings with him."

Brie chose her words carefully so as not to visit more pain on this oppressed woman. "To me it sounds as if he had decided never to forgive himself, so his only way out of pain was to obliterate his feelings. If that was the case, probably nothing you could have said or done would have changed the situation."

That opened the floodgates anew, and Clara sobbed as if her broken heart might be breaking all over again. "Watching his descent into alcoholism . . . well, I've just never felt that helpless, ever."

"Do you think the alcohol might have contributed to his death? Maybe he lost his balance out there that day and fell overboard. Or got tangled in his equipment?"

"You know, after Paul died, this detective came to the island asking questions. He asked that too, but I refused to comment on it. But the truth is, in my heart of hearts, I've always felt that Paul committed suicide."

At those words, Clara seemed to visibly deflate, as if, in finally telling the story, in speaking her piece, her last bit of buoyancy had escaped. She turned to Brie. "I think I would like to be alone. I don't think I'm the best company right now."

"Of course," Brie said.

"I'm glad we talked about all this, though. It feels good to have finally talked about it. Maybe it will bring me some peace."

"I hope it does," Brie said. "You deserve that peace. You did your best for him, you know."

Clara nodded slowly. "Yes, I know that."

Brie stood. "Let me help you clean up."

"No, that's not necessary. I'll take care of it. But I do hope we can meet like this again. Maybe talk more about your life next time."

"I'd like that," Brie said.

Clara showed her to the door, where Brie stepped into her boots and pulled on her coat. She thanked Clara for lunch and for sharing her quilting work, and then she was out the door.

As she drove slowly back to the house, the tragedy of Paul Le Fevre's life and fate sat heavily upon her. Clara had known him better than anyone in the last ten years of his life, and Brie trusted her instincts. But whether by suicide or accident, Brie had come to believe that Le Fevre's death might be an outlier, not connected to the other three. And with that thought, a new theory took shape in her mind. If victim one, Oslo Stumph, was eliminated because he was the island snoop and so posed a threat to the killer, and victim four, Abe Winter, was killed because he'd stumbled on the killer's identity and tried to blackmail him, and if Paul Le Fevre had committed suicide or died by accident, that left Cliff Gordon, victim number three, as the target. Of course it was just a theory, but theories are a detective's air and water. The question always is, will they stand up to the litmus test of scrutiny? This was only one of several theories that she and Jack had explored. Each of them was plausible. She knew that only time and more digging would bring the truth to light. But, as it had been since they'd stepped onto the island, the clock was ticking, and, for now, the spotlight was on Cliff Gordon.

*   *   *

John had been feeling his way through the sea smoke for several hours, locating his lobster buoys more by instinct than by sight. His only company today was the plaintive moan of his foghorn and the occasional pale specter of a gull that would swoop out of the mist. It is believed that seagulls carry the souls of mariners lost at sea, so each time one would appear, he was reminded of the men who had died in these waters. Between that haunting fact and grappling with the arctic fog, John, despite being in the middle of the ocean, began to feel the slow, clutching grip of claustrophobia.

Without Fin, the work progressed much more slowly. He had to maneuver the boat close to each buoy, dart out of the house and catch the buoy with his gaff, feed it into the hauler and wait for the traps—one after the other—to break the surface. Right now, he was among a line of traps, so he set the helm on autopilot, with the boat traveling at one knot, and focused on getting a rhythm going—clearing one trap and sending it back off the gunwale just as the second trap on the line would break the surface.

He didn't sense the boat ghost out of the fog, nor, with the noise from the hauler, did he hear it coast stealthily up to his port gunwale. The intruder stepped silently aboard, tied off, and crossed the deck. As John pushed the second trap off the gunwale, he sensed something was wrong and turned abruptly. Mo Thorn stood a hair's breadth away. John let out a startled cry and staggered backwards. He felt himself hit the low gunwale and begin to fall backwards. The gunwales of lobster-boats are dangerously low to make it easy to pull and process the traps. John grabbed for the upright pole of his hauler, narrowly stopping himself from falling overboard. He struggled to his feet, regaining his balance, and felt abject fury pump adrenaline into his bloodstream. With nowhere to go, this would be fight, not flight. He launched himself at Thorn, taking him down, and though Thorn was a giant of a man, John had righteous rage on his side. He slammed his fist into Thorn's jaw, and his hands went to Thorn's throat.

Thorn broke his hold and sent him flying backwards. They both struggled to their feet as the deck pitched beneath them.

"Stop!" Thorn yelled. "I didn't come here to harm you. This was meant as a warning."

"Warning?" John shouted. "How dare you board my boat without permission." He lunged at Thorn, fists raised, but Thorn pushed him off.

"Listen and listen well," Thorn growled. His eyes bored into John with the piercing intensity of an arctic wolf. "I've put up with you and those two detectives long enough. And by the way, you can tell your girlfriend that I will not be threatened or manipulated. I want you off my island. Now! And if you choose not to heed my warning, then next time this won't end so well for you."

"Don't you threaten me." John's voice was steel with a honed edge. "We are here under the auspices of the Maine State Police. Don't think you can't be arrested for impeding this investigation."

Thorn laughed. "You have no power here." He stepped over, freed his line, climbed up on John's gunwale, and jumped aboard his own boat. As he roared across John's bow, John saw his middle finger extended like an exclamation point through the side window. A second later, Thorn disappeared into the fog.

John took a deep breath to try and calm his racing heart. He thought about finishing his traps, but with the adrenaline rush abating, he suddenly felt completely exhausted and more than a little unnerved. "That's it for today," he said to himself. He shut off his hauler, headed into the house, and throttled up his engine. Steering by his compass and sounding his foghorn, he motored slowly southeast toward the harbor.

*   *   *

Jack Le Beau had gone to have dinner with Mary Geary at the general store that evening. While he'd mostly kept her at arm's length out of a keen desire to not deceive her, Brie had encouraged him to go this evening with the thought of keeping that channel open in case they might need her help.

Back at the house, after dinner, John told Brie what had unfolded on the water that day, with Thorn boarding his boat and threatening him.

"It scared the hell of me. I turned around and came nose to nose with him. No warning. I nearly fell overboard. And I have to wonder, if that had happened, then what? Would he have fished me out?"

Rage welled up in Brie like a storm tide. "I'll deal with him. And this time the gloves will be off."

"No you won't," John said, and the sharpness of his tone brought her head up.

Anger etched her words. "He can't be allowed to get away with that kind of intimidation. Period."

John studied her. "I can't believe that, in the middle of a murder investigation, he would do something that makes him look that guilty."

"He believes he's above the law. He's operated that way out here for who knows how long. He believes he can do any-thing, legal or not, and get away with it. He wants total and autonomous control over this island. If he could proclaim him-self king, he would."

"Look, what he did really pissed me off, but if you push him too far, I believe he *will* destroy our operation here."

Brie drummed her fingers on the table, staring past him at the darkness outside the window.

"I'll report this to Dent Fenton. He knows Thorn. He may be the best one to deal with the situation—to try and keep him contained until we can finish our investigation here. In the meantime, I'm putting Thorn back on the suspect list."

"Seems like he's asking for it," John said. "His actions today . . . well, I believe he was letting me know just how easy it would be for me to disappear from my boat, like the others."

His words were an advancing glacier around Brie's heart. Truth be told, she did not believe Thorn was the killer. But someone here was, and the incident showed just how vulnerable John was.

They cleaned up and headed for bed. John knew tomorrow would be a long day since he hadn't cleared all his traps today. But the seas were predicted to be calm, and if Fin showed up tomorrow, they'd get it done.

Chapter 23

The next few weeks passed uneventfully. While the team's initial weeks on the island had been replete with discoveries—somewhat like the first pass along the waterfront when beachcombing, where one finds all the good stuff just lying there for the taking—the following weeks produced little new intel in the case. Still, during this time the four of them were strengthening the ties they had formed and working at building new ones.

Brie had continued her work at the history center, slowly but surely becoming one with the warp and weft of the island's past. She had perused hundreds of articles while microfilming two decades of the *Starkhaven Signal* and had begun to develop a deep understanding of why people in such an isolated situation might wish to hide a myriad of emotions. But one thing she knew from her years as a detective dealing with domestic abuse was that repressed emotions tend to simmer inside a person, sometimes for years, slowly reaching a boiling point. Sadly, what happens then is often painfully predictable. During those weeks she often thought about Faith Babcock and her stooped shoulders, as she too began to feel the gravity of hundreds of years of interconnected relationships.

On a more joyful note, she had twice more encountered Hughie Bryce in the woods and joined him to watch for birds that wintered over on the island, both times walking back home with him. She had also taken time one day to bring the bird book she'd found at their house up to Hughie as a gift. He had been delighted with it and had given her one of his drawings in return, after his mother asked him if there was anything he'd like to give Brie. She had told Hughie that she would always treasure his gift.

During that time, Jack had shown up at the poker game most days and had developed a pretty keen sense of what made his three fellow players tick. While Marty Hawkins was steady as the trade winds, Dale Woodrow would often flare up unexpectedly, his hair-trigger temper getting the better of him. Marty Hawkins and Biddy Firth would then proceed to talk him down off his proverbial ledge. One thing became eminently clear to Jack during this time. It was that Dale Woodrow had harbored a deep and abiding hatred of Abe Winter, for the damage his drug dealing had visited on island families.

On another front, back at the house, Brie and Jack had put together a Murder Board—a visual representation of where they were in the case. They had used printer paper, taped together, and had mounted the 3-by-6-foot assemblage on a piece of cardboard. They had hung it on the wall of Brie and John's bedroom, where it would be out of sight of anyone who might casually stop by the house. On the board they had posted the pictures of the victims, with their names and the dates they had disappeared. They had also listed any possible suspects they had identified. Lines drawn on the board connected victims to potential suspects, and notes written beneath each suspect listed possible motives. More information would be added to the board as it was uncovered, but the board itself was as much psychological as it was informational, as it gave the two detectives some tangible proof that the investigation was underway and that they had a grip on the case.

During those weeks, Brie had showed up each Saturday at Tam Thorn's, where the Starkhaven Stitchers met. As time went on, she noticed a subtle but interesting interaction between

Bess Gordon and Sara Bellsby. Bess seemed to come to life around Sara, as if the mere fact of their association gave her permission to be a whole person. Brie noticed the glances of admiration between the two of them, and it was not hard for a detective to deduce that Sara was attracted to Bess Gordon and that Bess was not immune to those affections. After what Alan Bellsby had told her that day in his truck about Sara's inclinations, Brie had been on the lookout for some evidence of his claims. Bess Gordon's house lay between the general store and Brie and John's house, and Brie had twice seen Sara Bellsby leaving Bess's house early in the afternoon, long about the time the guys were due in off the water.

John and Fin had continued their lobstering work on the water. Fin had seemed more at peace, and John could only hope that he had listened to reason and sidestepped the admitted pressure to take a role in the island drug scene. As for Thorn, after trespassing on John's boat that day at sea, there had been no more threats from him. John and Brie could only assume that Lieutenant Dent Fenton had dealt with the situation, although Dent had chosen not to brief any of them on the matter, except to say that Mo Thorn would not pose a problem for them.

After hauling each day, John had taken up the habit of stopping into The Stern Man. Lars Bjorklund was often there, and John used the time to strengthen his ties with Lars, whom he saw as the antithesis of Thorn. While Thorn seemed intent on fraying the moral fabric of the island, Lars seemed bent on strengthening it.

One interesting development during this time was that Trulie Hyden disappeared from the island. George arrived at the harbor one morning, ready for his day's work on the water, to find no evidence of Trulie or his boat. He was beginning to fear the worst—that maybe Trulie had gone missing from his boat like the other four lobstermen and that no one had noticed. But then Lars Bjorklund showed up and informed George that

Trulie had left the island and that he had learned the news from Mo Thorn. George, having worked aboard Trulie's boat for over a month, was a bit hurt that he would up and leave the island without telling him. But if Trulie had gone to the mainland seeking drugs, maybe he wanted to avoid any questions. The fact that Thorn knew he had gone and that Thorn was suspected of having drug connections greatly concerned George. But there was little he could do for Trulie now.

So, after a few days, he had inquired of Kieran McTavish if he might be interested in letting him try his hand at cooking at The Stern Man, which had a well-equipped, albeit unused kitchen. George, so as to stack the deck in his own favor, had prepared a tasty resume of pub foods for Kieran to sample. His bill of fare ranged from haddock and chips to Scotch eggs, bangers and mash, and finally, fried lobster. After tasting George's cooking, it didn't take long for Kieran, who was part owner of the pub, to warm to the idea. Tasty fare meant folks would stay longer and drink more—every pub owner's dream.

From George's standpoint, the position would give him a chance to both observe and interact with the locals, and maybe, by keeping his ear to the ground, learn something of importance to the case. What was more, cooking was not just in his wheelhouse, it *was* his wheelhouse and, so, a far less stressful endeavor than the job of sternman.

During those weeks, as the operation moved deeper into the month of February, Brie found herself studying the calendar each day. She knew it was a pointless practice and one destined to increase anxiety, but the detective in her also knew that, in this case, time and success, like a covalent bond, were inextricably bound together.

Chapter 24

Wednesday, February 24

After a mid-February thaw that had lasted a week, during which high temperatures punched into the forties, Starkhaven Island had once again descended into the deep freeze. Clear winter light and blazing blue skies belied the truth of the thermometer, which seemed itself frozen at a daytime high of ten degrees.

Working under the direction of Faith Babcock, Brie had dutifully continued her microfilming marathon at the history center. Just last week she had crossed the millennium line with the filming of the *Starkhaven Signal*'s first issue of the year 2000. She and Faith had celebrated by closing up early that day. Faith had broken out a very respectable bottle of scotch whiskey, and the two of them had toasted each other.

This Wednesday morning Brie was at her regular routine in the microfilm room in the upstairs of the center. She had just picked up a copy of the *Signal* when the headline on the front page of the paper underneath caught her eye. It read *Girl Goes Missing from Island*. Brie set the paper in her hand aside to give the article her full attention. This had been a special edition of the *Signal*, dated April 17, 2000. The article beneath the headline read:

On Sunday, April 16th, Jema Hawkins, age 20, went missing from Starkhaven Island. Jema is the daughter of Marty and Denise Hawkins of Starkhaven Island and the twin sister of Jana Hawkins.

Brie paused, dumbstruck. She knew these names. Marty Hawkins was one of Jack's friends from the poker game, and Jana Hawkins had to be Jana Bjorklund, Lars Bjorklund's wife, because Jack had learned that Lars was Marty Hawkins' son-in-law. She studied the picture of the young woman. Even though twenty years had elapsed, the resemblance to Jana Bjorklund was striking. She read on.

An island-wide search has failed to reveal any clues about Jema's whereabouts. The authorities have been called in, and islanders are awaiting the arrival of the Coast Guard and the Maine State Police. Jema was home from college for spring break.

As Brie read the next line of the story, her heart sped up.

She was last seen talking to Cliff Gordon on the wharf yesterday afternoon.

Brie quickly finished reading the story. She pulled a small notebook out of her pocket in which she had been accumulating interesting facts from the newspapers as she microfilmed them. She wrote down the names and dates from the article. At the bottom of the notes, she wrote the name "Cliff Gordon—victim #3."

There was a copy machine in the room where she worked. She felt it imperative to make copies of this article but didn't want to be caught doing it. She went and looked out into the hallway. The door to Faith's office was closed. She quietly closed the door to the microfilm room and turned on the copier. Working quickly, she made a copy of the article she'd just read. She flipped through the special editions of the newspaper that had been printed in the days following Jema Hawkins' disappearance and copied the articles on the front pages, all of which pertained to the disappearance. She didn't want to push her luck as it was almost closing time, so she turned off the copier and carefully arranged the newspapers back in their stack. She placed the paper dated the week before the disappearance back on top of the stack, in case Faith came in to look around.

She folded up the copies and slid them into an inside pocket in her parka, which hung on the back of her chair. She debated how she might bring up the story of the missing girl that had emerged from the archive. She contemplated not mentioning it at all, but that in itself might send up a flag. After all, Jema's disappearance had to have been such a shocking chapter of Starkhaven's history that anyone stumbling on the story was bound to ask about it.

Still, she remembered the reaction she'd gotten one day when she had tested the waters by mentioning the deaths of the four lobstermen in what must have sounded like an inquiring tone of voice. Faith had cut her short by saying, "I'm here to watch over the island's history, not to comment on its darker chapters." That had closed the discussion of the matter, and Brie hadn't figured out a way to reopen the conversation since then. So, based on that, she decided she would hold off on asking about the tragedy of Jema Hawkins.

She checked her watch. It was going on three. She pulled on her coat and went and knocked on Faith's office door and stuck her head in.

"I'm heading out for the day."

Faith waved but didn't turn around. "Thanks, Brie," she called over her shoulder.

Brie had driven the old pickup truck to the center that day. She climbed in and headed for home, eager to share what she had discovered with Jack, wondering if this might lead to a break in the case. After leaving Clara Lyston's house that day several weeks ago, where she had learned more about Paul Le Fevre, she had posited a theory that Cliff Gordon might have been the killer's target. Was it possible that this case from so many years ago could be connected to the deaths of the four lobstermen, and, specifically, to Cliff Gordon's disappearance at sea? Her mind churned out questions as she drove. She noted the familiar spark of excitement inside her chest at the thought of a break in the case. A spark ironically juxtaposed with the tragedy of a young woman's disappearance so long ago.

*   *   *

Jack was in the kitchen when Brie arrived home. He turned from the sink and must have sensed her excitement.

"You've found something, haven't you?"

"I have indeed," Brie said.

While he dried his hands, she laid the articles out on the kitchen table. He stopped in his tracks when he saw the first headline. Brie watched him as he scanned through the story. When he got to Cliff Gordon's name, he looked up at her. "You certainly did find something."

"Gordon is the one victim we know little about. One has to wonder if all of this," she waved her hand over the table, "could connect to his murder."

"How old would Gordon have been when this young woman disappeared?"

Brie paused a minute, thinking. "Twenty-eight."

Jack nodded but said nothing.

The two of them sat together in the kitchen and read the rest of the news stories, which detailed the days following Jema Hawkins' disappearance. According to the *Starkhaven Signal*, the Coast Guard had spent three days canvassing the waters around the island, while detectives from the Maine State Police had interviewed virtually everyone who lived on the island.

"Should we take these upstairs so we can make notes as we go?" Jack asked.

"Good idea."

Angus must have overheard them because he rose from his bed in the corner and headed for the stairs, which he took in one great, unbridled surge of energy.

They gathered up the articles and followed him upstairs. The large bedroom that John and Brie shared now doubled as the war room. In addition to the murder board that they'd created and affixed to the wall, there was a six-foot table that they had found in the outbuilding and brought inside. It now held their laptops and the case files of the four victims. They had commandeered two extra dining room chairs and brought them up to the room so that they now had a permanent base of operations, where the working parts of the case could be spread out and remain close at hand.

They logged into the Maine State Police database on her laptop. The DSL connection on the island moved at a snail's pace but, using Jema Hawkins' name, age, and the date of her disappearance, they were able to locate the cold case file for her. Using their shield numbers, they were also able to access the reports filed on the case. The lead detective on Jema Hawkins' case back in 2000 had been one Ed Wilkes.

"Do you know him?" Brie asked.

"Vaguely," Jack said. "He was in a different division—robbery, I think—when I was with the department. He must have moved into homicide after I retired. I think he retired about ten years ago. Moved to Arizona, if I recall correctly."

The reports in the case file revealed that the ERTs, Evidence Response Team, had scoured every inch of Cliff Gordon's lobsterboat, looking for Jema Hawkins' fingerprints or DNA. While suspicion of Gordon ran high, mainly because he was the last one seen with Jema, the detectives could find not a shred of evidence with which to make a case against him. He'd repeatedly denied having anything to do with the young woman's disappearance, saying he had simply asked her how she was liking college and that they had talked for a few minutes. He had continued on to the pub and, according to Gordon, Jema had remained on the wharf, smoking a cigarette.

Brie went to the murder board on the wall and, with a black felt-tipped pen, drew an arrow down from Cliff Gordon's name. Below the point of the arrow she wrote *Jema Hawkins*, and under the name, the date of her disappearance and her age at the time. Below that she wrote *Last seen talking to C.G. on the wharf, the day she disappeared*. Brie drew an arrow out from Jema's name and wrote *daughter of Marty Hawkins*. Under that she wrote *twin sister of Jana Hawkins, now Jana Bjorklund, wife of Lars Bjorklund*.

Brie went back up and drew an arrow out from Cliff Gordon's name and there wrote *Suspects*, under which she wrote *Marty Hawkins, Lars Bjorklund*, and *Jana Bjorklund*.

"I think we can eliminate Jana as a suspect," Brie said. "She isn't tall enough, nor would she have the physical wherewithal to overpower Cliff Gordon."

"I agree," Jack said.

They crossed Jana off the suspect list.

Brie tapped her pen on Marty's name. "What do you think?" she asked. "You know him."

"I think he'd be physically able," Jack said. "But I don't know why he'd wait twenty years to do it. What's more, he seems to be the kind of guy who bears his burdens heroically. Now that I know about this, it helps me understand some of his interaction with Dale Woodrow, who lost his son to drugs. Now Dale? He's another story. Fierce temper on him."

"So, between the two of them, they had motives to do away with Cliff Gordon *and* Abe Winter."

"But remember, their boats were both out of the water by November when Abe Winter was murdered," Jack said.

Brie nodded. "But Lars' boat wasn't. So he had both motive and opportunity. What's more, Marty Hawkins could have had access to Lars' boat, being his father-in-law."

"But Lars would have been using his boat on those days— would have been out working his traps."

"So, that brings the focus back to Lars."

Jack crossed his arms on his chest. "But, again, why wait twenty years?"

"I don't know."

Brie sat back down at the table. "There's something I remember seeing in Gordon's case file." She retrieved it from among the pile of victims' case files on the table and began looking through it as Jack read over her shoulder. After a few minutes, she pulled two reports out of the file and laid them on the desk. She tapped them with her finger.

"While they used different wording, both detectives who worked the case reported a sense of something buried beneath the surface of Gordon's life. Something no one was willing to talk about, even though he was now dead."

"Jema Hawkins' disappearance," Jack said.

"I'd stake my ticket back to the mainland on it. And while the islanders won't talk about it, you can bet they've never forgotten." She remembered the strange tension she had sensed between Jana Bjorklund and Bess Gordon in her early days of attending the Starkhaven Stitchers. Now, she thought she understood the why of it. Had Jana always suspected that Bess Gordon knew something about what had happened to her twin sister?

Brie knew from the date on the Gordons' marriage license that they had been married when this tragedy unfolded. She wondered how the disappearance of Jema Hawkins and the unanswered questions about her husband's role in it would have unraveled their marriage.

They heard the door open downstairs and John come in.

"Yo, Brie. I'm home."

"We're up here working on the case, John. There's hot coffee."

"Perfect," he called. "I'll grab a cup and come up and join you."

A few minutes later he appeared in the bedroom. "So, something up with the case?" he asked, possibly picking up the vibe.

Brie handed him the copies of the articles about Jema Hawkins. His eyebrows went up when he saw the headline, "Girl Goes Missing from Island." He went and sat on the side of the bed and started reading.

When he was finished, he looked up at the two of them. "Do you think this girl's disappearance from so long ago could connect to the murders?"

"Well, since Cliff Gordon is one of the victims, we certainly can't discount it," Jack said.

"But do things like that really happen? Someone murdering someone after so many years?"

"It happens more than you'd think," Brie said. "I like to call it the 'Fester Factor.' Something that eats away at a person like a festering wound, year after year, until, well . . . something finally snaps inside them."

"But, in this case, there wasn't the slightest proof that Gordon was involved in the girl's disappearance."

"Believe it or not, it doesn't really matter," Brie said. "Sometimes someone gets an idea in their head and nothing is going to dislodge it. That person may become completely impervious to the truth. And the farther down that road he goes, the more dangerous he becomes."

"There's no missing the fact that this shines a light on Lars Bjorklund," John said. "He's Marty Hawkins' son-in-law. His wife was this young woman's twin sister."

Brie pointed to the board. "We've already added him to the suspect list."

"But what could his motive possibly have been to kill the others?"

"That's the burning question," Jack said.

Brie leaned forward. "Well, what are the things we know about Lars?"

"He's a good guy," John said. "Stands up for people even if it may make him unpopular."

"So, he's confident," Brie said. "Not likely to knuckle under. What else?"

"Supports new folks coming to the island," John said. "Again, not a popular stance in a place like Starkhaven, where families hand down their lobster territories generation after generation."

"Jana Bjorklund told me one day at the quilting get-together that Lars wants to bring new blood to the island. Believes that, without it, this community will not survive."

"So, if one wanted to make room for new blood, who would one be most likely to eliminate?" Jack posited.

"Lobstermen," John said. "Since there are only so many territories to go around."

"And who's been dying?" Brie asked rhetorically. She gave the answer. "Lobstermen. But not just any lobstermen. With the exception of Paul Le Fevre, they were troublemakers. A drug dealer, a guy who tried to drive new blood off the island, and a wife beater, who, coincidentally, may have been involved with a decades-old crime. In other words, men who diminished the character of the island. And there's one other interesting fact about those three victims," she said. "None of them had children. At least not ones who still live on the island. So, no one would be losing their birthright here."

"But to seriously pursue this theory would be to postulate that Lars Bjorklund is mentally unhinged, with a vigilante agenda," John said. "I'm not sure I buy it."

Brie let out a sigh. "You're right; it does seem outrageous. But the fact is, we have four dead lobstermen out here. So, there's one thing we know for sure. Something pretty outrageous has happened."

"You know, I've been getting to know Lars better the past few weeks," John said. "Hanging out with him at The Stern Man when we come in off the water. I've even mentioned your work at the history center to him. What if I were to mention the newspaper articles you found? Say how shocked you were to learn that this was Jana's sister. See what kind of a vibe I get from him."

"I think that's a really good idea," Jack said. "See if the topic seems to make him uncomfortable. Try to somehow connect Jema's disappearance with the idea of Gordon's disappearance at sea. Watch his facial mannerisms. See if he seems edgy or eager to get away from you. Or if he tries to change the subject."

John nodded. "I'll do my best. But right now I think I need to eat."

"We're done here," Brie said. "Let's go downstairs and put together a quick dinner."

There was some ground meat in the fridge, so they made hamburger patties. Brie slid them under the broiler and, when they were done, added slices of cheddar cheese to melt on top. They sliced up onion, lettuce, and tomatoes, and toasted the buns in the oven. Then they gathered around the table. John opened some beers for them, and they tried to put their minds on something other than the case.

Later on, Brie and John lay in bed, in the darkness, talking.

John spoke softly. "Can you imagine living here on this island for twenty years, knowing that there could be a killer at large? What would that do to the fabric of a place like Starkhaven?"

"It would cause people to shut down," Brie said. "Not ask questions. And not want to answer them, either. It's like that in small towns, too, when someone disappears and foul play is suspected. But it's worse on an island, because it's a closed community. No one can be passing through. In a small town, there's always the possibility of a transient. And believe me, people will cling to that idea, rather than thinking one of their neighbors is a monster."

"Could something else have happened to Jema Hawkins?"

"It's possible," Brie said. "Suicide is often considered with young people of that age. And living in a place surrounded by deep water and tides . . . well, it's possible her body would never be found. It's a terrible thing to never have that closure."

"Something that might lead to that festering wound you mentioned before," John said.

"Our killer either had one target among these men, or he had decided to eliminate problematic characters. The theory of Lars wanting to revitalize the island—bring new blood here—certainly is an interesting one. But we're going to need a lot more than a theory to make an arrest." She let out a troubled sigh.

"We still have time, Brie. You and Jack are good detectives. Let's not give up the ship yet. Don't you think that somewhere in the midst of all this information on all these various players, there's a nugget of gold?"

"I hope so," she said. "But is it buried so deep we'll never find it? We have plenty of theories, suspects, and motives, but without solid evidence, we're just playing a game of smoke and mirrors—a game the killer is winning."

John gathered her into his arms, and they lay there listening to the wind outside, and the warmth and comfort of the moment were so great that Brie slid effortlessly into a deep sleep.

Chapter 25

Faith Babcock had notified Brie that the history center would be closed on Thursday. But by midmorning on Friday, she was hard at work once again in the center's microfilm room. She had walked up to the center today, and as the road turned east to run along the spine of the island, a vicious wind had torn at her. Now, as she sat at her work, the onslaught of wind outside distracted her. Every time it would buffet the building, her thoughts would shift to John and Fin out on the water, grappling with their traps in what had to be dangerous seas.

Knowing that Faith Babcock was working on the displays downstairs, she had taken the opportunity to scan through the next couple weeks of the *Starkhaven Signal* and read the stories about Jema Hawkins' disappearance. Having pored over the cold case file with Jack Le Beau the previous night and again this morning, she already knew most of what there was to know. Her hope had been that the local newspapers might reveal something the islanders had chosen to keep from the police, but that turned out not to be the case. The fact was that Jema Hawkins seemed to have just dropped off the face of the earth.

The one and only question that had arisen involved an old dory that was seldom used, except for kids to mess around in, that seemed to have disappeared from the town dock. But no one could say when they had last seen it or even be sure if it had still been there when Jema disappeared. Much speculation went round about the forgotten dory, whose fame grew to somewhat mythic proportions during those weeks after Jema Hawkins' disappearance. Did she row out in it alone or with someone? Did it sink, or might she have fallen overboard? Lobstermen patrolled the waters around the island searching for the tiny craft, but finally all hopes of locating it faded along with the heart-sickening search for Jema.

Brie sat listening to the lament of the wind, haunted, as any detective would be, by a life gone without a trace. Did this young woman's disappearance lie at the heart of their current case? Did it somehow connect to the disappearance of the four lobstermen? Her gut was silent on the matter, and she took note of that. She was counting on John to both broach the topic of Jema's disappearance with Lars Bjorklund and to assess his reaction to it. Study whether the wound seemed to be fresh still, because that would tell them something. She wished she could be sitting across from Lars when this occurred, but due to the nature of this operation, that was impossible.

When she heard Faith next door in her office, Brie got up and took the newspaper with her that had heralded Jema Hawkins' disappearance. She didn't know what to expect from Faith, as she stood before the closed door, collecting herself, deciding how to play this.

She knocked softly on the door.

"Come in."

Brie opened the door. "Do you have a minute, Faith?"

"Sure, what's up?"

"I just came across this story in the *Signal*, from April of 2000, and well, it's just so terribly sad." She held up the newspaper with the headline about Jema Hawkins going missing.

Faith must have thought she looked stricken, because she said, "Come in and sit down, Brie."

Faith had a pot of tea to one side of her desk. She poured out a cup for Brie and handed it to her. "That was a terrible chapter in Starkhaven's history and a dark time for everyone on the island. I'm so sorry if finding it upset you. I should have thought about the fact that you would come across that story and told you about it in advance. I apologize."

"No, it's all right," Brie said. "It was just a shock finding it and, well, I felt compelled to talk to you about it."

"Of course," Faith said. "That would be natural, you being new to the island. And especially considering the recent deaths of the lobstermen that you had asked me about. I'm afraid I was rather sharp with you that day. I should have seen that your query had a lot to do with your concern over your husband's safety."

"It did," Brie said.

"I don't want you to think this island is cursed. That wouldn't give you and your husband much incentive to stay here and raise a family."

"Well, I don't think that, but the danger of John's work does prey on me. I'll admit that."

"You mustn't let the dark chapters in this island's history haunt you. We've had generations of families living here peacefully for four hundred years, with very little incident. But here and there, there is bound to be a tragedy. You can call it fate, or the law of averages, but sooner or later something tragic will happen."

"I suppose that's true in any particular place," Brie said. "I read a few of the other newspaper accounts from the days following her disappearance. Was there ever any clue as to what happened?"

"There never was," Faith said. "It was deeply troubling. And it changed life forever for Cliff and Bess Gordon. I expected at some point they might leave the island, make a life somewhere else. But they never did."

"It must have been terribly hard for them. And it sounds like there was no evidence that Cliff Gordon was involved in any way."

"There wasn't, but that didn't stop Starkhaveners from convicting him in their own minds."

Brie didn't ask, but she wondered how much the suspicion of Cliff Gordon had deteriorated his relationship with his wife. Had the stress of it in some way led to his abuse of Bess?

"Well, I guess I should get back to it. Thanks for discussing this, Faith."

"Look, Brie, if you're feeling upset about this, why don't you wrap it up for the day."

Brie checked her watch. "Well, maybe. I'll just finish up what I'm in the middle of though."

Faith nodded her approval, and Brie closed the door and went back to her work. Forty-five minutes later, at 2:30, she shut off the microfilm machine and got ready to leave.

Outside, she started down the road toward home, walking at a brisk clip. She'd decided to travel by foot today to get in some exercise, but also as a way to empty her mind and focus on the case. The cold air and the rhythm of her footfalls somehow helped her mental acuity. She was running through the facts about the Jema Hawkins case when she heard a vehicle approaching. She turned and recognized Alan Bellsby's truck. He slowed and came to a stop next to her and ran down his window.

"Like a ride?" he asked.

The possibility of discovering even a scintilla of information that might advance the investigation caused her to smile and say, "Sure." But, as she climbed into the truck, it was with keen awareness that Bellsby had not been eliminated as a suspect.

"Good to see you. How're ya doin'?"

"Doing okay," Brie said.

He put the truck in gear and drove on. "Would you like to go out to the overlook?" he asked, referencing the spot they'd visited before that overlooked the old settlement.

Brie looked out the side window, hesitating.

"Just to talk," Bellsby clarified.

"Well, okay," Brie said. Since, by truck, they were a whopping two or three minutes from the house, going straight home didn't provide much opportunity to collect information.

Beyond where the road curved south, Bellsby turned onto the gravel track that they had previously taken out to the overlook. It was compacted with snow, and he switched the truck into four-wheel drive. They bumped along through the tunnel of spruce for a few minutes, neither one of them speaking. When the forest fell away, Bellsby slowed the truck and edged out onto the granite overlook. The strong wind driving out of the north battered the top of the island. Occasionally, an unusually powerful gust would rock the truck, making their situation feel precarious and, Brie had to admit, a bit thrilling. The sea spread out to the horizon and even from this height, she could see it roll. They sat silently for a few minutes, taking in the drama of it.

"Was it bad out there today?" she finally asked.

"Pretty rough over on the east side of the island where my territory lies. Over here where John has his traps, it wouldn't have been quite as bad. Let's just say, on a day like this, none of us has it really great."

She nodded. "So, days like this, you still glad you moved here to the island?"

"Wouldn't trade it for anything," Bellsby said. "It's the gold standard of lobster fishing out here."

Brie could see that here was a man truly in love with his profession. *That's a rare thing in our world,* she thought. *And worthy of admiration.*

"What do you do there at the history center?" Bellsby asked, maybe trying to keep the conversation afloat.

"For the past month or so, I've been microfilming the issues of the island newspaper, the *Starkhaven Signal.* It goes back to the 1950s. Faith Babcock had been plugging away at it for the past couple of years, since the center got the equipment, but she's had to fit it in among her other responsibilities. Since I started volunteering, the work is really moving along. We just recently passed into the year 2000."

"The newspaper no longer exists, but we have some old copies of it up in the attic." Bellsby looked out the windshield at the sea. "It's too bad," he said wistfully. "I think it bound the island together."

"I came across a troubling chapter in the island's history as I was doing my work yesterday," Brie said.

Bellsby turned and studied her. "What was it?"

"The disappearance of Jema Hawkins from the island, twenty years ago. Do you know about it?"

"I was a young man when that happened. In my early twenties. Of course, it was in the papers and on the news on the mainland, where I was living. I hadn't thought about it for many years, but when Cliff Gordon disappeared from his boat out here, it brought the whole ugly saga up again. Sara actually found some of the old newspapers her dad had saved and showed them to me."

"You must have known Cliff Gordon," Brie said. "What was he like?" She had two reasons for asking. First, to get his impressions of Gordon, but also to see if the topic of Bess Gordon might come up. When Bellsby had made the choice to marry Sara and move to the island, he'd unwittingly put himself between a rock and a hard place, and Brie wondered just how long their relationship could survive. She had seen Sara leaving Bess Gordon's house more than once in the afternoon. If they were having an affair, seems like they weren't trying very hard to hide it. She wondered if Bellsby knew about the two of them. And if so, if he cared. She wasn't sure if it connected to the case, but since their focus was on Cliff Gordon, right now, any information could be pertinent.

Bellsby turned and studied her for a moment, possibly wondering why she'd be interested in Cliff Gordon.

"He was a pretty surly guy," he said, "but who wouldn't be if they'd been accused of what he had—being responsible for that girl's disappearance. Sara told me that there was never a shred of evidence against him, but once something like that starts in a place like Starkhaven Island, it's just gonna get ginned up more and more. Gossip, and hearsay, and conspiratorial theories. People start making things up. Who knows why? Reading wrong conclusions into what they've seen or think they've seen. Maybe because they're bored."

"I think you're right. I think boredom has a lot to do with it. People looking for a little excitement. But I've heard that Gordon abused his wife."

"Yeah, sadly, that's true. It started the last couple of years he was alive. Coincided with him drinking more and more."

"The two things go together like bad and worse," Brie said.

Bellsby smiled a sad smile. "Sometimes I wonder if Bess isn't better off without him."

Brie waited, hoping he might elaborate on that, but he didn't. A few seconds ticked by.

"So, did you kill Oslo Stumph?"

Bellsby jerked back as if she'd struck him. He gave her an unreadable look, one that momentarily chilled her to the bone. Up to this point she had sensed no malice in him, but in that moment she became keenly aware of the danger and isolation of her situation here, high on this desolate cliff. She felt her muscles tense, preparing to do battle if it came to that. But then the look was gone, as suddenly as it had come.

"Why would you ever think that?" he asked.

He waited a second for a response, but none came. "Of course, I disliked what Stumph was doing, cutting my traps, but I knew I could wait him out. That eventually the tide would turn." He studied her. "I have to say I'm hurt that you would think I'm capable of that."

Brie shrugged. "Sorry. I guess I've been thinking about the deaths of those lobstermen and wondering who might have had a reason to get rid of them."

He looked flabbergasted. "And what if I had said 'yes'? Here you'd be, out on the edge of a cliff, with a killer. How would that work out, do you think?"

"Well, when you put it like that, I guess it was kind of a careless question."

"Do ya think?"

"All right, next question. Were you snooping around my house during the night a few weeks ago, shortly after we moved here?

Bellsby squirmed in his seat. "Yes," he said "but not during the night. I came by one day to introduce myself. I admit I'd seen you around the island and wanted to meet you. No one answered the door, so I walked around the house and looked in a couple of windows. I know that crosses a line. I'm sorry if I caused any alarm."

The point of both her questions was to get a gut sense of his honesty. There had been that unreadable moment when she asked him about Oslo Stumph. As for the second question about the footprints, she had to wonder if he had just taken up where Stumph had left off—namely spying on his fellow islanders.

She was studying him quietly when he leaned across and tried to kiss her. She put a firm hand on his chest to stop him. "Be careful, Alan, or I'll have to use my kung fu on you," she said ironically.

"I think I'd like to see that."

"And I think we should head back."

"Shucks, just when things were getting good."

Brie gestured for him to start the engine, which he did. She knew one thing. If he *was* a killer, he kept that part of himself carefully compartmentalized from Casanova Bellsby. He maneuvered the truck away from the precipice. They drove back through the forest, neither of them saying a word, and turned onto the road where, a couple minutes later, he dropped her at the end of the driveway leading up to the Ross property.

"That's the first time you've used my name," he said as she climbed out of the truck.

Brie didn't remember doing it, and if she had, it certainly didn't mean anything. She regarded him from her place of neutrality outside the truck, then nodded briefly to him and closed the door. She leaned into the wind and headed up the long driveway, but she could feel him watching her the whole way.

Bellsby thought he had all the time in the world for the situation to unfold in his favor. Brie, of course, knew differently. Only one question mattered to her. *Was he a killer?* Because of his almost irrational love for this island, she wondered what he might be capable of and, despite what he'd said, how he might react to someone like Oslo Stumph trying to drive him off— destroy his dream. Then there was his wife's connection to Bess Gordon. Could *it* have created a motive for him to kill Cliff Gordon? She recalled his words: "Sometimes I wonder if Bess isn't better off without him." It seemed unlikely, but she planned to think on it—see what swam to the surface. In the meantime, she had no intention of telling John that Bellsby had tried to kiss her. They didn't need any more murders on Starkhaven Island.

*   *   *

Mo Thorn sat in the waiting room of Doc Ward's office. The pain in his shoulder, though excruciating, was still not enough to block out the seething anger that boiled inside him. The im-

276

potence he felt at not being able to take back his island stabbed at him like an ancestral Thorn in his side. The fact of that impotence had now taken up residence in his mind as a constant and eroding presence. A stark realization and painful reminder that he was not Old Man Thorn—that he was not his father—a man still missed and revered by the old-timers on Starkhaven.

He was being forced to give up the operation he had built on this island. Without that, he'd have to work harder. Catch more lobster. It meant more grueling hours on the water. His shoulder throbbed—a painful reminder of what that future meant, a future of gnarled hands and worn-out joints. He'd never wanted to grind away like the rest of them—hauling his living up from the ocean floor, one trap at a time. He felt entitled to something different, something better. And he had built that something better for himself. But now he was being robbed of that. Forced out of the drug business by one of Dent Fenton's minions. How had he allowed it to happen? How had he agreed to let them all come out here, undercover? He knew the answer, of course. Dent Fenton was one of his oldest friends—a friend since his troubled adolescent years. He hadn't felt he could deny him. But he certainly hadn't expected anyone as hardcore as this female detective who was heading up the operation. She was nothing like the other detectives who had come out here to investigate the deaths of the lobstermen. As far as he was concerned, she was the detective from hell. Where had Dent found her, anyway?

Just then Doc Ward stepped into the waiting room. "I'm ready for you, Mo. Let's take the first room here."

Mo Thorn followed the doc into the examining room. Doc Ward gestured toward the table, and Mo sat up there.

"So, what's up, Mo? Is it the shoulder again?"

"It's killing me, Doc. Is there anything you can do?"

Doc Ward stepped close to him and lifted his right arm, manipulating it up and down, his fingers probing the shoulder joint. Thorn winced when the doc hit a particularly painful spot.

"It's arthritis, Mo. But I've told you that before. Physical therapy might help, but you'd need to go to the mainland for that."

"I haven't got time for that, Doc. You know that."

"Even if it would help?"

Thorn waved that away.

"Well, we could try a cortisone shot. But you need to work at readapting your movements on the boat. Try to lead with your left hand sometimes. Give the right arm a rest."

Thorn nodded. "Okay, Doc. I'll work at it. But let's try the shot."

Doc Ward nodded and walked over to a cabinet where he kept meds and hypodermic needles. "You should begin to feel relief in forty-eight to seventy-two hours," he told Thorn. "If you don't, I want to see you back here."

"Got it," Thorn said.

"Try not to move as I'm doing this." Doc Ward sanitized the spot and injected the cortisone into Mo Thorn's shoulder. When he was done, he put a small bandage over the injection site.

He paused and studied Thorn as if intuiting something. "Is anything else bothering you, Mo? You seem preoccupied. Agitated."

Mo looked away. He deeply wanted to share what was bothering him. Well, up to a point, anyway. If the doc ever knew that he was the one behind the drug scene on the island, it would end their relationship. The doc might even pull up stakes, and that would be terrible for the longevity of the community.

He looked Doc Ward in the eye. "Anything I tell you stays between us, right?"

"Of course, Mo. Doctor-patient confidentiality."

Mo hesitated. "There's something going on here behind the scenes."

"You mean the drugs?" Doc asked. "With Abe Winter gone, things have gotten better, don't you think? Not that I would have wished such a fate on him."

"It's not that, Doc. Well, it relates to that in a way. To his death and all the others." He paused as if making a decision. "Here's the thing. There's an undercover operation underway here, on the island. It's being run by the Maine State Police to try and discover who's responsible for the deaths of the four lobstermen."

"But I thought they decided they were accidental deaths."

"No. They never decided that. The cases are still actively being investigated."

"By whom?" the doc asked.

Mo heard genuine interest in his voice. After a few moments, he saw light dawn in the doc's eyes.

"The Rosses?" he asked, dumbfounded.

Mo nodded. "You guessed it, Doc." He felt a misplaced sense of integrity that technically he hadn't divulged the fact. "The woman, Brie, is the lead detective, working with the Maine State Police. And Jack Beaumont is not her grandfather. He's a retired homicide detective from the Maine State Police."

The doc nodded and regarded him carefully. "I can see why this would bother you, Mo. You're used to being in charge of things here. But you must be part of this operation, somehow. They obviously didn't come here without your knowledge. Or did they?"

"No, I'm part of it. The lieutenant running the operation—his name is Dent Fenton—has been a friend of mind since my teen years. I didn't think I could refuse his request."

The doc nodded slowly, as if he were processing the information. "So, have they gotten anywhere?"

"I have no idea. They won't share any information. Police protocol, they say. But I feel I have a right to know what's going on. Who they're looking at, if anyone. What they've discovered, if anything."

The doc nodded again. "I don't know how to help you, Mo. I understand how you feel. You're the town manager and used to running the show here, in a sense."

"I actually confronted John Ross, or whatever his name is. Boarded his boat one day. Told him I wanted them off the island."

"Sounds a bit crazy, Mo. Do you think that was wise?"

"Probably not. I'm probably their chief suspect now."

The doc smiled. "If it helps to talk, I'm always here," he said. "In the meantime, try to live your life as usual."

Live my life as usual, Thorn thought desperately. *My life as usual and my operation is being dismantled by the female detective.* But he simply nodded and hopped down off the table. "Thanks, Doc," he said. "I'll do that."

When they came out into the waiting room, Kieran McTavish was sitting there. Thorn was startled to see him and wondered if he could have overheard what he'd just told the doc. If so, that would be very bad. McTavish was the biggest blabbermouth on the island. And being the island barkeep, everyone had been telling him their troubles for decades. He'd never be able to resist spreading such juicy information around.

Thorn gave him a curt nod. "Kieran," he said in his iciest voice, planning to convey a warning, just in case McTavish *had* overheard anything.

McTavish stared back at him, his expression blank, un-readable. Thorn continued to give him the stink eye as he passed. In his mind he had an image of McTavish with his ear pressed to the examining room door, overhearing everything that had just been said. Thorn continued on out the door and got in his truck, hoping he hadn't just made a colossal mistake. If he had, Detective Beaumont would carve him up and have him for lunch.

Chapter 26

About the time Bellsby was dropping Brie off at the house, John was heading for The Stern Man. He had seen Lars Bjorklund making his way there a few minutes ago and hoped to find him by himself. He felt exhausted from battling strong wind and wild seas all day, but he had promised Brie he'd try to find a way to talk to Lars. Bring up the topic of Jema Hawkins' disappearance. Try to read his reaction to the mention of Cliff Gordon and Gordon's possible connection to what had happened so many years ago. He knew Brie was counting on him. There was no way she could gather the information herself. He'd made a good connection with Lars from the beginning, and now he was depending on that connection to broach the topic of his wife's missing twin, gone so many years ago. But would he be able to sense anger or hatred? Would Lars even engage with him? And if so, would he be unguarded enough to reveal his emotions, or would suspicion get the better of him?

John decided he wasn't helping himself with all the second-guessing. He tried to push the doubts and questions out of his mind as he approached the door of the pub. He took a deep here-goes-nothing breath and let it out before opening the door and stepping inside.

He stood for a few moments letting his eyes adjust to the darkness of the interior. The Stern Man was the womb of the village, offering warmth and comfort and hot buttered rum to its cold and weary mariners. Old man Thorn had spared no expense in providing this jewel of a pub for the residents of Starkhaven Island. George had told him that even McTavish, who'd come complete with accent from Fair Isle, Scotland, where he'd been born, had been handpicked by the old man. And for decades it seemed McTavish had felt perfectly at home on this very remote island in the middle of the North Atlantic.

After a few moments, the interior of the pub came into focus, and he saw Lars across the room at a table, motioning him over. *Good start,* John thought. He headed toward Lars and just then George appeared from the kitchen carrying two baskets of food. He set them down on the table just as John arrived. There was a basket of potato wedges with some kind of creamy sauce and another basket with fried lobster.

George nodded to John. "How're you doin'?" he asked in a generic way, staying in character.

"Okay," John said.

"What can I get you?"

"Hot buttered rum," John said.

George moved off, and John sat down opposite Lars. This wasn't the darkest corner of the pub, for which John was glad. He noted that he could clearly see Lars' face and should be able to read his expressions.

"Help yourself," Lars said, motioning toward the food. "Wicked rough out there today."

"I'll say. Felt like we were inside a cement mixer most of the day."

Lars smiled at that and squared his broad shoulders. "If you can make it through the winter, it gets better. Still bad seas some days, but not so freezing cold."

John nodded. "Your wife worry a lot about you out there?"

"Nah. When we were younger, maybe. But you can't let yourself get in that place or you'd be worryin' all the time." He took a swallow of his scotch. "Of course, those fears have crept back in now, what with the missing lobstermen in the past couple of years."

George arrived and set a steaming mug in front of John.

"My wife, Brie. She doesn't say much, but I can tell she's worried about me."

Lars nodded like there was no remedy for that whatsoever.

But John realized he'd created the perfect opening for himself to discuss the death of Jema Hawkins.

"She's been volunteering at the history center," he said. "I think it's great. Takes her mind off me out there on the water."

"So, she's helping Faith up there," Lars said.

"Yup. Seems to like the work."

Lars nodded. "Faith is a good woman. Takes the life and past of this island quite seriously." He sat back and stroked his thick, blond beard.

"Brie's been helping her with microfilming lots of island documents and newspapers."

"It was a big deal when the center got that microfilm equipment," Lars said.

John studied him for a moment. "Brie came home quite upset the other day. She's been working on microfilming the back issues of the *Starkhaven Signal,* and she came to the articles on your wife's sister, Jema, going missing twenty years ago." John kept eye contact with Lars to see how he reacted at the mention of Jema's name. "We were so terribly sorry to learn about it, Lars."

Lars lowered his eyes to the tabletop and his gaze came unfixed, as if drawn back to another time. After a few moments, he let out a sigh and looked up at John. "I appreciate the thought, John. Thank you for that. It was a long time ago, though, and sometimes it's best to leave the dead buried. I always think fate is a lot like the sea. Unpredictable but also relentless in its power over us. Marty and Jana, they both still carry Jema with them. But we all had to make peace with the fact of her disappearance years ago, or we never could have moved on."

John heard the same fatalistic acceptance that he knew mariners here and elsewhere ascribed to. They daily put their lives in peril and saw no point in dwelling on what could happen. Providence was their anchor. He understood. He was one of them and, though not a lobsterman by trade, he'd been a mariner his whole adult life.

"I understand, Lars. Still, it's hard to learn about something like that. I felt I had to say something."

Lars leaned forward, placed his elbows on the table. "I appreciate that, John, and I will pass your and Brie's feelings along to Jana." He sat silent for a moment as if making a decision. Finally he spoke. "The terrible part is, I think the fact of Jema's disappearance may have ruined another man's life."

John took a slow breath and let him talk. He knew what was coming, but it was so much better that Lars had brought it up.

"Cliff Gordon came under suspicion in Jema's disappearance. Not for any real reason, except that he was the last one to talk to her down on the wharf that day. There was no proof of anything, but the islanders could not let go of the idea. Cliff was ostracized, and from then on his life started to slowly unravel. I tried to stand by him. We'd been friends in school, but when I married Jana, it got harder. I fault myself for that."

John knew that Lars was kind. He could imagine how the situation would have bothered him. But what he was most struck by was the authenticity with which he spoke. John doubted there was any way this man could have been involved in Gordon's death.

He looked at Lars, casting about for what to say. "I have a feeling that Cliff Gordon always knew you were on his side."

"Thank you for saying that, John."

Just then Fin stepped into the pub.

"I should be going," Lars said. "It was good talking." He drained his glass and stood up. "Say 'hello' to the missus. And encourage Fin to eat some of this." He motioned at the table where plenty of food remained, then donned his parka and headed for the door.

Fin had been standing just inside the door, letting his eyes adjust. He pulled the watch cap off his head and ran a hand through his dark shaggy hair as he started across the pub toward John.

Fin had been in a funk all day, so, between his mood and the weather, John's day had been doubly dismal. He could tell from Fin's pace across the floor that his disposition hadn't improved. When Fin was in one of his moods, he tended to move at a snail's pace. It drove John crazy when they were out on the water. Being the captain of a ship, he was used to his crew stepping lively, but he tolerated Fin's moods, knowing this wasn't a permanent arrangement. What was more, Fin had been a fountain of island information, and he didn't want to jeopardize the flow of that by antagonizing the lad.

By the time Fin reached the table, McTavish had set a pint of beer there for him. Fin pulled out the chair and slouched into it. John sometimes wondered how Isa Firth tolerated his childish antics. Fin still had a lot of growing up to do, and John couldn't help but reflect on his own life at Fin's age. There'd been no time to feel sorry for himself. After his dad died, he'd had to hustle to make ends meet while taking care of his invalid mother. But he fully realized that that'd been neither a normal nor an ideal life for a young man.

"Help yourself, Fin. There's plenty of food here. And thanks for finishing up those chores on the boat."

"No problem." Fin took a long swig from his brew and liberated a large piece of lobster from the basket. "How's Lars doing?" he asked.

"'Bout like the rest of us. Rough day out there."

Fin nodded and drank some more of his beer.

"You feeling okay, Fin? You seem down today."

Fin shrugged and stared into his beer. "Just thinking about Abe Winter and how I should have been with him out there that day."

"But you were sick," John said. "It wasn't your fault."

"Then why do I feel like it was?" His dark eyes bored into John.

"Tell me about that day, Fin."

"It was cold. Wicked cold for November. Plenty of sea smoke that day. No view of the sea at all. My bedroom is on the second floor and has a good view of the water, but that day it was like cotton candy. You couldn't see anything past the shore."

"When did folks realize Abe hadn't come in?"

"I heard Abe's mom came down to the harbor long about four o'clock. Went to the pub where she thought he might be. Found some of the men there, but no Abe. Said he was always home by 3:00. Said she'd radioed his boat at 3:30 but got no response. Lars told me she was worried. The men got up a search party, and Lars came to my aunt's house right away to see if I was there. He was mighty relieved to find me. I insisted on going out with the search boats. He didn't try to stop me."

"Do you remember who went out to search?"

"Sure. There was Mo Thorn, of course. Trulie Hyden. McTavish took his boat out. I went with him and Lars rode with Bellsby."

"Why didn't Lars take his boat?"

"Lars had his arm in a sling. He'd dislocated his shoulder a couple days before, so that's why he rode with Bellsby."

Fin kept talking, but John was fixated on that last statement, because with his arm in a sling, healing, there was no way Lars Bjorklund could have killed Abe Winter. And it would be easy enough to verify the fact of the injury with Doc Ward. So, if Lars was involved in the deaths of the four lobstermen, it would mean he hadn't acted alone. He was eager to share the information with Brie, hoping it might shed some new light on their remaining suspects. John tuned back in just as Fin continued his story.

"Within an hour we located Abe's boat, a mile off the island to the northwest. There was no one aboard. At that point we radioed the Coast Guard to report the situation, and they initiated a search and rescue operation."

"And the Coast Guard never found any trace of him?"

"Nothing. Like he disappeared off the face of the earth. Or I should say, the sea. Another nightmare scenario, just like the others. But this one hit too close to home." Fin studied John for a few moments. "I've never told you this, but every time I go out there now—go up that same side of the island where Abe also had his traps—I feel like the sea is just biding its time. Waiting to come for me. Sometimes I wake up at night in a cold sweat, and I think I hear Abe calling my name."

To John it sounded an awful lot like PTSD and some of the symptoms Brie had dealt with after being shot.

"I'm truly sorry, Fin. I didn't know you were experiencing those things. If you want to quit, not work stern anymore, I'll understand."

Fin was quiet for a moment. Finally he said, "I can't do that. I have to work my way through this. And I like working for you, man. I know some days I haven't been the best, but you've been patient with me. That means a lot."

John reached over and squeezed Fin's shoulder. "Don't mention it, Fin." He held the boy's eyes for a moment. "All I can say is I think it will get better with time. I know someone who went through something similar. It does get better with time."

"That's good to know," Fin said. "Some days I've felt pretty hopeless. After all, it's been my dream to get my own boat—have my own territory. But if I can't get past these feelings, I'll have to find another line of work. I can't even imagine where I'd start."

John was glad he'd been patient with the young man. All of a sudden, his dark moods and difficult days swam into focus. And having seen Brie's struggles, he felt a depth of compassion for Fin.

"Let me buy you another beer," John said. "And let's see if the cook can warm up this food."

Fin nodded. "Thanks, John."

It was the first time he'd heard Fin call him by his name. Aboard the boat he just called him "Cap."

John turned to signal McTavish for the beer, but as he did, he caught the barkeep studying him with what could only be described as a menacing look. The darkness of it startled John, as he'd only ever experienced McTavish as ebullient and gregarious. The man immediately morphed his expression, but not before John felt the full impact of it. The why of it troubled him. Had someone found out about their operation? How would that be possible, unless Thorn had spilled the beans? Or did McTavish's demeanor have its root somewhere else? Was it possible that he was somehow involved in the murders? He remembered George telling them about witnessing what seemed to be a close connection between Lars, Bellsby, and McTavish. McTavish was definitely a fixture on the island. Someone with a stake here, and John couldn't help wondering if Brie and Jack should look more carefully at him.

He signaled McTavish to bring two more of what Fin was drinking, and when the barkeep arrived at the table, asked if he would take the food to the kitchen and have the cook re-warm it. By now, McTavish was all smiles and light, but too late. John had glimpsed behind the mask.

*   *   *

That evening, after dinner, Brie, John, and Jack headed upstairs to the large bedroom that Brie and Jack had macabrely coined "murder central." At the far end of the room, they gathered around the six-foot table, set up beneath the murder board they had created on the wall. Angus knew the drill and had charged up the stairs in front of them and ensconced himself under the table, as if no meeting would be complete without him.

John had told Brie he'd had good luck talking to Lars Bjorklund, so he went first.

"I was able to bring up the topic of Jema Hawkins' disappearance by telling Lars about your work at the history center and that volunteering there took your mind off me being out on the water. That created a natural opening to bring up the topic of Jema's disappearance."

"And how did Lars react to the mention of that?" she asked.

"Somewhat philosophically, I have to say. And there was a strong thread of island fatalism woven into his words as well. As he talked, it was almost as if he'd been drawn back to another time—one that lay, if not forgotten, at least dimmed by the passing of years. His words were, 'Sometimes it's best to leave the dead buried.' He talked about fate being a lot like the sea in its power over us, and he said they'd all—himself, Jana, and Marty Hawkins—had to, long ago, make peace with the fact of Jema's disappearance in order to go on with life.

"But it was what he said after that that really surprised me. He said he thought the fact of Jema's disappearance had ruined another man's life. He talked about how Cliff Gordon had come under suspicion, even though there had been no proof at all of his involvement. But, of course, the islanders couldn't let go of it. Gordon was ostracized, and apparently that's when his life started to fall apart. Lars appeared to feel genuine guilt over it. Said he and Cliff had been friends in school and that he had tried to stand by him. I believed that because it seems to be in Lars' nature to stand by people. But after he married Jana, he said it got harder to maintain his connection with Gordon." He paused and looked from Brie to Jack. "Personally, I don't believe Lars could have had anything to do with Cliff Gordon's death. Everything he said today sounded heartfelt. It's hard to fake that kind of sincerity."

Brie leaned forward. "That's good work, John. It may not be what we were hoping for—in other words, a strong suspect —but if it's the truth, it's the best we can ask for."

"There's more, too," John said.

"Yes, go on."

"I also had an opening to talk to Fin about the day Abe Winter died. He's been in a dark place, and he admitted that, since Abe's death, he's been struggling with nightmares about dying at sea. I asked him to tell me about that day—the day Winter disappeared."

"Go on," Brie said.

"When Abe didn't come back that day, the men went to Fin's aunt's house to tell her. They were relieved to find Fin there. The men went out in their boats to search, and Fin insisted on going along. But he said Lars had to ride with Bellsby because he'd dislocated his shoulder and his arm was in a sling."

"So, that would rule Lars out for Abe Winter's death, and if we assume we are looking for one killer, it rules him out altogether," Brie said. She got up and put some notes on the murder board under Lars' name.

"But what if he didn't act alone?" Jack asked.

"Flesh that out for us, Jack," she said.

He leaned forward. "Remember what George said about observing Lars, Bellsby, and Kieran McTavish at the pub—about how tight the three of them were?"

"We do," Brie and John said simultaneously.

"It may sound outrageous, but what if they acted together, with the joint goal of ridding the island of problematic characters?"

"I don't really buy it," Brie said. "Here's why. The only man Lars had a firm motive to kill was Cliff Gordon. And from what

John has learned, Lars never believed Gordon was guilty. But go ahead, Jack. Run through their motives."

"Well, even if we assume Lars bore no animosity toward Cliff Gordon, he still has a cause to champion here. As his wife told you, he wants to bring new blood to the island. And what better way to make room for new blood than by eliminating problematic characters? As for Bellsby, he had a strong motive to kill Oslo Stumph, who was relentlessly cutting his traps—trying to drive him off the island. Lars would have wanted Bellsby to stay, so it gives him a motive in Stumph's death as well. As for McTavish, well, remember, old man Thorn brought him here a generation ago, back when this place had more integrity. McTavish may feel strongly about those times, want to bring them back. If so, he would have had a strong motive to kill Abe Winter, who was dealing drugs here and, so, destroying the fabric of the island."

"And, following your theory, he undoubtedly would have found both Stumph and Gordon less than stellar components in the island constellation," Brie said.

"There's something else you should know about McTavish," John said.

He told them about the baleful look he'd caught on McTavish's face at The Stern Man that afternoon. "It worried me. Almost seemed like he knew something."

"You mean about our operation?" Brie asked.

"I don't know. Maybe. It just seemed totally out of character for him."

"Huh. Strange. And a bit worrisome," she said. "Makes one wonder if he *does* know something about us. Also makes me wonder if he could have acted alone in the murders."

"He has a boat," John said. "Comes and goes randomly to obtain supplies. Sometimes also brings supplies for the general store between ferries in the winter. So, no one would question him going out on his boat early in the day."

"Good point," Brie said. "So, he had opportunity."

"What's more, he's able bodied. I'd place him in his mid-fifties. And he may be stronger than we might guess from hauling around crates of liquor and kegs of beer."

"So, he also had means." Brie got up and wrote McTavish's name on the murder board, and under it, his motive, means, and opportunity. She found him an interesting suspect and not one to be too quickly discounted.

She shifted gears. "There's something else about Alan Bellsby we may want to consider as well." She told them about seeing Sara Bellsby leaving Bess Gordon's house on a number of occasions, in the afternoon close to the time Bellsby would be due in off the water. "I think it's possible, in fact probable, that Sara and Bess are having an affair. I've noted the looks that pass between them at the quilting get-togethers. Now, I may be way out in left field on this, but assuming Bellsby knew about his wife's affair and assuming that the affair was going on before Gordon's death seven months ago, it could have given Bellsby a motive to kill Cliff Gordon." She looked from one to the other of the guys. "With Gordon out of the way, Sara and Bess could pursue their relationship. Bellsby would be bound to end up with a lobstering territory, and he could move on to another woman, if he so desired, which it would seem he does."

"Or Bess Gordon could simply have divorced her husband," John said.

"Frankly, I don't see that happening," Brie said. "Cliff Gordon was abusive. Bess would have been afraid of him. And living on an island far from the mainland, with no police presence, I don't see her risking it. Without leaving the island, she'd have had no way to really get away from him."

"I agree with that," Jack said. "And it lends credence to the idea of cumulative motives for those three. The problem with all of this is we have absolutely no proof of any of it. It's all conjecture. What's more, there's no evidence that anyone had a motive to kill Paul Le Fevre. From what I've learned, everyone seemed to love the guy."

"But we've always suspected that his death might be an outlier," Brie said. "There's a good chance that, due to his mental and emotional state, he may have killed himself or accidentally fallen overboard."

"Here's what troubles me about that theory." Jack stood up and went to the murder board. He pointed to each of the dates of death. "Oslo Stumph died in September. Paul Le Fevre died in February, five months later. Five months after that, in July, Cliff Gordon disappeared. And four months after that, in November, Abe Winter died."

"There's a pattern," Brie said. "We've known that from the beginning, though."

"Yes, but Paul Le Fevre's death is part of the pattern. Makes it hard to believe he died by accident or by suicide."

"And if he's part of the pattern, then he could have been the intended victim." She tapped her marker on the table. "Going back to one of our theories of the crime—i.e., there was one intended victim and the other murders were committed to muddy the waters—we need to allow for the possibility that Le Fevre, as unlikely as it seems, was the intended victim."

"I agree," Jack said. But it's getting late. Why don't we sleep on this and pick it up in the morning."

"Fair enough," Brie said. "John needs to get to bed, anyway."

She asked Jack if he wanted her to take Angus out for his nightly business, but he said he'd handle it. He bid them goodnight and headed downstairs with Angus in tow.

Brie made a few notes about their meeting while John showered and got ready for bed. When he came back into the bedroom, she turned off the lights and went to wash up. By the time she crawled in next to him, he was sound asleep, snoring quietly.

She lay in bed. It was a clear night and pale moonlight cast a ghostly glow through the window into the room. Her mind buzzed with the various theories they'd been exploring, not just tonight but throughout their work on the case.

There was the theory of a psychopath at work. One who killed indiscriminately and without reason. But she had long discounted this theory because there appeared, except in one case, to be very probable motives for the murders here.

Then there was the theory of one intended victim. That the killer actually had one target and that the other murders had been used as subterfuge. This was the theory Brie found most plausible.

Next was the theory of vigilante justice—a killer clearing the island of bad actors. Lars Bjorklund was the one who originally fit the profile. Strong, stands up to people, and stands up *for* people as well. Probably self-righteous with a bit of a savior complex—wants to save the island. But another and maybe better possibility had arisen in Kieran McTavish. A dark horse who also fit the vigilante profile. A surprising suspect, but not one to be overlooked. He had been brought to Starkhaven Island by old man Thorn, back when the island was a different kind of place—a place, at least to his way of thinking, of tradition and integrity. And to this day, he had maintained and run The Stern Man to a standard the old man would have approved of. McTavish had also had both means and opportunity to commit the murders.

Tonight they'd explored a new theory that was a spinoff of the vigilante theory. A three-man cabal that included Lars Bjorklund, Alan Bellsby, and Kieran McTavish working together. It was an interesting theory, but Brie was inclined to discount it. To her way of thinking, two of the three men had too much to lose to involve themselves in such a plot. Bellsby had waited his whole life to get out here, and Lars had a wife and family to think of. No, it didn't make sense.

But there was another view of the case that had emerged from information gathered since they'd arrived here. Tonight, Brie's gut was telling her to pay attention to it. Oslo Stumph, the first victim, had been the island snoop. The killer might have wanted him out of the way before going after his target victim. Furthermore, information had also come to light that Abe Winter might have discovered the killer's identity and decided, recklessly, to blackmail him. Winter obviously didn't mind taking risks. He ran drugs, so he might have been perfectly willing to try blackmail, if it seemed a quick way to get money. If that were the case, he would not have been an intended victim at all, but rather, an unexpected menace that the killer had to deal with.

That left the focus on either Cliff Gordon or Paul Le Fevre as the killer's intended target. Gordon had been the obvious choice, especially after she'd discovered the information about Jema Hawkins' disappearance. Were they missing something, though?

They were all respectable theories. Each had validity, and the recent appearance of Kieran McTavish as a suspect certainly had her attention. But what they needed was proof. Solid proof of something. In her estimation, they had done a good job here —uncovered both motives and suspects—but without proof, it all falls apart. There must be proof for prosecution.

She took a deep breath or two, willing herself to let it go for the night, and finally, with remnants of the case still swirling in her head, she fell into a restless sleep.

Chapter 27

Saturday, February 27

*A*ll around her, sea smoke boils off the surface of the ocean, obscuring her view. Brie spins in the freezing water, trying to orient herself. To the east she sees a diffuse red glow of light. *The sun, just climbing out of the sea. Its crimson hue heralding a warning. Storm ahead. She spins once more. The strong current claws at her, dragging her down. She battles against it, but her legs are numb. Now a strong wind clears a view for her. In the distance she sees Hughie. Again, he stands on the high cliff. Impossibly high. The white owl sits on his shoulder, not on his arm, as before. She tries to call out, but he does not hear her. He looks to the west, fixated on something there. The ghostly owl hoots, and now Hughie turns his head—sees her. But she is losing her battle. She sinks below the surface. It is warm down here. Welcoming. She thinks she will stay. She sinks deeper, deeper, into the warm lap of the sea. But now she feels the talons of the ghost owl, and she is rising swiftly, breaking the surface. They fly above the sea. Hughie beckons with his arm, sheathed in leather, like the falconer of old. The great snowy owl wings toward the land. Now they are over the trees. Hughie has disappeared—his job done. She is falling, slowly falling to safety.*

Brie wakes, but not in terror, as with the last dream. The images float around her in the dark—still electric with meaning. She reaches out for John, but he is gone—already risen. She sits up and feels for the small notebook and pen she always keeps beside her on the table and, in the dark, pens the images before they evaporate, like smoke over the sea. Hughie, looking away, blind to her plight; the white owl—this time on his shoulder; the cliff, impossibly high; the sea pulling her down, down, and her wish to surrender to it. She paused in her writing; then beneath the list, she wrote the name Athena. Something way back in her memory banks was flashing a signal, vying for her attention, but her brain was still fuzzy with sleep.

She rose and opened the curtains just a bit to let the first pale fingers of light insert themselves into the darkness, but not so much as to shock her from the reverie of the dream. She climbed back into bed and studied her jottings. She tried to focus her thoughts, but her brain was still sputtering along like a make and break engine. This was the second time she'd dreamt of Hughie and the white owl. She believed the dream had meaning, possibly carried a message. She believed there was a reason her subconscious had sent the dream again, like Hughie, sending the owl to her rescue a second time. There must be something that had triggered the dreams. Something she knew but didn't know, so to speak. Something that might rise to the surface if she followed the sign posts.

She studied the list of images again and underlined the name Athena. She thought back to her high school reading of Greek mythology. She wrote the name again and out flowed the words, "goddess of wisdom." And now she was remembering. In ancient Greece, the owl was the symbol of higher wisdom. An owl sat on Athena's blind side—on her shoulder—so she could always see the whole truth. Now the symbolism of the dream became clear. The impossibly high cliff—higher wisdom. Higher wisdom is synonymous with truth. The owl sits on Hughie's shoulder, so that even though he looks away—is blind to her dilemma—he will see the whole truth. He sends the owl to save her. She closed her eyes. *Hughie sees the truth.*

The dream was replete with symbolism. The sea pulling her down, down, and her desire to surrender to it. The sea as a symbol of her unconscious mind was hard to miss. Brie reflected on what would save her, save their operation. The truth, yes, but also proof, the last thing she had been focused on before falling asleep.

Suddenly, she was thinking about Hughie and his keen powers of observation, his ability to capture on paper, in almost photographic detail, what he had seen. A chill ran down her spine and the hairs stood up on the back of her neck. She felt fear. Not for herself, but for Hughie. Was it possible he had witnessed one of the murders? *Hughie sees the truth.* If so, was it possible he had drawn what he'd seen?

She was already out of bed, getting dressed, as her last thought was processing. She glanced at the clock. Seven fifteen. Way too early to do anything about the situation. She headed into the bathroom, washed up, brushed her hair into a ponytail, and headed downstairs with her notes. By the time Jack appeared downstairs, the coffee was dripping into the pot and she was beating up four eggs.

"You're up early today, Brie."

She caught the quizzical look on his face. He was usually the first one up. Well, second if you counted John, who was up and gone long before the crack of dawn.

"There's something I have to talk to you about."

"Sounds important. Let me just get Angus out and back in, and we'll talk."

Angus was doing his wiggle dance at the back door. Jack slipped on his parka and opened the door. Angus bounded forth, and the door closed behind them. Brie slid the eggs into a skillet and put down two pieces of toast. By the time Jack and Angus made their reentry, breakfast was plated up and the coffee poured out into mugs.

Over breakfast she told him about the two dreams she'd had. She had described Hughie to John and Jack and related her encounter with him, when he had shown her the Snowy Owl. She had also described her visit to his house, where she had met his mother, Annette Bryce, and seen his amazing sketches. She reminded Jack that, after that, she'd had two more encounters with Hughie, each as delightful as their first meeting.

Now she posited her theory, as well as her deep concern for Hughie's safety. "I think it's possible he could have seen something, Jack. His mother lets him roam the outdoors at will. It's his joy. His observations of the birds and his drawings are truly his *raison d'être*."

"You think he might have observed one of the murders?"

"He and Annette live up on the northwest side of the island. The cliffs are high. There's quite a vantage of the sea. A bird's eye view, you might say. So, yes, I think it's a possibility.

"Here's the thing, though. I think I'm going to have to tell Annette Bryce about our undercover operation, in order to get access to Hughie's sketch books. She's very protective of his privacy. She told me he doesn't always let her see his drawings and that she always respects his wishes. I know she would never violate that trust without a very good reason."

Jack was silent for a few moments, considering the situation. "Is it likely that she'll tell others?" he asked.

"I'll have to swear her to secrecy," Brie said. "Not that it's any guarantee she won't talk. But she seems quite reclusive. Hughie is her world. Helping him to feel whole, protecting him. If she thought he was threatened in any way . . . well, I'm pretty sure she would move heaven and earth to keep him safe. And, fact is, if he witnessed something, he may well be in danger."

"Then I don't think we have a choice," Jack said.

She saw the alertness in his eyes at the possibility of a break in the case.

"Do you want me to accompany you?"

"No, that might overwhelm his mother. I've made a pretty good connection with her. She can certainly see that I care about Hughie. I think I have a shot at getting her to co-operate."

"Well, okay then," Jack said. "As it so happens, I promised Mary I would help her with some inventory down at the general store. But I should be back in an hour or two."

"Good. When you get back, we'll do some more digging into Paul Le Fevre. See if there might be anything we've missed. Anything that might make him fit the profile of a murder victim rather than a suicide or an accidental death."

Jack nodded his agreement. They put the dishes in the sink and within ten minutes were both out the door. Brie told him to take the truck since she preferred to walk.

A heavy gray sky pressed down on her as she climbed the road toward Hughie's house. The air had that signature New England dampness that often precedes a gathering storm, and an easterly wind making up portended a blow. The Coast Guard weather forecast had not predicted a storm for today, but tomorrow, she thought, all bets would be off. The atmospheric omens were already in place.

She was glad to be on foot, as it gave her time to collect her thoughts and frame up the words she would need to say to Annette Bryce. She hadn't tried to contact Annette, because frankly, it was island convention for people to drop by. And if Hughie happened to be there, she would simply visit and leave. But with the temperature in the high twenties, she guessed Hughie would be out in the woods today, watching for birds.

In about ten minutes, she came to the gravel road that led to Hughie's house. The road ran west, slowly arcing north, and she followed it to the Bryce home, which was one of the last on the road. She turned in at the familiar driveway and made her way up to the house that enjoyed the seclusion of forest on either side of it. At the front door, she took a breath to calm herself and rang the bell. A few moments later, Annette Bryce opened the door.

"Well, Brie. This is a surprise."

"I hope it's okay to drop by like this," she said. "I wanted to talk to you. Is now a good time?"

"Sure. Please come in." She stepped aside and let her enter.

Brie saw a moment of confusion in Annette's face as she held open the door.

"I'm afraid Hughie is out exploring," she said apologetically, as if the thought that someone would stop by to see her was somewhat foreign.

"It's you I wanted to talk to, Annette. It's actually better Hughie isn't here."

Now Annette's confusion appeared to lean toward concern. "Okay," she said, uncertainly. "Would you like coffee? I just made some."

"That'd be great," Brie said.

They went out to the kitchen, where Annette poured out two mugs of coffee and handed one to Brie. "Is anything the matter?" she asked.

"Let's sit down, Annette."

They sat at the small table beneath the window that looked toward the sea.

"What I have to say is hard for me."

"Go ahead," Annette encouraged. "Whatever it is, I will listen. I owe you that for the kindness you have shown Hughie."

"Thank you, Annette." Brie let out a kind of sigh. "What I'm going to tell you needs to stay between us. Can you do that?"

Now Annette looked even more concerned. "I don't know. I think so."

"I'll get right to the point, then. John, Jack, and I have come here to Starkhaven for a specific reason. We are part of an undercover operation run by the Maine State Police to investigate what happened to the lobstermen who have died out here."

Annette's lips parted, her eyes riveted on Brie. She set down her mug. "But why are you telling me about this?" she asked. "What does it have to do with me and Hughie?"

"I'm not sure it does, Annette. But I need to explore all possibilities."

She told Annette about the symbolic dreams she'd had about Hughie and the white owl. "I believe something has triggered these dreams, and that it may have bearing on the case." She also told Annette about being shot and nearly dying, and how, after that, she had frequently had dreams that purveyed information. Information possibly known to her, at some deep level, that had not yet consciously registered. Information that might connect to something significant in a case.

"I know it may sound bizarre . . ."

Annette interrupted her. "You mean like something you know subconsciously, kind of like a sixth sense."

"It's possible," Brie said. "I don't fully understand it myself, but I've learned to pay attention to these dreams. Not to brush them off." She studied the suddenly frail-looking woman across from her. "Here's what I think, Annette. Hughie is amazingly observant. I suspect he has the ability to notice more than all the residents of this island combined may have. And I think there's a possibility that he might have witnessed something."

Annette looked truly shocked for the first time. "You mean something that might explain what happened to one of these men?"

"That's what I mean."

"If that were true, that would be terrible for him."

"I agree with that," Brie said. "Tell me, Annette. Was there ever a time you can remember in the past year and a half when Hughie came home upset? Or in some way acted out of the ordinary?"

Annette sat for a time, considering the question.

"You know, there was something," she said. "It was a few months ago. Hughie wouldn't go out of the house for over a week. I took his temperature to make sure he wasn't sick, but he seemed fine. You know, he's approaching adolescence, so

I'm always expecting to be surprised these days. Always wondering what will come up; how things may change." She looked down at her cup, her gaze unfocused. "I worry that when he gets to that age, he'll no longer hear the siren call of the birds."

"I don't know if that's possible, Annette. I've watched him in his observations. It's like nothing I've ever seen before."

Annette looked up at her, heartened by those words.

"Can you tell me about that day?" Brie asked. "The day before the period where he wouldn't go outside, do you recall if he drew anything that day?"

"As I recall, he came in that day, as usual, and went right to his sketchpad. I can't say if his mood was more urgent than normal." She stood and poured more coffee for them. "I do all the typing and correspondence for Mr. Thorn and the town office. It was a busy period, right then. I remember because, with Hughie here all the time, it was harder to get my work done."

"But to your recollection, he did draw something that day."

"Yes. I'm sure of that."

"We need to try and find what he drew that day, if possible," Brie said.

Annette hesitated.

"I understand you only look at his work when he gives you permission. But this is important, Annette. I'm afraid, if Hughie saw something that day, his life could be in danger."

A look of pure fear darkened Annette's face. "All right," she said. "It shouldn't be hard to find, because Hughie didn't draw anything for days after that. And even if he didn't let me see his work on that day, it's quite possible there's a date on the sketch from the day before. When Hughie lets me see one of his drawings, I always ask him if I can put a date on it. He always lets me. I mark it on the back of the sketch in pencil— it's kind of a chronology of his work that lets me know how old he was when a sketch was done."

"So, it's possible we could learn exactly what day he drew the last picture—the one before the hiatus," Brie said.

"Quite possible."

Annette stood up and headed for the dining room. There was a bookshelf under the window that held Hughie's sketchbooks. They were large format sketchpads with heavy-duty spiral bindings. She opened the back cover of several of the sketchpads, looking for dates. After a few seconds, she handed one pad to Brie and kept one herself.

"This one is from September and October. Yours has November and December."

They sat at the table and started their search. Brie was worried Hughie would arrive home before they finished, but she put that out of her mind and slowly turned the pages so as not to damage any of the sketches. The archive of drawings comprised a veritable ornithological tour of the island. Hughie had not just captured the land and seabirds that nested here on Starkhaven, but also the vast migrations he would have witnessed during these months in the fall.

The sketchbook that Brie perused had actually started in October. More than half of the drawings had a date on them, and she carefully turned the pages, studying the dates inscribed on the back, until she had entered the month of November. She had a date emblazoned in her mind, and as she neared that date, she could feel her heart rate increasing, as if she were sprinting toward a finish line. The date was November 14. It was the day Abe Winter had disappeared from his lobsterboat.

When she arrived at the penultimate picture—the one she guessed had been done on November 13, as the date on the back of the previous picture was November 12—she took a breath through her nose to calm herself and slowly turned the page. She suppressed a gasp at what she saw there. She glanced up at Annette to see if she'd sensed her alarm. The drawing depicted two lobsterboats, one off to port of the other. At the wheel of the posterior boat stood a shadowy figure, not at all recognizable, except as human, pulling away from the other boat. In the foreground of the drawing, to starboard of the other boat, floated a dead raven, but much larger than an actual raven would be. Its wing was broken and its head lay to one side on the surface of the water. To Brie the symbolism was unmistakable. She guessed that it might have been too frightening for Hughie to draw a dead body, so he had replaced it with one of his birds. The bird sometimes identified with death.

"Did you find something?"

Brie looked up to see Annette studying her.

"Yes." She heard the sound of her own word, infused with regret.

Annette got up and came around the table and stood behind Brie. "What do you think it means?" she asked.

"I'm not sure," Brie said, hoping to not alarm Annette. But the picture called up a scene in her mind. A scene she had conjured time and again while studying the case files of the men who had died.

"Annette, I need to take this sketchbook with me. It may be important evidence in the case. I don't want to take this drawing out because the chronology of the dates would be important."

Annette nodded slowly. "I guess if you have to. It's not Hughie's current sketchbook, so hopefully he won't miss it."

"I promise I will take good care of it and return it to you when we are done with it."

Annette nodded again. "Could I put it in a plastic bag, to protect it?"

"Of course. I was going to ask you for one."

Annette went to the kitchen, and Brie could hear her foraging around in a cabinet. She came back holding a good-sized plastic bag, along with a paper bag.

Brie carefully wrapped the sketchbook in the plastic and then slipped it into the paper bag.

"I should be going now," she said. "I wouldn't want Hughie to arrive home and wonder what I'm doing here."

Annette nodded, looking at a loss.

Brie reached out and squeezed her shoulder. "Everything is going to be all right, Annette. I promise." She looked her in the eye. "Please remember, this needs to stay between us."

Annette Bryce nodded again. "I promise. I won't forget."

"Thank you."

Brie pulled on her coat and boots and headed out the door. She tucked the bag under her arm and moved quickly down the driveway, hoping she wouldn't encounter Hughie along the way. She was afraid her face, her very energy, would send some kind of sign of unease that he might read.

As she turned onto the main road and headed south, her apprehension about encountering Hughie faded. The hum of excitement inside her that they had caught a break in the case was juxtaposed with a heaviness of heart at what Hughie had had to witness and what he might yet be called on to say or do. Preoccupied with those thoughts, before she knew it, she had reached the long driveway that led up to their property.

She came in the door and shed her boots and coat. The truck was parked outside, so she knew Jack had gotten back.

"I'm home, Jack," she called as she stepped into the hallway.

"I'm upstairs, Brie. Just got home."

In a few moments he appeared at the top of the stairs. As he came down, he noticed the bag she carried.

"Whatcha got there?"

"Hopefully proof of something."

She took the sketchbook out of the bag, laid it on the dining room table, and carefully opened it to the picture Hughie had drawn on November 14th.

"This is one of Hughie's drawings. They are all done from his observations, as I've told you before."

Jack's eyebrows went up as he looked it.

She pointed to the date on the previous drawing that Annette had placed there. It was November 13th.

"Is that the day before Abe Winter disappeared?" he asked.

"It is. And even though Hughie wouldn't let her see this drawing, Annette Bryce is positive he drew it the next day, November 14, the day Abe vanished from his boat."

"Wow."

"Yeah. I know. I think Hughie observed Abe Winter's murder." She pointed to the dead raven. "I believe this was his way of depicting the body. I think it was too scary for him to draw, so he used one of his birds."

"No mistaking the symbolism," Jack said. "The raven—death. Do you think he would know that?"

"No flies on Hughie," Brie said. "I think he's brilliant. A savant. He has the true soul of an artist. He observes his world. What's more, Annette reads to him every day, and the raven is a recurrent symbol of death, specifically violent death, in art and literature." She touched the drawing. "I think he's using it that way here. As an archetype."

Jack pointed to the drawing. "There are partial numbers on the boats." Excitement animated his voice.

"I know. You can imagine what I felt at seeing that. I have no doubt that Hughie could have captured the face of the perpetrator in exact detail, but like the dead body, the trauma of what he had witnessed may have precluded his ability to do so."

"We need to search the Maine boat registry. See if we can identify the owners of these lobsterboats."

"And if that fails, when John gets home, we'll send him down to the harbor to see if he can spot either of them there."

"Let's get to it," Jack said.

Chapter 28

B rie and Jack sat down at their work table in the upstairs bedroom and opened the laptop. Their first order of business was to check the Maine State Boat Registry to see if they could learn anything about the two boats in Hughie's drawing. But when they clicked into the portal at the Maine State Police website, they got a message that the site was temporarily unavailable.

"Darn," Brie said.

"They're probably making some changes to the site," Jack said.

She let out a sigh. "Well, it is Saturday, so maybe that's it. But let's send these partial numbers to Dent Fenton and see if he can get some answers for us."

Brie framed up an email to Lieutenant Dent Fenton, telling him it was urgent they get some intel on the boat numbers ASAP. She sent the email, and she and Jack looked at each other for a long, what's-next moment.

"While we have various motives for our various suspects, we're no closer to a core motive," Jack said. "Nor whether there was a specific target among the four victims."

"But we know there's a pattern to the deaths of these four men. So, have we been missing something all along? Maybe the least likely target is the one we should have focused on."

"Maybe," Jack said. "But investigations tend to start with apparent or obvious motives and suspects, because more often than not, that's where the solution lies. Obviously, three of the victims were such bad actors that they were bound to draw our focus. You've got Oslo Stumph, both a relentless bully and the island snoop—minding everyone's business; Abe Winter, complicit in destroying lives by selling drugs; and Cliff Gordon, a physically abusive spouse, connected or not to the disappearance of Jema Hawkins some twenty years ago. Frankly, my money's still on any one of them as the killer's target."

"Problem is, the investigation has revealed a disconnect between motive and opportunity for several of the suspects connected to those victims," Brie said. "So, maybe we're missing something." She reached over and pulled the case file for Paul Le Fevre out of the stack.

"The stone we haven't yet turned," Jack said.

"Because of the extenuating circumstances of Le Fevre's life, i.e., depression and alcoholism, and the likely possibility that he died by accident or suicide, it's been easy to focus elsewhere."

"Along with the fact that he was well-liked here," Jack said. "At least, that's what I've picked up by keeping my ears open."

"Still, we need to revisit his case—dig deeper, see if there's something we've missed." She opened the file. "Let's review what we know."

Together they read through the file.

"He's the second victim," Jack said. "Disappeared from his boat on February twelfth, approximately one year ago. Shortly after dawn, a fellow lobsterman spotted his lobsterboat with no one aboard."

Brie leafed through the file for the weather and seas report. "There was a swell running that day. Seas six to eight feet. Would have made his boat unstable."

"Which would play into our accident theory," Jack said. "And if it was still dark it would have been more dangerous still."

"We have testimony from Le Fevre's neighbor, Clara Lyston, given to the detective who originally investigated the case and backed up by what I learned when I met with her. There's little question that Le Fevre was both depressed and an alcoholic. Ms. Lyston, who it appears was the person closest to him, told me that, in her heart of hearts, she felt he had committed suicide. His spiral downward began with the death of his wife and unborn child, ten years before he died."

Jack shook his head. "How does one ever recover from such a thing?"

"I think he might have had a chance with Clara. It's clear she loved him. But I think he was too consumed by his grief, and eventually the alcohol, to see how she felt. That she was there for him. That she might be his way back."

"As you recall, I looked up the death certificate for Le Fevre's wife," Jack said.

"I remember we talked about it at the meeting with Dent Fenton, but I didn't see a copy of it in the case file."

"Let's take another look," Jack said. He logged into the Maine State Police site and entered the public records database. Within minutes he had brought up a copy of Julianne Le Fevre's death certificate as well as the medical examiner's report. "The cause of death was cardio respiratory collapse, resulting from coagulopathy caused by an amniotic fluid embolism."

"She bled to death," Brie whispered. "So terribly sad."

She suddenly leaned forward. "Look here." She pointed to the date of death. Julianne Le Fevre had died on February 11, 2010. She flipped back to the Coast Guard officer's report for the day Le Fevre had disappeared. "Paul Le Fevre went missing from his boat on February the twelfth, exactly ten years later, but for one day."

"Coincidence?"

"You know me, Jack. I don't believe in coincidence. Still, it's not the exact date."

She tapped away at her keyboard and brought up the National Weather Service site. She clicked on Maine on the map and then on "Past Weather" and brought up the report for February 11 of the previous year.

They read the data.

"There was a gale blowing that day. Small craft warnings had been issued," Brie said.

"So, you think the killer could have been planning on killing Le Fevre on the tenth anniversary of his wife's death?"

"I think it's a possibility we can't overlook."

"How could I have missed the fact of those two dates?" Jack asked.

"Lots of victims. Lots of details. We were just getting our feet wet with this case when you looked up the death certificate. We hadn't even finalized the details of the op yet."

Jack sat back, looking disgusted. "Still, there's no excuse for that."

"Well, we're seeing it now, Jack. Question is, does it mean anything?"

"But if the killer was taking retribution for Julianne Le Fevre's death and the date was important, why wouldn't he wait till the next year? Or go out after him, despite the gale?"

"Chances are, Le Fevre didn't go out to pull his pots that day, because of the weather. So, theoretically, the killer had a choice. Do the deed the next day or wait another whole year. Assuming there's actually something significant about the date." She looked at Jack. "We have to remember that Oslo Stumph was already dead. So if the killer was working some grand plan, he would have gone ahead with Le Fevre, even though he'd been robbed of the symbolism of the date."

"All this suggests a possible connection between the killer and Julianne Le Fevre."

They went back into the public records database and instituted a search for the Le Fevres' marriage certificate, as they had done for Cliff and Bess Gordon, when Gordon had been the focus of the investigation.

The seconds felt endless as they waited for the painfully slow internet connection to catch up with their search. Brie could hear the wind outside battering the windows, whistling up a storm. The melodrama of it seemed tailor-made for the moment.

Finally, the document appeared on the screen in front of them, and they both leaned in to read it. They turned and looked at each other for an astonished moment. The maiden name on the certificate read Julianne Ward.

"Wow." Brie sat back, stunned. "Whatever I was expecting, it would never have been this."

"Doc Ward?" Jack asked quietly. "Could it be possible?"

Brie shook her head slowly. "I don't know," she said, bemused. "But we both well know from our years in law enforcement that anything is possible. It's a common name, though. Do we know of any other Wards on the island?"

"Not that I've heard about."

"How about the lobstermen who are off-island for the winter?" she asked.

"There's still frequent scuttlebutt about all of them," Jack said. "As if the umbilical cord to Starkhaven is never quite severed. To my knowledge, the name Ward has never come up."

"Nor have I seen it in any of my work at the history center, poring over back documents and old newspapers."

"So, if the thought is that Doctor Tobias Ward could be Julianne Ward's father, and if he *were* the killer, then his motive for murdering Paul Le Fevre would be the death of his daughter."

"Undoubtedly based on a belief of negligence on the part of his son-in-law," Brie said. "What's more, under this theory of the crimes, Le Fevre would have been the primary target."

"Do we know anything about the doc's history here?" Jack asked. "Or how long he may have been on the island?"

"Actually, we do. That night when I cut my hand and went to have it stitched up, we talked about the doc's time on the island. Just small talk, mostly, probably to take my mind off what was going on."

"Or maybe the detective in you is just hard-wired to gather information."

Brie shrugged. "Maybe."

"Anyway, John asked if he'd grown up here. He said 'no.' That he had left the clinic in Rockland, where he practiced, and come here out of a desire to be more essential. He said he'd been an Army surgeon in the Middle East and that once one has been a battlefield surgeon, it changes everything. His words were, 'every day it's life or death.' After his wife died of cancer he said he wanted to go where he'd be . . . I think 'indispensable' was the word he used. And then he said something that didn't register then, but it does now. He said that people die in these remote communities, from things like heart disease, diabetes, prenatal care. Said he felt like he'd made a difference out here."

"Certainly an ironic statement if he were to turn out to be our killer," Jack said.

"I'll say. I did ask him that night how long he'd been on the island. He said he'd been here almost nine years. Le Fevre died a year ago, so that would put Doc Ward coming out here approximately two years after his daughter's death."

"Huh. So the two things could be connected."

"Possibly," Brie said. "But what strikes me now, looking back, is what he said when I went back to get my stitches out. Something like, 'life is a cycle' and how some die and some are born. How some leave and others arrive. At the time I wrote it off to the islanders' fatalistic bent, but the ease with which he said it . . . well, it almost seemed in that moment that he was as comfortable with death as with life."

"Interesting," Jack said. "I guess someone who'd been a battlefield surgeon might get that way."

"He also took the stance that drugs were behind all the deaths of the lobstermen out here. Of course, if he turns out to be our killer, we'll know that was just a smokescreen."

They sat for a moment staring expectantly at the computer monitor, as if they could conjure up an email from Dent Fenton with the mysterious boat numbers.

But now Brie was thinking about something else. Something that had happened that same day, when she went back to have her stitches out. Something that must have implanted itself in her subconscious. Something that may have triggered the symbolic dreams. That had been the day she had first met Hughie and his mother, Annette. They had come out of one of the examining rooms as she waited, and she recalled how agitated Hughie had been. At the time it wouldn't have struck her as out of the ordinary, considering his autism. But in the light of what they'd just discovered and considering Hughie's drawing, it had profound significance.

She told Jack about the incident. "I didn't know Hughie at all then, so his demeanor that day wouldn't have sent up any alarms. But his behavior on that day doesn't jibe at all with the boy I've come to know. Looking back now, he was clearly afraid that day; in fact, I would say terrified. Think about it, Jack. If he *had* witnessed the doctor murder Abe Winter, and he was keeping that secret inside him, imagine how frightening it would have been for him that day. It was probably a routine medical visit, but chances are Hughie hadn't been in the presence of the doctor since the day he'd witnessed the murder."

"You're right. Assuming the doctor could be the killer, that would have been completely terrifying for him." Jack shook his head slowly. "That poor kid. He may need some help to put things right."

"Believe me, I'll make sure Annette has some resources to find help for Hughie after this all shakes out."

Brie sat back in her chair and closed her eyes for a few moments. She was thinking about the first dream she'd had. Hughie on the cliff with the white owl, like a falconer of old. There was an image in that dream she could never make sense of. The wound on her hand was bleeding. Now a possible answer presented itself. If you're bleeding, you see the doctor. *See the doctor*, she thought. But to Brie the detective, "see the doctor" could also mean "be aware of the doctor."

"Whatcha thinking?"

"Just processing something." She leaned forward and clicked open her email. "Nothing from Dent yet."

"It's Saturday. He may be off doing something. So it's a waiting game."

"Something I'm not very good at," she admitted.

"You know what? We need to search for Julianne Ward's birth certificate," Jack said. "If Tobias Ward is her father, he'll be listed there."

"Why don't you stay here and work on that, Jack. I think I'll pay a visit to Clara Lyston—the woman who lived next door to Le Fevre. She was closer to him than anyone on the island. She would know if Tobias Ward was his father-in-law."

"Might also know how strained the relationship between the two of them was," Jack offered.

Brie nodded. "Good point."

She stood up and headed downstairs. She was putting on her coat when she had a thought. She went into the dining room where her sewing machine and quilting fabrics were and selected a beautiful piece of deep red batik fabric, about two yards in size, to bring to Clara as a gift. She folded it carefully and, using a long fragment of another color, tied a bow around it. Then she was out the door and climbing into the truck. She backed up and headed down the driveway and out onto the road.

Strong gusts of wind buffeted the truck as she drove toward Clara's house. She was thinking about how she could direct the conversation so as to ask about the connection between the doctor and Le Fevre. If in fact there was one, she assumed lots of people on the island would have known about it. Would it seem unusual that she was asking about the wife's maiden name? *Darn*, she thought. *I hate this being undercover. Every move has to be so carefully calculated.* She knew one thing. If this theory of theirs bore fruit, Clara Lyston would most likely be called as a witness for the prosecution, so she wanted to be very careful how she handled their interactions.

Before she knew it, she'd arrived at the east end of the village. She turned onto one of the short streets that ran up the hill. In about a quarter of a mile, she turned right and almost immediately pulled into Clara Lyston's driveway and drove up to the house. As she got out of the truck, she could hear the sound of an ax at work. Last time they'd visited, Clara had told her that she liked to split wood, that she thought it was good exercise. Brie headed around the tall white house. As soon as she turned the corner behind the house, Clara saw her. She was leaning on her ax, taking a break, and a smile broke out on her face.

"Brie. This is a nice surprise. It's good to see you."

"Hi, Clara. Hope I'm not catching you at a bad time."

"Not at all. Let's go inside. I'll make some coffee."

"That'd be great," Brie said, although she was plenty caffeinated already. She didn't know if it was her imagination, but Clara seemed somehow brighter, happier. There was a light in her clear blue eyes that hadn't been there before, and even her sandy, shoulder-length hair seemed to have come to life. Brie followed her in the back door, through a long hallway where they deposited their boots and coats, and into the kitchen.

"I brought this for you." She held out the small bundle of fabric. "I thought it was a color you'd enjoy."

"That's so kind of you," Clara said. "Thank you. It's lovely. I'll find a special place for it in my next project."

Brie nodded. "You're welcome." She looked down at the dark pine floor. "I felt bad that I had inadvertently brought up something that made you so sad last time I was here."

"You shouldn't feel that way," Clara said. "The truth is, I think it helped me." Brie must have looked a bit surprised, because Clara said, "Really, I think it did. I've somehow felt happier since that visit with you. I don't know why, but maybe, finally being able to share how I felt about Paul Le Fevre with somebody has lifted a burden off of me."

"If anything I said or did helped in that way, I'm glad," Brie said.

They got busy making coffee, but it seemed like the perfect opening to ask about Julianne Le Fevre.

"It's really tragic that there was no help for Paul's depression here on the island."

"You know I tried more than once to get him to go to the mainland to see someone there. Even told him I'd go with him. But his answer was the same one most men give about everything—'I'm fine.'"

Brie smiled. "Yes, I'm quite familiar with those two words. It's just too bad he didn't at least try to get help or maybe some medication from Doctor Ward, here on the island."

Clara turned away, but not before Brie saw anger darken her eyes.

"That never would have happened," she said. "You see, Doctor Ward was Paul's father-in-law. He came to the island a couple of years after Julianne died. Supposedly to go somewhere his skills were truly needed, but . . ."

"But what, Clara?"

She hesitated as if making a decision. "But while he may have moved here with good intentions, wanted to be of help in a place that had no doctor, I think he may have had other motives, too. I think he hated Paul. Blamed him for his daughter's death. Paul thought so, too. He said once that he wished Tobias had never come to the island." Clara's words came out in a rush as if under pressure, as if they'd been held back for a long time. "All I know is that after the doctor moved here, things went downhill fast for Paul. That's when his descent into alcoholism really accelerated. I think the doctor's presence was a constant reminder of the guilt he felt. A constant reminder of how he believed he had failed his wife."

"So, kind of like a mind game," Brie said.

"Exactly like that. And whether that was the doctor's intent . . . well, I guess no one can know that. But the longer it went on, the more tormented Paul seemed to become."

They took their coffee and sat at the table, and Clara put out a plate of cookies.

When Clara revealed that the doctor was Paul Le Fevre's father-in-law, Brie had felt her heart rate pick up. And everything else she had said just now went toward establishing a strong motive for the doctor. Whether he'd come to the island with a plan to gaslight his son-in-law or whether the idea had evolved after he arrived, the fact was that, according to Clara, Tobias Ward at some point had started down a dark road that eventually led to Paul Le Fevre's death.

"It seems like the situation would have stopped Paul from feeling like he could move on with his life," Brie said.

Anger flashed again in Clara's eyes. "That's what I thought, too. And to this day it makes me sad and angry. After he'd had a certain amount to drink, Paul would sometimes open up, give me a glimpse into his tormented life. After Doc Ward moved out here, things just went from bad to worse for him, psychologically speaking."

Brie sipped her coffee and let Clara talk. While what Clara was saying was certainly compelling, she reminded herself that this was the viewpoint of a woman who had been in love with Paul Le Fevre. Still, Brie sensed that truth might underpin everything she was revealing.

Clara went on. "Paul once told me that the doctor blamed him not only for his daughter's death but the death of his wife, Paul's mother-in-law, as well. It was after Julianne died that Esther Ward developed cancer. I guess the doc believed that the stress contributed to his wife's cancer."

Brie shook her head. "That would have been awful for Paul."

"If you recall, last time we talked, I told you that, in my heart of hearts, I believe that Paul had committed suicide. Now you can understand how I came to that conclusion. I think, finally, it was more than he could take."

Eventually they moved on to lighter topics. Clara described what spring was like on the island, and Brie talked about her work at the history center with Faith Babcock and why she found it so interesting. After about an hour, Brie said she should be heading home. She thanked Clara for her hospitality.

"It's been really nice getting to know you, Clara." She wanted to say more but couldn't and hoped when it all shook out that Clara wouldn't feel betrayed. But she guessed that Clara would be one of the first to want the killer brought to justice.

"Thanks for stopping by, Brie, and for listening. It really means a lot. And thank you for the lovely fabric."

At the back door, Brie pulled on her coat and boots and headed out to her truck and back through the village. She was thinking about everything Clara had said, and while not directly incriminating of the doctor, it certainly contributed to a picture of him, a side of him, that was less than benevolent. But the last piece of the puzzle was still missing. Until they learned about the numbers on the boats in Hughie's sketch, the final answer would continue to elude them. She could feel the strong easterly wind shaking the truck from behind. The weather gods were mixing up a good old New England cocktail— North Atlantic wind and water pressurized in that great barometric crucible.

Chapter 29

F ive minutes later, Brie turned left and headed up the access road. She parked the truck next to the outbuilding and ran for the house, head down against the wind.

"I'm home, Jack," she called.

"Still up here, Brie."

"I'll be right up."

Just then Angus appeared at the top of the stairs and came careening down the long flight. At the bottom he wiggled and thrashed around her. You have to stand strong when a large Newfoundland dog decides to love you, or down you'll go in a jiffy.

"Should I give him a run outside?" she called up the stairs.

"Couldn't hurt."

She headed for the back door, where Angus, having heard the word "outside," was doing his dance of joy. Any chance for a close encounter with a snow drift brought unbridled enthusiasm. He bounded out the door when she opened it and headed straight for the deep snow on the perimeter of the yard.

Back inside ten minutes later, she shed her outerwear, drank a large glass of water, and headed upstairs. She found Jack where she had left him an hour before, in the war room corner of the bedroom. He was typing up a report about what they had discovered through their records search and what had triggered the search, namely Hughie's sketch drawn the day Abe Winter had died.

She sat down next to Jack. "Well, I learned from Clara Lyston that Tobias Ward is indeed Paul Le Fevre's father-in-law." She told Jack about the psychological torment that the fact of the doctor living here had wrought on Le Fevre.

"Think about it. He would have always felt watched. And it sounds like, from the picture Clara drew, that was the doctor's intent. To never let Le Fevre free of the guilt he bore for the death of his wife."

"Cruel."

"Yes, it would have been."

"It took me some searching, but I found Julianne Ward's birth certificate. Turns out she was not born 'Ward.' When I couldn't find a birth certificate under that name, I searched for a marriage license for Tobias Ward, M.D., thinking that maybe Julianne was his stepdaughter. Once I found his wife's maiden name—Ester Townsend—I searched under that name and located Julianne's birth certificate. Her name there was Julianne Townsend. There was no father listed on the birth certificate. So the doc must have adopted Julianne when he married her mother. According to my math, the girl would have been about four years old when they married."

"Nice work, Jack. We may need those documents as evidence to prove the relationship between Tobias Ward and Paul Le Fevre. Very interesting, as well. Obviously he loved that little girl like his own blood."

"Not uncommon for good stepparents."

"So, we're just waiting on info on the boat numbers, but we know there are now several things that point toward Tobias Ward as the perpetrator. First off, there's Hughie's behavior in the doctor's clinic that day. Because I didn't know him, it didn't set off any alarm bells. But now that we know about Ward's connection to Le Fevre, it certainly does. But there's something else that occurred to me on the way home from Clara's."

"What's that?"

"The doctor was the only one who knew that Abe Winter would be out alone on the water that day in November, three months ago. Fin was his sternman and always would have been on the boat. But remember that the day before Winter died, Fin came in off the water sick and went to see the doc. He related the whole incident to John because he still feels guilty he wasn't on the boat that day. Anyway, the doctor told Fin he had the flu and to stay home and rest the next day or two."

"So if the doc is our killer, he created his own opportunity right then, by telling Fin to stay at home."

"And assuming Fin went directly home, no one else would have known that Winter would be alone on the water that day."

"Well, potentially someone could have seen him alone the following morning in the harbor, making it a crime of opportunity for one of the other lobstermen. But it's a strong point and certainly a damning fact for the doc."

Brie slid a yellow legal pad over and jotted some notes she knew would be helpful when it came to writing her report.

"Don't know about you, but I'm starving," Jack said. "Breakfast feels like a distant memory."

"Let's grab some lunch." She nodded toward the email screen. "A watched pot never boils."

Jack chuckled, and they headed downstairs to make some sandwiches.

There was just enough bread left for two sandwiches. They got out the ham and sliced some cheese, and Brie heated up the skillet so they could toast their sandwiches. Jack sliced up a couple of apples, and in a few minutes they settled at the kitchen table with their plates and coffee.

"I hope John gets home soon. The wind is up out there, and the seas will be building." Brie stared out the window, feeling that inexorable fear that always accompanied thoughts of John on a small lobsterboat on days like this.

"He'll be home soon, but if you're worried, you could call him on the radio." Jack nodded across the kitchen to where the ship-to-shore radio sat on the end of the counter.

Brie stared at it for a moment. "That's okay. I shouldn't bother him. Let's get back upstairs."

They put their dishes on the counter and headed back up to their work.

They sat down behind the table. To their right lay Hughie's sketchbook, open to the drawing he had made. They brought up the email screen. There was an email from Dent, and they clicked on it. Brie's heart rate picked up at the thought of what it might contain. After a few seconds it appeared on the screen, and they both leaned in. Dent had placed the two partial boat numbers there. The first, from the boat in the foreground of the picture, was registered to Winter, Abraham M. And there, listed next to the partial number from the second boat was the name, "Ward, Tobias J."

"We have our killer," Jack said, *sotto voce*.

They both sat back, and Brie felt a tremendous sense of relief. "We do indeed, and we have proof."

"Good work, Brie. Without your connection to Hughie— the most surprising of witnesses—I fear this case might have gone unsolved."

"Thanks, Jack. But this was a true joint effort. And we're not done yet."

She leaned forward and started typing an immediate reply to Dent, telling him they had their man and that they had hard evidence. She refrained from mentioning Hughie's name or the drawing out of an abundance of caution. "Please advise concerning arrest," she wrote. "We will need transport to mainland and uniform backup. Please also advise about possible timeline."

Within a couple of minutes, a reply came back. "Good work, team! I will put the wheels in motion here and get back to you. There are gale warnings posted, and day's end is fast approaching. We'll hope the seas are passable tomorrow. Stand by for more information."

Brie wrote back. Three words. "Roger that, Dent."

She had just clicked "Send" when she heard the door open downstairs and then that ubiquitous winter sound, the stomping of feet.

"I'm home, Brie. I brought lobsters."

"We're upstairs, John."

"I'm gonna grab something hot to eat."

"There's beef vegetable soup in the fridge and French bread on the counter."

"Sounds perfect," he called up the stairs.

A few moments later she heard the refrigerator open and close. She turned back to Jack. "Once we hear back from Dent Fenton, I'll email Mo Thorn and set a meeting with him. We owe him the courtesy of informing him about the arrest."

"I agree with that, Brie. But I don't like this waiting."

"Nor do I, Jack. The cop in each of us is hardwired to act once we identify a perpetrator. But with no way to hold Tobias Ward here on the island, we have no choice but to wait for transport from the Maine State Police or possibly the Coast Guard."

In about ten minutes, John appeared in the room. He grabbed some warm sweats and went into the bathroom to shower and change. When he came back, Brie asked, "How were the seas out there today?"

"Not too bad on this side of the island, but there are gale warnings out for tonight, so all bets are off for tomorrow." He must have read something into the look that she and Jack exchanged. "Why. What's up?"

"Pull up a chair," Brie said. "It's been a productive day."

There was an extra chair in the corner, and John brought it over and sat down at the table. First, Brie showed him the sketch that Hughie had done and explained the significance of it. Then she and Jack detailed their search through the public records and what it had revealed about the connection between Tobias Ward and Paul Le Fevre. Brie also told John what she had learned from Clara Lyston about the deteriorating relationship that had unfolded between the two men over the years. And finally about the email from Dent confirming who owned the two boats in Hughie's sketch.

"Wow. It's almost unbelievable." John sat back in his chair as if suddenly exhausted—as if a long day on the freezing North Atlantic could not begin to compete with such news. "Of all the people here we've looked into, speculated about, or established motives for, who would ever expect this?" He was silent for a moment. "And the other three murders?"

"It's hard to understand the motivation of a madman," Brie said. "And believe me, killers are mad. That said, it's not too hard to see why the doctor picked who he did. Oslo Stumph was a notorious bully who liked to mind everyone's business. I think the doc would have wanted to eliminate him in order to feel secure about going after his prime target—Paul Le Fevre. As for Cliff Gordon, it occurs to me that, when Jema Hawkins disappeared, she was close to the age of the doctor's daughter, Julianne, when *she* died. That could have struck a nerve for the doc, and if he bought into the island narrative that Cliff Gordon had had something to do with Jema's disappearance, it could have created a motive."

"Along with the other more obvious motive the doctor would have had," Jack said. "Namely that Gordon abused his wife. Being a doctor, that wouldn't have sat well with him."

"But killing four people did?" Disgust and anger stained John's voice.

"Look, John, there's a part of every killer that's completely divorced from logic," Jack said.

"Yeah, the madman part," Brie added.

She told John about the doctor's comments when she went back to get her stitches out—comments about how some are born and some die, that were said with an almost casual kind of acceptance of the fact.

"Maybe not that surprising," John said. "As a battlefield surgeon, that would have been his day-to-day reality."

"Exactly what I thought," Jack said.

"He may actually have managed to convince himself that the island would be a better place without those other two men—Stumph and Gordon." Brie said. "And as for Abe Winter, the doc had a passionate hatred of the opioid trade, which would have been reason enough for him to go after Winter, even if Winter wasn't blackmailing him—something we have no proof of so far."

"He got careless, though, when he went after Winter," Jack said. "Maybe he'd become overconfident, or maybe with Fin ashore that day, sick, it was his only opportunity to go after his blackmailer. But he somehow miscalculated, didn't use darkness or the sea conditions as cover, and Hughie Bryce was able to observe him."

"Fin said there was heavy sea smoke that day," John said. "But up on the northwest side of the island where Winter had his traps, who knows? A strong gust of wind could have made the boats visible long enough for Hughie to witness the murder."

"Yes, and remember, Hughie always has his binoculars with him," Brie said. "Plus, the cliffs up there are right near where he lives. That's his main stomping grounds."

"So, what's going to happen now?" John asked.

Brie leaned back in her chair. "I've put Dent on notice. He's organizing transport and will send a couple of officers for backup. We will have to coordinate the arrest with their arrival, and with the gale warning issued for tonight, it's uncertain when they will be able to get out here. But I'm hoping the seas will be passable and the arrest can take place tomorrow. One thing's for sure. With this storm brewing, no one's leaving the island tonight."

As if to confirm what she said, a strong gust of wind buffeted the house and whistled around the eaves. In the forest behind the house, she heard the trees creaking and groaning.

John lay down on the bed to take a nap, and Brie and Jack worked on their reports while the information was fresh in their minds.

Later on they all headed downstairs to start dinner.

"I doubt we'll hear back from Dent until he has a lock on weather conditions for tomorrow," Brie said.

Jack filled the big lobster pot—the one that resides in every Maine kitchen—with water and some seaweed that John had brought home to add to the boil.

"The lobsters are out back, chilling in the snow bank," John said.

Brie cut some potatoes, coated them with olive oil, salt and pepper, and put them in a hot oven to roast.

When the pot was boiling, John plunged the lobsters in head first and slapped the lid on. They kept a good-sized rock on the countertop to weight down the lid. They got out salad greens and some veggies and put together a salad, and Jack melted some butter for the lobsters. Brie put a plastic-coated tablecloth on the dining table to make for easy cleanup, since lobster boils can be messy business. Extra napkins and nutcrackers were added to the table, and when the lobsters were done, they went onto a big platter. John cracked open some beers and they headed into the dining room to eat.

"I'm gonna miss the lobster dinners," Brie said.

"Ditto that," Jack added.

"Well, we'll just have to meet for lobster now and then and reminisce about Starkhaven Island."

Brie wasn't sure if John was being facetious, but before she could respond, Jack said, "That'd be great. Let's do it."

"Here's an update," John said as they cracked into their lobsters. "Trulie Hyden has returned to the island. Fin told me about it today. I guess he arrived back yesterday."

"Did Fin know where he'd been?" Brie asked.

"Yeah. At a drug treatment center on the mainland. Apparently he checked himself in there shortly after he left the island."

"Good for him," Jack said. "That had to take guts."

"Fin said he's like a new man. Said he came by his aunt's house last night. He apologized to Fin for how he'd treated him and for accusing him of having something to do with Abe Winter's death."

"He'll want George back as his sternman," Brie said.

"Speaking of George, shouldn't we let him know what's going on?" John asked.

"We will, as soon as I hear something back from Dent Fenton about the timeline."

She told John she'd have to notify Mo Thorn as well, and that she planned to request a meeting with him, in person, once she knew when the arrest would go down. She cautioned John that they needed to keep the situation under their hats till then.

"Got it," John said.

When they were done eating, they cleaned up from dinner. Brie and Jack went upstairs to check for word from Dent, and John went into the living room to read.

At 7 p.m. an email came through from Dent Fenton. He had received the marine weather forecast from the Coast Guard. The storm was now expected to track south of them, missing northern New England. Seas were expected to be passable tomorrow. He had put together a team for the arrest. Their ETA at Starkhaven Island was 10:30 a.m.

Brie immediately framed up an email to Mo Thorn. It read: "Urgent I meet with you tomorrow morning at the town office. Would 8 a.m. work?"

Within fifteen minutes a reply came back from Thorn. "I'll meet you there at eight o'clock."

Brie replied back. "Roger that."

She then sent George a somewhat cryptic email saying that the "storm" would be coming to an end and they should meet tomorrow. She thought he would get the gist of it, and sure enough, a reply came back within fifteen minutes saying, "Understood." He said he had promised Trulie Hyden that he'd go out with him in the morning to check the status of his traps but would check his email later tomorrow.

Shortly after that, John appeared upstairs. He didn't have to say anything. Brie knew he needed to get to sleep. She and Jack closed their laptops and went downstairs.

At ten o'clock she crawled into bed. John was fast asleep, but the escape she craved would not come easy that night. Faces of the dead lobstermen seemed determined to haunt her on this eve of resolution, as if to say, "What took you so long?" As if to say, "We're restless down here, in our watery graves, waiting for justice."

Chapter 30

Sunday, February 28

B rie woke at 6:30 a.m. feeling like she hadn't slept, her thoughts clouded by a low-grade headache. She crept out of bed so as not to disturb John on the one day he could sleep in a bit, and headed in for a shower. The hot water on her head and neck began to dissolve the pain and clear the cobwebs from her brain. There was plenty of time before her meeting with Mo Thorn, so she stood under the water for a few extra minutes, feeling the comfort of the warm steam that slowly filled the small room. This was the big day. They'd solved the case. All that remained was the arrest of Dr. Tobias Ward. But because of the logistics, things were not as straightforward as they would normally be. The location of the island, the weather, and the seas all played a role in making the staging of this operation more troublesome.

Once out of the shower, she brushed her teeth, dressed, and took her hair dryer downstairs so she wouldn't wake up John. Down in the kitchen, she started the coffee, put a pot of oatmeal on to cook, and sat at the table and dried her hair. By the time she'd finished, Jack and Angus appeared in the kitchen.

"Well, today's the big day," he said.

"It is indeed. Let's hope all goes according to plan."

331

Jack pulled on his coat and boots. "I'll just get Angus out to do his business, and then we'll talk." He opened the back door, and Brie felt a blast of cold air rush in. But the sky outside was clear with just a few patchy clouds. The storm, as Dent had predicted, had tracked south of them.

She went to the stove and stirred the oatmeal and got out bowls, milk, and brown sugar. Within five minutes Jack and Angus came through the door in a rush of foot stomping and fur shaking. Jack peeled off his coat and boots and came over to the stove.

"I checked the marine forecast online this morning. Seas are running three to six feet."

"Should be passable," Brie said. "Are you coming with me this morning?"

"I think I'll let you handle Thorn, and I'll stay here and monitor communications from the lieutenant."

"Probably a good idea. One of us should hang here in case the plan of action changes."

By the time the oatmeal was cooked, Brie heard John moving about upstairs. In a few minutes he came down. They ate their oatmeal and drank their coffee while standing in the kitchen, speculating about how the day would unfold. There was an air of excitement but with something else mixed in—something that tempered the adrenaline. Brie knew it well. Jack would have too. It was caution.

*   *   *

At five minutes to eight, Brie pulled up and parked across from the town office. Mo Thorn's pickup truck was parked outside, so she got out and headed across the street. She took a deep breath and let it out before stepping inside. She shed her boots on the mat there and walked the length of the meeting room and rapped on Thorn's office door with its brass door plate that said "Town Manager."

"Come in."

Instead of his normal gruffness, the words held a hint of welcome. *Of course they would,* she thought. *He knows he's close to getting us off his island.*

"Good morning, Mr. Thorn." She had decided to keep it formal since this was official business. "Thank you for meeting here so early."

"No problem. Eight a.m. is lunchtime for us lobstermen." He gestured to the chair across the desk from him, and Brie sat down. "But I assume it's something important to bring us both out at this time on a Sunday."

"It is," she said. "We've reached a conclusion in the case."

"You've found the killer?"

"Yes, we have."

He leaned forward in his chair. "So, don't keep me waiting. Who is it?"

"I'm afraid I can't tell you who the perpetrator is until we make an arrest."

His hand came down hard on the desk. "Dammit, yes you can. I demand to know who it is."

"Demand all you want, but protocol dictates I withhold that information until we make an arrest."

He sent daggers across the desk at her.

"But I wanted you to be informed about how and when the arrest is going down today. We certainly owe you that."

Thorn sat back in his chair with an air of surrender. "Fine. So tell me."

"Lieutenant Dent Fenton will be arriving at the island at ten thirty this morning, with two uniformed troopers, to make the arrest. Either the Coast Guard or Maine Marine Patrol will provide transport. I assume that will depend on sea conditions."

Thorn nodded seriously, as if the gravity of the situation was sinking in. "It will be good to see Dent again," he said, sounding more reasonable now.

Thorn has pulled in his thorns, Brie thought. *A rare occurrence.*

"This information needs to stay between you and me," she admonished. "You just need to carry on as normal and let the operation unfold. Understood?"

"Understood."

The word was said with reluctance, and Brie held his gaze for a few moments, conveying the necessity for compliance.

They sat for a moment, regarding each other.

"There's one other matter we need to address. I think you know what it is. When we met before, I told you I expected you to provide the name of the person who runs the drug operation in Maine waters."

Thorn reached in the drawer to his right and handed her a piece of paper with a single name on it and a phone number.

She studied it and then gave him a look that said she meant business.

"Look, that's all I have," Thorn said. "It's not the top dog, but it's one of his henchmen."

"If this turns out to be nothing, you know I'll be back."

"I know that. It's not nothing."

"Very well, then. I assume you'll be in your office here throughout the morning as things unfold?"

"I'm not going anywhere. Believe me, I'm as eager to have this be over as I'm sure you are."

"Something we can agree on," Brie said. It was as good a place to stop as any. She stood up. "We'll be in touch as things wrap up."

Thorn nodded and busied himself with something on his desk. It was her cue to exit, and she did.

Outside, she checked her watch. Eight twenty. Two hours before things started to pop. She crossed to her truck but then remembered they were out of bread and instead headed down to the general store. As she stepped in the door of the store, she missed seeing Doc Ward park his truck just up the street and head into the town office.

*   *   *

Tobias Ward walked through the meeting room and knocked on the door to Mo Thorn's office.

"What now?" Thorn's exasperated voice rang out.

Ward opened the door and stuck his head in. "It's me, Mortimer."

"Oh, Doc, sorry. I thought you were that annoying Beaumont woman, back to bother me some more."

"Beaumont woman?"

"It's Brie Ross's real name. She was just here."

"Well, it's just me. I had to come in for a few supplies. Saw your truck and thought I'd stop in and check on your shoulder." Doc Ward walked over to the desk.

"Thanks, Doc. It's much better since you gave me that shot."

"Good to hear. Can I check the shoulder?"

"Sure." Thorn started to stand.

"No, just stay seated."

The doctor hung his coat on the chair and came around the desk. He pressed on some spots on Thorn's right shoulder. "Any pain?" he asked.

"Nope."

Then Ward lifted the arm and moved it in different directions—up, down, front to back. "How about now? Anything."

"Nope. Feels fine, Doc. Guess you know what you're doing."

"Well, I hope so, after all these years. So, any progress on the undercover case? I know how frustrated you were about it when you came to see me."

Thorn let out a sigh. "They keep me outside the loop. It makes me angry. After all, I'm in charge of things here."

"Yes, you are," Ward affirmed.

"It'll be over soon, though. I've just had word this morning that they are making an arrest."

"Really? That is big news. Don't suppose they told you who?"

"Of course not," Thorn spat out. "Doc, this info has to stay between us. Those detectives would have my head."

"My lips are sealed, Mo."

The doc moved hastily around the desk, put on his coat, and headed toward the office door.

Thorn wondered what the rush was.

"I'll leave you to your work," Tobias said.

"Thanks for stopping by, Doc." But Ward had already closed the door. Thorn heard a rapid retreat on the other side of it. For just a moment he wondered if he'd made a mistake. But he quickly shrugged that off and went back to his work.

*   *   *

Just inside the general store, Brie stomped her boots on the mat and headed back to the bakery and deli.

"Good to see you, Brie," Mary said when she saw her heading down the aisle. "It's been a while."

"I know. Good to see you, too." She wondered how amiable the greetings would be after the day unfolded. "Jack is down here so often, he usually picks things up for us."

"He's such a nice man. It's wonderful to have him here on the island."

Brie wasn't sure what to say to that, so she changed the subject.

"John told me that Trulie Hyden is back on Starkhaven."

"Yes. It's all around the island about him going in for drug treatment. So I'm not breaking any confidences."

"John filled me in about it. Wonderful thing, don't you think? Shows courage."

"It certainly does. I'm hoping he'll be a beacon to others here who struggle with substance abuse. He's been in the store a couple of times already, buying fruit and vegetables. He seems like a changed man. Said he's working on a healthy diet as well."

"That's great to hear."

They talked on for a few more minutes about Brie's work at the history center and how John was doing on the water. At 8:40 Brie checked her watch. Time to head back home, see if Jack had heard anything new from Dent Fenton. She asked for a loaf of Italian bread and some deli ham. Mary bagged everything up, and Brie paid her.

By 8:45 she was back in her truck. She made a U-turn and headed for home. She was deep in thought when she recognized Tobias Ward's truck approaching. She'd seen it outside the clinic the two times she'd been there. As he got closer, she saw the doc behind the wheel. As he passed, he turned and smiled at her and waved as if everything was normal as pie.

Probably headed to the store for some of Mary's coffee and danish, Brie thought. *Well, he has a couple more hours of normal as pie. I hope he enjoys them.* She felt a flash of anger, and even though the sun was out and the sky blue, the reality of those four men dead at the bottom of the sea cast a deep shadow across her heart.

A couple of minutes later, she turned into the driveway that led up to the house. She parked the truck and headed inside. Jack was sitting at the dining room table with his laptop, typing away.

"Any news?" she asked.

"ETA is still the same. Ten thirty. The seas are rough, so they've asked the Coast Guard to provide transport. Dent is supervising the operation and will have two uniformed troopers with him as previously stated."

Brie nodded. "Just passed the doc on the way back from the village. He smiled and waved."

"He won't be smiling in a couple of hours," Jack said, carrying on with his work.

As he said it, though, Brie felt a faint sense of alarm. "Where was he going?" she asked under her breath.

"The store? For some of Mary's danish she makes on Sundays," Jack offered.

"That's what I thought. Still . . . I think I'll drive back into the village, check it out."

"There's no way he could know, Brie. No one but the three of us knows who our perp is."

She didn't say anything but stepped into the entryway and pulled on her coat and boots. "Where's John?" she asked as she opened the door.

"Went out for a run. He just left."

"Hold down the fort. I'll be back in a few."

In less than ten minutes she entered the village and slowed to a crawl. Down the street, she saw the doc's truck parked in front of the general store. She felt a sense of relief, knowing that Tobias Ward was just exercising the Sunday morning rite of pastry. Even so, she parked her truck and headed across to the store, just to check things out. She certainly didn't want to get into a *tête-à-tête* with him, fearing he might intuit that something was off, but she could confirm he was there and then be on her way. Still, she didn't want him to get the sense that she was checking up on him, either. *Don't overthink it, Brie. He doesn't know you're the law.* Even so, maybe best to buy some danish. The guys would just have to deal with it.

She stepped inside the store and looked around. No sign of the doc. She walked along the front windows, looking down each aisle. When she got to the last aisle, Mary spotted her from back in the bakery/deli.

"Did you forget something, Brie?"

"Sure did. I forgot to get danish." She walked back toward the bakery. "The guys need their fix." She peered into the pastry case. "Doc Ward's truck is out front," she said by way of conversation. "Was he just in here?"

"Nope. Haven't seen him this morning."

Brie asked for three apricot and three cherry danish. Mary bagged them up, and Brie paid her and headed out of the store. She stowed the pastries in the truck and stood for a moment looking up and down the street. There was no sign of the doc, so she headed back up the street to the town office, walking at a good clip.

Inside she stomped her boots but didn't remove them and headed for Thorn's office. She knocked on the door and waited for a few fidgety seconds until she heard, "Come."

She opened the door and moved quickly across to the desk.

"What now, Brie? I thought we were done."

"I'm trying to locate Doc Ward. Have you seen him this morning?"

"Yeah. He was in here shortly after you left. He wanted to check on my shoulder. He gave me a cortisone shot last week and wanted to know if it was working."

"You didn't mention anything about our meeting this morning, did you?" She watched him carefully. "You haven't told him anything about our operation."

Thorn's eyes shifted to the side, and he worried some papers around on his desk. "I might have," he mumbled, sheepishly.

"Not about the arrest?" Brie's voice moved up the decibel scale.

"Might have. What would it matter?" he said defensively. "He's just the doc."

Brie placed her hands on the desk and leaned in. "He's the killer." Each word struck like an ax.

Thorn bolted out of his chair. "What? No!"

"Yes. Tobias Ward is the killer. His truck is outside, down the street. Where is he?"

Thorn grabbed a pair of binoculars from the far side of his desk and raced toward the front door with Brie close behind. Outside, he rushed across the street and trained the glasses on the harbor below—on one particular spot.

"His boat's gone. He's fleeing!" He turned and ran back across the street with Brie in pursuit. He burst through the door. "I'll radio the men. We'll go after him." He darted toward the ship-to-shore radio in the corner of his office.

"Alert the Coast Guard!" She didn't wait for his response but turned and ran for the door. "We'll follow in John's boat."

She thought Ward would head for Rockland. He'd lived there. He would know that harbor. Might even have a vehicle on the mainland. That was not uncommon. But what if he headed down the coast or farther down East toward Canada?

She raced to the truck, jumped in, and headed out of the village in the opposite direction from home. John liked to run the island circuit. She knew what time he'd left home and guessed he'd be nearing the opposite end of the island, where he'd drop down through the village and then back toward home. If she was wrong in her estimate, he had already passed through the village, and that would cost her precious time. But she kept going, up the hill toward the spine of the island, where the road turned and ran west.

The road here seemed more desolate than usual as she strained to see farther along it than was possible. And while it basically ran in a straight line, it rose and fell just enough to arrest a long view down it. After what seemed like far more than the three or four minutes that had elapsed, she came up a short rise and spotted John down the road. She stepped on the accelerator, and gravel shot out behind her.

He saw her approaching and stepped to the side of the road. She came to a lurching stop next to him, and he opened the passenger door.

"What's up?"

"Get in. Tobias Ward is fleeing the island."

John hopped in and she stepped hard on the accelerator, once again rocketing gravel into the air behind them. She told him what Thorn had done and that he was calling the men to go after Ward.

"I need to get my gun, and we have to go after them in your boat."

"But which direction?"

"I think Ward will head for Rockland. He used to live there. What do you think?"

"He's not a mariner. Chances are he'll go to the port he knows."

They drove west in tense silence for the next few minutes along Starkhaven's spine and followed the road as it bent south toward their house. Brie turned in at the driveway and gunned the truck up the hill. They piled out and headed in the house, and she took the stairs two at a time up to the bedroom, where she kept her gun in its lock box. She heard John telling Jack what had happened. She clipped the holster and gun onto her jeans and was back downstairs in a flash. John had pulled on his Bean boots and squall jacket and waited, hand on the doorknob.

"Inform Dent what has happened," she said to Jack.

"Will do. Be careful."

Brie caught his words just as they shut the door. And then they were in John's truck heading for the harbor.

Chapter 31

John parked unceremoniously at the foot of the wharf. They jumped out and headed for his dory. Brie went down the ladder, stepped aboard the tiny craft, and perched in the bow. John freed the docking line and stepped aboard. He pulled hard for his mooring and in no time they were climbing aboard his lobsterboat. He went forward to the house and turned over the engine while Brie released the mooring line and tied the dory to it.

While he gave the engine a minute to warm up, she looked around the harbor. "Do you know who's gone after him?"

John scanned the harbor to see which boats were missing. "Thorn, for sure, and Lars Bjorklund." He looked to starboard. "Bellsby's boat is gone, too, and Kieran McTavish's." He throttled up the engine, and they motored out of the harbor. Once clear of it, he opened her up all the way and they surged forward. The waters just south of Starkhaven were calm, but John was already steering a northwest heading toward Rockland. Things would get rough once they left the shelter of the island.

As the boat careened over the water, Brie, feet spread wide, leaned close to John. "Do you think they'll be able to catch him?"

John kept his eyes on the sea ahead. "How much lead time do you think the doc had?"

She was silent for a minute, estimating things in her head. The time it would have taken the doc to get to his boat and leave the harbor after he passed her on the road. The time it took her to get back to the village, check the store and alert Thorn, and the time it would have taken to get the posse launched.

"If the men responded quickly, the doc might have had a fifteen- to twenty-minute lead," she said.

"The doc's boat is an older one, and the seas will be rough, which will slow him down. Thorn and his posse all have big powerful lobsterboats. The time to the mainland, even in a fast boat, is at least an hour. If their heading is correct, they should overtake him." He picked up the handset to make a radio call, but Brie stopped him.

"No," she shouted over the roar of the engine. "If you call the men, you'll alert the doc."

"Right. Good thinking."

In her former life as a flatlander from the Midwest, she might not have so quickly remembered that a call going out over VHF is heard by all vessels in radio range. After all, it had been many years since her familial sailing of Lake Superior. But after a full season aboard *Maine Wind*, that fact was keenly in sync with her detective instincts for radio silence.

She looked at the compass. Their heading was north northwest, bearing 325 degrees magnetic. They were on a bead for Rockland, Maine. Starkhaven Island fell away to the east of them, and now the seas toughened up. John maintained his speed even though they were taking spray and the occasional sea across their bow. Overnight the wind had turned to the west, so at least they weren't driving straight up into it.

As they pounded across lumpy seas, Brie was left to her thoughts. She felt responsible for what had unfolded—guilty that Tobias Ward had gotten away. How could she have prevented it? What could she have done differently?

"This isn't your fault, you know," John said, as if reading her thoughts. "Thorn has been a loose cannon from the start."

"I should have warned him more often not to divulge anything about our operation."

"Do you really think that would have mattered?"

Brie was silent for a few moments. "Probably not," she finally said.

"Guys like Thorn, they feel entitled. He was destined to run the island. It was his birthright. That's not always the best thing for character development."

After that they fell silent, John focused on the seas ahead, and Brie holding on to the side of the house with one hand to steady herself while training the binoculars on the sea ahead every twenty seconds or so. For fifteen minutes they held to their heading. Brie started to feel desperation coming to a slow boil in her gut, burning its way up into her esophagus. She took a deep breath, told herself it was just the rocky seas. She raised the glasses again, holding her breath as much to steady them as to steady her own hope.

"There. I see something. North of our heading."

John took the glasses and trained them on the sea ahead for a prolonged moment and then corrected course to the new heading. He raised the glasses again to be sure and checked the compass bearing so he could steer that course.

"Keep watching, Brie. We need to know if it's them."

She let go of the house, using her wide stance and strong legs and core to steady her as she trained the glasses on the sea ahead. In the distance a picture started to come into view. First one boat, then another and another. As they advanced on the position, she realized she was seeing a group of boats.

"I'm seeing several boats, looks like they're stationary, in a circle, maybe. That has to be them."

John took the glasses and trained them on the sea ahead while maintaining his course and speed. "It's a group of boats, all right. Looks like they might have Ward's boat surrounded." He handed the glasses back to Brie. "We're still several miles away."

Brie kept the glasses trained on the boats, trying to see what was unfolding. But they were still too far off to glean any details. Even though John was traveling at 25 knots, which is really hauling on the water, it could never have been fast enough for her. Her anxiety mounted as each nautical mile sped past.

Four or five minutes ticked by, and finally she could make out some details. Now she saw a fifth boat in the middle of the others—presumably Ward's boat. There appeared to be two men aboard near the stern of that vessel. She assumed one of them must be Tobias Ward and that one of the lobstermen had gone aboard to detain him until she arrived.

"What are you seeing?"

"They definitely have Ward's boat surrounded, and there are two men aboard his boat. Can't make out who they are."

They were closing on the scene fast, though, and John throttled back his engine as they made their final approach. Brie trained the binoculars on the boats, and now she could make out the two men aboard the boat in the middle. Mo Thorn and Lars Bjorklund.

"I see Thorn and Bjorklund aboard Ward's boat, but no sign of him."

"They've probably stowed him below. Maybe they tied his hands and feet just to be safe."

John made the final approach, slowing his boat to a near idle as he made his way up to the group. Brie headed out on the bow and got ready to throw their line across to the men aboard. There was an open spot near the stern of Ward's boat, and John nosed his bow in there, reversing the engine at just the right moment to bring the boat to a dead stop. Brie threw the line, and John headed to the stern and threw a second line. He pulled a large fender out of one of the lockers and hung it between the two boats. Brie stepped up on the gunwale and jumped across to the other boat. She noticed Bellsby and McTavish watching intently from their boats. Thorn and Lars were stone-faced.

"Where's Ward?"

No answer came back.

"Where's Ward?" she asked again, a knot taking shape in her gut.

"His boat was abandoned when we got here."

She looked at Lars, but he didn't make eye contact. "That right?" she asked.

"Yup." Lars towered over her like a mountain man, feet spread wide, arms across his chest.

"McTavish thought he saw the doc jump overboard as we were approaching," Thorn said.

"That right?" she called across to McTavish.

"Thought I did. Happened pretty fast—kind of a blur."

"Uh-huh. Was his boat still underway when you thought you saw that?"

McTavish darted a look toward Thorn. "No, it was stationary," he said.

"Boat was dead in the water when we approached," Thorn said.

"I see." She turned to Alan Bellsby. "That what happened?"

"It's what happened," he said.

She held his eyes for a few moments, trying to divine what lay behind them. She looked back at Thorn and then Bjorklund, waiting for someone to elaborate.

"So, you're saying he took his own life."

"He's not here," Lars said. "Doesn't leave too many possibilities."

She turned and looked to the northwest. The mainland was still just a shadow on the horizon. Beneath them, the boat rolled in the seas. A Northern Gannet wheeled overhead, circling momentarily, curious about the unusual floating island far below. She glanced back at John, but whatever he was thinking was unreadable.

"I'm going below and look around," she said.

She stepped past Thorn and into the house, also known as the standing shelter on lobsterboats. She looked around at the console, the windows, the sole beneath her feet. There was nothing here to give a clue of what had happened. She ducked down into the trunk cabin that sat beneath the house and ran forward toward the bow. It was a tiny, cramped space, full of lines, lobster buoys, and equipment. There was a V-berth forward under the bow, also covered with all kinds of flotsam and jetsam.

She was looking for anything that might tell her what had unfolded. A note, any sign of a struggle, and of course, blood. She'd been below decks for a few minutes when she sensed she was not alone. She turned abruptly, her hand automatically going to her gun. Thorn and Lars Bjorklund loomed unusually large in the claustrophobic space.

Lars took a step forward. "What are you doing down here?"

Brie stood her ground. "Looking for evidence."

"Evidence of what?" Thorn asked.

"I'll know when I find it." Her eyes traveled from Thorn back to Lars and held there.

"Those four men," Lars said, "they were our friends. Our fellow lobstermen."

Brie studied him. "So, you're glad Tobias Ward is gone."

"Didn't say that. Said they were our friends." The words were like the closing of a door. Lars turned and headed topside. Thorn followed.

Brie searched the space again, but there was nothing to be seen down here except a tangle of disorganized equipment.

She climbed back up on deck and walked slowly toward the stern of the boat, again looking for any signs of struggle, checking the coaming for blood trace, looking for anything that might have been dropped, anything that seemed out of place.

The wind came strong out of the west. The entire flotilla was drifting east, and the tide was going out, taking them farther and farther from where Ward had gone into the sea. Virtually erasing any possibility that his body would ever be found.

She turned abruptly to Thorn. "Did you have something to do with this?"

"Course not," he blustered.

She turned to Lars. "How 'bout you? You have anything to do with Ward's disappearance?"

Lars was stoic. "Nope."

A moment passed. It bristled with passive hostility.

A smile crept slowly onto Thorn's face. "Look at it this way. The State of Maine won't have to lock him up. Davy Jones has taken care of that."

Brie turned on him. "You find this amusing?"

"It is what it is."

And I'd like to know exactly what it is, she thought to herself.

"Did you alert the Coast Guard?"

"We didn't want to tip Ward off. We knew he'd be monitoring the Coast Guard channel."

She nodded. It was the same reason she and John had maintained radio silence.

"Who's going to tow his boat back to the island?" she asked.

"I'll do it," Lars said.

John gave Brie a hand back aboard. Thorn released the lines and threw them across to John.

Lars boarded his lobsterboat and maneuvered his stern up to the bow of Tobias Ward's boat. Thorn threw him the docking line, and Lars belayed it to a cleat at the stern of his boat. He stepped back to the helm, and once Thorn had reboarded his boat, slowly motored free of the rest of the group and headed southeast.

"We need to alert Dent Fenton to call off the mission," Brie told John. "They're probably already underway."

"We'll use the satellite phone. That way we won't reveal the situation to everyone on the island who's tuned in to their radio."

When they'd come out to the island, John had brought the satellite phone he carried aboard *Maine Wind*. The phone allowed for private communication with someone on shore or with the captain on another vessel who had a satellite phone. Brie entered Dent Fenton's cell number and sent the call. She hoped the team was still close enough to the mainland to pick up the call. If not, they'd hail the Coast Guard vessel on the radio. But within seconds, Dent answered. Brie filled him in on what had happened and waited for instructions. She heard Dent talking to the skipper, telling him to abort the mission. Then he was talking to her again.

"When you were aboard Ward's boat, did you see anything suspicious?" he asked. "Anything that would suggest a different narrative from what the lobstermen told you?"

"Nothing, Lieutenant."

"So, the supposition is that Ward saw the lobstermen overtaking his boat and decided to end it himself."

"That's the supposition. One of the men said he thought he saw Ward jump overboard, but they were a ways off, and he couldn't be sure."

"What do you think, Brie?"

Silence stretched between them.

"I'm not sure what to think, Dent."

"When I get back to the mainland, I'll put the Evidence Response Team on notice. I want to send them out there to go over that boat."

"Roger that, Dent. I'll send all the details that led up to the situation in a report later."

"Thanks, Brie."

They ended the call.

As they motored slowly back toward the island, Brie felt deeply troubled by the outcome. A question hung in her mind. A question she knew would never be answered. John was silent, but she sensed he, too, was troubled.

"Do you think that's how things really unfolded?" she asked.

He kept his eyes on the sea for a time before he spoke.

Finally he said, "I think four lobstermen were sent to the bottom of the sea by Tobias Ward. Interesting that he should end up there, too."

They fell silent again, the seas passing beneath them.

"Remember that first meeting with Thorn, on the island?" John asked.

"What about it?"

"Remember what he said?"

Brie nodded slowly, remembering but not wanting to un-earth the words. Not wanting to repeat them, as if the vocaliz-ing gave them some terrible power. "He said, 'Out here, we like to take care of things ourselves.'"

To the southeast, Starkhaven Island swam into view. Brie had read once that it's the people that make a place. For good or for bad, it's always the people. She watched as the island climbed slowly out of the sea. It sat as it had for millennia. A hard knob of granite, sometimes crowned by snow, as it was now, sometimes by a haze of dark green spruce. But forever sur-rounded by the cold, insulating, deep blue sea. The islanders insulated, too, by the remoteness of the place. Bent and shaped by the will of the sea. *For good or for bad*, she thought. *For good or for bad.*

Chapter 32

The harsh winds of reality blew over the island, delivering the cold truth of what had happened. Revealing the guilt of Doctor Tobias Ward, as well as the undercover operation, led by Brie and Jack, that had uncovered the truth.

The Evidence Response Team from the Maine State Police was sent to the island, but no further evidence was found as to what had unfolded aboard Tobias Ward's lobsterboat. Brie, for her part, would always believe that four men had decided to take the law into their own hands and mete out justice to a killer in an eye-for-an-eye kind of retribution. And even if one of them had gotten there first and done the deed, the other three had closed ranks to protect him. The outcome was a bitter pill for her and Jack—that after solving the case of the murders, they could not bring the perpetrator to justice.

She also strongly suspected that, had the investigation never been launched, had an answer not been found in the deaths the missing lobstermen, the residents of Starkhaven would have gone on as they had for generations, simply denying what was not helpful to the island narrative. Like all dark parts of its history down through time, the island would have absorbed those deaths and moved on. And maybe, in such a remote place, survival depended on that approach.

The case was officially closed, but a number of questions lingered in her mind. Had Tobias Ward originally gone to the island innocently or even symbolically to place a doctor where his daughter had so desperately needed one? Had the general lawlessness of the place begun to work on him so that, after years, he finally decided to take retribution for his daughter's death? Was there a killer inside him all the time, or did the nature of the island itself turn him into one? They were questions with no answers. The kind that haunt detectives late at night when sleep is elusive, trapping them in the grim web that only human nature can spin. As with all difficult cases, Brie would have to make peace with them—lay them to rest so she could move on.

During the week and a half in which the team prepared to leave the island, she did sense that a weight had been lifted from the collective consciousness. Even so, she still experienced a mixture of gratitude and resentment from the natives. The investigation had unraveled part of the island fabric, cut out a piece that, while defective and malevolent, was essential to the status quo. As the island doctor, Tobias Ward had been both broadly depended on and one of Starkhaven's most trusted residents. The fact of that brought a variety of reactions.

While Annette Bryce, Lyla Stumph, and Clara Lyston made a point of thanking Brie, others were not so forthcoming. Faith Babcock clearly felt betrayed and possibly believed that Brie had taken advantage of her position at the island history center to gather information. She didn't say as much, but she didn't have any praise for Brie or the operation either. Mo Thorn could never bring himself to say "Thank you," which didn't surprise them, since he had been a reluctant participant in the operation all along. Anything likely to diminish his power on the island was bound to have been met with resistance.

The day after the operation came to a head, Jack went to visit Mary Geary at the general store to apologize for having to deceive her about his identity.

She studied him with interest and said, "You know, I wasn't that surprised to learn about it."

"Why's that?" Jack asked.

"I guess it's the way you ask about things," she said. "Like there's something inside the question. Something more than meets the eye."

Jack nodded, realizing that while you can take the detective out of the work, you can never take the detective out of the man.

Brie visited Hughie several more times before they left the island. She found another book at the house—one about ducks and other coastal birds—and gave it to him. In return, he gifted her a picture of a pair of Common Eider ducks that he had drawn during the winter.

Starting in March, the ferry from the mainland visited the island twice a month. George agreed to stay on the island until the second ferry and work stern for Trulie Hyden, to give him enough time to find a new guy. Considering Trulie's recent rehabilitation, George said he wanted to do whatever he could to keep Trulie on track. The mutual respect between them, formed on the icy waters off Starkhaven Island, had become the basis for friendship.

In mid-March the rest of the team, packed for departure, were waiting at the town dock for the ferry, when Tam Thorn and the Stitchers unexpectedly arrived and presented Brie with the quilt they had just finished. And whether or not Clara Lyston had been the driving force behind the gesture, Brie decided to see it as a show of good faith and gratitude.

The ferry steamed away from the dock, and Brie watched as Starkhaven Island slowly disappeared astern. She was thinking about Locard's Exchange Principle. It states that a perpetrator at a crime scene both leaves something behind and takes something with him from that scene. She was thinking about the principle in terms of human interaction. They had taken something from the island—a killer, but also a doctor. She hoped they had left something of value behind. She hoped it was peace.

Epilogue

In the weeks and months that followed the team's departure from Starkhaven Island, several things unfolded that related to the operation and to their time on the island.

At Brie and John's request, and facilitated by Lieutenant Dent Fenton, an arrangement was reached with the county for Fin—Jim Finrude—to purchase Nathan Ross's property, lobstering territory, and boat, with financial support from Fin's aunt and Biddy Firth, Isa Firth's grandmother.

Brie talked to Joe Wolf—the medical examiner she had worked with on several cases in Maine—to see if he had any connection to medical residency programs in the state. To see if a young doctor might be interested in practicing on Starkhaven Island at a well-established clinic that offered living accommodations. Later she would learn that several candidates had come forward and that a committee, including Mo Thorn, Faith Babcock, and Annette Bryce, had been formed to interview the candidates.

Brie also learned from George that Trulie Hyden had approached Mo Thorn about starting a chapter of Narcotics Anonymous on the island. Thorn, following through with his promise made to Brie, agreed to fund the program. On another front, Brie gave Dent Fenton the name Thorn had given her—a name supposedly key to the greater drug trafficking operation in the Gulf of Maine. She trusted the lieutenant would take it from there.

Back at John's boatyard, work resumed on the spring haul out of *Maine Wind*. Ed and Scott scraped the hull, ridding it of layers of barnacles, while Barney, John's dog, lay in the sun, supervising the operation. The woodshop buzzed with activity, and under John's watchful eye, the new foremast was sanded and finished. Using the crane, the mast was passed through the deck and stepped to the ship's hull. By the beginning of May, newly inspected and sporting a fresh coat of navy blue bottom paint, *Maine Wind* slid down the rails into the sea, ready for another season of adventure. Brie was ready too.

The sea called.

Acknowledgements

Sea Smoke and Mirrors has been taking shape in my mind for a number of years. Sometimes I know exactly where a story has originated. At other times, it seems to be a slow coalescing of many experiences of various parts of Maine and its culture.

I'd like to thank the staff at the Island Institute in Rockland, Maine for all the information and help I have received from them over many years, about diverse aspects of the Maine islands. Also many thanks to both the Maine Lobstermen's Community Alliance and their publication "Landings," and to the Maine Lobstermen's Association for a wealth of information and resources.

The following resources have been invaluable to me in my research. *Well Out to Sea: Year-round on Matinicus Island* by Eva Murray. *Our Point of View: Fourteen Years at a Maine Lighthouse* by Thomas Mark Szelog and Lee Ann Szelog. *Islanders* by Virginia Thorndike, and *Lobsterboats* by Virginia Thorndike. "Violence on Matinicus Island"; Article by Geoffrey Douglas; Yankee Magazine, Sept./Oct. 2011. "Matinicus Island"; Article by Jason Brown; June 2010 (https://www.themainemag.com). "The Story of *Bajupa*" (a Maine lobster smack) by Melissa Waterman; published by the Maine Lobstermen's Community Alliance in *Landings*, October 22, 2018.

Finally, many thanks to my wonderful editor, Jennifer Adkins, who works tirelessly on my manuscripts, and my cover artist Rebecca Treadway. Thank you both for putting up with the perfectionist in me. And to my very thoughtful readers, Jeanette Brown, R.J. Kinderman, and Christopher Valen. Finally, to my wonderful husband and first reader, Craig Granse, who is always willing to live in the story with me until it comes to completion.